A Heart's Rebellion

A REGENCY ROMANCE

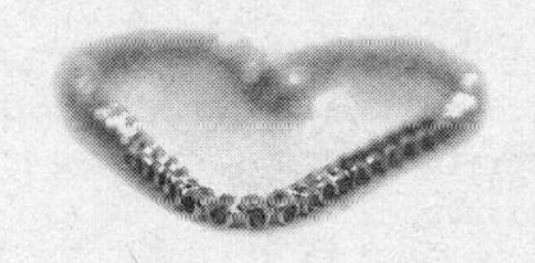

RUTH AXTELL

Revell
a division of Baker Publishing Group
Grand Rapids, Michigan

Published by Revell
a division of Baker Publishing Group
P.O. Box 6287, Grand Rapids, MI 49516-6287
www.revellbooks.com

Printed in the United States of America

Library of Congress Cataloging-in-Publication Data

Axtell, Ruth.
A heart's rebellion : a Regency romance / Ruth Axtell.
pages cm.
ISBN 978-0-8007-2090-2 (pbk.)
1. Aristocracy (Social class)—Fiction. 2. London (England)—Social life and customs—19th century—Fiction. 3. Great Britain—History—George III, 1760–1820—Fiction. I. Title.
PS3601.X84H43 2014
813′.6—dc23 2013039638

The author is represented by MacGregor Literary.

14 15 16 17 18 19 20 7 6 5 4 3 2 1

For Tom,

my Lancelot

There is therefore now no condemnation to them which are in Christ Jesus, who walk not after the flesh, but after the Spirit.

Romans 8:1

1

April 1815

"If this is what a London season is, I'd say it's a silly waste of time." Jessamine Barry folded her arms in front of her, frowning at the hordes of people milling past her in the Grecian-style drawing room, their edges slightly blurred since she was forbidden to wear her spectacles in society.

"It is rather difficult to speak to anyone in this situation," admitted her closest friend, Megan Phillips.

If it weren't for Megan, Jessamine would know not a soul in this mass of glistening, gleaming faces. Her handkerchief was already limp from patting it against her forehead and neck. "All this trouble to dress one's finest just to be ignored. I don't know how long I shall be able to stand it."

Megan turned worried eyes toward her. "Don't say that. You know it's such an opportunity we've been given by your godmother. I'm sure things will soon improve." Megan craned her neck above the crowd. "Where did she go? I haven't seen her since we arrived."

"In the card room, I would say," Jessamine said dryly. The picture Lady Bess had painted Jessamine's father of a London season was far from the reality. If her father could see her now, he'd utter a Scripture verse on man's vanity; her mother would lament the cost of her gowns and all the other furbelows to accompany them.

Jessamine flicked open her fan, eyeing the ivory brisé sticks as she remembered how dearly it had cost, and stirred some of the warm air against her face.

"Look at that gentleman there." She snapped the fan closed and pointed it toward a young man whose florid jaws bulged over his neck cloth. "He looks close to asphyxiating any moment from his own cravat. How can men be so ridiculous?"

Megan swallowed a giggle behind her own fan. "Careful, he'll hear you."

"How anyone can hear anyone in this babble is beyond me, yet they all go on as if anyone cares what they say." She narrowed her eyes at the ladies and gentlemen making a slow progression past her, bringing them into sharper focus. As far as she could make out, a rout was merely a place to see and be seen. No one seemed to be listening to anyone, yet their mouths kept moving, their smiles pasted on their faces like painted dolls.

She shuddered at the amount of rouge she observed on women's faces both young and old. What went on in London! And the gentlemen were worse, dressed like popinjays with more jewelry flashing from them than the women.

"Perhaps if we smile at some of the young ladies our age, we'll be able to meet them."

"My lips hurt from all the smiling I've done since arriving in London," Jessamine muttered. "I refuse to do so any longer, since it hasn't done us a bit of good." To illustrate her point, she scowled at a lady sporting an emerald-green turban with three pink ostrich plumes thrusting themselves against her male companion's upswept curls, curls so full of pomade they reflected the light from the chandeliers hanging above them.

"I know you're not in the best frame of mind, but things will get better, I'm sure. Things just . . . take time."

Jessamine's lips tightened in displeasure at Megan's reminder. How she wished on occasion Megan weren't her closest friend. It would have made things easier. To be constantly reminded—but no, she would not think about *him*! *He* was as good as dead to her.

She felt like one of those families that had exorcised a wayward son from their midst, the father banning the mere mention of the loved one's name in his hearing.

It would be humorous if it still didn't hurt so much—and weren't nigh on impossible to avoid hearing her beloved's name, since he was Megan's brother. Thank goodness he was no longer in England.

This should have been the happiest time of her life, yet she was miserable. A year and a half ago she would scarce have imagined herself among the fashionable world in a London drawing room, enjoying a season. Indeed, she'd never wanted a London season, even when Mama and Papa had broached the subject. At eighteen she'd pooh-poohed such a notion as frivolous. What need had she to parade around London drawing rooms, advertising herself to eligible young bachelors, when her heart was faithfully committed to a man far superior to any simpering dandy?

How little she'd imagined that a few months shy of one-and-twenty, she'd leap at her godmother's invitation to London, proving herself no better than any young miss hanging out for a husband.

The tears that were never far threatened to cloud the vision of the glittering array of ladies and gentlemen parading before her.

A year and a half ago, she'd envisioned herself betrothed by now, perhaps even married, to the finest, handsomest—no! The streak of rebellion and bitterness—a streak new and foreign to her which had invaded her nature when she'd heard of Rees's marriage and poisoned everything around her—reasserted itself.

The man in question—Rees Phillips—was not the finest, handsomest, noblest gentleman. He was the lowest, most despicable, shabbiest cad she'd ever known! He had no right to be happy when he had made her so miserable.

"Your frown could crack marble."

Jessamine jumped at the low masculine tone. Turning, she glared to see if the gentleman standing beside her had indeed had the temerity to address her.

Glaring in this case entailed craning her neck upward if she didn't want to waste the effort on a bleached white shirt front and pristine cravat.

"Are you speaking to me, sir?"

Amused blue eyes stared down into hers. They might have been attractive if the pale forehead hadn't been topped by a mop of light red hair—that shade that could not be described as anything but orange.

The gentleman's slim lips quirked upward. "You recognized the description of yourself?"

Jessamine drew herself up. How dare he mock her! "Excuse me, sir, we have not been introduced." With that set down, she turned away, her chin in the air, and took Megan by the arm.

Before she could move, he stepped in front of her and bowed. "I beg your pardon."

He turned and left her open-mouthed.

She fumed, watching him move with ease across the crowded drawing room.

Lancelot Marfleet strode away, seeking to put as much distance as possible between himself and the two young ladies he'd been listening to.

Eavesdropping, his mother would say.

He wouldn't have stooped to such behavior, much less spoken his thoughts aloud—he recoiled inwardly at his indecorous behavior—if he hadn't been so bored.

He'd been dragged to the rout by his elder brother, who had soon disappeared, leaving Lancelot to stand like a wallflower beside the profusion of potted greenery.

The young lady whose words had caught Lancelot's attention had moved to stand so close to him, it had been impossible not to overhear her complaints—remarks he heartily agreed with.

His mother would doubtless soon know of this latest social blunder from one of the dowagers who'd been standing near him. He could hear her aggrieved tone. "*You've been too long among the heathen. In England a gentleman does not address a young lady he has not been introduced to.*"

He'd thought by now he'd mastered his fault of speaking first and thinking later, but clearly he had a ways to go and was not ready for a London drawing room.

It wasn't the heathen of India among whom he'd spent the last two years who'd taught him to speak out of turn. If anything, he'd learned to listen and observe, hampered as he was by not speaking the language.

Speaking of observing, he dug into his coat pocket and drew out a pair of round, thin-rimmed, black metal spectacles. If he'd been fashionable, he'd have used only a quizzing glass, but he found the one-eyed look ridiculous and ineffective.

But now he needed to search for his hostess to rectify matters with the young miss before word of his ill manners reached his mother.

His eyes scanned the room, everything once more in sharp focus from the feathers atop ladies' headdresses to the fobs dangling from men's watch chains. His mother had forbidden him to wear the spectacles in public, but he was getting weary of nodding and smiling like a witless fool until the person drew near enough to be recognized.

Before searching for Lady Abernathy, he sought the young lady whom he'd insulted. It didn't take him long to spot the black-haired girl. He could feel his cheeks going ruddy as he identified her. The drawback of being a redhead—every emotion showed immediately on his cheeks.

The young miss continued talking with her companion. The two appeared typical of all young ladies making their coming-out. They were dressed similarly in white muslin gowns, only their colored ribbons setting them apart.

She had a pretty, though dissatisfied, face. Slim, pert nose, decided little chin, smooth pale skin with rosy lips and cheeks, the latter more likely due to the stuffiness of the room than to a healthy glow.

As she faced forward again, he shifted his gaze away, searching for his hostess. Not seeing her, he headed to the card room.

After two years traveling from Andhra Pradesh to West Bengal, living in a variety of primitive conditions, he'd acquired a certain self-possession, but a few weeks in London drawing rooms had him feeling as awkward and ungainly as he had in his youth, trailing behind his elder brother. Harold, who was only three years his senior, delighted in ragging Lancelot over his clumsiness at sports and awkwardness with the fairer sex.

Pushing aside those memories with the same single-mindedness he used to push through the crowded drawing room, Lancelot arrived at the saloon filled with card tables.

He located his hostess, a tall, stately woman walking among the green baize tables and stopping to chat with the card players.

When he approached Lady Abernathy, she held out her hands to him. "Marfleet! How delightful to see you among us. I haven't had a chance to properly welcome you back. Your mother wrote that you were terribly ill and recuperating in Hampshire." His hostess's pale brow furrowed briefly as she scanned his face. "I must say you look in fine fettle now." She clucked her tongue. "We Europeans are not meant for those ferocious climes overseas, so I hope you are home for good."

"I'm much better now, thank you, ma'am."

She looked around the room. "What do you think of my little gathering?"

"You certainly draw a lot of people to your evenings."

She laughed. "I like to think so." She patted his hand. "Now, what may I do for you, dear?" Her light-blue eyes looked shrewdly into his. "Your mother has made it no secret that she and your father wish you to settle down. I'm surprised to see no bevy of young ladies on your arm."

His cheeks warmed, but she had given him the opening he needed. "Well, it's precisely to beg an introduction that I come to you."

Her finely plucked eyebrows rose a fraction. "Oho, which of our young ladies has caught your interest? I shall present her to you forthwith."

He cleared his throat. "There are two young ladies in your drawing room. I'm not familiar with them, so I thought perhaps . . . ?" He left the request dangling, his heart thumping.

He had no need to say more. She tucked her hand in his arm and began to steer him back the way he'd come. "Show me. I am all curiosity."

When they stood in the doorway of the drawing room, he said, "Over there, straight in front of us, the two brunettes in the white gowns."

"Yes, I see them. They are new in town. I am not acquainted with them personally. Lady Beasinger brought them. She is sponsoring their season." Lady Abernathy turned to him, her eyes serious. "They have nothing to speak of. One is a vicar's daughter from some little village, I forget which Lady Beasinger mentioned; the other a merchant's daughter." Her fine lips thinned. "With little dowry since he died bankrupt." She gave him an appraising look. "Are you still interested in an introduction?"

A vicar's daughter? His interest rose as he wondered which of the two. "Yes, very much so."

She straightened her shoulders as if resigned. "Ah, love is blind to those practical matters a parent thinks about."

He said nothing, his gaze on the young lady he'd offended.

"Very well, since you remain silent, let us hence."

On their way, she caught her butler's attention and whispered something to him. He replied and she nodded. "Ah yes, I remember now. Miss Jessamine Barry and Miss Megan Phillips," she said to herself as if to memorize the names.

The first name caught Lancelot's attention. Jessamine. *Gelsemium sempervirens*, yellow jasmine. Would it be the one he'd spoken to, with her dark curls set off so appropriately by yellow ribbons?

It took a few moments to navigate across the room, but finally they stood in front of the two young ladies, who looked wide-eyed at them, their glances shifting from him to Lady Abernathy. Finally, the one Lancelot had not spoken to smiled. The other remained serious.

"My dear Miss Barry, Miss Phillips"—Lady Abernathy nodded to each in turn—"Mr. Lancelot Marfleet begs an introduction." As their gazes fixed on him, she addressed him. "May I present Miss Jessamine Barry." With a flourish of her hand toward the young lady in yellow ribbons, she paused before proceeding to the other young lady. "And Miss Megan Phillips."

They each curtsied as Lancelot bowed.

"Well, I shall leave you to become acquainted. Pity we have no dancing this evening," his hostess murmured as she departed.

"Thank you, my lady," he said to her retreating back.

Feeling as awkward as at his first dancing lesson, he turned to the two young ladies. Now what? He didn't even remember why he'd wanted an introduction.

Ah yes, so his mother would have nothing to reproach him with on the morrow. "I . . . beg your pardon for addressing you so rudely a few moments ago," he said to Miss Barry as she stared back at him.

She had green eyes, he noticed, fringed by black lashes. Her dark hair caught the light from the chandeliers and reflected like the polished gaboon ebony cut and shipped from West Africa and made into chess pieces and piano keys for Europeans.

She only tipped her head in acknowledgment.

Fiddling with his watch chain, he found nothing more to say. He'd always found small talk excruciatingly difficult. Flippancy came more easily to him, as evidenced by his first remarks to her, which had led him to this awkward situation.

He cleared his throat. "Lady Abernathy said you are lately come to town?"

She nodded.

As if embarrassed by her companion's reticence, the other young lady volunteered, "Yes, sir, we've been in London but a fortnight."

She was a pretty girl, her countenance friendly. Although of similar build and coloring as Miss Barry, the likeness ended there. Her chin was squarer, her nose straighter, her eyes gray, her hair dark brown.

"You have been in town about the same amount of time as I. I haven't seen you, though, until this evening," he said in stilted tones.

"That is not strange," Miss Phillips replied with a little laugh. "We spent our first week sightseeing with a guidebook and know scarce anyone in London so have attended few parties."

His lips quirked upward, feeling a little more at ease by her friendly candor. He chanced a glance at Miss Frosty, as he was beginning to call her. Instead of smiling, she was looking fixedly at her companion as if trying to transmit a message without words. Surely, she couldn't object to Miss Phillips's attempt to make conversation?

"Where do you hail from?" This time he addressed Miss Barry directly to see if she would deign to speak to him.

"Alston Green," she murmured, barely moving her lips.

"In Horsham," Miss Phillips added helpfully.

"Ah yes, West Sussex. Pretty country round about there. My family is from a little west of there, in Hampshire."

Miss Phillips nodded, then with a glance at Miss Barry, volunteered,

"Jessamine—Miss Barry—was born and bred there, but I moved there with my mother and brother almost fifteen years ago. My mother is originally from the village."

Miss Barry's compressed lips and flared nostrils confirmed her displeasure at her friend's offering of information.

"But we've been the best of friends ever since. I can hardly remember a time I didn't know Jessamine—Miss Barry—so feel as if I'm originally from the village."

He nodded. "Where did you live beforehand?"

A shadow crossed Miss Phillips's pretty gray eyes. "Bristol."

He raised his eyebrows. "That must have been a change for you from the city to a village."

"Yes, though meeting Miss Barry, who is our nearest neighbor, made all the difference." Her expression sobered. "My father was a merchant in Bristol, until he passed away."

"I'm sorry." He remembered Lady Abernathy's words. Miss Phillips's father had died bankrupt. Bristol, a city dependent on its seafaring trade, had been hard hit from so many years of the blockade with France.

"It was a difficult time for my mother, brother, and I. Of course, I was but a child so do not remember it so well as they. It happened many years ago."

"Still, the loss of one's father must be a terrible blow." He was grateful he still had both of his parents even when they didn't always see eye to eye on his way of life. Thankfully, being the younger son put him under no undo obligation to conform to their manner of life—until lately.

"Do you live in London?" Miss Phillips asked him in friendly inquiry.

His nervousness disappeared. It wasn't hard to feel at ease with Miss Phillips. She had a generous smile that bordered on the saucy but didn't cross over into flirtatious. "No, my parents have a place in town—on Grafton Street—so I have spent a fair amount of time here, though not lately." He cleared his throat again, reluctant to offer any more about himself, afraid he'd appear to be boasting. "I've been in India the last two years."

That got Miss Barry's attention, but it was Miss Phillips who expressed her curiosity. "India? What took you there, the East India Company?"

"I went out with the Church Missionary Society." He looked down, experiencing the familiar hesitancy at explaining. "I'm a vicar and felt called to go as a missionary." He raised his gaze as he finished, curious to gauge Miss Barry's reaction. Experience had taught him he'd either face disbelief or embarrassed silence.

His words appeared to have neither effect. Miss Barry's green eyes narrowed as if she were assessing him. Miss Phillips's eyes shone. "A missionary, how exciting! You must tell us about your time there."

He shrugged, feeling ill at ease again. "It was not an easy task," he said slowly, finding it hard to encapsulate his experience in a few sentences, which was all people usually wanted to hear.

In an effort to turn the topic, he addressed Miss Barry, remembering her words of dissatisfaction. "You are enjoying your season thus far?"

"It is certainly different from what we're used to in Alston Green," she answered in a careful tone.

"We attended assemblies there and in neighboring Billingshurst, but they were nothing like these parties," added Miss Phillips when Miss Barry said nothing more. "It is a bit difficult to fully appreciate these great houses when one is a stranger in town."

He nodded, his sympathy engaged. Even when one had grown up among the "ten thousand," the parties of the ton were intimidating. "I daresay. Your patroness is—"

"Lady Beasinger," Miss Phillips finished for him. "She's Miss Barry's godmother. It was very sweet of her to include me in her invitation to Miss Barry."

Lancelot nodded. "Yes, my mother knows her. She seems a kindly person. She's a bit on in years, though, and perhaps is not acquainted with the younger set."

Miss Phillips nodded eagerly. "That's precisely so. She goes out very little in society these days except to a few card parties among her small circle." She indicated the crowd around them. "This is our first evening at a real society event. Unfortunately, she left us here for the card room and thinks just by standing around, young gentlemen will come flocking to us." Her cheeks dimpled again. "But it seems to have worked."

He couldn't help chuckling, but he saw that Miss Barry didn't share the joke.

Before he could think of some appropriate rejoinder, Miss Barry spoke to him directly. "If you will excuse us, Mr. Marfleet, I believe I see someone we must greet."

He swiveled around.

"Oh? Who?" Miss Phillips asked.

Miss Barry gave her companion a sharp look.

Realizing Miss Barry was only trying to get rid of him, he stepped back. He had probably outstayed his welcome in any case. "I shall not keep you. It was a pleasure meeting you both."

Miss Phillips looked disappointed but said nothing to contradict her friend. She held out her hand. "It was a pleasure indeed. I hope we see you again."

He bowed over her hand and then turned to Miss Barry. But she neither offered her hand nor smiled. "I look forward to it," he murmured, moving out of their way.

He observed them crossing the room, delayed several times by the throng. Miss Barry was in the lead, her hand upon her friend's arm as if she were towing her along.

Only when they reached the doorway did he realize he was still wearing his spectacles. His face heated up and he swallowed, imagining the sport Harold would have if he were with him.

Sir Lancelot, you managed to converse for a quarter of an hour with not one but two *pretty ladies, and you ruined it all with those spectacles.*

Then he'd throw back his blond head and roar with laughter.

Hang it all! What did Lancelot care what Miss Barry and Miss Phillips thought of his appearance? It was worth it to see them both clearly. And *clearly*, Miss Barry didn't care if she ever saw him again.

Miss Phillips hadn't seemed to notice his spectacles at all.

Remembering his brother, Lancelot decided it was time to hunt for him.

After searching all the public rooms in the elegant town house, he realized Harold had left, probably as soon as he'd deposited him here. No doubt to some gaming den.

Jessamine bit back her annoyance as she pushed herself in front of a bejeweled lady, ignoring the lady's exclamation as she accidently trod on her satin slippers.

"Impertinent chit," the lady said to her escort. "I vow, Lady Abernathy is allowing all sorts of nobodies at her routs these days. Probably a mushroom's daughter by the looks of her."

"Did you hear that?" Megan whispered.

Jessamine nodded abruptly, keeping her pace up. All she wanted was to exit this room with its odious people. Never had she felt so out of place. "Some people, even in London's best homes, have no manners," she said shortly.

"Why are you in such a hurry?" Megan asked when they were halfway across the room.

"I wanted to get away from that impertinent gentleman."

Megan stared at her. "Mr. Marfleet? I thought he was quite charming."

"Charming? With all that red hair and—and spectacles?"

Megan's gray eyes twinkled. "Spectacles?"

Jessamine felt herself blush to the roots of her hair, thinking of the pair she carried in the leather case in her reticule. "But no one wears them in public like that, not to a rout!"

"I thought it showed a refreshing honesty. He's a vicar and a missionary. He probably doesn't care about his appearance."

"Yes, a vicar."

"What's wrong with being a vicar? Your father is one."

Jessamine shuddered. "I'm not interested in meeting a vicar." Nor in giving her heart to anyone else.

"But to think he's been to India. I wonder who his family is," Megan mused, "if they have a house in town and in Hampshire."

Jessamine concentrated on maneuvering past a dawdling couple in front of them before she replied. "He can be the Duke of Marlborough's son for all I care. His hair is unruly, he has a bran-faced complexion, and he sports his spectacles at a rout!" A vicar was the last man she would look at. Not after having lived life by the rules and having it turn to ashes. With her words, she reached the doorway and grabbed the jamb as if arriving at a finish line.

Megan looked around. "I thought you wanted to greet someone?"

Jessamine blushed again, looking away, ashamed of having told a fib to her friend. "It was just an excuse to get away from Mr. Marfleet."

Megan's eyes widened. It was no wonder. Jessamine had never told such a fib. But those days were over. Being good got one nowhere.

"I'm sorry," Megan said. "I didn't realize you were uncomfortable with him. I was so relieved to be talking to someone closer to our age."

"He looked closer to Rees's age—" she blurted out then stopped, realizing she was the one who had brought up Megan's brother this time.

Megan laid a hand on her arm. "I'm sorry. I didn't think. He just seems so different from Rees. I didn't think he resembled him at all."

He didn't. Mr. Marfleet was nowhere near as handsome as Rees Phillips with his dark looks and gray eyes, so like his sister Megan, but in a tall, masculine form. Try as she would to blot out the hurt, it still lay behind her heart like a smoldering acid and turned her every thought acrimonious.

"I found him old," she said abruptly, turning away from Megan. "How long do you think Lady Bess will be?"

"A few hours if we're fortunate."

Jessamine's lips turned downward. "Too bad she has nowhere else to visit tonight."

"It would only mean hopping in and out of a hackney in the rain to do the same thing we're doing now."

The night loomed before them. Jessamine's shoulders slumped as she admitted defeat in the face of her friend's realistic assessment. "I wish we could play cards."

"It wouldn't matter. Young ladies are not expected to sit like dowagers at the card table here in London the way we do back home."

"Instead we are supposed to be standing like storks, to be seen by eligible bachelors who happen by." She pasted a false smile on her face and batted her eyelashes.

Only to have her glance land squarely on that odious redhead and find him observing her across the room. She flushed, realizing her falsehood had been discovered.

Once again, she took Megan by the elbow. "Come along, let's find Lady Bess and pray she's on a losing streak."

2

Lancelot descended the hack chaise and faced the nondescript door in the nondescript town house in a row of others like it. After visiting the reputable gentlemen's clubs along St. James's Street, he invariably ended up at one of the private gaming rooms in barely reputable neighborhoods. They showed their wear in the peeling paint of their doors and window frames and odor from the kennels lining the streets.

These gaming rooms were usually located in some widow's upstairs drawing room.

With the head of his walking stick, he rapped on the door.

"Good evening," he said to the footman who was eyeing him to determine if he was a regular or a newcomer. "Is Mrs. Smith holding an open house this evening?"

"Yes, sir." The footman, after a last careful look, stepped back and allowed him entry.

Knowing it was useless to ask the man if he'd seen Harold, since discretion was key in these gaming saloons, he stepped inside the vestibule. "Dashed cold this evening."

"That it is, sir. Don't hardly seem as if spring is even here."

Lancelot removed his hat and cloak, hoping he wouldn't have

to go through this routine much more this evening. By now he was beginning to know Harold's favorite haunts.

He paused on the threshold of the upstairs drawing room and scanned the tables. The men gathered around the tables didn't even look up.

He could understand why his brother favored Mrs. Smith's establishment whenever he was tired of the play at Brooks's, Boodle's, or White's.

The four-story town house on Duchess Street, though not in a fashionable part of town, was nevertheless tastefully furnished within. Its interior was warm and well-lighted. A buffet of varied dishes was replenished frequently by a couple of footmen.

In return for the convivial atmosphere, gentlemen came to spend their money, and Mrs. Smith, a lady of indeterminate years, was able to live comfortably and in a style she desired without compromising her standards. A young gentleman's losing his parents' money was not considered a sin, merely a rite of passage.

The fair-haired woman, who was still quite attractive, approached him with a smile. "Ah, Mr. Marfleet, how nice of you to join us this evening. Care to try your hand at a bit of whist or faro?" She chuckled, knowing he didn't play faro nor whist at the stakes played at her establishment.

"Thank you, no," he said, summoning a polite smile. "I'm simply looking for my brother. Ah, there he is." Pretending an affability he didn't feel, Lancelot excused himself and crossed the carpeted room.

Reining in both exasperation and relief at seeing Harold hunched over one of the tables, Lancelot cast about in his mind what reasoning to use to drag him away. Several other gentlemen ringed the round table, their eyes intent on the player sitting in the curved indented space reserved for the banker.

Lancelot's jaw tightened. Baccarat. Judging by the pile of chips in front of Harold, his brother would not be leaving anytime soon. It would be useless to remonstrate. He consoled himself that at least he wouldn't have to track him down to a cockfight or rat-catching ring in less savory neighborhoods.

Harold didn't glance up at Lancelot's approach, his gaze fixed on the cards laid out on the green baize.

With a sigh of resignation, Lancelot looked around for an empty chair. He retrieved one along the wall and placed it near his brother, nodding to those present who chose to acknowledge him. Most were too intent on the cards being dealt.

Upon his return from India, Lancelot had been grieved to see Harold had not changed from the man he'd left two years ago. He continued to live the life of a young gentleman about town rather than a married man of thirty with an estate to learn to manage.

Even though he knew he could do little to influence his older brother, still he kept hoping his presence might compel his brother to get up from the gaming tables before he lost everything.

As the hour dragged on, Harold's pile of counters diminished then grew high again and now was once again on the ebb. He wouldn't leave unless convinced he was on a losing streak.

The wait gave Lancelot ample time to relive his earlier fiasco with the two young ladies at Lady Abernathy's rout. If Harold hadn't matured in two years, Lancelot acknowledged ruefully that neither had he himself grown any more attractive to the fairer sex.

Lancelot imagined the scene with Miss Barry and Miss Phillips if Harold had been there in his stead. With his dark blond curls arranged à la Brutus and his innocent blue eyes, Harold had inherited all the looks in the family. With a mere lift of his lips, he would have had Miss Barry gazing in adoration.

Lancelot shifted in his chair to ease the stiffness in his legs. He had long ago stopped railing at the fate that had brought him into the world with a thatch of pale-red hair. No one in his immediate family had it—only his paternal grandfather whom Lancelot had never known but whose portrait graced the gallery at Kendicott Park. At least no one could question his birthright.

He observed Harold's intent profile now, comparing the strong, evenly proportioned features to his own longish face—all cheekbones, jaws, and knobbly nose. His mother always used to say, "Poor dear, never mind, it's your mind and heart that people will notice. You were born with all the brains and sensibility your brother seems to lack. He is all Marfleet, excelling at physical prowess but thoughtless and careless about people's feelings."

The comparison had been no comfort to Lancelot during his first years of adulthood. Thankfully, he was past that now, having found solace, as his mother had predicted, in his books and then at Cambridge under the inspirational preaching of Charles Simeon. That encounter had changed his life.

Lancelot was roused from his reminiscences by his brother's lazy smile. "That you, Lancelot? Got tired of playing the wallflower at Lady Abernathy's?"

Lancelot grimaced. "Especially when you dumped me there and absconded before the coachman had even gone around the block."

Harold's grin only deepened. "I'm only discharging my duty toward you, as I promised Mama. I have no need to procure a wife by the end of the season. It's enough I take you to these functions. You can't expect me to endure them." He picked up his cards and examined them. "Nor is it my fault if you refuse to lift a finger on your own behalf."

Impatience rising in him, Lancelot blurted out, "You needn't trouble yourself anymore. I have met two charming"—at least Miss Phillips fit the description—"young ladies. I think I shall ask Mama to invite them to her dinner party. That should satisfy her."

Harold's golden brows lifted. "What's this, not one but *two* young ladies? Don't tell me, one is cross-eyed and slack jawed and the other weighs fourteen stone." He guffawed before turning to place his bet.

Lancelot bit back a retort. It annoyed him that even after all these years, Harold had the ability to rouse his ire. Since boyhood,

Harold's teasing had always gotten a rise out of Lancelot, which only made people point out that his temper matched his hair.

Only years of disciplining himself through prayer and Scripture reading had helped curb his temper. It was disheartening to think how little he'd progressed and that any self-possession had more to do with having been away from his big brother than any spiritual maturity.

Exclamations around the table drew Harold's attention back to the play, and Lancelot was forced to sit back once more and wait.

An hour later when Harold was ready to leave, his pockets flush, he brought the subject of the two young ladies up again.

In the meantime, Lancelot had had plenty of time to repent his loose tongue. What had he been thinking of? Of course he wouldn't invite the two young ladies to dinner. As they drove home in his brother's curricle, Harold chuckled. "So, you've set your eyes upon two lovelies? Do give me the particulars."

"I've done no such thing." Lancelot turned away with little hope that Harold would let the matter rest. "They are just two young ladies in London for the season and scarce know a soul. I took pity on them."

Harold's lips curled upward. "Always the compassionate clergyman." He glanced sidelong at him, clucking his tongue. "Taking pity on them won't fadge with Mama. You'd best take my advice and tell her you fancy yourself violently in love with at least one of them. It will put her in alt, and you may do as you please for the rest of the season."

Lancelot shoved his hands in his pockets, resigned to hearing Harold's unwelcome advice until he tired of the topic.

Jessamine and Megan joined Lady Bess in the breakfast room late the next morning. The older lady greeted them with a cheerful smile from her place at the round table at the back of the comfortable town house in the parish of Marylebone, London.

Though her real name was Lady Beasinger, when Jessamine had first met her godmother, the name had been too much for her child's tongue to pronounce, so her godmother had suggested Lady Bess as a satisfactory substitute, and the diminutive form had stuck.

As they poured themselves coffee or tea, they responded to Lady Bess's inquiries of how they'd slept. Jessamine felt tired, her body still not used to town hours. She usually awoke too early after a late night and had difficulty going back to sleep again.

"What a crush last night!" Lady Bess's aqua-green eyes twinkled at them across the table. Her graying brown hair curled around her face beneath a sheer lawn cap.

Thankfully Megan's enthusiasm for the rout made up for Jessamine's less vocal murmurings of assent. As they made their way to the sideboard to serve themselves from the hot dishes, Lady Bess read to them from her morning papers.

"There will be a Queen's Drawing Room later in the month. What a pity you are not going to be presented."

Jessamine glanced at Megan, hoping the remark did not hurt her feelings. While Jessamine as a vicar's daughter was eligible for court presentation, Megan as a merchant's daughter was not. Of course Jessamine had no intention of being presented, having neither the funds nor connections to do so, and not wishing to do anything her best friend would be excluded from.

But Megan seemed not to be bothered as she heaped some eggs onto her plate. When they sat down with their plates, Lady Bess was riffling through the morning post. "A letter for you, my dear," she said, handing a sealed missive to Megan with a compassionate smile to Jessamine. "Nothing for you today, dear."

"I expected none, since I owe my mother a letter." It was getting more difficult to write home since there was so little to tell. Having jumped at the chance to escape to London, she disliked now having to pretend to her parents that her days were crammed with activities.

How different from two years ago, when she and her mother

had come with Megan to London for a fortnight. Brimming with all the hopes and expectations of an eighteen-year-old, she had spent the days shopping and sightseeing, awed and thrilled with everything she saw.

Now she only felt guilt at all her parents had sacrificed to provide for her season. As a vicar in a small village, her father had a modest income. At least she was an only child, she consoled herself, so they didn't have other offspring to provide for.

Jessamine glanced at Megan, wondering what news she might have received from home. Little changed in the village from week to week except the weather.

Lady Bess broke the seal on a note she had received. A moment later she lifted her eyes to Jessamine with a smile. "You two must have made quite an impression at last night's rout."

Megan looked up from her letter. "What's that, ma'am?"

Lady Bess tapped the stationery before her. "I have here an invitation to dine tomorrow evening at the home of none other than Sir Geoffrey Marfleet, baronet, and Lady Marfleet."

They turned to stare at each other.

Lady Bess read them the invitation. "It's signed by Lady Marfleet herself. The Marfleets are a very ancient and well-respected family." She peered at the two of them over her spectacles. "If you have managed to catch her attention, your season is complete."

"But we never met—" Jessamine began.

"Wait." Megan's eyes rounded as she looked at Lady Bess. "Do they have a son?"

Lady Bess nodded, her eyes matching Megan's in wonder. "They have two, as a matter of fact, though one is married. Wait, let me look them up."

She rose from the table and brought back her copy of *Debrett's Peerage and Baronetage* from a small round table, where it held a place of honor for answering any questions that came up in her correspondence or in the society pages of the *Morning Post*.

When she located the entry for the baronet, she read to them: "Marfleet, Geoffrey Alexander James, baronet, of Kendicott Park, Kingsclere, in the county of Hampshire."

She continued reading as she scrolled down the entry with her forefinger. "Ah, here is the gentleman in question, no doubt: 'Lancelot Beresford Marfleet, F.R.S., born 5th February, 1788.' Unmarried, and his brother lists no issue." She continued perusing the entry. "There is also a younger sister, Alice Delawney Marfleet."

Lady Bess looked up from the book with satisfaction. "What a stroke of luck to have met the baronet's son last night, even if he is but the younger son. You are sure he is the one you met?"

Megan laughed. "We are sure of nothing. All we know is Mr. Marfleet requested an introduction to us from Lady Abernathy."

"He did! Do tell me all."

With a smile, Megan recounted how Mr. Marfleet had approached them.

"Why I never! You don't say! To address you without an introduction!" Lady Bess interjected throughout Megan's story. "That doesn't sound at all like a Marfleet." She clucked her tongue. "His mother would be appalled. It just shows he has been among the heathen too long."

Jessamine's irritation resurfaced as she remembered Mr. Marfleet's impudence. She didn't know why it rankled her so, but the fact remained that he had made her feel childish and petty. How little he understood how she'd hurt.

"He told us he had spent some time in India," Megan said.

"I know very little about him since he has not been in society lately. But if one of you has caught his attention, your season may be assured."

Megan eyed Jessamine with wonder. "You made more of an impression than you supposed."

Jessamine's fork clattered against her plate. "You are mistaken.

You are the one he spoke with most. I found his company tedious." She didn't care if he was a baronet's son, not that awkward, bespectacled redhead! She picked up her fork and speared a piece of ham.

"No matter, you are both invited, as am I," Lady Bess announced, picking up the invitation again.

"I'm so glad," Megan said. "I'd be too intimidated to go with only Jessamine."

Jessamine chewed slowly, puzzled by the invitation. Mr. Marfleet doubtless had wished to further his acquaintance with Megan, she reasoned, even as she remembered the faintly mocking look in his slate-blue eyes every time he glanced her way behind those steel-rimmed spectacles.

"It's a fashionable address, Grafton Street, not far from Piccadilly," Lady Bess said, studying the note.

"Do you know the baronet and his wife?" Jessamine asked. Lady Bess seemed to know everyone, though she didn't venture much into society anymore.

"Oh yes. Sir Geoffrey is a most charming man, both he and his wife, though quite high in the instep. That's to be expected, otherwise they'd have all sorts hanging on their coattails. She's of the Hallowells of Northamptonshire, a very old family in their own right."

She sat back in her chair, musing, "The eldest son, Sir Harold—for he has the courtesy title of knight until he comes into the baronetcy, you know—was always a dashing young blade, but so was his papa before him." She chuckled with a reminiscent shake of her head. "Sowing his wild oats, I imagine. Pity Sir Harold and his wife have had no sons."

She consulted *Debrett's Peerage* again. "They've been married these past ten years with no issue. I am sure the baronet and his wife are anxious to see the younger Marfleet married and setting up a nursery." Her gaze rested on Jessamine and Megan in turn, her tone thoughtful. "Some girls don't 'take,' but I'm sure that will not be your fate. You are both charming girls."

With a sigh of satisfaction, Lady Bess picked up another newspaper and began to read the society column. Jessamine only half listened to her comments on various members of the fashionable world, her feelings mixed about attending the Marfleets' dinner party. A part of her resented the fact that she would be in Mr. Marfleet's debt if this invitation led to others. Another conceded that she was tired of attending Lady Bess's card parties. Perhaps at last things were going to change.

"Aren't you coming?"

She started at Megan's question. "I beg your pardon?"

"If you're finished with breakfast, I was wondering if you were ready for our walk. I wanted to share Mama's letter with you."

Jessamine brushed the crumbs from her hands and stood. "Forgive me, I was woolgathering."

Megan smiled archly. Jessamine had to bite her lip to keep from retorting that she was *not* thinking of Mr. Marfleet and his odious invitation to dine.

When they'd changed into walking dresses and pelisses, she and Megan took a hackney to Hyde Park. Used to the country where they took long walks every day, they'd felt stymied at first having to take Lady Bess's maid Betsy every time they stepped outside. They'd finally persuaded Lady Bess that they did not need the young maid. The poor woman took care of the town house almost single-handedly, with only a cook and scullery maid to see to the kitchen.

Both Megan and Jessamine had further scandalized their hostess when they'd offered to help with housekeeping and kitchen tasks. They were accustomed to doing so at home since neither family kept many servants.

During the first week in London, they had taken their travel guide everywhere, scrutinizing its pages until they'd become confident navigating the streets of Marylebone and Mayfair.

They were let down at Cumberland Gate now. As soon as they

entered the vast parkland, Jessamine inhaled. "No fog, just a whiff of smoke. Why, I almost could believe I'm back in Alston Green."

They preferred coming to the park before noon when no one was about but nursemaids with their charges. By three in the afternoon the main paths began to fill with carriages and pedestrians. By five o'clock they were choked with traffic.

London was also difficult to get used to with its sooty atmosphere. A gray pall seemed always to hang overhead. The large park was the only place that resembled the countryside.

They slowed their pace, strolling along a tree-lined path to a reservoir.

"It's a pity so many of the trees are being cut down," Jessamine said of the large walnut trees forming a row on either side of their path. Some of the venerable trees still stood, others were felled, and some were only a wide stump.

"Lady Bess said it is because they are so old, each storm brings a few down."

"I do hope they replant them." Jessamine sighed, discovering she preferred village life to that in the city.

They paused at the circular reservoir placed midway down the avenue of trees. Megan looked skyward. "I spy a patch of blue sky. We haven't seen that in a week. Pale, but blue nonetheless."

"What does your mother say?" Jessamine asked after a moment, always yearning yet fearing to glean some news of Rees from Megan's letters from home.

"She is well. She has recently begun helping your father at the village school, since he lost the schoolmaster last week." Megan sighed. "It helps to keep her busy. With me gone, she is quite alone, though she never complains."

Jessamine gave her a sympathetic glance. "I know it was hard for you to leave her. It's a pity she couldn't come with us."

Megan merely nodded. She was looking quite fetching in a poke bonnet with a wide pink ribbon around the base of its crown. "She wouldn't leave. She says she prefers her quiet village life."

Before Jessamine could comment, Megan brightened. "Isn't it exciting to be invited to a dinner party? Perhaps it will be the beginning of a successful season. You have to admit, up to now it has been sadly flat—to be among so many people and feel you know no one. Poor Lady Bess has done what she could, but she is invited to so few places."

Jessamine frowned at the dark body of water encircled by an iron railing. "How awful to be only remembered by your friends when you are young and in funds. Now that she is widowed and has lost most of her wealth, she seems to be utterly forgotten."

"She seems content with her small circle of whist-playing friends." Megan chuckled. "They enjoy their gossip of people who no longer take them into account, yet they follow their lives as if they were the closest of relations."

"Busybodies."

"I think they're harmless old widows, since they only talk among themselves. Isn't it interesting Mr. Marfleet's being the son of a baronet?" Megan said, returning to the topic that interested her most. "And to think he's a vicar and a missionary! I confess there was a certain air about him, a gravity that marked him as a clergyman."

Jessamine snorted. "A clergyman would never have addressed a young lady so—and what he said!"

"You never did tell me." Megan's gray eyes, so like Rees's except more lively, danced with mirth.

"He was insufferable. Remarking upon my frown. Who wouldn't frown at such a tedious event?"

Megan burst into a peal of laughter, but seeing Jessamine's scowl brought a gloved hand to her mouth. "Forgive me," she said. "I shouldn't make sport of you since I was feeling as bored as you. But, admit it, you must have charmed him for him to ask his mother to issue an invitation to a dinner party."

"I did nothing of the sort. You were the one talking to him most of the time."

"We shall soon see who has caught his bespectacled eye," she said with a knowing look. "By the bye, what shall we wear? Your sea-green crepe is lovely. You haven't yet had an opportunity to wear it." She tapped a finger against her chin. "For me, I'm thinking about the pink satin with the rosettes along the hem."

Jessamine nodded. "That one is quite becoming. I don't think it matters overmuch what we choose to wear, since the gowns we worked so hard over back home will look sadly countrified among the *haut ton*."

Megan turned worried eyes to her. "Do you really think the Marfleets are so exalted?"

"You heard Lady Bess. They are an old and distinguished family with a country estate."

"I suppose so, though Mr. Marfleet didn't sound proud at all. I wonder how many guests will be present. I hope they are not all old and prosy."

Jessamine, tired of all the conjectures, resumed walking. "We shall see soon enough. Come, let's go down to Piccadilly. We can return home by Bond Street. Remember Lady Bess's commission."

Megan nodded, and they continued their walk. As they approached the gate at Hyde Park Corner, she clutched Jessamine's arm. "I have an idea."

Jessamine waited, used to her friend's spontaneous suggestions.

"Let us locate Grafton Street and get a glimpse of Mr. Marfleet's residence before the dinner party."

Jessamine stared at her friend, hardly believing what she heard. "What a preposterous idea."

"It's not at all preposterous. We can see what kind of house the baronet lives in. If it's a simple town house, maybe it will be a simple dinner party. If it's a grand one, then we know it will be a grand party."

Jessamine shook her head. "I can tell you right now it will be a grand party—grander than any dinner party either you or I have ever attended."

"But are you not the least bit curious?"

"Any curiosity I have can be satisfied when we attend their dinner. Come, let's cross the street while it's clear." Taking Megan's arm, she picked up her pace, hoping her friend would forget her outrageous notion. What if they were caught? She blushed to the roots of her hair, imagining the humiliation if Mr. Marfleet saw them dawdling outside his residence.

When they reached Piccadilly, she said, "I should like to stop in at Hatchard's and see the latest books. We shan't have time to be looking for street addresses if we are to shop."

Megan said no more, and they arrived at the renowned bookstore that was frequented by learned scholars. It still took courage to step across its threshold. It was reputed that Lord Byron patronized the store. They had not caught a glimpse of the notorious poet yet—not that Jessamine would recognize him if she did. But since his marriage, he had been seen little in London. His *Hebrew Melodies* had made a stir upon its publication the previous month, but at a guinea, it was beyond her and Megan's means.

At that hour, the bookshop was devoid of all but a few patrons, who lounged by the empty fireplace, perusing the newspapers laid out for them by the owner.

Megan and Jessamine bypassed these in favor of the books arrayed along the shelves. They had never had the luxury of so many recently-published books at their fingertips.

Jessamine deliberately took more time than she needed, peering into every conceivable title to read a portion of the text, hoping Megan would forget her idea of looking up Mr. Marfleet's address.

When they left the bookshop, she continued to linger at every shop window. At a print shop, she edged forward between other onlookers to read the latest caricatures displayed in the bowfront window.

All to no avail. When they arrived at the corner of Albemarle, Megan motioned down the intersecting street. "We can go this way. I asked the clerk at Hatchard's, and he told me that Grafton Street is at the end. If we continue down it, we shall end up at Bond Street, where we can purchase Lady Bess's commission."

Jessamine stared at her friend, her feet refusing to move, even as her mind raced, trying to come up with reasons not to go down that street. The pedestrians moved past her on the busy street corner until Megan propelled her forward.

"I don't think it's a good idea to go sneaking around to take a peek at someone's house," Jessamine said, pulling back.

"We're not. We are merely taking an alternate route to Bond Street."

"Aren't you tired?" Jessamine asked with little hope of dissuading her friend, who was known to be persistent when she decided upon a course of action. "Perhaps we should hail a hack. We've already walked quite a distance this morning."

Megan made a face at her. "Nonsense. We walk this distance most every day, and at least it's warm and sunny today. Come along. You know it's amusing to explore new streets."

Jessamine still hung back. "What if someone should see us?"

Megan rolled her eyes. "Who is going to recognize us?"

Jessamine reluctantly began to follow her down the flag way.

"And if we happen to run into Mr. Marfleet himself, maybe he won't be wearing his spectacles and won't even see us!" Megan said with a giggle.

That reminded Jessamine that she was still wearing hers. She preferred to see clearly when she was sightseeing or looking into shop windows, although it horrified Lady Bess that she should wear them. Lady Bess carried a quizzing glass in her reticule, which she only pulled out when she wanted to peer at something in a shop.

As she walked alongside Megan, Jessamine chewed her lip, debating whether to take off her spectacles or not. Finally she gave herself an impatient shake. She was not so vain. What did she care about running into a gentleman she cared nothing about! Megan was right, too, that the chances of his being about were little to nil. It was just noon, and they had found that the fashionable world scarcely stirred before three.

She continued looking about her at all the interesting buildings and shop windows. This street was quieter than Piccadilly with fewer shops but many imposing buildings, including the large Grillion's Hotel across the street.

Megan pointed to it. "Look, that's where we stayed two years ago when we came to London with your mother to visit your uncle, who was on leave at the time. What fine style our visit was then. It was so nice of your uncle to host us all at this hotel."

The street did look familiar. "Yes," she said slowly, remembering the excitement of that weeklong trip to London, even though Rees had written his sister that he would not be in town.

It was much later that she had discovered he had been in London all along, busy falling in love with a Frenchwoman who was likely a spy to the British Crown. Bitterness rose in Jessamine's throat at the memory of that first trip to London.

As if reading her mind, Megan said, "How long ago it seems now. Just to think a couple of months later, Louis XVIII stayed in the same hotel when he came for the victory celebrations."

Thankfully, Megan mentioned nothing of the other, more personal changes their lives had undergone since that visit. Jessamine pushed back the memories. She must move forward, the way Rees had done with his life.

They continued walking, passing small art galleries, a publishing house, and a few less distinguished hotels. They paused at the end of the street to look at an imposing colonnaded building.

Jessamine read the words carved along the top. "The Royal

Institute." Her father always talked of the lectures given at this bastion of scientific discovery. "That's where Papa heard Sir Humphrey deliver a talk."

"I wonder if they still hold laughing gas parties," Megan speculated aloud.

"Surely not here. This is for serious scientists."

"We don't have anyone to escort us to such a place, though I should love to give it a try," Megan said with a sigh as they resumed their walk.

The road ended at Grafton Street. To Jessamine's relief, they were the only pedestrians visible, although a carriage stood midway down the street toward Bond Street.

"What a charming street," Megan said as they stood a moment, looking down both directions of the short street. "It seems quiet, likely only residences."

"The invitation said number fifteen." Jessamine looked doubtfully around her at the pretty stucco buildings. "There's number ten," she indicated, "but it leads away from Bond Street. Do you suppose it's in that direction or toward Bond Street?"

As she spoke, she turned to face the latter direction and smothered a gasp.

At the same moment Megan clutched her hand. "It's Mr. Marfleet!"

3

Jessamine froze. Two gentlemen were exiting a white stucco town house about midway down the block. A curricle stood in the road, a tiger at the horses' heads.

Could she and Megan back down Albemarle before being observed? Even as the thought raced through her mind, it was too late. Both men stopped speaking, their gazes drawn toward them.

As the only other individuals on the pavement, there could be no mistaking who had drawn their attention.

For a moment Jessamine had the hope that Mr. Marfleet wouldn't recognize her since he was not wearing his spectacles. But before she could turn back from whence they'd come, Megan broke into a smile and walked boldly toward the gentlemen.

Usually Jessamine appreciated Megan's more outgoing personality, but at that instant she wanted nothing better than to yank her back. Her worst nightmare had come to pass.

Gritting her teeth as she imagined Mr. Marfleet's knowing smile, Jessamine followed Megan. As they drew close enough to be recognized, Mr. Marfleet's eyes widened in visible surprise. He recovered quickly. Saying something to the other gentleman, he stepped forward.

Touching the brim of his tall beaver, he inclined his head to each one. "Good day, Miss Barry, Miss Phillips. What a pleasant surprise to see you here."

Megan's smile widened. "We were just returning home from our morning walk and we took this route instead of continuing on Piccadilly to return to Bond Street. It . . . it's quieter."

A perfectly reasonable excuse, but to Jessamine's ears it sounded contrived. Her face heated at the thought that he would think they were hunting out his residence.

"I see. How nice." He turned to Jessamine, and too late she remembered her spectacles. Her cheeks flamed. All she could do was brazen it out, staring back at him without blinking. Except for an initial blink of his own, he gave no sign that he noticed anything different about her appearance. Instead, he turned to the other gentleman, who had approached them and stood smiling. "May I present my brother, Sir Harold Marfleet?"

They murmured their greetings as Mr. Marfleet explained to his brother that she and Megan were in London for the season. Sir Harold was indeed handsome, as Lady Bess had said. Closely cropped golden hair curled beneath a tall beaver. His cravat was perfectly stiff with a few careful creases below his cleft chin. His dark-blue coat of superfine outlined broad shoulders. Buckskin breeches molded muscular thighs. Shiny black boots with a width of white tops completed his outfit. He appeared a dashing London buck, and made her think Brummell would have approved in his day.

Her observation turned to Mr. Marfleet, who wore a more somber black coat and breeches and crumpled cravat. He looked like a poor parish vicar. Her father would doubtless approve.

"Are you staying far from here?" Sir Harold asked.

"We are staying with Lady Beasinger on Weymouth Road in Marylebone," Megan replied.

"That's quite far." He glanced at his curricle. "I would offer to take you home but it only seats two. I could call for the carriage."

She and Megan protested at once, telling him they enjoyed walking, being used to it in the country.

He tilted his head, eyeing them through a quizzing glass. "You have no maid accompanying you?"

"No. I mean, she—we left her at home. We are used to going about on our own at home." Megan tossed her curls. "She protests after a mile of walking, and it became quite tiresome."

"London can be a dangerous place with its cutthroats and pickpockets. You must have a care," Sir Harold said in a serious tone, though the twinkle in his blue eyes belied his brotherly admonition.

"We are quite careful where we go," Jessamine said, bringing both men's attention to her. Again, she remembered her spectacles and wished she could hide behind Megan.

"We go out early too, before the streets become too crowded," added Megan.

"Bond Street can be a bit unsavory for unaccompanied females in the afternoon. I should stay away from there unless you are in a carriage."

"Yes, of course. Thank you," Megan murmured.

Mr. Marfleet cleared his throat. "Did you receive my mother's invitation?"

"Yes," they both answered at once, then fell silent as if they'd answered too eagerly. Jessamine determined to let Megan do the talking from then on.

Megan continued in a calmer tone. "Thank you. Lady Bess—that is, Beasinger—our hostess, received it. It was very thoughtful of you."

Ruddy color suffused his pale cheeks. "I thought perhaps being new in town you might not have many acquaintances."

"London is a town that depends wholly on introductions," his brother put in. "Depend upon it. My mother knows everyone worth knowing. If she approves you, the invitations shall pour in."

Sir Harold's words would have been insulting if they hadn't

been delivered with humor in his crinkling eyes. "What have you seen in London since you arrived?" he asked.

As Megan described some of their outings, Jessamine wished there were some way of discreetly removing her spectacles. But all she could do was look at her friend, studiously avoiding the eyes of the two men. When she stole a glance at Mr. Marfleet, she found his gaze upon her. Quickly she averted her own.

"You must go to the theater and Astley's Amphitheatre," Sir Harold said. "Don't you agree, Lancelot?"

"Yes, I should think you'd find those amusing."

Sir Harold chuckled. "If you asked him, he would have you sitting at the Royal Institute or Somerset House listening to stuffy lectures all day."

Jessamine eyed Mr. Marfleet. Was he interested in scientific pursuits? He sounded more and more like her father.

"My brother exaggerates. I find as much amusement in a night at the theater or circus as anyone."

Feeling a stir of compassion for his obvious discomfort, Jessamine volunteered, "This is only our second visit to London, but both times I have fallen in love with the parks. I thought London would be nothing but buildings crowded together, but I am amazed at the number of parks and squares. And Kensington Gardens is lovely."

"Have you been to any of the botanical gardens?" Mr. Marfleet asked her.

She shook her head, embarrassed to have the focus back on herself.

"Lancelot fancies himself an amateur botanist," his brother said. "Our house is filled with exotic specimens he brought back from India."

"You were able to bring back plants?" Megan asked. "Jessamine's father would jump at the chance to see them."

Once again she was the recipient of Mr. Marfleet's slate-blue gaze. "Your father is a botanist?"

"My father is a vicar. Botany is only a hobby."

"As with me. Botany is but an interest. I would be delighted to show your father my specimens if he ever is in London."

"My father rarely travels." She despised herself for her short answers, but she would give him no encouragement. The last thing she desired was a suitor who was both a clergyman *and* a botany enthusiast.

Let him set his sights on Megan. With that resolve, she shifted her attention to her friend.

"Those scraggly plants are worth their weight in gold, considering Lancelot almost died procuring them," Sir Harold said, clapping his brother on the shoulder. "I suppose we should be thankful for that fever, otherwise he'd still be over there preaching to the heathens. If Mama and Papa have their way, he is back to stay, settled in a cozy vicarage for the rest of his days."

As a pause descended, Sir Harold stepped back. "Well, I must be off. Are you sure I cannot offer you a ride? It will be no trouble to call for the carriage."

As they continued to insist it was unnecessary, Sir Harold said, "At least let my brother escort you. It won't do to go unaccompanied on Bond Street—not at this hour." He glanced at his pocket watch again and shook his head. "The Bond Street beaux will be emerging by now."

When Jessamine began to protest, he added, "He hates driving with me anyway. I'm off to Tattersall's to see a horse. Lancelot would be no help at all there. You'll be doing me a favor by taking him off my hands."

Before Jessamine could think of a graceful way to refuse, Megan replied, "If you put it like that, Sir Harold, we should be grateful of your brother's company." She hastened to assure Mr. Marfleet, "Even if only for a short way. We really don't want to put you out."

With a few more assurances, they finally were off. Mr. Marfleet walked between Megan and Jessamine.

When they turned onto Bond Street, Jessamine had to admit she was glad of his escort. The wide thoroughfare had filled with pedestrian and carriage traffic. It was the most fashionable place for shops. Neither she nor Megan had yet tired of looking in all the windows. As they made their way along the crowded pavement, it soon became impossible to walk three abreast. Mr. Marfleet took the cobbled street, allowing the two of them the flagstone pavement.

His action contrasted sharply with the behavior of the young dandies Sir Harold had warned them about, who strutted along the pavements arm in arm, ogling the young ladies through their quizzing glasses, unmindful of pushing older matrons onto the street.

"Tell us more about your time in India," Megan said. "What made you decide to go as a missionary?"

Mr. Marfleet studied the knob of his walking stick a moment before replying. "I can best attribute it to a sermon I heard the Reverend Charles Simeon give while I was at Cambridge." He glanced at them, adding lightly, "It quite changed my life."

"Changed your life? However so?" Megan looked at him, her curiosity no more keen than Jessamine's unspoken one.

He flushed, his smile abashed. "I didn't mean to imply I had received a bolt of lightning. Simply that the rector's exhortation about the need to take the gospel to the ends of the earth convicted me in such a way I'd never felt before, as if I were hearing Jesus's commission to reach the lost for the first time. I was sent to several outposts—Serampur, Danapur, Cawnpore—all in northeast India."

"How awe inspiring," breathed Megan. "When did you decide to go into the church?"

"It was either that or the law, as a second son, you know," he said with a quirk of his lips. He had a mobile face, every nuance of self-disparagement or irony reflected in an expression of his lips or eyes. Against her will, Jessamine found herself studying it, even as his words drew her attention.

"My brother could have gone into my father's business," Megan said. "He was a merchant in Bristol, but the war ruined his business. My brother chose instead to run off to the navy."

Mr. Marfleet took their arms as they crossed the street. "The war gave many young men the opportunity to advance. That is," he added with a wry grimace, "if they survived. I'm sorry, I hope your brother is all right."

Megan smiled. "He is quite all right, thank you for your concern. He left the navy after being wounded and taken prisoner some months in a French jail near Calais. He is with the British Embassy in Paris now, serving under the Duke of Wellington."

Jessamine listened to her best friend recite the accomplishments of Rees Phillips, pride evident in her voice. Poor Megan, who had to be so careful of Jessamine's feelings when they were together, now had someone to whom she could openly boast about her brother.

"That must be an interesting career. I'd never thought of it myself, but perhaps as a lawyer, I could have made my way in the diplomatic field."

"My brother was in Paris at the liberation with Wellington, and then he was invited to Vienna for the congress under Lord Castlereagh. His wife is French, which is of great benefit, he writes, both in Vienna and Paris."

Mr. Marfleet quirked an eyebrow. "He met someone while he was in France?"

"Actually, he met her while they both lived here in London a couple of years ago. Mother and I were both stunned when he wrote us a letter after arriving in Paris last summer that he had met up with her again and was planning to marry her. She had returned to France shortly before the war ended. We haven't seen him since he left England—and have not met her at all."

"It sounds like a romantic tale."

"Indeed it does." Megan's eyes sparkled. "If you knew my brother, you would say he is the least romantic person in the world!"

Their conversation scraped against Jessamine's heart like a dull knife, abrading her scars afresh. Why should Rees want a poor country girl, who was only passably pretty when he could have Lady Céline Wexham, by all accounts an exotic, dark beauty? With all the accompanying wiles of a Frenchwoman, Jessamine was sure.

She had lost track of Megan's conversation with Mr. Marfleet and had to stop abruptly when Megan thrust her arm in front of her, pointing to a shop window. "We have a commission for Lady Bess—our hostess," she explained to Mr. Marfleet. "If you could wait for me a moment while I run into this linen draper's?"

She included Jessamine in her apologetic smile. "You wouldn't mind keeping Mr. Marfleet company so he doesn't get bored if I'm delayed? You know how Lady Bess says I have an eye for color?"

Megan left her with little choice but to murmur, "Very well," even as she fixed her eyes on the shop window, remembering how she was wearing her spectacles. Would Mr. Marfleet make an observation on them?

As soon as Megan entered the store, an awkward silence descended between them. Jessamine pretended to study the display of fabrics and notions.

Mr. Marfleet cleared his throat.

Wondering if he meant to get her attention, she lifted her gaze. A tentative smile hovered around his lips. "You wear spectacles."

She stared at him. A polite gentleman would *not* have noticed. "I should think it obvious," she said between her teeth.

Color suffused his cheeks once more. If she were as outspoken as he, she'd point out how his skin reflected every emotion he felt.

"I—I beg your pardon. It's just that you weren't the night I spoke to you. I just find it interesting because . . . because of the fact that I do too."

Did he think that implied they had anything else in common?

She turned back to the shop window. Unfortunately, it only gave her a reflection of her oval spectacles. She quickly looked down, mortified at her predicament. Why did this gentleman make her feel so gauche and ill-mannered?

"I'm sorry if I offended you."

"You didn't." She kept her gaze fixed on a beaded handbag displayed against a velvet backdrop.

"I find it refreshing to see a young lady wearing spectacles instead of groping about half blind."

"Is that why you are not wearing yours?" she asked, giving him a pointed look.

He twisted his lips. "Harold does not allow himself to be seen in public with me if I do. That's why I wasn't wearing them at the rout, but then I had to put them on to search for Lady Abernathy."

"I see." She fought to keep from smiling at his awkward explanation. "Lady Bess is the same with me," she finally admitted. "She makes it sound like the gravest sin to be seen wearing spectacles in public. I'm only a trifle shortsighted so I don't really need them unless I want to focus on something particularly."

"Mine comes from years of too much study, poring over books till the wee hours."

Jessamine shrugged. "I haven't any such excuse, although I help my father with his botanical notes and sermon notes and prayers for services."

His light red eyebrows lifted a fraction. "Are you interested in botany too?"

She turned away from his scrutiny to study the passersby, regretting her words. She did not want him to think they had anything in common. "I like flowers. My father takes it to the scientific level."

"I should like to meet your father. He sounds a very interesting man."

"He is a very good man."

Another silence fell between them. After a moment, Mr. Marfleet cleared his throat. "Miss Phillips speaks very fondly of her brother."

"Yes," she answered shortly, dreading to have to discuss Rees with this gentleman. Striving to keep her voice devoid of emotion, she added, "He is her only sibling, so it is natural."

He gave a wry laugh. "I confess I don't think I could speak in such glowing terms of Harold, nor he of me—not that we are not fond of each other. We have seen so little of one another since our school days."

Her gaze returned unwillingly to him as he spoke. "He seems very different from you."

His lips twisted. "I used to wonder if we were born of the same parents. He was the true Marfleet since he so resembled my father in both looks and temperament. I was the foundling my mother had rescued from the doorstep one wintry morn."

Her heart caught at the wistful image of a young boy questioning his place in such an august family. "Do you think you could have been a . . . a foundling?"

His blue eyes took on a thoughtful look. "I tried to discover it for years but must confess I never found proof of it. Still, one never knows when a new fact may emerge."

She narrowed her eyes, wondering if he was making fun of her. But his eyes had a perfectly serious cast as he rubbed his chin, as if considering.

"I should think there would have been some clues along the way if you were really not your parents' offspring."

"My parents are quite closemouthed about many things, especially anything that hints of scandal. No," he said, a speculative look in his eyes, "if there were clues, I didn't find them. Perhaps I was left on the doorstep by a maid who didn't want to give her baby up to the orphanage, hearing the horrors of that place. And she didn't want to lose her job—"

"She would hardly be able to keep her condition secret in your household all those months." As she realized the indecorous topic she was discussing with a young gentleman she scarcely knew, she clamped her lips together and turned away from him. "This is an unseemly subject."

"You brought it up with your suspicions."

"I?" She flashed him a look of outrage only to find his eyes filled with amusement. "You were making all that up."

He tugged on an earlobe, looking sheepish. "I confess, no matter how uncertain my heritage, I'm afraid the proof of it is undeniable. A portrait of my grandfather hangs in the family gallery. I resemble him to a great degree, including my coloring. Thus, despite the more romantic appeal of being a foundling, I am only the ugly younger son of Sir Geoffrey Marfleet."

"Younger and ruder," she muttered, looking away again.

"You do seem to bring out the worst in me."

"Then I would suggest you stay away from me. I do not like to be thought of as detrimental to a person's conduct," she ended stiffly. She wished she were better at parrying and thrusting his mockery.

"You are not detrimental. It is I who am at fault. Being away from civilized London society seems to have turned me into a person who cannot keep a proper rein on his tongue. I do beg your pardon once again."

When she said nothing, he added quietly, "My time in India has also made me more keenly aware of the ridiculous. I don't say this to boast. I am merely stating a tendency I don't seem able to control since returning to England. India has made me see things from a different perspective. Manners and behavior I took for granted as the way they are supposed to be appear absurd to me now."

As he spoke, her irritation diminished, replaced by a grudging fascination for what he said.

"I have lost the ability to behave as I should around young ladies—if ever I had the ability, which my brother is quick to point out I did not."

She lifted her chin. "You don't treat Miss Phillips with ridicule."

His reddish eyebrows drew together. "Ridicule? It was not meant so, believe me. It was just . . . just that the situation appeared ridiculous and my tongue ran away with me, taking the matter to its conclusion."

Jessamine pressed her lips, resolving to say no more to him. His explanation might satisfy—and even move her—but she was not disposed to render herself up to his ridicule another time. She had no interest in garnering the admiration of a vicar. She was grateful for the dinner invitation he had procured for them, but that was all.

"I see I have offended you," he said gravely when she maintained her silence.

Before she could think of a suitably indifferent reply, Megan exited the shop, her face alight. "I haven't kept you two waiting too long, have I?" She turned to Jessamine without waiting for a reply. "I found the shade of primrose Lady Bess desired. It matches the sample she gave me perfectly."

"I'm glad."

"Shall we continue on our way?" she asked Mr. Marfleet.

"If you are ready," he answered courteously.

Jessamine searched for the slightest hint of mockery in his look or tone, but his demeanor looked as polite as his words sounded.

She gave a pointed look as if to say, *See? You save your mockery for me.*

He only lifted a brow in bland inquiry.

They resumed walking, Jessamine positioning herself on the far side of Megan, away from Mr. Marfleet. Let him continue the conversation with her friend, with whom he seemed to manage to control his mocking tendencies.

After bidding farewell to Miss Phillips and Miss Barry at their brick town house not far from Portland Place, Lancelot decided to return home on foot.

He needed the time a walk would afford to mull over his encounter with the two young ladies. He'd been surprised—pleasantly so—to find them on his street earlier. He'd been going back and forth about having asked his mother to invite them to one of her exclusive dinner parties.

He cared nothing for such things as pedigree and portion, but his parents did. After quizzing him for a good quarter of an hour on the two young ladies, his mother had finally agreed to the invitation. "I suppose I should be thankful you are evincing the slightest interest in any young lady who is of sound mind and limb." She sighed, picking up her pen. "You are seven-and-twenty and still unmarried. Your brother will no longer have any offspring. What is to become of the estate if you don't settle down and start a family?"

He turned off the familiar litany he'd heard all during his convalescence, thankful at least that his mother would issue the invitation.

As he walked along Oxford Street, he wasn't sure whether to be put off or annoyed with Miss Barry. Miss Phillips was a pleasant companion, but there was something about Miss Barry that drew him. Whether it was her flashing green eyes which could as quickly show annoyance as a hint of humor, or whether it was the way she listened to his tale of the doubts of belonging to his family, she evinced empathy and a depth of understanding he had not yet encountered in a young lady of the ton.

But now he doubted his instincts, realizing he was probably reading more into her glances than they conveyed. The likeliest thing was that she despised him for his tendency to ironic humor. He hadn't meant to tease her and regretted his words.

With a shake of his head, he tried to dismiss their conversation from his mind. He had too many other things to think about to get stirred up over a young lady making her come-out in London.

When he arrived home, he took up the journal he'd kept during his travels in India and went in search of his younger sister.

He went first to the solarium which their parents had built to satisfy his hobby of cultivating plants and hers of painting them.

Delawney sat on a stool before an easel in a narrow aisle hemmed in on either side with lush green foliage. Beside her stood a small table filled with brushes and tablets of watercolors.

"There you are," was all she said as he walked between the potted plants, the moist air enveloping him.

"I hope I haven't held you up."

Instead of replying, she asked, "What do you think?" Moving aside, she held up her brush to allow him to view the watercolor she was working on.

It was a picture of the vine that grew from a pot she had placed beside the easel. Along its stem, a pink flower resembling a morning glory blossomed at intervals.

He'd brought it back from Bengal. "Exquisite," he said, satisfied that she'd reproduced it accurately. "The colors are perfect."

"I'm glad you approve."

"I do."

She let out a breath. "Good. I just need to put a few finishing touches on it." She glanced up at him. "How are your notes coming?"

He grimaced. "Slower than your watercolors."

"It's because you are spending all your time chasing after Harold, trying in vain to stop him from his certain destruction."

"Don't say that!"

She raised an eyebrow at his retort.

"Nothing is 'certain' in this life," he said more gently.

Her lips thinned in an uncompromising line. "You must let Harold squander his life as he wishes. Your preaching to him shan't change him, you know."

Lancelot contemplated the soft tones of the watercolor. "I can't just stand back and see him run headlong to that destruction. It's time he matured."

She snorted. "Why should he? Mama turns a blind eye, and Papa thinks that's the way any gentleman of the ton behaves."

Lancelot ran a hand through his hair. "Actually, it was Papa who asked me to try and curb his excesses."

"If he wants you acting as his guardian angel, it's only to curb his behavior, not to stop it entirely." She set her brush into the water jar and got up to stretch. "And Mama feels only a tragic sympathy, believing he is only trying to hide the failure of still being childless after so many years of marriage. What a burden," she said with exaggerated sorrow.

Lancelot fingered the edges of his journal he'd brought with him. "Yes, since my return I feel an ever-increasing pressure to marry and fill the lack."

Delawney picked up the brush and swished it in a watercolor to dab on a spot. "They have given up on me—besides which, a child of mine couldn't inherit."

She cocked an eyebrow at him. "Any progress on that front? Mama hinted that you'd met someone the other night."

Lancelot stared at his sister, feeling like a cobra caught by a snake charmer's flute.

4

A spurt of annoyance rose in Lancelot's chest at his mother's indiscretion. "Don't tell me you are going to join Mama and Papa in their campaign."

Delawney chuckled. "If it means they leave me in peace, I shall do so wholeheartedly."

His sister was an attractive woman, especially when she smiled. Her hair was a tawny shade like their mother's, but she kept it carelessly pulled back in a knot, sometimes with only a pencil holding it up. She wore a faded muslin gown with a ruffled white kerchief along its neckline. A wide white apron splotched with watercolors covered most of her gown. Her fingers, nicely shaped, were stained brown and gray from the amalgamation of colors.

"What is it?"

He shook his head, realizing he'd been staring. "Nothing. I still fail to understand your refusal to go out into society at all."

"If you don't understand it, then it is useless to try to explain."

"Just because I have little use for ton parties does not mean I renounce society completely. Our Lord commands us to take the message of salvation to everyone. How are we to do that if we shut ourselves from the world?"

She had no reply to that. His heart went out to her. She was not yet five-and-twenty, but it was doubtful she would ever marry. Instead of a young lady's usual pursuits of parties, shopping, and outings, she devoted herself to her gardens and watercolors of every specimen she discovered, which at present included the ones he had brought back from India. She had eagerly assented to his plan to put everything into a folio to be published.

"Which plant should I attempt next?"

Seeing she wanted the subject changed, he opened his notebook, leafing through it to the page he desired. "I thought perhaps this one the natives call 'tulsi.'" He walked over to the plant he referred to. It had grown to a few feet high and was now sprouting small pink flowers. "It's very aromatic, and they use it in both cooking and religious ceremonies. It's similar in coloring to the morning glory you just finished."

She touched one of the spindly clusters of tiny whitish-pink flowers gracing a stalk. "Very well. I shall begin it as soon as I'm satisfied with the other."

"Thank you."

"My pleasure."

He smiled at her, and she returned his smile. Sometimes it felt as if she was the only one in the family he had anything in common with. "I shall be in my room endeavoring to do some more work on my notes, before the lecture at the Royal Society."

"Don't let me keep you."

Accepting the dismissal, he bowed and left her, glad that everything was right between them.

"A pity there was no time for new gowns," Lady Bess said with a sigh. Jessamine had lost count of how many times Lady Bess had emitted an audible sigh in the stuffy hackney they had been obliged to hire for the drive to the Marfleet residence.

Across the shabby coach, Lady Bess eyed Megan and Jessamine through her quizzing glass in the fading light. "You do look very pretty, I'm sure. There is nothing like youth, which no gown or adornment can improve or take away from." She sighed again, as if remembering her own vanished girlhood.

"The sea green suits your dark hair and green eyes," she said to Jessamine, "and the pink your complexion and gray eyes," she said with an approving nod at Megan.

They murmured their thanks to their hostess, even though she'd already given them the same compliment upon first seeing them this evening.

"The important thing is that Mr. Marfleet will find you charming," Lady Bess said for the dozenth time. "I have been asking around about him, and he seems the opposite of his rakish brother. He's had the best of education—Harrow, Eton, then Cambridge to take orders, as a younger son, naturally, and one who didn't seem suited for the military."

She paused, her lips making a small moue of distaste. "I did hear that it was while at Cambridge that he came under the influence of one of that Clapham Sect with all their evangelical zeal. The next thing, he tells his poor parents he is becoming a missionary and heading off to Calcutta or some such place." She shuddered. "It's a wonder—a miracle—he didn't perish. Most do, you know. And some take their poor wives, who don't last long."

Jessamine couldn't help smiling, contrasting Lady Bess's account with Mr. Marfleet's.

"Lady Villington-Rhodes—she's cousin to Lady Marfleet—says the family didn't expect him to survive the fever he succumbed to. He was all winter recovering on their estate in Hampshire. Did he look ill?"

"Yes," said Jessamine at the same time Megan said, "No."

Lady Bess looked from one to the other and smiled. "Ah, I see how it is. Well, at least you shan't have to fight about him. Let us hope his mother seats you beside him, Megan. Perhaps there will be another young gentleman there for you, Jessamine. I won't be satisfied till you both end the season with a betrothal."

Giving them no chance to respond, Lady Bess pushed down the carriage window. "Good, we are almost there. It's a pretty street, one I rarely travel since it is not a main thoroughfare." She sat back against the squabs. "I wonder what the older brother is worth? I must inquire. A pity he's married. As for your Mr. Marfleet, I was informed he has no living at present since he was in India. I should think his father would be able to find him a competence on one of his own estates. Likely they are all filled." She shook her head, setting the lacy trim around her cap atremble. "I do hope his evangelical zeal has dimmed."

Jessamine leaned toward the window just as the carriage came to a halt. They were behind a line of carriages making their way to the Marfleet residence.

Megan was looking out the other window. "I should say there are at least a dozen carriages, Lady Bess, and they look so grand. Some even have a crest on them."

Lady Bess leaned forward once more, trying to see over her shoulder. "Can you see the color of the hammer-cloth or the footmen's livery?"

"I see blue with gold on a carriage two ahead of us."

Lady Bess pondered, sitting back and flicking open her peacock-feathered fan, which matched the color of her gown. "That could be the Earl and Countess of Withycombe or perhaps the Marquess of Grenfell."

Unable to stifle her own curiosity, Jessamine put her spectacles on and peered out her window again. The coaches did indeed look grand, many with the coats of arms upon their doors and elegant liveried footmen on the footboards. Her heart began to thud as the reality of a dinner party sank in. "How many guests will there be, do you think? There seem to be an awful lot of carriages pulled up."

Lady Bess closed her fan and said with satisfaction, "Any respectable dinner party will have at least a dozen guests. This one, by the number of coaches here already, will have at least twenty, I'd wager."

A heavy, leaden sensation settled into the pit of Jessamine's stomach.

"Twenty," breathed Megan, excitement sparkling in her eyes.

Why hadn't Jessamine pleaded indisposition and stayed home? Why had she insisted on a London season and not been content to remain in her small village where she knew everyone and was comfortable with them all?

"The baronet has a seat in the House of Commons, so there will be other members present, I'm sure. He is a Tory, so I wouldn't expect any Whigs."

Before Lady Bess could launch into another summary of all she'd gleaned in the past two days about the Marfleet family, the coach lurched again, sending her forward.

As she settled herself once more upon her seat, the coach moved only a short way before stopping. They waited in silence, tense. Even Lady Bess looked subdued, her fan clutched in her pudgy, beringed hands.

"At least we are not the first nor, hopefully, the last guests to arrive," she said when the coach moved forward.

After a quarter of an hour of stopping and starting, their hired coach pulled in front of the entrance. Jessamine leaned over Megan's shoulder, recognizing the fluted pilasters on either side of the door, which stood wide open this evening. A red carpet led down the steps onto the pavement to the carriage.

"Take off those hideous spectacles!" hissed Lady Bess.

Hurriedly, Jessamine complied, having seen enough, and stuffed them through the drawstring of her beaded reticule with shaking fingers. She quickly pulled the twisted silk cords closed just as a footman opened their door.

Wearing blue velvet livery and a powdered wig, he let down the step and handed out first Lady Bess then Megan and lastly Jessamine, who had deliberately hung back.

This would be her first real foray into London society. What would she say and do? How to behave? Would she meet someone to take her mind and heart off Rees Phillips for the first time since he'd dropped her for that Frenchwoman?

As these thoughts scurried through her mind like a mouse over a dining table, never stopping for long at any one dish, the footman handed her down, and she smoothed her gown before proceeding up the wide carpet behind her godmother and Megan.

Another footman met them at the door. He looked identical to the first, both tall and broad shouldered. He took their wraps, though Lady Bess retained her shawl, declaring one never knew when there would be a draft, even in the best of houses.

This footman led them up a wide, semicircular staircase to the first floor, where an older man, undoubtedly the butler, met them and took them into a room brightly lit by dozens of wall sconces and a chandelier hanging from the plastered ceiling.

He announced, "Lady Beasinger, Miss Barry, Miss Phillips."

A sea of faces seemed to turn their way. How many were titled ladies and gentlemen, members of Parliament or high-placed officers, she wondered, spotting a red coat in the midst.

It was not quite a sea, she amended, seeing not a crowd but well over at least two dozen individuals. Lady Bess turned to greet their hosts. At the same time, Mr. Marfleet came up to them with a hesitant smile.

"Good evening." He bowed to both Jessamine and Megan as Lady Bess spoke to Sir Geoffrey and his wife. "I'm glad you could come. May I present my parents, Sir Geoffrey and Lady Marfleet? And my sister, Miss Delawney Marfleet?"

Jessamine faced a distinguished-looking couple and a young lady at their side. She made her curtsy alongside Megan.

Sir Geoffrey reminded her of Sir Harold in a mature, fiftyish way, his dark blond, wavy hair graying at the temples. Still handsome, his chiseled features were ruddy as if he spent time out-of-doors, hunting perhaps. Blue eyes stared into hers, a blond eyebrow raised appraisingly.

Lady Marfleet was a tall woman with upswept hair a shade darker than her husband's under a diamond and sapphire tiara. Miss Marfleet was tall like her mother, her hair a similar shade, but the resemblance ended there. She wore no jewels, and her hair was pulled back tightly, doing nothing to soften strong features like her father's.

"How lovely to meet you two young ladies. Lancelot tells me this is your first season," Lady Marfleet said in a cultivated voice.

As they murmured their polite affirmatives, Jessamine felt every detail of their toilette taken in by those seemingly warm brown eyes. Fleetingly she remembered her conversation with Mr. Marfleet about his being a foundling on the doorstep, and almost burst into laughter. She stifled it just as Lady Marfleet dismissed her and Megan with a slight movement of her patrician chin.

They followed Lady Bess farther into the room. The carpet was so plush that Jessamine's slippers sank into it without a sound.

All around came the steady drone of voices. The room continued to fill with entering guests, the black or dark-blue coats of the gentlemen relieved by the brightly colored gowns of the ladies. She and Megan seemed to be the only ones in pale-colored gowns as befitted unmarried young ladies.

Everyone around them seemed to know one another in contrast to her and Megan, who stood huddled beside Lady Bess as chicks under a hen.

Mr. Marfleet appeared at her elbow. "Thank you for coming. I hope it doesn't prove frightfully boring for you. They're mainly my father's guests, fellow MPs, you know." He seemed ill at ease, and again she remembered their last conversation, this time remembering his words "ugly younger son of Sir Geoffrey Marfleet."

Did he feel like an ugly duckling among his handsome parents and brother? Even his sister had a striking look about her, though she hid it behind an unfashionable coiffure and gown.

"My dear boy, we are tickled that you had your mother include us in your party," Lady Bess told him. She had no qualms about lifting her quizzing glass to her eye and subjecting him to the same scrutiny his mother had given Jessamine and Megan.

His sister stood at his side, looking at Megan and Jessamine with frank curiosity.

Lady Bess's quizzing glass focused on something beyond Mr. Marfleet's shoulder. "Isn't that Lady Gouldsborough? I haven't seen her in an age. Not since she remarried."

Mr. Marfleet turned a fraction. "Yes, it is she with Henry Dalton. She is Mrs. Dalton now."

"I must say hello, if the two of you will keep the young ladies company for a moment?"

"With pleasure," he murmured.

Lady Bess was off in a flurry of lace.

Megan giggled. "You mustn't feel compelled to stay with us. We are quite accustomed by now to standing about not knowing a soul, are we not, Jessamine?"

Jessamine smiled with effort. She did wish at times that Megan weren't quite so forthcoming about their lack of social standing. "Indeed."

"Then you are in good company," he returned with an easy smile that included them both. "Since my return to London, I scarcely know anyone."

"And is not particularly desirous of remedying the situation," his sister added.

He looked abashed. "Not particularly. You heard the despair in my brother's tone, and now my sister betrays me."

Megan looked around her. "Where is he, by the way?"

"Harold isn't here. He rarely attends my mother's dinner parties. He has his own town house—he and his wife."

"I see. Is she in town?"

"No," Miss Marfleet answered. "Lady Rosamunde Marfleet is at their country place in Hampshire. She prefers it to London."

Megan nodded.

"If you think I am unwilling to go into society, my sister here is worse. The only reason she condescended to come to dinner this evening was that it is under her own roof and she must eat."

"My brother exaggerates. He has the luxury of running off to places like India where he can escape British society, and then has the temerity to come back and criticize me."

Jessamine blinked at the raillery between brother and sister.

Mr. Marfleet gave his sister a lopsided grin. "And yet the moment I return and am well enough to be on my feet, I obey the pater and accept invitations high and low." He addressed Megan and Jessamine. "My sister stays ensconced in our solarium and paints. She is an accomplished watercolorist."

Jessamine eyed her with new curiosity. Miss Marfleet shrugged off her brother's words. "I am passable. But at the moment he flatters me, since he needs me to illustrate the dozens of plant specimens he brought back from India."

Mr. Marfleet took no offense at her words, merely smiled indulgently and said, "She is very gifted in her abilities."

Miss Marfleet raised her eyebrows with an expression of "you see?"

Jessamine said, "My father would love to see your paintings, I'm sure. He is . . . somewhat of an amateur botanist, though he does not travel. But he frequently experiments with new varieties of flowers in our small glasshouse at the vicarage."

"I should like to see his collection," Mr. Marfleet said at once.

"I'm sure it is nothing like what you have brought back with you."

"If my brother has his way, he shall publish his findings in a folio," Miss Marfleet said. "That is why I am doing my best to illustrate them for him."

"How fascinating," Megan said. "I look forward to seeing it. I can't paint worth a straw, although it is an accomplishment all young ladies are supposed to have."

"Since it is my only accomplishment, I do not feel any overweening pride in it."

"You look very pretty this evening," Mr. Marfleet said in the pause that followed, his glance encompassing both Megan and Jessamine.

Megan executed a curtsy. "Thank you, sir, but we feel quite dowdy ever since arriving in London."

Jessamine envied her friend her easy manner.

"You wouldn't feel so in India," he said, "unless you felt overshadowed by the brightly-colored cloth some of the women attire themselves in. They can be quite pretty."

"It must be terribly exotic," Megan said.

"Even the colors of the land are intense. It's such a vast area that the regions vary enormously."

"I've heard it is very hot," Jessamine said, just to contribute something.

"Except for the mountains to the north, yes, it is," Mr. Marfleet replied. "That is why Europeans quickly succumb to the various diseases that are so prevalent. Our constitutions don't seem able to withstand the oppressive heat."

Before she could ask him anything about his health, his mother requested that they find their partners for dinner.

"I'm to escort you," he told her, "and my friend Donald Emery"—he indicated another young gentleman who approached them—"is to escort you, Miss Phillips."

The brown-haired gentleman bowed to Megan. "At your service, miss."

"Thank you." She returned his smile and placed her hand on his proffered arm.

Jessamine felt a pang. All Megan had to do was smile. It lit up her face and looked so genuinely warm that both men and women were won over. Jessamine knew the smile was sincere. By contrast her own smile felt as stiff as the plaster molding the ceiling.

"Shall we?"

"Oh—yes, thank you."

Mr. Marfleet stood waiting, his bent arm held out. She placed her gloved hand atop it. He was dressed in a black coat and pantaloons, looking, except for his cravat, every inch a vicar. She should have spotted it immediately, she who'd grown up in a parsonage and had been around vicars all her life.

"You are very quiet this evening. I hope this company doesn't intimidate you."

She started at his words. He would think she was addlepated if she didn't start paying attention to what was going on around her. "Not at all," she answered tartly.

"Is it because you can't see them?"

"What!" Her gaze flew up to his. He was wearing his spectacles, but they did not hide the amusement in his eyes.

She had a good mind to whip hers out of her reticule and put them on to show him she didn't care a fig what she looked like. What a pair they'd make! But she wouldn't give him the satisfaction.

She looked straight ahead of her as they walked to the dining room. "I told you, I am not so shortsighted, as you perhaps"—she glanced sidelong at him—"and only wear my spectacles when I need to focus on some minute object in the distance."

Before he could reply, she continued. "I didn't wear them tonight since I didn't expect to address those sitting across the dinner table, but then again, a gentleman who speaks to a lady he has not been introduced to perhaps expects his guests to do the same."

She had the satisfaction of seeing his cheeks turn a ruddy hue.

"I have already asked your pardon about that," he said in formal tones, all amusement erased from his eyes. "I don't know why I did it. I can assure you I am not in the habit of addressing young ladies I have no acquaintance with."

They arrived in the dining room, and Mr. Marfleet showed her to her seat. As she had expected, both she and Megan were seated near the foot of the table as their lack of rank demanded. She was surprised when Mr. Marfleet took his place beside her. She thought as son, he would be seated closer to the head of the table.

As if reading her mind, he cocked an eyebrow. "Did you not expect me to sit beside you when you are my guest?"

She felt her cheeks warm. "I didn't know what to expect, to be perfectly frank." She sought Megan, who was sitting directly across the table from Mr. Marfleet. Mr. Emery sat beside her across from Jessamine. She smiled in their general direction before looking around for Lady Bess.

She made out her peacock-blue gown and fan farther down the table; Lady Bess was already feeling at home among her dinner companions from the sound of her voice. "Thank you for including Lady Bess in the invitation," Jessamine said in a low tone to Mr. Marfleet.

"It was nothing. Besides, I could not very well invite you and Miss Phillips without a chaperon, could I? I am not so far gone from propriety, no matter how long I've been in India." The wry humor had returned to his tone.

She fixed her attention on the table instead of replying to him. She did not wish to appear too friendly to him. It would do no good to encourage him. Her supposition that his interest lay in Megan must have been wrong, yet she did not want him to think she was available.

Everything on the table was exquisite from the white damask linen to the gilt-edged plates, heavy silverware, and fragile crystal goblets atop it. The center of the long table held crystal vases filled with arrangements of flowers cascading over their sides and ivy trailing along the tablecloth.

The footmen began serving the first remove, a creamy soup. There were many other dishes on the table, and Mr. Marfleet did his duty offering her a selection.

Accustomed around her father's table to say grace before meals, she discreetly bowed her head and uttered a short prayer.

When she took up her fork, Mr. Marfleet said quietly at her left, "Amen. I'm sorry my parents do not generally say a blessing over the meal—especially not at a dinner party."

"There is no need to apologize. I didn't expect it of them."

He swallowed a spoonful of soup and then said, "Your father is a vicar as well as an amateur botanist?"

"Yes," she replied after taking a spoonful.

"That is perhaps why he named you as he did?"

She nodded cautiously, surprised that he had made the association.

"Jessamine. Yellow jasmine. *Gelsemium sempervirens.*"

"Or plain wild woodbine, not nearly so exotic."

"But just as beautiful."

She dabbed at her lips with a napkin, feeling uncomfortable with his notice. "My father's passion—besides that for the Lord—is flowers. He loves the beauty of them. He has developed a couple of new varieties of roses and a peony."

"I shall have to look up his name."

"He hasn't any renown. He hasn't sought publication, and if I didn't keep his notes straight, he'd probably have forgotten half of what he's done."

"He is a devout man? Forgive my asking," he added quickly, "but being a member of the clergy does not guarantee devotion. I have found sometimes quite the reverse."

"No, indeed," she was quick to agree. "My father, however, is devout. That is perhaps why he has remained a lowly vicar in a small village when he could have moved to a bigger parish when the opportunity presented itself. But he knew his flock would be neglected . . . under the present rector."

Mr. Marfleet nodded, as if understanding perfectly what she said without having to hear more. She knew her father would not want her to malign his overseer.

When she had eaten more of her soup, she ventured to ask, "Are you a member of the Clapham Sect?"

He set his spoon down, cocking an eyebrow at her. "Where did you hear that?"

She made a vague motion with her hand. "Lady Bess heard it somewhere and concluded it had something to with your having become a missionary."

He toyed with the handle of his spoon before replying. "She was not far from wrong. I have been influenced by them, certainly, but am not myself a member. My greatest mentor, as I told you, Reverend Simeon, however, is a member of the Clapham Sect."

As the first remove was cleared and a Dover sole served, Jessamine sat back. "How long were you in India?" she asked, telling herself that if she had to sit beside him through dinner, she might as well get to know him. He did appear to have led an interesting life.

"A little over two years. Not nearly enough to do anything that would seem on the surface to amount to much, in terms of souls won—especially when I was sick half the time," he added with a grimace. "I can only trust that the Lord used me to plant seeds that may someday bear fruit."

"It must have been very difficult, with India being so different from England."

"Imagine if you can a land completely alien to our Christian world—not only in religious traditions but in every tradition we hold dear. A land where people have none of the modern advances we begin to take for granted. Everything is primitive, barbaric to the European eye—and yet, as a person representing the gospel, one is called to view the natives through the loving eyes of the Savior, who wants their salvation as much as our own."

The more Mr. Marfleet spoke, the more he reminded her of her father, whose gentle character cared deeply about souls. Jessamine sighed. After her heartbreak over Rees, she did not want to wed a man who preached patience, resignation, and submission to God's will above all else. All those virtues had brought her nothing but pain and a sense of wasted years.

It was clear her virtue was not enough to incite a man's love. No, a woman of beauty and charm and other worldly allurements was what won a man's heart.

A footman hovered between them, holding out a platter of thinly sliced roast beef, which Mr. Marfleet served her before serving himself. "I worked alongside some fine men who have sacrificed much to bring the gospel to the native population, among them Henry Martyn. He was a chaplain with the East India Company. Have you heard of him?"

"Yes, my father has mentioned him to me. He died there, didn't he?"

He seemed impressed that she should know the name. "Yes. It is most unfortunate. He was still quite a young man. But in the short time he had, he accomplished an astounding amount, including translating the Scriptures into many languages and dialects of the region. His will be a legacy of long duration."

"He must have been very dedicated."

"Yes, all of the missionaries over there are—they and their wives. Many have perished." He cut a slice of his meat. "I would still be there if not for the recurring fever."

"I'm sorry," she said in a polite tone, although her spirits were sinking the more he spoke.

"I'm sorry, rather, to be boring you. I hadn't meant to go on about being a missionary."

"You weren't boring me."

His lips curved upward. "Your scowl suggested otherwise, unless it is something on your plate."

She glanced down at the slices of roast beef on her plate. They were done to a turn, small roasted potatoes and onion beside them. "Everything looks delicious."

"I am relieved. So, it must have been the conversation."

She met his gaze, noticing the striking color of his eyes. His irises were a pale slate blue ringed in a deeper midnight blue. "No, it was not the topic of conversation. It was just that for a moment you reminded me quite forcefully of my father."

He quirked a pale red eyebrow upward, but rather than explain, she picked up her fork and knife and began to cut her meat. It would do no good to attempt an explanation, since she didn't fully understand it herself. All she knew was that she was dissatisfied with the life she had led up to now in her sheltered vicarage.

"You do not get along with your father?"

"I get along splendidly with my father." That much was true as far as it went.

"Your tone of voice did not suggest a compliment."

"It was neither a compliment nor insult. It was merely an observation."

"I see."

Out of the corner of her eye, she watched him chew his meat.

Unwilling to pursue the topic of her father, she took the moment to turn to her other dinner companion. He was a middle-aged gentleman who was eating with relish. As if sensing her attention on him, he wiped his mouth with the napkin tucked into his collar. "Delicious roast. Lady Marfleet has the best table in Mayfair."

"Yes, it is delicious," she agreed and took another bite to show her agreement.

In a lull in the conversation around her, a distinct female voice reached her across the table.

"The Parisian citizenry has welcomed Napoleon with open arms."

"Silly frogs," the man beside her muttered in a tone of disgust. "You would think they'd had enough war."

Sir Geoffrey directed his words to the lady. "Louis certainly proved his mettle, turning tail and sneaking off to Brussels."

The company around them laughed.

Knowing that Rees was on the continent, Jessamine had been following the news of Napoleon's escape from the island of Elba a few weeks ago. The newspapers had filled everyone with alarm as they predicted what he would do with the remnant of his loyal soldiers.

"Knowing Wellington is in Brussels should reassure Louis no matter how hot things get in Paris. Louis knows there is no better man if things come to war," the man beside her said in a loud voice.

Another guest raised his fork and pointed it at them all. "I wager Napoleon is going to attack the Allies before they attack him."

The lady exclaimed in horror, "Is he mad? He can have no troops left!"

"The French are a rabid lot—all glory, regardless of how few men he has left. Napoleon is a madman," Sir Geoffrey said in disgust.

"I've heard the troops sent out to arrest him dropped their arms and joined him as soon as he appeared in France," the lady said.

"Fools!" harrumphed the man beside Jessamine. "They deserve him!" He put a forkful of roast in his mouth and chewed with a vengeance.

Jessamine glanced to see how Mr. Marfleet was reacting to the topic and found him listening to each speaker. He smiled slightly at her but said nothing. The same way her father would have reacted, she thought. He rarely engaged in political disputes.

"What we've heard from the Foreign Office is that Napoleon is struggling to form a new government in Paris. Let us hope he is kept busy with that and has no time to think of war," another gentleman said in a quieter, more reasoned voice. "Perhaps that will give Wellington time to get our army in order and join forces with the other allied troops."

Jessamine remembered that Lady Bess had said members of Parliament would be present at the dinner, and she surmised that this gentleman was one.

Jessamine heard Megan's voice. "My brother is in Brussels with Wellington."

Jessamine's breath caught. Rees was in Belgium? The last she had heard he was in Vienna with the congress. When had he gone to Brussels? She stared at Megan. How long had Megan known? Why hadn't she told Jessamine?

Even as she realized why Megan would have said nothing, to avoid reminding her of Rees, Jessamine felt hurt. It was all Rees's fault, she thought. He had come between her and her closest friend.

The lady who had started the conversation leaned across Mr. Emery and said to Megan, "La, my dear, if your brother is in Brussels, he'll be having the time of his life. Brussels is nothing but a round of parties. Anybody of any consequence is there now. I have half a mind to cross the channel myself."

"Then you don't think there is any danger for him there? He is with his bride of a few months."

"What is her name, my dear?"

"Céline de Beaumont, formerly the Countess of Wexham."

The French name stabbed Jessamine's heart, yet she couldn't help straining forward to catch every word about the woman who had wrecked her dreams.

"Céline! I know her well, though I haven't seen her since she left England for France. There was some talk at the time, but I'm sure that is all over. Who is your brother?"

"Rees Phillips. He is with the British delegation. He was working with Lord Castlereagh at the Congress of Vienna until Lord Wellington took over for him there."

The lady nodded. "Your brother must be a special man to have won the Countess of Wexham."

"He is. I haven't met her. They have not returned to England since the peace."

"Your brother is fortunate to be with Wellington in Brussels at the moment," the lady said. "The duke is the darling of society from Vienna to Brussels. Your brother shall have a stupendous career—especially if he has Lady Wexham at his side."

"I trust it is as you say."

Jessamine strained to listen to their conversation about Rees and his bride, imagining the world Rees now inhabited, a world of parties and important world events among brilliant people, doing what he'd always dreamed of doing, with the beautiful countess at his side.

From the time she was seventeen, Jessamine had refused to look at another man, deciding she would wait until the day Megan's older brother would notice she had grown up.

She had loved him since she was thirteen. The Phillips family had moved to their village when she was a young child. Megan and she had quickly become playmates, living next door to each other. Megan's older brother, Rees, years older than the two of them, had been away fighting the French with His Majesty's navy.

It wasn't until he left the navy and begun working in London, when Rees was about twenty-five and Jessamine thirteen, that she had developed a *tendre* for him. He was such a handsome, good brother to Megan—kind and patient with his young sister, who was only eleven at the time. He was always bringing her a gift when he came home to visit, even though she knew from Mrs. Phillips that he didn't earn much as a junior clerk in the Foreign Office and every penny he earned was for his mother's and sister's support.

Jessamine had grown to have the same respect and admiration for Rees that Megan had for her older brother, and wished her parents had given her an older brother too.

Jessamine's respect and admiration had grown into love until she looked forward to Rees's visits with a beating heart and trembling expectation that someday he might look upon her as more than his sister's closest friend.

And that miraculous, longed-for day had arrived a few years ago. Rees had begun to look at her with a special something in his gray eyes.

She'd turned eighteen and he was well-nigh thirty. But to her he didn't seem too old at all. On the contrary, he was grave and mature compared to the awkward, pimply young gentlemen at the local assemblies. Jessamine lived for Rees's visits and for bits of news Megan read from his frequent letters home.

Her hopes had almost born fruition until that fateful day he'd met that Frenchwoman, Céline Wexham, an earl's widow in London, under most suspect circumstances involving spying and intrigue, which she and Megan still didn't know the half of. To the shock of them all, Rees found her again in France after the war.

He had put his career, his entire reputation at risk, since there had been rumors that Céline had spied on the British during the war. Jessamine could not imagine the serious, disciplined Rees throwing away all he'd worked so hard for for a woman, certainly not for Jessamine herself, she admitted with the same bitterness that had plagued her since she'd heard of his sudden marriage. Rees's life had been one of self-denial and sacrifice as he toiled for years as a lowly clerk. What had this Frenchwoman done to make him behave like a madman? In less than a month, he had written from Vienna that he was married.

Jessamine stared unseeing as a footman removed her half-empty plate, as the familiar feelings of inadequacy flooded her. What could she, a nondescript country miss, have hoped to offer a distinguished man like Rees?

The conversation around her once more merged into a buzz of

voices while the footmen cleared the removes and laid out clean plates and cutlery.

She looked over at Mr. Marfleet, but he was engaged in conversation with the lady on his left. Would he leave everything for love of a woman? She couldn't imagine so. His life was tied to the Lord's work.

Her gaze traveled over the table, lingering on each gentlemen. Could any of them leave everything behind—their families, their country—for the woman they loved?

Her gaze came to rest on the lady who had spoken to Megan. Perhaps for a woman as beautiful, intelligent, and charming as she. She imagined this was what the Countess of Wexham must look like—dressed in a red gown with a low décolletage, diamonds glinting in her dark tresses. Had she enthralled poor Rees with her female allurements the way this woman seemed to captivate the men sitting near her?

Jessamine remembered Mr. Marfleet's words earlier in the evening: "You look pretty tonight." Dry, insipid compliments, just as Rees's had always been to her—the few he'd paid her. What would it be like to have a man gaze upon one with admiration and more, the way the men did to this woman?

5

Lancelot awoke early the next morning and lay a few moments thinking about the previous evening.

He was beginning to like Miss Barry more than he'd expected to. He'd only asked his mother to invite the two young ladies with the aim of putting things right, but the more he talked with her, the more she drew him.

Prickly one moment and keenly discerning the next, like a cactus in bloom. When he'd spoken of India, he'd felt for the first time real interest from a female—not the oohing and aahing of someone wanting to hear of tigers and cobras but the genuine interest of a fellow Christian.

Of course, it was because she was a vicar's daughter, he told himself. She had grown up hearing the message of the gospel—or had she? He wasn't sure if she had expressed approval or disapproval last night over the Clapham Sect, that evangelical arm of the Church of England, but he'd sensed a withdrawal in her at that point. She had not gone into detail about her father. He sounded like a pious man, but was he of evangelical leanings? Some of the strongest resistance he'd encountered from the pulpit both in an English village and among the English settlements in India was to the message of salvation and God's grace through the suffering, death, and resurrection of Jesus Christ.

The church he'd grown up in was a comfortable place of tradition, where the church calendar was celebrated every Sunday with its cycle of holidays sprinkled throughout—Epiphany, Easter, Whitsunday, Trinity Sunday, Advent, Christmas . . . No rousing sermons were accustomed. Instead, edifying homilies were read from the pulpit and the Eucharist celebrated at certain services.

But did it mean anything? When he'd administered the bread and wine, did the people understand anymore the meaning behind them?

Lancelot had not realized how cold and indifferent he'd become to the meaning of the gospel until he'd gone one Sunday on the advice of a college mate to hear Charles Simeon preach at Trinity Church.

For the first time in his life, he'd been confronted with the message of a personal salvation and with his own inability to save himself because of his shortcomings and inherent sin.

What he'd scornfully dismissed as the emotionalism of the Methodists, Baptists, and other radical dissenters was coming from one of his own Anglican priests.

Lancelot had left that church service convinced he would not come back. But he'd returned Sunday after Sunday until he'd fallen on his knees in his room, asking for that salvation Jesus had bought for him on the cross.

There followed a period of euphoria and such peace as he'd never known in his life. For the first time he'd felt a sense of being justified—his life with the potential for true purpose and meaning.

New and deep friendships had arisen with the Reverend Simeon and those close to him—deacons, curates, and fellow divinity students of Cambridge, all like-minded men because they'd experienced the same transformation in their own lives.

They'd had ambitious dreams to preach salvation through grace alone from the pulpits across England and to win the heathen across the seas. Up to then the Church of England had not considered its mission to take the gospel to far-off lands the way the Baptists were beginning to do.

But he and his fellow students were filled with zeal and saw no limitations to the harvest field.

But once he'd been ordained and served, first as a deacon and then as a vicar in a country church, he'd been confronted with the reality of complacent congregations resistant to any kind of change. They did not want their lives turned topsy-turvy. Those who did had already left for the Methodist chapel at the other end of town. They did not want that kind of emotional preaching in their own sanctuaries.

It had been a difficult and lonely time for Lancelot, his only support the letters from his old mentors and fellow students now scattered about the British Isles.

It had been one of those friends, who'd left as a chaplain for the East India Company, who had written asking him to come, telling him there was a massive field to sow in India. As soon as his curacy period was over, Lancelot had applied to the London Missionary Society and, to his amazement and awe, had been accepted, certain it was a sign of God's will.

The voyage was long and arduous and fraught with dangers. Once he landed, he'd confronted a land so different from everything he'd ever known; he'd been overwhelmed.

How could a few men and women ever hope to change the hearts and minds of these people with their innumerable gods, their temples and pagodas dotting the countryside and cities, their slavish adherence to sometimes barbaric rituals?

Sickness and fever had plagued him almost from the first day and driven his spirits even lower.

He'd had to rely on God as never before, his soul frequently weak and despairing. Thankfully, he'd found sweet fellowship in the small community of other Christians. Most surprising and eye-opening had been the community and collaboration among those sects viewed with disfavor back home. He'd worked closely with Baptist missionaries, traveling through the countryside, preaching the gospel and establishing Bible colleges.

He'd been forced to return after the last bout of fever had almost finished him. He doubted he could go back. The doctor had bluntly told him it would be the end of him. Neither would the missionary society accept him if his health was not good.

Since his convalescence he'd been waiting for a position to open somewhere in England. It could easily take years. In the meantime, his parents were pressuring him to marry.

He remembered his mother's words last evening when the dinner guests had departed.

"Well, Lancelot, those were a pair of sweet young ladies you had me invite. No portion either of them, I'm sure," she added in a dry tone, "and you with a vicar's living will be as poor as church mice, but I'd prefer you choose one of them than remain a bachelor."

"Since I have no plans to marry either of them, I have no idea what their portion is."

She heaved an impatient sigh. "But you must marry *someone*, and as long as she is respectable, your father and I do not care if she is indigent or plain—only healthy and young enough to bear children."

His father, who had said nothing until then, spoke up, "Your brother and Rosamunde are in their thirties." He stood before the mantel in the drawing room and stared up at the portrait of the late baronet. "After ten years, I doubt they'll begin a family now." He looked at Lancelot over his shoulder. "All I know is God had the grace to spare you. Now it is your responsibility to beget an heir for this family."

Before Lancelot could make a suitable reply, his mother added, "I shall endeavor to introduce your misses—what were their names?"

"Miss Barry and Miss Phillips," he answered automatically, his heart still heavy with his father's pronouncement. It was not that he didn't wish to be married. Many times he'd yearned for a companion and helpmate. He'd seen with almost envy the strong partnerships some of the missionaries overseas had enjoyed with their spouses. But the life had been hard on the women, and he couldn't have brought himself to ask a woman to sacrifice her life so. Thus, he'd chosen the single life throughout that time of seeking God and living for him. He hadn't yet met the woman who shared his dedication in that area.

But now that he was home for good, he'd begun to reconsider his bachelor state. Yet, he didn't wish to be pressured into a hasty marriage just because his parents were afraid they would be left without an heir.

Marriage was too sacred a covenant for Lancelot to go into without the certainty that God had chosen his mate for him.

"Yes—Misses Barry and Phillips—to the right circles," his mother continued. "This will give you the opportunity to pursue an acquaintance and determine which one you prefer."

"Yes, Mother," he said quietly. He hated the whole business, but as he'd found with his mother over the years, it was easier to agree with her when she had made up her mind to something, and then simply go one's own way.

It had been what he'd done when he'd decided to go to India.

In this case, he realized, it was in his interest to have his mother introduce Miss Barry and Miss Phillips to society, where he could continue his acquaintance with Miss Barry and see if she continued to interest him. Or if he could ever interest *her*—a much more daunting thought.

Jessamine sat at the breakfast table with Megan and Lady Bess, only half listening to them go over last night's dinner party again. It was all they'd talked about on the ride home, past midnight.

As she buttered her toast, she ignored the names of the important members of society Lady Bess had spoken to, hadn't seen in an age, and whose lives—births, deaths, weddings—she'd been able to catch up on during the evening.

But Jessamine's thoughts had been fixed elsewhere ever since the dinner party. She'd thought long and hard about the lady who'd spoken to Megan about Brussels. Jessamine had continued to observe Lady Angelica Dawson when the ladies rose from the table, leaving the men to their port, and afterward when the men rejoined them in the drawing room.

Jessamine had found a seat closer to Lady Dawson. Even her name—Angelica—sounded French, like Céline. As soon as the gentlemen joined the ladies, she never had fewer than three gentlemen around her.

"Jessamine, are you all right? You've been awfully quiet since last night." Megan's voice intruded her thoughts.

"What?" She looked over the piece of toast still held at her lips unbitten. "Yes, I'm quite all right," she assured her friend.

Lady Bess smiled. "Are you so wrapped up in thoughts of Mr. Marfleet that you aren't hearing a word that goes on around you?"

Jessamine blinked, hardly remembering the vicar. "Mr. Marfleet? No—of course not." She determined to nip that notion in the bud. "In fact, I thought it was Megan he took an interest in," she added, hoping to turn the focus from herself.

Megan held up a hand to her breast, her gray eyes wide. "Me? I think you are being too modest. Mr. Marfleet sat with you at dinner after fobbing me off on Mr. Emery, a very pleasant though dull individual," she said with an impish smile.

"Well, whoever Mr. Marfleet fancies is no concern of mine, since I don't fancy him," Jessamine replied with firmness. Mr. Marfleet might be the worthiest of young gentlemen, but she was no longer interested in impressing a worthy gentleman. She was interested in being a Lady Dawson, with a gaggle of men fawning over her.

"You don't?" Lady Bess looked crestfallen beneath her lacy cap. "But he's such a nice young man, even if he is a redhead."

"If he is such a nice man, he will have no trouble at all in snagging any of the numerous young ladies out this season."

"Are you sure you wish to relinquish him so quickly, my dear? He's a most eligible young man, though he hasn't much as a vicar." Lady Bess's face brightened. "But he is a baronet's son. A pity there were not more eligible young men at Lady Marfleet's dinner. But perhaps we'll receive another invitation." She tapped a finger to her lips, thinking aloud. "I could drop a line to one or two of the guests I spoke with last night." She drew in another long breath. "There was a time when my drawing room was full. Alas, what age and a loss of fortune can do."

She put on her reading glasses and picked up the *Morning Post*. Megan and Jessamine ate in silence while she opened the paper.

"Let me see if there is any mention of last night's dinner." She flipped through the pages and began to peruse the society columns. "There was a rout at Lord and Lady Brougham's last night . . . the Duchess of Stathemore was seen at the Drury Lane in company of—" She cleared her throat and didn't read on. "Oh—here it is. 'A distinguished and lively gathering was seen at Sir Geoffrey and Lady Marfleet's Grafton Street residence. A line of carriages lined the block into Bond Street.

"'Lord Palmerston's crest was spied on one carriage; Lord Grey walking up the steps in company of his wife the countess; and the divine Lady Angelica Dawson on the arm of Richard Cavendish, lately of Kingston, West Indies. We are sure the most scintillating conversation took place around her as she holds court wherever she goes.'"

Even the gossip columnist knew this!

"Who is she?" she ventured to ask Lady Bess.

Lady Bess lowered the paper to peer at Jessamine. "Who, my dear?"

"Lady Dawson."

"Lady Dawson? She's a widow of the late Sir Dawson, a baronet. He left her immensely wealthy and with entrée into all the best places. She was nothing when he met her but a young, penniless miss from the country. He was besotted when he first beheld her in a London drawing room and married her almost immediately. He was quite some years older and died a few years later. They had a child, a son, who is being brought up by a governess on their country estate."

Lady Bess shook her head at the vagaries of the nobility. "Lady Dawson pursues a life among the ton in London and Brighton. I wouldn't be surprised if she dashes off to Brussels as she said last night." She glanced at Megan. "It was quite a compliment she paid you to take such an interest."

Her words brought to mind the other thing that had kept Jessamine awake long after Megan had fallen asleep. "I didn't know your brother was in Brussels."

Megan colored. "Yes. A letter came only yesterday," she hastened to say. "The congress received news of Napoleon's escape almost a fortnight after he'd sailed from Elba. Rees writes of the great disarray this news put the members of the congress in."

She turned to Lady Bess. "It was more than a week after Bonaparte's landing in southern France that they were informed of his escape. My brother writes that everyone is in a panic. His letter is already a few weeks old. He sounded quite rushed. Wellington has just received orders to leave the congress and join the allied troops in Belgium when the congress hasn't even concluded its business!"

"Goodness gracious, what is the world coming to?" Lady Bess clucked her tongue.

Megan kept her eyes fixed on Lady Bess as if unwilling to meet Jessamine's gaze. "Rees sounded concerned in his letter. He said no one trusts Napoleon—neither the Prussians nor Austrians nor

Russians—and they want to be prepared to stop any ambitions he may still harbor."

"Do they really expect war?" The whites of Lady Bess's eyes were visible all around her aqua-green irises above her spectacles.

Megan gave a helpless shrug. "Rees doesn't say. He only wrote that the congress passed a resolution before he left Vienna declaring Napoleon an 'international outlaw.' That was the wording he used."

Lady Bess fanned herself with one of her letters. "So many years of war to face the possibility once more. I don't think I could bear it!"

Megan sat back, her expression troubled. "My brother's biggest concern is his wife, Céline. You see, she's in a . . . in a family way." She stumbled over the words, her glance flickering to Jessamine and away again.

Jessamine's world collided in on itself. Rees and his French wife were expecting a child! She gazed down at her plate, everything blurring.

Lady Bess's exclamations of delight and Megan's quieter replies swirled around her.

Why was it so shocking? People married and babies followed. That was how it went. Jessamine clenched her fists under the tabletop, willing herself to calm, but her insides felt twisted. For a moment she was afraid she would be sick.

"Jessamine, are you all right?" Lady Bess's solicitous voice came to her as from afar.

She stood, finding it hard to swallow, much less speak. "I'm sorry, I—I don't feel well."

Ignoring their expressions of concern, she hurried from the room.

She ran up the stairs to her room and flung herself across the bed. *Please, God, don't let Megan follow me! I don't—can't—see her right now.* She curled into a ball, rocking back and forth, a fist to her mouth, a pillow clutched to her breast, wanting only to blot out the image of Rees and his beautiful French bride.

Jessamine moaned, imagining his tender concern for her now that she would bear his child. That woman should have been Jessamine.

Why had he stopped loving her? She knew he had been fond of her—no, it was stronger than fondness. The last times Rees had visited her, he had shown a distinct preference for her company. He had sought her out. He had made his intentions clear by the look in his eyes, by his warm words. If not expressly those of a suitor, then certainly those of a man singling her out with that purpose.

Even her mother and Megan had remarked upon it. They had all been so happy with the thought of the two families joining through marriage. Jessamine had been content to wait until Rees felt able to marry. She had heard him say more than once over the years that he wouldn't think of marriage until he had enough saved up to take care of his mother and Megan's coming-out. But in that last year before he'd met that Frenchwoman, he had told Jessamine that he had saved enough money to think about settling down very soon.

Then everything had changed. He'd gotten an assignment in Lady Wexham's household and ended up falling in love with her—a woman who had more than likely been a spy against the British even though nothing had ever been proven.

The tears came hot, squeezed from her eyes and running down her cheeks, soaking her pillow. All the tears she had suppressed since that last visit of his when he had gently killed all Jessamine's hopes and dreams.

How her heart had soared when he'd asked permission of her mother to take Jessamine out for a turn in the garden. There was only one reason for a gentleman to speak alone to a lady. But his words had sounded so strange. *"I know that someday . . . soon, I imagine, a young gentleman is going to come along and . . . desire you for his wife."* As his gray eyes regarded her, she had felt puzzled at first, but as his gaze continued to pierce her with its intensity, fear had mushroomed in her chest as the meaning of his words had penetrated.

He was telling her there was no hope for the two of them. If she had been left in any doubt, his next words sounded the death knell. *"I thought for a while that I might be that man."* He'd drawn in a breath as if seeking courage to continue. *"But I am not that man."*

He had gone on to tell her how deserving she was, but she had not let him continue. No pretty words could erase the fact that he didn't want her. That she was not good enough, that somehow, somewhere, he'd fallen out of love with her and his affections had been replaced by pity and compassion. She hadn't realized then that his heart was now filled with thoughts for someone else.

That had come later, almost a year later, after the peace had been declared and Rees had found his French love across the channel.

The sobs racked Jessamine's body. She clutched her pillow tighter. And now they would have a baby, and the portrait of a loving, happy family would be complete. Jessamine would never be that woman to Rees. She would never bear his children and watch them grow up with him as their father.

The door opened quietly and the next second Megan was behind her, wrapping her arms around her. "Please don't cry, Jessamine, please don't cry." She rocked her, repeating the words. Jessamine tried to shake her off, but Megan held her fast, her words soothing.

"I-I'm sorry . . . I'm sorry," Jessamine sobbed. "I k-know I sh-should rejoice for h-his happiness," she said with a hiccup, "but I love him so, and now—now I know I can never have him." Somehow the fact of a child added a finality to Rees's new life without Jessamine. As long as he'd been far away in Vienna and she had never seen his bride, there had been an unreality to his love story.

"I'm so sorry too," Megan said with feeling, smoothing the hair off her brow. "Mama and I wished for the two of you to be together, but it was not meant to be—"

Jessamine pushed away from her, turning to stare at her. "What do you mean, not meant to be! It wasn't Rees's fault. It was that woman—she ensnared him."

Megan looked troubled. "I don't know. Until I meet her and see how she and Rees are together, I can't judge her."

Jessamine lay back, staring at the ceiling, wiping her nose and eyes, too spent to hang on to her outrage. Emptiness filled her. The rest of the season in London held no pleasure for her. Their plans to visit the zoo today, the theater tonight . . . All she wanted was to lie there and not have to do anything ever again.

She sniffed and turned her head on the pillow to look at Megan. "What else did he write?"

Megan was silent a moment. "Not much else. He is worried for Céline's safety but otherwise busy with diplomatic affairs. So much was still unsettled in Vienna, so he is sorry to be called away so suddenly but is happy to be on Wellington's staff. He has found much favor with the duke and the others he worked with in Vienna, including Lord Castlereagh."

She fell silent again. Jessamine thought how it would have been. All Rees's hard work as a clerk in the Foreign Office was finally bearing fruit. With all that had happened during the Congress of Vienna, he would be promoted, and his career in diplomacy was all but assured. He could have married her now.

Before the tears could begin to fall anew, Megan said, her words hesitant, "He said that he hopes—depending on what transpires in Brussels—to see us soon in person here in England."

Jessamine's body tensed at the words "see us." "He is coming here?" she whispered.

"Yes. He said if there's the least sign of war, he wants to bring Céline to England, though he added that she wouldn't want to leave him, but for the sake of the baby, she could probably be prevailed on to come here."

The baby. A woman so in love with her husband she didn't want to leave him despite the dangers, who now carried another life, a precious unborn life, within her.

Another tear slid from her eyelid down her temple. She brought her handkerchief up to her face.

As if sensing her distress, Megan put her arm across her, hugging her to herself. "I know how much you cared about him, dear, but perhaps you'll meet someone else someday."

"That's what he said! I'll never meet anyone like Rees." She sniffed again. "It's been over a year and a half, and I still feel the pain of that last interview."

Megan's eyes were filled with sadness and compassion. "He's my brother and I love him, and I understood why you should love and admire him too, but Jessamine, what if the Lord has someone better for you?"

At those words, well-intentioned but so hurtful to hear, Jessamine sat up. "Then why did He have me wait so long for Rees?"

"I don't know. Yours is a faithful nature. God made you so, but perhaps you fixed your affections on the wrong man."

"So it's my fault!"

"No, dear Jessie. I know we can't control with whom we fall in love—"

Jessamine glared at her friend. "I had a father who instilled me with the notions of patience and resignation, and you and your mother encouraged me in my affections to your brother." She knew her words were unreasonable, but she couldn't help herself. For too long, she'd kept everything bottled up inside, putting on a brave face to her family and Rees's mother and sister, who all meant well. But all it had meant was keeping the bitterness brewing inside her. She knew Megan and her mother must be overjoyed to finally see Rees and his bride, and now a grandchild.

Megan flushed. "Perhaps Mother and I did wrong, but you two seemed so right for each other. We felt keenly how much Rees had sacrificed all these years in order to provide for us. We knew how lonely he must be. We hoped so much for a woman as faithful and true as you for him. You seemed God-ordained for him, apart from the difference in your ages."

Jessamine blew her nose again. "If I had only been born a few years sooner, or he a few years later, perhaps we would have been married before he ever met that—that Frenchwoman!"

Abruptly, she turned away from Megan and swung her legs off the bed. "Well, we were all wrong about 'God's will.' I sometimes think God must be laughing at all our petty hopes and schemes."

"Jessamine!" Megan sounded truly shocked.

Jessamine did not take her words back, although they shocked her as well. It was the first time she expressed aloud what had simmered below the surface all these months. The thoughts that had plagued her the night before resurfaced. "I can tell you this," she said, standing and facing her friend. "I will not make the same mistake again. I will not pledge my heart to a man who gives nothing in return. The next time a heart is broken, it shall not be mine!"

She crossed the room to her dressing table and looked at herself in the mirror. The face staring back at her looked awful—eyes swollen, hair tumbling down, nose red, skin splotchy.

She yanked at the rest of her hairpins, allowing her hair to fall down past her shoulders, then grabbed up her hairbrush and pulled it through her locks, welcoming the pain.

Feeling calmer with her resolution taken, she sat at her dresser and twisted her hair into a knot. As she held it up in one hand to repin it, she paused, picturing Lady Dawson's fashionably cropped curls.

"I am going to cut my hair."

"What?" Megan scrambled off the bed and came to stand behind Jessamine, meeting her eyes in the mirror.

"Do you remember Lady Angelica Dawson last night?"

"The lady you were asking Lady Bess about?"

"I want to fashion my hair like hers. She looked very smart."

Megan nodded slowly as if afraid that disagreeing with her would bring on a new storm of tears. But Jessamine could have told her the time for crying was over.

"It did look nice on her," she conceded.

"Do you think the style would suit me?" Jessamine looked at herself in the mirror again.

Megan took up her hair from her, considering. "I think so. Your hair is so pretty, it seems such a shame to cut too much off."

Jessamine loosened her hair. "Well, I think it's time for a change. High time for a change."

6

When she left the hairdresser's salon, Jessamine's head felt lighter, freer than she could ever remember. She kept putting her hand up to the nape of her neck to feel her hair. As promised, the hairdresser had cut the back portion of her hair to a length slightly past her shoulders, long enough to still draw up in a knot, which he had done. But the sides and top were very short.

She still marveled at how it curled around her head and forehead like a boy's.

"How does it feel?"

She smiled at Megan. "Light."

"It looks quite boyish, a bit like a gamin."

They left the side street they were on and turned onto Bond Street. Jessamine stopped in front of a shop window and looked at her reflection.

"I hope not a street urchin."

"Oh no, like a charming young fawn." She gave her an impish grin. "A bit like Caroline Lamb."

Jessamine brightened, liking the notion of being notorious. Of course she wouldn't be fool enough to fall in love again and make a cake of herself the way Lady Caroline had for Lord Byron. They resumed walking. "I want to get some new gowns made." Since taking a decisive step toward a new life, a new outlook, she felt better.

"But we brought so many new dresses with us," Megan said.

"Have you noticed how simple they appear beside those of the ladies of fashion like Lady Dawson?" When Megan considered, Jessamine added, "I want to find a seamstress."

Megan's brow puckered. "It could prove expensive to compete with someone like Lady Dawson."

She nodded glumly. "I know. Perhaps Lady Bess or one of her friends knows of a good seamstress. I don't want a woman who makes up the fusty old gowns they wear, however."

Megan laughed, probably glad to find her in a better mood than she had been in earlier. Jessamine shuddered, not wanting to go back to that pathetic, sniveling figure she had cut. "I want someone who can give me a new style. I don't want to look like every young miss on the marriage mart." She paused again before a shop window and twirled a curl around a finger.

Megan stood beside her. "It would be nice to stand a little apart from them, but what can we do? Only the most pale pastels and whites are allowed us."

Jessamine didn't reply. Instead, she said, "Perhaps a French seamstress, an émigré, with a Parisian sense of style but who would be grateful for our patronage."

"Still, how can you afford it? I know you don't want to ask your father for any more pin money."

Jessamine touched the pearl drop pendant that hung from a gold chain around her neck and swung it between her fingers. "I have spent very little of my allowance. Let us first price some muslins and see how much a gown or two would cost."

She began walking again, picking up her pace. "Come, let's look at bolts of material at the Bond Street Bazaar." With a lighter step, she skirted past the pedestrians, eager to put her plan into action.

Lancelot walked back from Soho Square a few days later on his return from one of Sir Joseph Banks's "mornings." While abroad Lancelot had missed those informal gatherings of botanists and naturalists in the great naturalist's library, where a variety of British and foreign periodicals were laid out for their perusal and discussion. The latest findings of those commissioned to collect plant specimens from their voyages around the world were eagerly disseminated and discussed.

As president of the Royal Society, Dr. Banks had invited Lancelot to become a member after Lancelot had sent him his first treatise on plants, and later nominated him as a fellow of the society.

Now, he had greeted Lancelot with enthusiasm and insisted he regale the company present with a description of all he'd brought back from India. Sir Banks had promised to help him find a publisher for the work he and Delawney were compiling. He'd also asked him to speak the following evening at the meeting of the Royal Society at Somerset House and to give a lecture to the public at the Royal Institute at a later date.

His mind bubbling over with ideas for these presentations, Lancelot turned onto King Street and halted at the sight of Miss Barry across the street. He was usually so deep in thought that he rarely noticed anyone, even with his spectacles on, until he was upon them. But he had been intending to cross the street so had been scanning the opposite side.

He frowned, noticing Miss Barry was alone. She had just emerged from a rundown shop in a part of town he would not expect to see an unaccompanied young lady. He narrowed his eyes to read the sign above the window. Harris & Sons, Pawnbrokers.

He crossed the street, lengthening his stride to reach her before she disappeared.

"Good afternoon," he said, drawing abreast of her.

"Good afternoon, Mr. Marfleet." She nodded to him, unsmiling, and looked away.

She looked different to him but he wasn't quite sure how. Perhaps it was her hair, which looked curlier around her face but was mostly hidden by her bonnet. Remembering the reason he had hailed her, he indicated the shop behind her. "What are you doing here?"

She turned around as if not sure what place he was referring to. "Where?"

"At a pawnbroker's shop," he added helpfully.

She swallowed. "Nothing." Her hand went to her throat and then she brought it back down again to clutch the strings of the reticule she held in her other hand.

His concern grew. Only people in financial straits frequented pawnbrokers. "Do you find yourself in the hatches, having to pawn your mother's jewels?"

Her gaze flew to his, her green eyes wide. They were a deep green like a Scots pine in the Caledonian forest. *Pinus sylvestris*, he thought automatically.

"No, certainly not!"

Before he could think how to proceed, she stepped away from him. "I must go. Good day to you, Mr. Marfleet."

"Wait, I shall accompany you home. You shouldn't be alone on these streets. Where is your maid?"

She was already several paces away from him. "There is no need, thank you."

He took a step after her, debating whether to insist. But as if sensing his resolve, she broke into a fast walk and turned the corner.

He uttered a prayer for her safety even as his thoughts puzzled over why she had seemed so dismayed to see him. He had thought they had gotten on rather well the other night at his mother's dinner.

He walked back to the pawnbroker's shop, peering into its smudged window, which held an odd jumble of articles from old watches to men's hats and ladies' gloves. People of the gentry only visited them if they were desperate for some ready cash.

His experience as a clergyman and his skills as an amateur

scientist made him rarely accept things at their face value. He opened the door and entered the dim shop.

A musty odor of things old and never cleaned or aired greeted his nostrils. The bell above him tinkled, and a dark-haired, middle-aged man looked up from behind the counter. "Good day, sir. What may I do for you?"

"That young lady"—Lancelot motioned to the street—"who just left here." He cleared his throat, feeling both idiotic and unforgivably inquisitive. "Did she come here to pawn an article?"

The man gave him a measured look, scratching at the days-old growth of salt-and-pepper beard covering his cheeks. "Young lady, sir?"

Lancelot flushed, feeling more foolish. "Yes, not a minute ago she stepped out. I'm—I'm acquainted with her and wouldn't want her to have to pawn an article which might be of value to her." He fumbled with the words as he grasped for a good reason to be inquiring into Miss Barry's affairs.

The man continued to regard him, his fleshy lips puckering and twisting.

Lancelot's gaze dropped from his obsidian stare and fell upon the article the man had been examining. It was a narrow rope chain with a small pearl hanging from it. He remembered seeing it around Miss Barry's slim neck—and how her hand had gone to her bare throat earlier. "How much did you give her for it?"

The man didn't glance at it. "Poor young thing. She did seem a bit broken up about having to pawn her necklace. Still wearing it, she was. Said something about its being her grandmother's and meaning to redeem it in a few months' time. I'd hate to disappoint her."

"That's all right. I shall redeem it for her. How much?"

The man named the sum.

Lancelot realized the man was probably hiking up the figure, but without questioning it, he drew out his purse and extracted some banknotes.

The man took the bills from the counter, counted them, and put them away in a drawer. "What shall I say if the young lady returns for it?"

"I'll have restored it to her by then."

"Very good, sir. You alleviate my mind."

Ignoring the trace of mockery in his words, Lancelot put the necklace away in a waistcoat pocket. "Good day to you."

"Good day to you, sir. It's been a pleasure doing business."

Lancelot nodded and stepped away from the counter. The bell tinkled above his head once again.

He continued down the block, thoughtful about why Miss Barry should be so short of funds she'd pawn something obviously dear to her and of some real value.

Jessamine stood surveying herself in the glass, hardly recognizing the young lady before her. She used the quizzing glass instead of her spectacles to inspect her appearance. Even though seeing clearly through only one eye was better than none, it still demanded an adjustment over having two lenses to see through.

Nevertheless, it was a vast improvement over not wearing her spectacles at all. She had practiced in the last week before her dressing table mirror so she now felt confident in using it as a fashion accessory to her new, stylish self. The small, circular glass was tied to a narrow silk ribbon affixed to her gown, a ribbon whose color would match whatever gown she wore.

Tonight she wore a new ball gown confectioned by Mademoiselle Clare. Jessamine turned slowly, admiring the wild rose sarcenet skirt and its ruby red bodice. She hadn't shown it yet to Lady Bess and hoped the color wouldn't scandalize her.

A soft tap on the door checked her movement.

"Come in."

Megan poked her head around the door. "Oh!" She entered and shut the door behind her. "I came to ask if you needed any help with your hair or gown, but I see you do not." She stopped. "You look beautiful."

"Thank you," Jessamine said shyly, a hand going to her hair, which had artificial sweetbriar roses woven through it on one side. "I'm still not used to the shorter, boyish look. Betsy helped me dress it."

"I think you shall rival any *élégante* at the ball."

"What do you think of the gown?" She touched the edge of the bodice, hoping it was not too low. It was lower than anything she'd ever worn and showed a lot more skin than she was accustomed to. She blushed just thinking what her parents would say if they saw her.

Megan had not yet seen the finished gown, as Jessamine had taken only Betsy with her for her fittings.

"It's the most beautiful gown I've ever seen. The colors are wonderful. They truly become you." Megan circled around her. Jessamine resisted the urge to tug upward at the bodice. "Mademoiselle Clare is a genius." She frowned at Jessamine's neckline. "You aren't wearing any jewelry. Where's your pearl?"

Jessamine made a careless gesture with her hand. "I thought the flowers alone would be more elegant."

"Perhaps you're right."

When Megan made no remark on her décolletage, Jessamine said, "You look very pretty too." Her white satin gown had a wide band of colorful embroidery at the hem and neckline.

"Thank you." Megan made a pretty curtsy. "Let's hope our dinner at the Marfleets ensures we are not wallflowers tonight. Shall we go? Lady Bess is waiting for us downstairs, I believe."

With a last glance at the glass, Jessamine turned down the lamp and took up her shawl, fan, and reticule.

Downstairs, they had to show their gowns to their godmother. "Lovely, the both of you," the older lady said, clasping her hands over her breast. "How it takes me back to my own youth and coming-out balls." She wore an azure demi-turban, her graying curls visible above and beneath it, and an amber gown with carnelian ornaments. "How lovely to receive the invitation to the Fortescues' ball. I'm sure Lady Marfleet is to thank for it. You may be pleased that you have made at least one conquest since your arrival," she added with a wink. "Let us hope for a half dozen more this evening."

Thankful that Lady Bess had said nothing of concern over her gown, Jessamine wrapped her shawl around her shoulders. A niggling doubt assailed her when she thought of her mother and father, but she told herself that in Lady Bess's and her mother's day, women had worn brighter colors and more scandalous necklines.

They arrived at the large mansion in Berkeley Square only to be forced to wait on the other side of the square behind the dozens of carriages in line around the street.

"Everyone who is anyone must be here tonight," Lady Bess remarked with satisfaction, peeking out the window. It was still light outside, and the interior of the carriage was stuffy. Jessamine was glad that Lady Bess never lacked for conversation since she herself didn't feel like talking, too nervous about her new appearance. Would anyone notice her tonight?

Lady Bess continued commenting on every carriage she recognized by the footmen's livery. When she was close enough to see the guests descending, she reported it to Megan and Jessamine. Jessamine let Megan reply. With each jolt of the carriage drawing them closer, the flutters in Jessamine's tummy grew.

The sale of her grandmother's pendant still hurt. Her hand kept going to her throat, forgetting it was bare. She bit her lip, remembering Mr. Marfleet's appearance outside the pawnbroker's shop. Why was it he always managed to be where he was least wanted? She had not precisely lied to him. It had not been her mother's jewelry. It had been her grandmother's—who'd handed it down to her mother, who'd presented it to her on her eighteenth birthday, she reminded herself.

It was none of Mr. Marfleet's business, anyway. But Jessamine still felt the guilt when he'd accused her of selling her mother's jewels. He may have been joking, but his words had hit too close to the truth.

Jessamine rubbed her moist palms against her mantle, focusing on her new gown beneath it. It had been worth it, she reminded herself, thinking of the two other new gowns hanging in her clothespress.

She would have to wait until her next month's allowance before she could redeem her necklace. What if she and Megan "took" tonight and they were invited to a round of balls and parties? Would she need more gowns? She bit her lip, fretting over this new possibility. Perhaps she could offer to sew the gowns if Mademoiselle Clare would make the designs. If not, she would just have to copy what she saw at the ball tonight. She shook her head at the direction of her thoughts. She and Megan would probably not be noticed, and they could return to the dull round of card parties Lady Bess attended.

Would Mr. Marfleet be there? She had seen no sign of him in the intervening week. And had not missed his company! She hoped he was absent this evening. She wanted—needed—to meet other eligible gentlemen.

If she were ever going to get over Rees Phillips, she needed to meet men who were handsomer and better than he. No more falling in love for her. But she needed to prove she could win a man's heart, so she could forget Rees and cease to torture herself over the felicity he had found with his French bride.

Their stuffy rented carriage finally pulled in front of the well-lit grand entrance of the limestone mansion fronting the wide square.

The footmen handed them down, and they went up the steps to the wide marble foyer. Jessamine brought her quizzing glass up to her eye and surveyed its large dimensions, vaster than the whole ground floor of Lady Bess's town house.

One footman took their wraps and another led them up the

broad circular staircase, following the many people going up before them. Bright candlelight flickered from hundreds of gilt wall sconces and dozens of crystal chandeliers.

When they reached the ballroom entrance, Jessamine saw it already held a crowd. She needn't have feared calling attention to herself. In this crush no one would notice her or her new gown.

It would be like the rout. Standing on the side, watching everyone else enjoy themselves. Her spirits sank to the toes of her satin slippers as they waited to be announced. So much sacrifice for a new ball gown that just blended in the vast array of colorful gowns.

Once the butler had intoned their names, they entered the ballroom. A quadrille was playing and the dance floor was filled with sets of dancers.

"What an elegant crowd," Lady Bess said once she found them a place along the gold satin wall. "The Fortescues are one of the finest families." She craned her neck, looking around with her quizzing glass. "I knew his father once upon a time." Her eyes twinkled. "He had a *tendre* for me. Oh, there is Lady Swanborough. I must say hello to her later. I don't see Mr. Marfleet. I'm sure he will be in attendance. You mustn't dance more than twice with him," she warned them both with a tap of her fan.

There seemed to be an awful lot of young ladies, all vying for attention. With the added advantage of family name and portion, it didn't matter what kinds of gowns they wore, Jessamine concluded as she surveyed the crowd.

A passing footman carrying a tray loaded with refreshments stopped before them.

"Thank you," Lady Bess said with a smile, taking a glass of orgeat from him. "Take some, my dears. You'll soon develop a powerful thirst from dancing."

Megan took a glass of lemonade. Jessamine eyed the crystal goblets. "What is this?" she asked the footman, pointing to a pretty pink liquid in a widemouthed glass.

"It's champagne, miss."

Jessamine had never tasted champagne. She remembered a comment of Lady Dawson's: "I only drink pink champagne."

On the heels of it came her father's gentle voice, admonishing his congregation against the excess drinking of spirits.

Silencing the voice, Jessamine reached out and took a glass. Perhaps the champagne would bolster her courage. She was determined that her efforts to present a new image of herself would not be in vain.

As of tonight, her life would change.

"It matches your gown," Megan said.

Jessamine held the glass up, liking the way the tiny bubbles rose to the surface of the pale pink liquid. "So it does."

Lady Bess raised her glass. "May you meet many eligible bachelors worth at least one thousand!"

After lifting their glasses in the toast, Jessamine took a careful sip. The pink liquid tickled her tongue and tingled down her throat, spreading warmth throughout her body. Liking the sensation, she took another small sip.

"Careful, my dear, champagne is heady stuff."

"I will," she promised, lowering her glass. Already she felt able to conquer, if not the world, then this ballroom.

The dance floor filled again. Jessamine tapped her foot to the lively music, wishing she could be dancing.

"I don't see Mr. Marfleet or Mr. Emery," Lady Bess said, her quizzing glass eyeing all the gentlemen passing them by.

Megan rose on tiptoe. "Neither do I. I wonder if they came. I haven't seen either since the dinner party, but then neither have we been invited anywhere."

Jessamine lifted her quizzing glass, although part of her preferred the indistinct edges of the colorful room, the soft aureoles of the candlelight making everything appear magical.

Everything clarified at once. The ballroom was immense, spanning the length of the mansion, she judged. Its ceiling was painted with frescoes of clouds and nymphs. Three massive chandeliers hung from it. Dozens of wall sconces lit the sides of the room.

She studied the faces, unsure whether to feel relieved or sorry that Mr. Marfleet's was not among them. "Nor do I," she said, lowering her quizzing glass, "but they are not the only gentlemen here tonight." It would be best *not* to see Mr. Marfleet, she decided, her hand going to her bare throat.

What if he mentioned seeing her coming out of the pawnbroker's shop?

Jessamine took another sip of champagne, bracing herself for the encounter. If Mr. Marfleet was here, she'd have to trust his discretion. If he did let something slip, she'd have to brave it out.

Lancelot eyed the crowded ballroom when he arrived with Harold. They were fashionably late since Harold had insisted they dine at his club beforehand. That had led to a stop at the faro table. Only by intimating that he wanted to see Miss Barry and Miss Phillips at the ball was Lancelot able to pull his brother away.

He put on his spectacles now and scanned the ballroom, seeking Miss Barry. He didn't see her and swallowed a sense of disappointment. Hadn't they received an invitation? His mother had promised to drop a hint to the ball's hostess, a close school friend.

He touched his pocket, feeling the slight lump of the necklace's pendant there. He meant to give it to Miss Barry this evening, if he could find a moment alone with her. He grimaced, wondering how she would react at seeing him tonight.

Harold disappeared into the crowd. Deciding to wait a bit before making a foray into the ballroom himself, Lancelot backed out and headed to the card room.

He was a coward around women, he knew, but even as he acknowledged this, he kept moving away from the ballroom, his hand patting his pocket once more.

7

Jessamine tapped her foot against the parquet floor to the beat of the Scotch reel. She and Megan were still standing where Lady Bess had left them when she'd gone off to the card room with a friend with the parting admonition, "Don't sit out too many dances."

That had been an hour ago. Jessamine had finished her champagne, the euphoria long since worn off. The evening was promising to be like all the others since coming to London.

When a passing footman laden with a tray of glasses crossed in front of them again, she snatched another glass of champagne. Her abrupt gesture jarred the tray and set the glasses shaking.

The footman halted, startled at her sudden movement. She glared at him, and his features took on the impassive look of a well-trained servant.

"Are you sure you should have any more?" Megan whispered after he'd moved away.

Jessamine stared at her over the rim of her glass. "If I am to stand here bored until supper, yes, I think I should indeed." She took a healthy swallow.

Megan returned to watching the dancers.

A moment later she touched Jessamine's arm. "There is Sir

Harold." Her hold tightened. "He has seen us." She raised a hand in acknowledgment.

If he was here, it meant his brother must be too. Jessamine resisted the urge to lift her quizzing glass. Instead she took another swallow of champagne.

A moment later, Sir Harold bowed before them. "Good evening, ladies, how pretty you both look." His glance rested on Jessamine. "Ravishing, I should say. What have you done to yourself?"

Her already warm cheeks felt warmer as his eyes drifted downward and lingered on her neckline. She had the urge to tug it upward. Instead, she touched her hair. "Shorn my locks."

"So I see . . . à la Caro." His gaze returned to her face with a lazy smile. "I hope you don't fall in love with Byron and make a cake of yourself as she has done."

"Running besotted after a poet? I can assure you I shall not be so foolish."

His dark blond brows drew together. "Why are neither of you dancing?"

"Because no one has asked us," she replied, emboldened by the champagne.

"Where is that slowtop brother of mine?" He craned his neck around. "I swear he was following me just now. Ah, well, I'll find him presently. In the meantime—" He snagged the arm of a passing gentleman. "Reggie, I need your services."

Sir Harold turned back to them with a flourish. "May I present Reginald Layton. Reggie—Miss Phillips, Miss Barry."

The handsome young man bowed to each then asked Megan, "May I have this dance?"

Sir Harold made a courtly bow to Jessamine. "Can you content yourself with me until I find my wayward brother?"

"You mustn't feel obliged to ask me—"

"Nonsense. It is my pleasure. Come, let's set down your drink and kick up our heels."

They followed the other two onto the dance floor and joined a set.

It was a lively dance that kept them moving constantly so she did not have to worry about talking to Sir Harold but for brief snatches.

The champagne made her giddy but light on her feet as well. "How is your sister?"

"Delawney?" he said. "She never comes to these things. She is worse than Lancelot. She refused a season and now is squarely on the shelf and says she doesn't care."

"Refused a season?" Jessamine could scarcely imagine it, especially if one's parents were as important as the Marfleets.

"Said she couldn't abide being looked at by a bunch of worthless gentlemen who had the temerity to judge if she'd make them a suitable wife."

By the time the dance ended and he asked her for the next, the new quadrille, Jessamine felt better. After that, Sir Harold introduced her to another friend. Mr. Allan led her out for a country dance.

At the end of it, the slower strains of a waltz began.

She had never danced the waltz. It was not permitted at the assemblies at home.

"Do you know the waltz?" Mr. Allan asked her.

She shook her head.

"There is nothing easier."

She refused to try it, but he stayed with her. She studied the couples as they moved in the short march that preceded the dance. As each one paired off and went through a set of graceful movements, Jessamine was enthralled. What would it be like to be held in one's partner's arms as he twirled and promenaded one in a small circle?

An image of Rees filled her thoughts. No! She mustn't think of him. She tried to conjure up someone else, and all she succeeded in doing was picturing Mr. Marfleet. He would probably step all over her feet.

When the waltz ended, two acquaintances of Mr. Allan's stopped by, and he introduced them, Lord Fane, whom they called "Cubby," and Mr. St. Leger, a tall, dark-haired man who appraised her through his quizzing glass.

"Charmed, I'm sure," he drawled after a full minute of perusing her.

"Allan said you are from West Sussex?" Cubby asked her.

"Yes, a small village."

"It is a pretty countryside," St. Leger said, dangling his quizzing glass.

"Are you familiar with it?"

"No, I can't say that I am."

She couldn't help smiling at his droll reply.

"How do you find London?"

"London is . . ." She searched for a word. "Crowded and cold."

He cocked an eyebrow at an exaggerated height. "Do you find it cold?"

She smiled. "Not physically, not at this time of year."

"Ah, you mean its citizens. We shall have to remedy that so you do not take an unfavorable impression back with you to your hamlet."

Her tongue loosened by the champagne she had drunk earlier, she asked, "And where are you from?"

"My family hails from Nottinghamshire for the last several centuries. Since Henry I, to be specific."

"No outlaws among you?"

He eyed her appreciatively. "None in such noble lawbreaking endeavors as Robin Hood. But we do boast many questionable characters throughout the age. Our portrait gallery is filled with these reprobates."

She couldn't imagine living in a house with its own portrait gallery, much less knowing her ancestors from so long ago.

After a moment, he said, "Excuse me if I don't ask you to dance, but I find it exceedingly nonsensical to be cavorting about an open area for amusement."

"Why then do you come to a ball?" Mr. Allan asked him with a smile.

"To watch the ladies cavorting," he drawled, his gaze taking in Jessamine's gown.

"That's quite all right," she managed. "I have been cavorting for a good hour and could stand a rest."

"And some refreshment too, I'll be bound. All that jumping about the dance floor must have you parched."

"Indeed it has," she admitted. "I had a glass of champagne but have no idea where it went . . ." She glanced about her, but it had long since been cleared away by a footman.

"No matter. I shall fetch you another." Before she could protest that a lemonade was all she desired, he signaled a footman then took a glass of champagne and handed it to her. "For the parched lady."

She looked longingly at the lemonade but said nothing, taking the glass from him. She didn't want to appear unsophisticated.

"For myself, there is nothing like a punch," Cubby said, taking the small glass from the tray.

Mr. Allan raised his glass to her, and the others followed suit. "To a country miss—may she soon dance her first waltz."

"Hear, hear!"

She smiled shyly and took a sip, determining that she must learn the waltz.

Mr. St. Leger lowered his glass. "A country miss come to town. How delicious. We shall be most happy to initiate you into the ways of the city."

She joined in their laughter even though she knew they were teasing her. But at least she was no longer standing against the wall.

Soon more gentlemen approached, and she found herself surrounded. To her surprise, she made them laugh with her pert remarks.

By the time the music started again, she was being called a wit. One of them asked her for a dance. After that she lacked no partners for the next two sets. She had not had such fun in an age. If her season continued like this, soon Rees's memory would fade.

As Cubby turned to lead her off the dance floor, she came face-to-face with Mr. Marfleet.

"Good evening, Miss Barry."

His black evening clothes of tailcoat and breeches, white waistcoat and neckcloth were as elegant as the other gentlemen's. His unruly red hair was neatly brushed, but he wore his spectacles, reminding her again that he was a clergyman and botanist. She remembered her own spectacles, but insisted that didn't signify, since she had now learned to handle a quizzing glass.

"Good evening, Mr. Marfleet."

"Hallo there, Lance. You here tonight too?" Cubby, his plump cheeks red with exertion, eyed him in surprise. "I didn't know you were back—from where was it, Arabia?"

Mr. Marfleet spared him a brief look. "India. Hello, Cubby."

"I heard you were laid up with a fever. Only seen you a few times with Harold. Wouldn't think dancing was quite the thing if you've been abed."

"I'm over it now, thank you."

An awkward pause descended.

Mr. Marfleet's attention returned to her.

He seemed to be looking at her bare neck—or was it her neckline? Would he notice her quickened heartbeat thumping against her chest?

"I didn't see you earlier," she said, then could have bitten her tongue. He would think she had been looking out for him.

"I was in the card room." His gaze stayed fixed on her.

Once again, her hand rose to her neck to fiddle with her necklace before recalling that it was not there. "We saw your brother some time ago." That was worse. It sounded as if she was reproaching him for not looking for them sooner. To banish that impression, she waved a hand. "He is around here if you are in search of him."

He smiled faintly. "I am not, thank you all the same."

When Mr. Marfleet didn't move or say anything more, Cubby took her lightly by the elbow. "If you will excuse us—"

Mr. Marfleet put a step forward, blocking their path. "I wanted to ask you for the next dance, Miss Barry."

"I—I'm sorry, I feel a bit fatigued." In truth, she felt a bit too queasy to dance anymore.

"I see. I shall not trouble you further." With a clipped inclination of his chin to them both, he left them.

"Poor old Lancelot, such an old parson. It sticks out all over him. Nothing at all like Harold or the rest of us. Suppose it was inevitable, being the second son and all, to be obliged to enter the church."

She stiffened. "There is nothing wrong with entering the church."

"But no one expected him to take it to such lengths. Going off to India, upon my word." He shook his head, his jowls trembling above his starched shirt points.

"Perhaps he felt compelled to." She bit her lip, annoyed that she found herself defending Mr. Marfleet.

Cubby blinked at her. "What's that?"

"Perhaps he felt a conviction to—to take the gospel to the heathen." The more she spoke, the more awkward she felt at the growing puzzlement on his round face.

"A 'conviction'?' 'Pon my word, Miss Barry, you sound like a Methodist. Don't tell me you are one." He chuckled as if the joke was on him.

She smiled in reassurance. "Not at all. I am merely a vicar's daughter."

He opened his mouth, then burst out laughing. "That's a good one—a vicar's daughter."

They had rejoined the other gentlemen by this time. "Did you hear that? Miss Barry's a vicar's daughter."

Mr. St. Leger eyed her. "How curious. You don't look like a vicar's daughter."

"Not at all," Mr. Allan echoed, taking her measure.

"What does a vicar's daughter look like?" she asked, feeling their ridicule.

"Deuced if I know," Mr. Allan murmured.

"Prim and drab," maintained Cubby. "Certainly not wearing a fashionable gown like yours."

Once again she was the center of attention. She made a mocking curtsy, remembering Lady Dawson.

"Certainly not enjoying a season in London," Mr. Allan said.

"Nor flirting with gentlemen of questionable repute," Mr. St. Leger added softly.

"Am I flirting?" She batted her eyelashes at each of them. If they were going to tease her, she would show them she was not fazed. "With gentlemen of questionable repute? I had no idea."

"We are shockingly disreputable reprobates, dear Miss Barry," Cubby said, folding his hands before him as if he were sincerely penitent.

She lowered her lashes. "I have read that flirting is an art."

"Which you have mastered, Miss Barry," Mr. St. Leger murmured. "I applaud you."

At that moment Megan approached with Mr. Emery. "Look who is here," she said, glancing at the men around Jessamine as she spoke. "I wondered if you cared to join us for supper, Jessamine. Mr. Marfleet is with our party."

"Is it supper already?" Mr. St. Leger studied Megan through his quizzing glass as if she were a curious insect.

She blushed. "Yes, indeed."

"Hello, Emery," he drawled to her escort. "Who invited you?"

Mr. Emery smiled, unruffled. "The same person who thought fit to include you on the guest list."

"We may as well make it a party," he said, yawning. "Lady

Fortescue, whatever her indiscriminate taste is in her guests, is known to put on a decent collation."

Mr. Allan put out his arm to Jessamine. "Shall we, Miss Barry?"

"Thank you," she murmured, looking forward to sitting down. Hopefully, a bit of food would settle her stomach.

Lancelot watched the group head for the supper room. His friend Emery looked around, doubtless searching for him. But Lancelot remained standing where he was, as he considered joining the supper party.

He wasn't sure if he could endure a half hour or so watching Miss Barry flirt with Harold's set.

He'd been watching her for a while before asking her to dance. He'd scarcely recognized her in her getup, her hair shorn, her bosom half exposed. And drinking champagne.

The group hovering around her like a pack of bloodhounds were wealthy young men who cut a dash about town in their sporting curricles and dandified appearances. They played hard and deep into the wee hours at the clubs on St. James's before heading off to less savory neighborhoods to bet on cockfights and badger baiting.

Lancelot didn't like it one bit that their attention was focused on Miss Barry. Where was Lady Bess?

His fingers fiddled unconsciously with the necklace in his pocket. What had she been doing pawning her jewelry? She couldn't have racked up debts already. Or could she?

Every young man who came to London for the first time fell prey to that temptation. Lady Bess was known for her love for cards, but he found it hard to believe she'd allow her charge to indulge in gaming.

Turning away in disgust, Lancelot wandered the deserted ballroom for a quarter of an hour before heading to the supper room. He was hungry and it was foolish to avoid the room because of some silly chit.

He served himself a plate of food from the vast array—though most serving dishes were now half empty. Standing well away from the tables, he ate mechanically, his eyes scanning the crowd.

Miss Barry still sat amidst the dark-coated gentlemen. At least Miss Phillips and Emery sat at the same table. They seemed to be having a hilarious time by the sounds of their laughter.

Lancelot continued taking up forkfuls, though the food tasted like mush in his mouth. Finally, his plate still half full, he set it on a passing footman's tray.

Instead of leaving, he remained standing near the entrance, continuing to observe Miss Barry's table, telling himself he was only doing so because he needed to return her necklace to her before the evening was over.

Jessamine had eaten the plate of delicacies, thinly sliced ham and turkey, pickled vegetable, miniature puff pastries filled with crabmeat, and various sweetmeats. But instead of helping ease her discomfort, it had made her feel worse.

"If you will excuse me," she said, pushing her chair away.

Megan looked at her, concern in her eyes. "Are you all right, Jessamine?"

She nodded and forced a smile to her lips. "I'm fine."

"Can I get you anything?" Mr. Allan asked.

"No, I don't need anything, thank you. Just let me excuse myself a moment." If she didn't get away from them soon, she would be sick over the table. She would never outlive the humiliation and would have to leave London for good.

She stood, and all the gentlemen followed suit. Feeling embarrassed at the attention, she quickly moved away, motioning Megan back. "Please, I am quite all right. I shall return forthwith."

She walked resolutely from the room, glad Megan didn't follow her. By the time she reached the corridor, she was tempted to run. She hurried toward the stairs to the ladies' retiring room. Footsteps sounded behind her. She glanced back to see Mr. Marfleet at her heels. Of all people!

"Are you all right?"

"I—I'm fine."

"You look pale."

"I am fine. I just need the retiring room." Feeling her stomach begin to heave, she didn't wait for his reply but picked up her skirts and dashed up the stairs.

To her consternation, he followed behind her, but she was too much in a hurry to snub him. She found the room set aside for the ladies and pushed open the door.

He stood behind her, looking helpless.

"Leave me, please." She closed the door in his face.

She pushed past a maid and entered the water closet, thankful for such modern facilities in this opulent residence.

She was immediately sick.

Horrified she might ruin her new gown, she did her best to protect it. Finally, feeling relief, she stood on shaky knees and groped for the washbasin.

After cleaning herself up, she stood a moment, leaning against the basin, a cold, wet washcloth to her forehead.

Weak, but with her stomach settled, Jessamine exited the lavatory and spent a few minutes in front of the dressing table, accepting the maidservant's assistance to tidy her appearance. She pinched her cheeks to put some color back in them.

The maid stepped back. "There, miss, everything in place."

"Thank you." Jessamine let out a breath, realizing she should not have drunk so much champagne. It had seemed so harmless going down. *Forgive me, Lord.* She uttered the prayer while staring at her still-pale cheeks.

As much as she hated admitting she was wrong, she had learned from her parents that it was best to ask forgiveness sooner rather than later, and move on. If only she could move on so quickly in matters of the heart.

She had not been able to talk to the Lord about Rees. The words lodged in her chest and refused to find an outlet. She had spent too many years worshipping him from afar.

Now, she stood and smoothed the gown, eyeing her reflection from all angles to make sure her gown was not ruined. She breathed a sigh of relief that no harm seemed to have been done.

She opened the door and stopped short to find Mr. Marfleet still standing in the corridor.

"What are you doing here!"

He looked taken aback but only stared at her neckline. She put a hand to her throat.

"You aren't wearing any jewelry."

She started at his abrupt words. His gaze seemed fixed upon her bare throat. "No."

"You usually wear a necklace—with a pearl. I should think it would look nice with your gown." His gaze drifted downward.

He had noticed her necklace. She lifted her chin, her gaze unflinching. "I—I disagree. It wouldn't go at all."

She took a step to move by him.

"Are you feeling better?"

"Yes, thank you." She began to walk toward the stairs.

"The champagne didn't bother you?"

She swiveled around, her eyes wide. "How do you know I drank champagne?"

He swallowed. "I watched you."

"You watched me!" Her mouth opened than snapped shut. Of all the nerve! "What right do you have to stand there—censuring me!"

He flinched. "I'm not censuring you. I was merely concerned if you were feeling sick from drinking too much champagne."

She planted her hands on her hips, her annoyance growing. "First of all, I was not drinking *too much* champagne. I was merely not accustomed to it."

"So you were feeling unwell."

"Only a trifle. It was the—the rich food I had just now."

"As long as you are feeling better now."

"I am, thank you." Why did he make her feel as if she was in the wrong? As if her parents were here watching her? With a swish of her skirts, she turned and resumed walking.

"I . . . wanted to give you something."

She looked over her shoulder without stopping. "What?"

He fished something out of his pocket.

A fine gold chain dangled from his hand.

8

Jessamine fumbled for her quizzing glass and stared at the pearl suspended at the end of the chain Mr. Marfleet held. "Where did you get that?"

His gaze traveled to meet hers, and she remembered. "You—you went into the pawnbroker's shop?" Even as she said the words, she could scarcely believe he'd do such a thing.

He swallowed visibly. "I wondered what you would be doing coming out of a pawnbroker's shop."

She approached him warily, wanting to get a closer look at the necklace, even now disbelieving it was hers. It looked incongruously delicate in his large hand. "And the man showed it to you? He was supposed to put it away—save it for me." Her voice rose at the man's untrustworthiness. She should have known people in London couldn't be trusted.

"I had to . . . to convince him." Before she could react, he hurried on, as if afraid she wouldn't let him speak. "I redeemed it for you. Here, take it." He held it out to her.

She recoiled but then thought better of it. Slowly she extended her palm, and he dropped the necklace into it. She clasped it tightly, relief flooding her. She'd hated what she'd done and had been afraid she'd never have enough money to redeem it.

Slowly her eyes rose to meet his. "How much did . . . did you have to pay for it?"

His gaze shifted and he shrugged. "You needn't worry about it."

"Of course I need to. I shall pay you back . . . only I can't yet." Her face felt hot. How could she be indebted to Mr. Marfleet? It was worse than having to deal with a shifty pawnbroker. Mortification filled her.

"You needn't trouble yourself. You may pay me when you can, in the amounts you can. Please don't trouble yourself. I don't need the money at present." His mouth quirked upward. "I'm living at home and have few expenses."

She stared at him, feeling sicker to her stomach than she had when she'd run to the lavatory. To be beholden to this man she scorned for no good reason except that he reminded her of all she was trying to run away from.

Shame filled her. She knew she ought to say something, but the words of gratitude stuck in her throat, wedged tighter than a chicken bone.

His smile slowly disappeared, and his slate-blue eyes gazed earnestly into hers. "Is something the matter?" He gave a nervous laugh. "It—it is your necklace, isn't it?"

The words gave her an excuse to look downward. "Yes," she whispered. "It is. It was . . . was my grandmother's. Thank you. I'll repay you, I promise," she added quickly before turning around and almost running from him.

Lancelot stood staring after Miss Barry, feeling as confused as a blind man in a crowd. Harold was right. He would never know the first thing about women.

He'd waited the whole evening, the necklace feeling like a hot coal in his pocket, hoping for a moment alone with her to restore the necklace.

He'd imagined the smile that would finally grace her fine lips as she met his eyes in gratitude. Even though she had said the necklace wasn't important, the last few moments had proved otherwise. It was a family heirloom.

But instead of looking happy to have it back, she could hardly choke out her thanks and had run from him as if he would do her some harm.

He should leave her alone. Wash his hands and be done with her. He didn't know why he persisted. He wasn't even sure if he liked her.

But there was something in her green eyes when she stared up at him that awakened all his protective instincts. It was the look of a little girl who has lost something precious and didn't know where to find it.

Shoving his hands in his pockets, he strode down the hall. He wouldn't disturb her anymore with his company this evening. He'd carried out his purpose. Harold had clearly taken off long ago. He'd walk home and spend time with his botanical notes. There was no confusion there.

Jessamine awoke with a pounding headache between her temples and an awful taste in her mouth. But worse was what she felt inside. Shame at her behavior. What had she tried to be at the ball? Worse than drinking champagne and flirting with the young gentlemen had been being confronted by the necklace.

She buried her head in her pillow at the memory of seeing her grandmother's necklace in Mr. Marfleet's hand. Her mother had entrusted it to her. How could she have done such a thoughtless thing as take it to a pawnbroker? She cracked her eyes open and looked across the room at the gown hanging over the back of a chair.

What had seemed so beautiful last night now reproached her. How was she ever going to pay Mr. Marfleet back? She would not remain in his debt. That was unthinkable.

He'd looked at her with such pity, as if he knew exactly what she'd done and why. He'd admitted to watching her behavior.

He'd worn that wise, knowing look so much like her father's, when she was a little girl and had misbehaved. Instead of anger, he'd looked sad, which made her feel ten times worse than if he'd whipped her. It had compelled her to obey in order to avoid disappointing him, until obedience and a desire to please had become second nature to her.

She sat up in bed, ignoring her throbbing head, and hugged a pillow to her chest, her knees drawn up. She was tired of seeking to please. And she didn't need someone like Mr. Marfleet hovering around her as if she was still that little girl!

She punched at her pillow, wanting to sob in frustration. Only by an effort of will did she hold back the tears. She didn't need puffy, red eyes on top of everything else. She'd cried enough since finding out that Rees and Céline were expecting a child.

She bit her lip, holding back a longing for how things had been. When her father had gotten an inkling of how the wind blew between her and Rees, he'd counseled her to be patient, for Rees was a man worth waiting for.

She'd obeyed him, and been good and done everything as she ought. All for nothing!

Knowing it was useless to stay in bed where her thoughts would continue torturing her, Jessamine threw off her covers. Thankfully, Lady Bess had not witnessed her indisposition of the previous evening, and Megan was too kind to say anything.

Kindness—ugh! Jessamine preferred a good, bracing dose of sarcasm or censure to pitying words and looks. An immediate vision of Mr. Marfleet came to her mind, and his teasing words on Bond Street. But she erased them, preferring instead to conjure up Mr. St. Leger's subtle derision and world-weary air. There was a sophisticated gentleman, and one who had appreciated her wit.

After struggling with her garments, she descended the stairs to the breakfast room in the hopes that a cup of tea would help her head.

She was thankful only Megan was there so she didn't have to feign lightheartedness in the face of Lady Bess's unfailing morning cheer.

Megan smiled, but a second later her smile faded. "Are you quite well? You look pale. Maybe you should have stayed in bed a bit longer the way Lady Bess has this morning."

"Only a bit of a headache," Jessamine said, advancing into the room. "It will pass, I'm sure, once I've had a cup of tea."

"Let me get it for you, and perhaps some dry toast." As she spoke, Megan bustled about serving her.

"Thank you," she murmured when the tea and toast sat before her. She bowed her head to say grace then took a sip of the strong, hot tea.

"Do you think it was . . . the champagne?"

Jessamine stared at her friend. Between Megan and Mr. Marfleet, it would seem she'd been observed the entire evening. "I'm sure a couple of glasses of champagne can do a person no harm."

"No, of course not. Unless you are not accustomed to it." Megan fell silent after her hesitant comment.

Jessamine nibbled at a corner of her toast. A letter from home lay at the side of her plate. She broke the seal and unfolded it. Recognizing her father's hand, a wave of homesickness came over her as she read about the Sunday services, a sermon he'd prepared, a prayer he'd written, and the calls he'd made on parishioners. All the while he lamented her absence.

My plants are sadly neglected too. I've had to be away so much with a spate of illness in the village that I've had little time to water the seedlings we sowed. They are crowded and looking reedy. I miss my able assistant, but your mother assures me that a London season is a necessary step at this time of life in order to find a suitable husband.

I was content with finding a wife in my own corner of the world and have been blessed with your mother all these years.

Yet, I understand that it was good for you to be away for a season. Too many memories here, I imagine, the hopes and dreams of youth being dashed.

By now I hope you've met a number of young gentlemen to allow you to begin to understand God's wisdom in taking Rees away. Resignation to God's will is sometimes hard, but if one trusts in His ultimate wisdom, one will see that the ways of Providence are best . . .

Her father went on in this vein for a few more paragraphs, but Jessamine stopped reading, her fingers crumpling the edge of the paper as she curled them into a fist.

The ways of Providence. What man had she met in London to rival Rees? Those silly dandies and bucks of the evening before?

Mr. Marfleet—her father would doubtless approve of him. They were cut from the same "cloth." Her lips twisted at the unintended pun. Quiet, unassuming parsons. Her father had been content to live in a tiny vicarage at the mercy of a rector who lived several hours away in a thriving town and rarely came to see how her father fared.

And Mr. Marfleet had left the comforts of his family name and wealth to go as missionary to a foreign land. Yet, likely back home, he'd receive a comfortable living in some prosperous parish because he was a baronet's son.

No, she did not consider Mr. Marfleet superior to Rees. Not that Mr. Marfleet was interested in someone like her, someone who imbibed champagne and pawned the family jewels, she thought with a bitter laugh.

"Good news from home?"

She looked across the table at Megan. "Only the usual things. Papa's sermons and his plants. Thankfully both he and Mama are well. There has been some illness affecting several parishioners, so I'm glad it has not touched them. I hope your mother is well."

"I'm thankful your parents are well. Mama writes the same. She is keeping busy visiting neighbors. They had a strawberry picking party at the squire's, and she has put up several jars of jam."

"How nice."

"Jessamine—"

She looked up from the rim of her teacup at the serious note in Megan's voice. "What is it?"

"Rees is on his way to London . . . with Céline."

Lancelot was eating his breakfast of cold slices of tongue, a boiled egg, and toast, his mind on his plans for the day, when his father walked into the breakfast room dressed in a riding outfit as he habitually did at that hour, his top boots shining, his cravat spotless, his cheeks ruddy from the outdoors.

"Good morning, Lancelot. I'm surprised to see you up so early," he said in a jovial tone, glancing down at the *Morning Post* and a tray of correspondence the butler set before his place.

"It is past ten."

His father helped himself at the sideboard. "Ah, but I know you had a late night. I don't expect you to burn the candle at both ends. You're still getting your strength back."

"I was home shortly after midnight, so no need to worry."

His father brought his heaping plate back to his place and sat down, rubbing his hands together. "Mm. Nothing like sitting down to a good breakfast after an early morning ride in the park."

He dug into his food as Lancelot continued his own breakfast.

His father paused to take a sip of coffee. "Did you have a successful evening?"

Lancelot finished chewing before replying. "I'm not certain what qualifies as a successful evening."

His father chuckled. "In my day it meant dancing with all the pretty girls making their come-out, promising to call on a few on the morrow, then making the rounds of a few clubs and if my luck wasn't holding, leaving the tables without having written too many vouchers, and trying my luck with the ladies in Covent Garden. But we won't go into that, since you are a respectable clergyman."

"It doesn't sound as if the life of a young gentleman about town has changed much from your generation to mine," Lancelot said dryly.

"I suppose it hasn't. I think Harold is a prime example. He may forgo dancing with the young ladies, but as for gaming and . . . the rest of it . . ." His father sighed heavily before turning his attention back to his plate.

Lancelot leafed through a botanical periodical that had come in the mail. He was reading an article on *Aloe picta*, "spotted aloe," a native of the Cape of Good Hope, easily confused with the common soap aloe, when his father spoke again.

"Your mother tells me you're dangling after some chit—or is it two? Doesn't do to muddy the waters, you know."

Lancelot pulled his attention from the foreign plant with a scowl. "I don't believe my behavior qualifies as 'dangling after a chit.'"

"You must excuse the expression, but I'm afraid you've gotten your mother's hopes up, and I just wanted to see if there's any substance to the tale. Both she and Harold say the young ladies in question are presentable enough."

Lancelot stared at his father. "They were present at your own dinner table."

His father's light-blue eyes widened and his light-brown eyebrows rose as he searched his memory. "I seem to recall a pair of young things here. Were those the ones? Well, they seemed pretty enough."

Lancelot said nothing, used to his father's obliviousness when it came to anything not within his immediate sphere.

"I don't want to pry into your affairs, my boy, but since you are seven-and-twenty and have evinced no interest in the fairer sex until now—or kept very quiet about it—you can understand if your mother is snapping like a turtle at a cricket at the merest whisper of any interest on your part." He smiled gently. "Come now, is there any reason for us to hope?"

Reluctantly Lancelot faced his father again, remembering the look of disdain on Miss Barry's face as she snatched back her necklace. "I rather think not. The lady in question has taken me quite in dislike, and I really am not sure of my own feelings at this point." As he'd walked the streets of Mayfair last night, he'd gone from chagrin to a desire to wash his hands of her.

His father mulled over his words before sighing. "Well, thank you for the honest answer, at any rate." He cocked an eyebrow. "And the other young lady?"

Lancelot shrugged, at a loss. "She is a nice young lady, but—"

"But you are not in love with her. No chance to change your mind?"

Feeling his face redden, he looked down at his empty plate. "I think *love* is too strong a word at this juncture."

"Well, don't be surprised if it sneaks up on you before you're aware." His father chuckled again. "So, the young lady has got under your skin, has she?"

Lancelot shrugged and flipped over a page of the illustrated periodical. "She wants nothing to do with me, and I begin to think I want nothing to do with her."

"What's her name again?"

"Jessamine Barry." *Jasminum*. Jasmine. He could still smell the heady scent of the jasmine garlands made by the people in India and sold on the streets, used as offerings at their temples and heaped upon their funeral pyres.

His father thrust out his lower lip. Finally he shook his head. "Never heard of her. Barry is an old enough name. Could be a distant relative of any number of Barrys of my acquaintance. Didn't your mother say she was a vicar's daughter?"

He nodded.

"Probably as poor as a church mouse, but with that upbringing she should suit as a vicar's wife if you manage to get a new living soon."

His father picked up his letter opener and twirled it against his fingertip. "In the meantime, your mother is right. You must find a wife. You are no longer a young man. Even without a living, you have an adequate allowance. But the most pressing thing is to ensure the succession." He sighed heavily, his eyes somber as he gazed across the table. "It is clear Rosamunde will not give Harold any children."

Lancelot tried to interrupt, but his father held up a hand.

"It's been more than ten years Harold has been married with no issue. They live separate lives these days. If one of you doesn't beget a *legitimate* son soon, the estate and all the lands risk passing to a lesser Marfleet branch—some distant cousin of mine, I shudder to think."

"Harold is hale and hearty."

His father gave him a pitying look. "But a few years older than you and living a more reckless life. Of course, jaunting off to India was probably more dangerous than anything he ever undertook. But the good Lord saw fit to bring you back in one piece, if not precisely hale. But it won't do to tempt fate any longer. I will not accept that both of you fail to produce a son of your own." His father's blue eyes fixed on him under his bristling brows.

"I am telling you as your father and head of this family, that before anything else, you must marry and begin producing a family. If this girl won't have you, look to another. The season's in full swing. London must be bursting with young ladies of marriageable age. If you can't attract one young miss with your name and pedigree and a respectable income, you have no right to call yourself a Marfleet!"

"Yes, Father." Lancelot fixed his eyes on the periodical but could no longer focus on the words. His parents wished him to marry, yet he felt he had already proven a failure this season and he had little heart to attempt a new pursuit.

Jessamine's jaw dropped at Megan's announcement. The next second she snapped it shut. "Rees is on his way to London?"

Megan nodded, her gray eyes filled with concern. "I received a message by courier from Rees. They landed in Dover. He said they'd be here tomorrow or the next day since he is taking it in easy stages, because of . . . Céline's condition."

Her condition. Carrying his child. Jessamine looked down at the remains of toast crusts on her plate. Her fingers curled into her napkin. "I see. Where will they stay once in London?"

"I'm not sure. I know Lady Wexham—my goodness, I don't even know what to call her. Mrs. Phillips sounds so odd and too formal, seeing as she is now my sister." Megan's eyelids fluttered downward as if embarrassed to remind Jessamine of the new relationship. "And she's so much older than I." She gave a strangled laugh. "More an aunt than a sister, I should say." Megan cleared her throat. "I know she has a town house here in London, but I don't know if they'll stay there. Rees says very little in his note." She brightened. "Well, I shall soon find out."

"He will probably call on you right away," Jessamine said in a wooden voice.

Megan swallowed. "I imagine, unless he has to report to the Foreign Office first. I imagine he'll be very busy, what with this crisis in France."

"But not too busy to see his only sister."

Megan swallowed, her gray eyes large as they gazed into hers. "Will you mind very much?"

Jessamine dusted the toast crumbs off her fingertips. "I shall be fine. I have an idea I wished to discuss with you," she said in an effort to change the subject. "I wondered if you would care to engage a dance master to teach us the waltz."

Megan's eyes widened. "The waltz?"

"Yes. I found it so elegant when I saw it performed last night. But I dared not attempt it without some lessons first." She looked down at her plate. "But I haven't much money left since I had the gowns made, so I thought, if you cared to share a dance master with me, perhaps Lady Bess could recommend someone for us at not much cost."

"I don't know what Mama would say, or Rees, if they saw me waltzing."

"I don't think it was so scandalous. I found it ever so graceful."

Megan pondered this a few minutes, then finally nodded her head slowly. "Very well. I have most of my allowance."

Jessamine wasn't sure whether Megan agreed only to placate her and take her mind off Rees and Céline's arrival, but she didn't care. All that mattered was being able to dance the waltz at her next ball.

"Perhaps Mr. Marfleet will ask you for the waltz."

Jessamine's lips turned downward. "I wish you wouldn't keep bringing up his name as if he were a suitor. If you're so interested in him, you may waltz with him."

"Perhaps I may, if he asks me." Her look sobered once more. "You shall have to face him sometime, you know."

Jessamine knew she didn't refer to Mr. Marfleet. She sucked in air. "I know. But I'd rather it be later than sooner."

Megan nodded. "Perhaps I can call on him and that way prevent his coming here."

"Nonsense. You live here and you shouldn't be afraid to have anyone call on you. It's been over a year. I shall be fine."

She was kept occupied that afternoon with gentlemen callers whom she'd danced with the evening before. Wearing a gown of moss green that brought out the color in her eyes, her hair dressed in careless curls atop her head, she felt confident that she looked her best.

There was talk of a ball, an assembly, and an excursion to Vauxhall. She showed the proper enthusiasm for them all. She would keep herself so busy she wouldn't think of Rees's return and would likely miss his visit if he did call. By the time she was forced to face him, she'd have a dozen swains following her about, and perhaps Rees would realize what he'd lost.

When she entered the house the next afternoon after a trip to the circulating library, the maid was coming in from the service area at the back of the house. Jessamine took off her hat and arranged her hair in the mirror.

"Oh, miss, there's a gentleman in the drawing room with Miss Phillips."

9

Jessamine looked over her shoulder at Betsy, her breath caught. Had Rees come so soon? "Is it someone we know?"

"It's Miss Phillips's brother, miss."

Jessamine drew in a lungful of air, her heart thudding against her chest. The moment had arrived. She moistened her lips, needing to know the worst. "Is anyone with him—his wife?"

"No, miss. He came alone."

"Thank you, Betsy."

She finished arranging her hair, glad that the walk had left her cheeks rosy. Her outfit suited her coloring. What was she thinking? She could never compare with that Frenchwoman who had stolen Rees from her—except on one count. Céline Phillips was old, near thirty at least.

Drawing comfort from that fact, Jessamine squared her shoulders and headed up the stairs to the drawing room, feeling as if she were going to face an execution squad.

She could continue on to her room, but that would be the coward's way. Sooner or later she'd have to see Rees. Better here than in a public place.

She stood a moment in front of the closed door, hearing muffled voices through the panels.

Dear Lord, help me get through the next few moments. If I can just get through those, I shall be all right. Thank You.

Taking a deep breath, she pushed it open.

The moment she entered the room, the conversation ceased and she was the focus of all eyes. But she only had eyes for Rees Phillips.

His penetrating gray gaze locked with hers as he stood. "Hello, Jessamine, how nice to see you again."

Continuing to pray for strength, she walked across the room, extending her hand. "Hello, Rees. Welcome back."

His larger hand clasped hers warmly and he smiled. Was it relief she saw in his eyes? "Thank you. You are looking well."

She forced her lips upward, keeping all emotion locked down deep where no one could be aware of her inward turmoil.

Their hold loosened, and she stepped back a pace. "As are you," she said. He was indeed, appearing more elegant than she'd ever seen him, in a dark blue, well-cut coat of superfine with brass buttons; a crisp white cravat with just the right number of folds under his chin; a silk waistcoat of a silvery gray that matched his eyes; and close-fitting, fawn-colored pantaloons tucked into top boots.

"Thank you." His lips tilted up on one side in that familiar way that made her traitorous heart lurch with longing. "I must say you are looking very elegant. Full of town bronze, the both of you." He turned toward Megan. "I'd hardly recognize you if I met you on the street."

Megan laughed. "Perhaps to your inexpert eyes, Rees, but we are still but country bumpkins here in London."

"Nonsense," Lady Bess, who had sat quiet until now, said from her place behind the tea service. "I'm so glad you have returned from your errand, my dear, in time for Mr. Phillips's call. Why don't you ring for some fresh tea and you can catch up with your old neighbor. I'm sure there is much news to exchange."

Jessamine did as she was bid, glad for an excuse to turn away from Rees. It had been worse than she'd thought—though she was glad the first moments were over. She had faced him and not given way to her emotions. But it had cost her. Oh, to see him so close and still want him as desperately as she had a year ago—two years ago. Nothing had changed. If anything, he seemed more attractive than ever. It was more than his fashionable clothes, although those certainly added to his allure. He had never worn a watch fob before, she noted. The old Rees would have considered it a bit of frippery reserved for dandies. Had his wife perhaps given it to him? Bitterness cast its shadow over her thoughts.

It was more than clothes and haircut. He had an air of contentment and confidence that he'd lacked before. He'd always been so serious, as if bowed under the weight of responsibilities toward his family and ambitions for himself. Now he seemed more relaxed and at ease with himself. He laughed and smiled more readily.

Jessamine turned away from the embroidered satin bellpull and took her seat, in an armchair neither too far nor too close to Rees, to show him and Megan—and herself—that she was indifferent to his presence and treating him like any guest in Lady Bess's drawing room.

Rees retook his seat beside Megan on the sofa. "I find it hard to believe the two of you haven't turned a lot of heads since you came to London."

Megan rolled her eyes. "I am beginning to conclude that with a few exceptions, London gentlemen are either already married, fops and dandies, or merely hanging out for a wife with a sizable dowry."

Rees shook his head. "I do hope you exaggerate."

"Of course she exaggerates," Lady Bess said stoutly. "They have met some fine gentlemen. Things started a bit slowly, but that is understandable, since I myself no longer go out in society the way I used to." She fluffed up the lacy fichu at her neckline. "I was quite a renowned beauty once, though you'll find that hard to believe now, I'm sure."

"Not at all. My mother and I are very grateful to you for taking our Megan under your wing." He glanced at Jessamine then away. "You had no obligation to include her in your kind invitation to your goddaughter."

"Nonsense." Lady Bess waved a hand at him. "It has been my pleasure to introduce both young ladies into society. Such pleasant girls. They have made me feel young again. And they have had quite an amusing time lately, whatever your sister will have you believe." She smiled indulgently at Jessamine. "We've had a string of gentlemen callers since the ball the other night at Lady Fortescue's. Jessamine was quite a hit in her new gown and hairstyle—and, of course, Megan looked delightful as always."

Jessamine could not control the blush creeping up her cheeks as Rees's assessing gaze turned once more to her. "I am not surprised."

"Lady Bess grossly overstates it." Jessamine fiddled with one of the buttons on her cuff as she recalled how sick she'd been at the ball.

As if sensing her discomfiture, which only proved how discerning he was to her moods, Rees turned back to Megan. "What else have you two been up to since arriving in London? Besides dancing till dawn?" he teased.

"Lots of things. Since we knew no one but Lady Bess, we went sightseeing together, taking along the travel guide." She began describing some of their outings, her hands gesturing and her eyes shining as she described the places they'd visited.

Jessamine was thankful for Megan's enthusiasm. It saved her from having to speak, except for filling in a detail or an impression here or there so neither would suspect what she was suffering inside. Nothing would appear unusual to Rees, since he was used to his sister's more boisterous nature and Jessamine's quieter one.

It could almost be old times, she thought sadly. His wife's name had not even been mentioned.

The maidservant brought in a fresh pot of tea, and Jessamine busied herself with her cup. When she sat back, she was able to observe Rees over the rim of her cup without appearing obvious about it, since both Megan and he were facing each other.

He looked handsomer than ever. His dark, almost black, hair was brushed back off his square forehead, yet it didn't hide the distinct wave. His strong jawline was neatly shaved, though his sideburns were longer than she remembered.

His gray eyes glanced her way now and again, and she forced herself not to look away but smiled slightly before shifting her gaze to Megan, as if she were giving them both equal attention.

But as Megan's voice died down, Rees leaned forward, allowing Lady Bess to pour him a fresh cup of tea. "I'm sorry I won't be in London long, so I shan't be able to escort you many places. Things are very uncertain in Belgium right now."

Lady Bess's lacy cap trembled. "Will there be war?"

He shook his head. "There is no telling what Napoleon will do, especially if he thinks himself surrounded by his enemies. He is not the type to sit idle if he feels his borders are threatened."

Megan sighed. "I wish you didn't have to go back to Brussels so soon."

"I really shouldn't have come, but I wanted to bring Céline away, no matter how remote any danger."

It was the first mention of his wife, and Jessamine thought she detected a slight hesitation before he said her name. He hadn't glanced at her. Throughout his conversation, he had maintained a balanced focus among the three of them. Neutral, she would describe it, like a good diplomat. No wonder he had advanced in that field. Had all feelings he'd once had for her disappeared? It would appear so if she went by his demeanor and tone of voice.

"I hope the trip across the channel didn't tire her out too much," Lady Bess said as soon as he mentioned his wife. "Poor thing."

"She is fine, thank you, ma'am, and resting today."

"I . . . I would like to meet her," Megan said, stumbling only slightly, her gaze flitting to Jessamine and away again.

"Yes, she is eager to meet you too." He glanced at each one of them without pausing on Jessamine. "In fact, she would like to do anything to help introduce you into society—while she is still able to go about." A flush crept along his jawline at mention of his wife's condition. "She has been out of London for almost two years now, but her connections are very good, especially since she has been very active both in Vienna and more recently in Brussels among the cream of society."

"I'm sure she has. She was most admired here in London." Lady Bess clucked her tongue. "We were all so surprised when she left for France so suddenly, but thankfully, the war was almost over. Rumor had it she hastened to the side of a relative."

His look shuttered as he stared down at his teacup. "Yes, she found herself forced to return to France." Then he seemed to recover and addressed Lady Bess directly once more. "I was able to locate her when I was sent to Paris after the peace to work with Wellington. Céline has proved a fine asset to the British diplomatic efforts since we've been together."

"I think it's so exciting." Megan clapped her hands together, ending any awkwardness in the atmosphere.

"You have always wanted to be in the diplomatic service," Megan continued. "And after so many years working in the Foreign Office here in London, your dream has finally come true—and the Lord has blessed you with a true helpmate at your side." She sighed as if it had all been divinely orchestrated.

"Yes, I am a blessed man. I could hardly have imagined how my life would change." He looked at Lady Bess again. "But that's enough about me. I'm sure despite living a more retired life, ma'am, you have still been able to introduce your two charges into society."

Lady Bess batted her eyelashes, as if she, too, were falling under Rees's quiet charm. "I am not completely forgotten in society, it is true. But the real credit of the invitations that have begun to grace our mantel comes thanks to the girls themselves."

"Though if it hadn't been for Lady Marfleet, we'd still be waiting to receive our first invitation," Megan said with an arch look at Jessamine.

"Lady Marfleet?"

"She is quite a leader in society. I'm sure your wife is acquainted with her," Lady Bess explained.

As he nodded, Megan added with an impish look in her direction, "The credit for her attention belongs solely to Jess, who made quite an impression on her younger son, Lancelot Marfleet, at a rout we attended not long ago."

Jessamine's first impulse was to deny any such attraction on Mr. Marfleet's part. But pride came to her aid. Let Rees think a leading member of the ton was courting her. It would not make up for hearing about his wife and what a blessing she was to him, but it would help ease the pain of this first meeting. "Once again, Megan is given to hyperbole," she murmured, looking modestly at her lap.

"Not in this case," Megan asserted. "He is a most attentive, eligible gentleman. Best of all, he is a vicar! He has even been to India as a missionary. What better suitor for our Jessamine?"

Rees lifted a black brow. "I am indeed impressed. I knew there was someone special for you."

For an instant Jessamine's gaze clung to his as she felt the knife thrust anew at his words. She forced herself to look away, even as her breast seethed with resentful anger. How convenient for him to think she had already fallen in love with someone else, so he could wash his hands of all responsibility for breaking her heart!

"He is just . . . one among many," she managed to say in an offhand manner. "I am in no rush to settle with any. I prefer to enjoy my season."

"That is wise," he said quietly.

Later that afternoon, after Rees had left, Megan knocked on Jessamine's door.

"Come in."

Megan crossed the room and stood looking down at her. "Are you all right?" she asked hesitantly.

Jessamine sat propped up in her bed against her pillows, an opened book in her lap. She attempted a careless tone. "Yes, of course. I am glad I could see Rees and know he no longer affects me in that way."

She withstood Megan's searching look until finally her friend seemed satisfied. "I am glad."

"When shall you pay her a visit?"

Megan didn't ask to whom she referred. "Tomorrow." Thankfully she didn't ask Jessamine to accompany her.

Instead, Megan sat down beside her on the counterpane and began to pluck at a thread. "He's asked me to . . . stay with them."

Jessamine stared at her friend's bowed head. Before she could rally herself to express her best wishes for her, Megan hurried on, "I have so little chance to see my brother, and he is to be in London so short a time."

Jessamine covered Megan's hand with her own, stilling its nervous movements. "Of course you must go."

Megan's gray eyes still looked troubled—in the same way Rees's had the day he told her to forget him. "It's not just for the time Rees is here. He—he wants me to stay on and accompany Céline."

Slowly, Jessamine removed her hand from her friend's. "I see."

"He asked me especially. He says he doesn't want her to be alone when he leaves since he doesn't know how long this crisis is to last."

"Doesn't she have anyone of her own?" Jessamine couldn't help blurting out, then bit her lip, regretting the question, which sounded so ungracious.

Megan shook her head. "Her mother is in France and she has no one close in England. No one but the late Earl of Wexham's family, and they are not close. Her former sister-in-law used to live with her, but from what Rees told me, she has always been jealous of Céline and done her much harm. At any rate, her sister-in-law has gone to live with the new Earl of Wexham and his wife."

Jessamine stared down at the counterpane. "Well, you must do as he wishes."

"I wouldn't if he hadn't asked me expressly. He knows I don't want to leave you."

Jessamine forced a laugh. "I shall be fine with Lady Bess. And it's not as if we shan't see one another." Except now it would mean having to see her usurper as well.

"Of course not!" Megan let out a breath of relief. "I shall visit you every day." Her enthusiasm quickly returned, although it sounded a bit too cheery to Jessamine's finely attuned ears.

Megan jumped up from the bed with a final pat to Jessamine's hand. "Well, I shall meet Rees's wife tomorrow. She's probably a haggard old shrew," she threw out as final sop before leaving the room.

Jessamine was only able to muster up a lackluster smile, which faded as soon as Megan shut the door behind her.

When Megan returned from visiting her brother the next day, she said little about his wife except that she seemed nice. Jessamine knew Megan was trying to spare her feelings, because if there had been anything the least unfavorable, she would have been sure to mention it and even exaggerate it.

Jessamine and the maid helped Megan pack her belongings. Rees would come with a carriage later to collect her.

"It's a lovely house on Berkeley Square, so close to Hyde Park. I hope you come to visit me."

Jessamine pretended to bend down to retrieve a handkerchief off the floor to avoid answering.

Megan changed the subject to an upcoming ball. They'd both received invitations, confirming their success at the first. "I think I shall wear this ivory crepe. I haven't worn it yet." She held it up to herself. "What do you think?"

"It's very pretty. The color looks most becoming against your complexion and hair."

"Which gown will you wear?"

"Perhaps the new amber sarcenet with the blonde lace."

Megan breathed in. "It's so lovely. I can't wait to see it on you."

They spoke some more about what accessories they would wear with their gowns and how they would dress their hair. Jessamine thought about her restored necklace and how well it would match her gown.

She still hadn't come up with a way to repay Mr. Marfleet. She did not want to be in his debt any longer than absolutely necessary. It was an intolerable situation.

Every time she met Mr. Marfleet at a ball or assembly, she would be reminded of that awful night of her first ball.

When the fancy coach came to collect Megan in the early evening, Jessamine braced herself to face Rees again, but only a groom accompanied the coach.

"Rees had a late meeting at the Foreign Office," Megan read from a note. "I shan't see him until later this evening."

With a sense of relief, Jessamine turned her attention to helping Megan collect all her smaller articles of luggage. Then the two embraced.

"I shall see you tomorrow," Megan promised, then quickly bit her lip. "Perhaps if I come by early, we can go for our usual walk before anyone else is up, the way we are accustomed to?"

Jessamine withdrew from the embrace though she kept a loose hold on her friend's forearms. "Why don't you wait and see what M-Mrs. Phillips's schedule is first?" she suggested, tripping over the name. The only Mrs. Phillips she'd known was Rees's mother. She took in a breath, plowing on. "If you have time during the day, feel free to call, but if not, we shall see each other at the ball."

Megan nodded slowly. "Very well." Then she giggled. "If we

don't see each other before then, we can surprise each other with how beautiful we look."

"You shall probably have a French maid to dress your hair, so it is not a fair contest."

Megan's smile widened. "I shall use every means available to look my best—not to outshine you but to find my prince charming at the ball." Reluctantly, Megan pushed away with a sigh. "I shall send a note over tomorrow to tell you how everything is."

"Thank you, but there is no rush. I know you shall be fine and I don't expect much to alter here."

With a final nod and tentative smile, Megan allowed the liveried footman to help her into the coach. Jessamine watched the step being lifted, the door shut, and the footman take his place at the rear with a call to the coachman to depart.

The horse hooves clopped over the cobblestones, the iron wheels grating. Megan pushed down the window and waved.

Jessamine forced a smile and waved back.

When the coach was out of sight, Jessamine reentered the silent house with a weary sigh. Lady Bess was out dining with a friend and attending a card party afterward.

Jessamine faced her first evening in London alone.

Despite what Megan had told Rees about their popularity, their calling card tray had remained empty the last couple of days.

Determined not to mope, she climbed the stairs slowly, trying not to notice how quiet the house seemed without Megan's lively voice.

In her room, she opened the oak clothespress and took out her ball gown to examine it, already thinking of having to dress without Megan's help.

She would doubtless see Rees at the ball. Surely he'd escort his sister. And Mrs. Phillips? Would she be seen in society? It all depended on her condition.

Whether Jessamine would see her or only Rees, she was determined to look her best.

To her surprise, the next afternoon Mr. St. Leger called on her and invited her to ride in the park in his phaeton. She latched onto it as a lifeline thrown to her. Mr. St. Leger, handsome, fashionable, appearing bored by all society had to offer, had singled her out. Perhaps her fortunes were finally about to change.

She quickly ran upstairs to change her gown for something more appropriate to be seen riding in Hyde Park at the fashionable hour.

She donned a sprigged muslin with jade trim and over it a jade spencer. She gave herself a final inspection in the mirror, adjusting the angle of her poke bonnet, which was trimmed with a matching shade of ribbons and small pink rosettes. She did not want to appear to disadvantage beside Mr. St. Leger's elegance.

When he was announced, she ran down the stairs to the drawing room, where he waited. "I am ready," she said, feeling suddenly shy at the thought of going with this elegant dandy on a ride in an open carriage. He was dressed nattily in buckskin breeches, top boots, and a dark brown jacket fitted snugly over his broad shoulders. He took his time inspecting her outfit and finally declared, "You are looking fetching."

Her cheeks flushed, understanding how a young gentleman must have felt when given a nod of approval by Brummell himself. "Thank you."

Remembering Lady Bess's caution about rakes and young blades about town, she had a few qualms about going alone with a gentleman, but they disappeared as soon as she stepped outside and saw his shiny phaeton standing on the curb, a beautiful chestnut pair harnessed to it. Her spirits lifted. To drive in Hyde Park with an eligible gentleman of the ton, that was favor indeed.

The presence of his tiger reassured her as well. She allowed him to help her up and took her place beside Mr. St. Leger.

"Are you ready to be ogled by every driver on Rotten Row?"

He had been astounded to know she'd never ridden on the famous riding path in Hyde Park.

"I'm sure there are too many others to be ogled," she demurred.

His tiger took his place in the rumble at the back, and Mr. St. Leger took up the reins, setting the horses in motion. They kept up a smart pace down the cobbled street but slowed as traffic increased on Oxford Street.

They didn't speak much after that as he concentrated on maneuvering the busy streets. Jessamine relaxed, taking pleasure in seeing everything from the view of a high, open carriage. People stopped to watch the smart vehicle drive by. As they turned onto Park Avenue, he was able to pick up the pace again. He saluted other drivers of his acquaintance with his whip. Hyde Park's vast fields spread before them to her right.

They didn't enter the park until they had reached Hyde Park Corner at the southeast corner. "There's Number One, Apsley House," he said, pointing his whip at a large brick mansion before the park. "It belongs to the Duke of Wellington's older brother."

"I wonder if the duke will be obliged to face Napoleon in battle."

"There is no telling. If he does, it will be the first time."

A moment later, he pointed out Tattersall's.

"The horse auctioneers?" she asked hesitantly.

"The very one. It is where I purchased this fine pair."

"They are beautiful horses." She had never thought too much of horses except as farm animals. But since hearing the conversation of the gentlemen at the ball, she realized horses were a passion among them.

The traffic was congested before the Hyde Park Corner tollhouse gate, but they turned in beforehand near the formal gardens at the rear of Apsley House. Here the park traffic forced Mr. St. Leger to slow to a crawl.

Riding on Rotten Row proved an eye-opening experience, vastly different from her morning walks in the park with Megan.

Now the sandy path was crammed with carriages inching along. Mr. St. Leger nodded and tipped his hat as a landau passed them.

Two ladies seated within smiled before eyeing her. One drew close to the other to say something.

Jessamine was soon distracted by the other vehicles jamming the driving lane. There were several gentlemen and uniformed soldiers riding horseback and a few more daring ladies doing the same. The traffic was further slowed by all those who were walking on the footpath alongside the Row, the two dirt paths separated by only a low row of wooden posts. The carriages stopped frequently for their occupants to chat a few moments with their acquaintances on foot.

Jessamine recognized almost no one.

Mr. St. Leger, however, seemed to know everyone, especially the gentlemen on horseback. He always introduced her first. There was a speculative look in the eyes of the gentlemen for a few seconds before they would get busy talking horses or races.

She smiled when she finally saw a familiar face from the ball. Cubby drew up in a yellow curricle. "Hallo there, Miss Barry. If I'd known you like to drive, I'd have invited you myself."

"Hello, Cubby," Mr. St. Leger drawled as Jessamine smiled her greeting. "Finally taking your grays out for air?"

Cubby looked proudly at his horses. "I exercise them regularly."

"You mean your groom does."

They bandied about insults for a few more moments before Mr. St. Leger greeted another rider.

Cubby drew his curricle closer to her side. "How have you fared since Lady Fortescue's ball?"

Jessamine blushed, wondering if he were referring to her indisposition. "Very well, thank you."

"We missed seeing you at the rout last night at the Buxtons."

She had known of no rout but merely smiled. "I'm sure it was a sad crush I'm glad to have missed."

"Not so tired from the dancing that you won't be ready to kick up your heels at the Waverley ball?"

She laughed in relief, having received an invitation to that ball. "No, indeed. I look forward to it." On impulse she added, "I wouldn't want my new gown to go to waste."

Cubby's eyes lit up. "A new gown, eh?" He waggled his eyebrows. "I await in anticipation."

He touched his gloved hand to the brim of his top hat. "Until then, Miss Barry."

They continued moving along the drive. The day was clear and warm, and Jessamine's spirits lifted at being out-of-doors in an area that seemed far from the city. She had received a brief note from Megan just as she'd promised, but it had contained few details. Jessamine assumed she must be very busy in her new surroundings.

"You have made a favorable impression on Cubby. He is not easily taken with young ladies in their first season."

She arched an eyebrow at Mr. St. Leger. "How unfair of him. Here we try our best to primp and do everything in our power to fascinate and please the company, only to have those like Mr. Fane disdain our efforts."

Mr. St. Leger smiled down at her, a glint of humor in his blue eyes. "We are awfully hard to please, are we not? But you must see it from our point of view. The least bit of interest we pay a young lady and her mama is already planning the announcement of her betrothal in the *Gazette*."

"I am certain you exaggerate."

"I assure you I do not."

"If that is so, it is a wonder you dared invite me to ride with you in the park."

He surveyed her under the brim of his hat. "Ah, but your mama and papa are not in town, are they?"

"No, they are not." For a moment, she wondered whether he was teasing her or in earnest.

But he chuckled, and the puzzlement disappeared. "I have only

Lady Beasinger to fear, and she is a delightful if scatterbrained goose."

"You mustn't say such things about my hostess. She is a dear woman."

Instead of replying, he turned with a smile to chat with an acquaintance who had drawn abreast of the phaeton.

"Jessamine!"

Jessamine started, recognizing Megan's excited voice. Turning in her seat, she wished herself anyplace else. Megan waved and smiled from a barouche with its top down. Beside her sat a dark-haired, very elegant beauty.

Jessamine's mouth went dry as she took in the sight of Rees's bride.

10

Jessamine forced a smile to her lips as Megan's carriage pulled up to Mr. St. Leger's. To her dismay, Mrs. Phillips sat on the side closest to Jessamine.

"How wonderful and convenient to see you here this afternoon," Megan said, "since you are precisely the person I've most wanted to see. I wished so to stop in at Lady Bess's, but this is even better."

Megan's exuberance ebbed a notch as she turned to her companion. "Céline, may I present my best friend in all the world, Jessamine Barry? She is like a sister to me." She smiled at Jessamine. "Jessamine, Rees's wife, Céline Phillips."

As she murmured her greetings, Jessamine took in every detail of her rival's appearance.

Rees's wife was even more beautiful up close. This was no old hag. However old she was, whether five-and-twenty or five-and-thirty, Jessamine could find no flaw. Her complexion, slightly darker than her own pink and cream, was nevertheless smooth as silk. Her features had classic perfection yet were strong enough, from the full lips to the dark, slashing eyebrows above amber-colored eyes, to give her an exotic look.

"Megan has been telling me so many wonderful things about you. You must come by and visit us."

Even though Jessamine knew she was French by birth, Mrs. Phillips's speech revealed no accent. It was soft and cultivated. "Thank you, ma'am," she said, clutching her reticule in her hands.

Mrs. Phillips laughed, a clear, tinkling sound like refreshing water. "Please, call me Céline if we are practically sisters."

Jessamine must have shown her puzzlement, for Céline said, "If you and Megan are as close as sisters and now she and I are sisters through Rees, then the two of us share a common sisterly bond."

Jessamine attempted to smile, but the sound of Rees's name on her lips opened the wound afresh. "Yes, I see. Of course."

Céline turned to Mr. St. Leger. "Hello, St. Leger, still about town, I see, escorting the prettiest ladies."

Mr. St. Leger smiled. "Where have you been all this time? I heard rumors that you'd absconded to France right before Boney's fall."

The Frenchwoman didn't betray by a flicker that the question ruffled her. "Yes, I hurried across the channel to be in France. I knew there would be a vacuum of power in the interim. Although Britain was backing Louis, there were many who were not pleased to have him on the throne. They feared a return of the *ancien régime* and the worst of the aristocracy's excesses."

"Do not dare say you are a Jacobin?"

She lifted her chin a notch. "I am a Republican." Before he could express any shock, she smiled. "But now I am a British subject, as I was before, married to an English diplomat and working very much at his side for peace for the continent."

As Jessamine and Megan listened to the conversation between her and Mr. St. Leger, Jessamine saw that her rival was not merely a woman of beauty but had charm, intelligence, and a firm grasp of the politics of Europe—all things that would attract Rees more than beauty. No wonder he had fallen for her.

But did she have heart?

Jessamine's glance fell to Céline's waistline. Despite the loose gown with its high empire waist, a slight bulge was visible. A bitter acid rose in Jessamine's throat.

As if sensing her regard, Céline's hand went to her stomach in a move Jessamine had seen expectant mothers do. Her gaze met Jessamine's as Mr. St. Leger continued speaking of the situation in France and Belgium, unconscious of the silent communication between the two women who loved Rees Phillips.

Mr. St. Leger brought Jessamine back home and left his tiger with the phaeton as he walked her to the door.

"I hope you had as pleasurable an excursion as I. Shall you be at the Waverley ball?"

"Yes, I believe so." She mentally pictured her gown and wondered how it would measure up against whatever Céline Phillips wore, doubtless a Parisian creation.

Her doubts were momentarily dispelled when Mr. St. Leger smiled down at her. "I shall look forward to it then."

She tossed her chin. "I thought you didn't dance."

He raised dark eyebrows. "There are always exceptions to one's rules." With those enigmatic words, he lifted the brim of his beaver with his fingertip before returning to his vehicle.

Megan promised to call on Jessamine before the ball, though Jessamine had little hopes of this. Megan would want to spend as much time with her brother before he had to leave for Brussels.

To Jessamine's surprise, Megan did come by early the next afternoon. Lady Bess prevented any confidences between the two, since she was eager to hear all about Céline's household—how many rooms, the number of servants, and who called upon them.

Megan did her best to fill her in although she had been there a very short time. Jessamine received the impression of a very comfortable town house, luxuriously furnished with a full staff to meet every need. "But they do try to live simply, mainly because Rees doesn't want Céline to overdo in her condition."

Lady Bess nodded. "She will probably retire soon from society until her confinement."

After Lady Bess's curiosity had been satisfied, Megan and Jessamine were able to excuse themselves for a walk. As they made their way down Harley Street to Cavendish Square, Megan sighed. "Just like old times."

Jessamine smiled but made no reply, because she felt all the opposite. They would never be able to recapture "old times."

They crossed the wide, cobbled street to the center of Cavendish Square and walked along the perimeters of the black wrought-iron fence enclosing the circular green within.

"I have the most wonderful news!"

Jessamine's heart stopped for a moment, wondering what could possibly have happened. The next second her fears were relieved when her friend said, "Céline has offered to hire a dance master to teach us the waltz before the Waverley ball!"

Jessamine looked away from her toward the green. "That is very kind of her." To have Rees's wife pay for her lessons?

Megan touched her arm. "I didn't even bring it up. She is the one who asked me what I thought of the waltz. After she discovered it hasn't even come to Alston, she suggested hiring a dance master. I told her what we'd discussed and she urged me to include you. We have very little time to learn, but she said with only a lesson or two we should be all right. Our first lesson is tomorrow morning. Please say you'll be there."

Jessamine turned to meet the look of entreaty in her friend's eye. She really had no choice. "Very well," she said slowly.

"Céline is really very sweet. She may look sophisticated, but she is the kindest person. She is at great pains to make me feel welcome and wants me to consider the house my home. Even though it is hers, you can see immediately that she doesn't lord it over Rees that she had a much greater fortune than he when they married. She respects him so much and defers to him in everything." Megan smiled. "He is certainly made to feel 'lord and master' of his castle."

"I never thought of Rees as an overbearing sort," Jessamine pointed out quickly, curious despite herself about his married life.

"I was being facetious, because really, the two of them defer to each other, so an outsider wouldn't be able to tell who owned what before their marriage. They have achieved a true union of minds and hearts."

"I'm glad." Jessamine was able to make her good wishes sound natural now that she'd had time to recover from meeting Céline. Besides, she wanted to show Megan she was completely over Rees, for it was the only way Megan would open up and tell her all she wished to know about the new couple. "It must be nice to be with your brother again."

"Yes." Megan's voice took on a sad tone. "But it is all too short a time, alas, for he leaves next week for Brussels."

Jessamine's heart staggered. "So soon?"

"Céline is so worried, though she doesn't let it show around me, of course, but I've overheard them talking a time or two. If it weren't for the baby, she wouldn't have allowed him to bring her back to London."

Jessamine ventured to ask, "Did you ever find out if any of those rumors were true—about the reasons she left London so suddenly?"

Megan shook her head. "Rees told me only that Céline is loyal to him and his work for Britain, that whatever she did before the war was not against the British crown but between the different French factions vying for power. He says that she has proven an immense help to him on the diplomatic front in Vienna and now in Brussels. He claims that if he has advanced at all in the Foreign Office, it is in large part due to her skills as hostess to all the top diplomatic emissaries in Vienna, otherwise he'd be nothing but an aide among several with finer pedigrees than a merchant's son."

"I'm sure he is being overly modest about his own skills."

Megan smiled. "I'm sure he is, but it doesn't take away from the fact that they are well suited to each other." Her friend eyed her. "Do you mind very much that I speak so candidly?"

Jessamine squared her shoulders. "No. I am over my sadness . . . now that I have met Céline. She seems a . . . very fine person." The words cost some effort but were worth the sacrifice when her friend's face cleared.

"I'm so glad. There is so much I'd like to tell you about my new life but was so afraid of causing you pain."

Jessamine mustered a smile though each word stabbed her. "I do hope you can tell me all you wish. I'm happy for Rees, truly I am."

When they returned to Lady Bess's, Céline's carriage stood at the curb waiting to take Megan back to her new home. "My, how we have arisen in the world," Jessamine teased her.

Megan grinned back. "I am enjoying it while it lasts." She gave her a quick hug. "I shall see you at our first dance lesson."

Jessamine nodded. "I hope it's not very difficult."

"Céline assures me it is not, though of course having a good partner makes all the difference, she said. I wonder if Mr. Marfleet dances the waltz, since he is a clergyman."

"I wonder if Mr. St. Leger waltzes," Jessamine countered.

Megan raised a brow. "Do you fancy him?"

"Haven't you noticed how handsome he is?"

"Yes, of course, who would not? But doesn't he seem a trifle aloof, as if he is above us all?"

Jessamine shrugged. "That is part of his allure."

With a puzzled look, Megan let the topic drop and stepped into the awaiting carriage.

The evening of the Waverley ball finally arrived.

Jessamine and Megan had only had time for a few dance lessons, but the dance master assured them they had mastered the basics of the waltz and with practice should acquit themselves well.

Jessamine had spent much of the afternoon at her toilette. As she stood back from the mirror, she knew she looked her best. She and Betsy had experimented with several hairstyles until satisfied. Her curls were swept up in a deceptively careless array atop her head, leaving one long strand to fall along her nape to the front, drawing attention to the gown's neckline.

The color of the gown enhanced the tone of her skin, giving it a warm glow. She put the pearl necklace on, with only a brief thought to Mr. Marfleet and his reaction to it if they should meet tonight.

Lastly, she donned the fine kidskin gloves which cost her most of her remaining income from the necklace and took up her lace shawl and reticule and went down to meet Lady Bess.

The ballroom was crowded when they arrived. She and Lady Bess each took a glass of ratafia and began to mill about the room.

"How warm it is in here already." Lady Bess fanned herself, her color high. "Ah, there is Adele MacGiver. I must say hello. Come along, dear."

Jessamine was not obliged to stand too long listening to the two older women's gossip.

Mr. Allan came up to her and greeted her with a smile. "I say, you look quite fetching tonight."

"Thank you," she answered demurely, looking down at her glass, still unused to the admiration she saw in men's eyes.

"Would you care to dance?"

"Very much." Setting aside the drink, she followed him onto the floor. It was a lively hornpipe, and she was laughing and breathless by the time the dance was over.

Cubby asked her next. As she stood in the line waiting for their part in the dance, she spotted Megan. Her breath caught. Rees and Céline stood with her. What a handsome couple they made, he tall and distinguished in his evening clothes, his demeanor smiling and more lighthearted than Jessamine had ever known, and Céline beautiful in a gauzy silver gown and jeweled tiara. The bulge under her high-waisted gown was more apparent now, although not unseemly large.

It gave Jessamine a pang to realize Rees would soon be a father, with a little baby to be doted on, uniting him and his bride as nothing else could. Céline held on to his arm in a possessive way, but Rees's hand covered hers in a way equally possessive—or protective—Jessamine was forced to concede.

So much for the ton's habit of husbands and wives not appearing affectionate with each other in public. From their gestures and glances at each other, Rees and Céline clearly disdained such conventions.

Jessamine stumbled in her figure.

"Are you all right?" Cubby's concerned tone registered.

"Fine, thank you, my mind merely wandered."

When the dance was over, she didn't know where to turn. She ought to walk over to Rees and Céline, to greet Megan at least, but her feet remained glued to the parquet floor.

As she was debating what to do, Mr. Marfleet stepped in front of her. "Oh—it's you. Good evening," she said, flustered.

"That glad to see me, I see."

She flushed. "No, it's not that. You startled me." Her hand went to her necklace in the automatic gesture she had when she was nervous. Seeing his gaze follow her movement, she snatched her hand away, remembering that in truth, the necklace belonged to him.

"You look very pretty."

Before she could react to the compliment, he said abruptly, "Would you care to dance?"

Too late she noticed the music beginning was a waltz. She had not thought her first waltz would be danced with him. As she debated, she saw Rees taking Céline onto the dance floor. She would be forced to stand watching them dance arm in arm if she refused Mr. Marfleet.

"Yes," she said abruptly, but quickly added, "but I'm not very good. I have only just learned the steps."

He smiled crookedly. "That's all right, neither am I. I shall endeavor not to tread on your slippers," he said as he held her hand and led her to the other couples taking their places. She noticed Rees and Céline stood farther down the line.

She flinched as Mr. Marfleet placed his arm around her shoulders, unused to having a gentleman touch her so.

She had been so intent on the similar movements of Rees and Céline, she had forgotten that she must do the same with her partner. Slowly she placed her arm along Mr. Marfleet's back since he was too tall for her to reach his shoulders. She put her feet in fifth position.

He took her hand in his other in front. In this close embrace, they promenaded behind the other couples in the opening march. For a moment she forgot all about Rees in the awareness of Mr. Marfleet's hand on her bare shoulder, his other tightly clasping hers.

As soon as the four steps of the march were completed, Mr. Marfleet began the pirouette of the slow waltz. She had no more time to think of Rees and Céline as she concentrated on following with her three pas de bourrées.

Mr. Marfleet next placed his right hand on her waist, and she tensed at the feel of his hand through the thin silk. Now she understood what all the uproar was against the dance. And yet, as the music guided their movements, she felt graceful performing these steps so perfectly synchronized with her partner's, although they were not simultaneous but alternating, each performing the pirouette and pas de bourrées while the other performed the previous steps. Then they joined right hands, lifting their free arms in a graceful curve.

The tempo quickened, their steps following suit. At times they were encircled in an intimate embrace, at others they were apart performing their little jetés. Her breath hitched as Mr. Marfleet's body brushed hers.

He was not a faultless dancer and made mistakes at times, as did she, but they were able to rectify and guide each other in the nick of time. By the time the music was over, she was sorry it had ended.

He stepped away from her and bowed. "Thank you, Miss Barry. You are a—"

"If you say flawless dancer, you are an abject liar."

He chuckled. "Well, you danced it credibly."

She made a mock curtsy, still feeling breathless from his proximity during many of the steps. "As did you."

"May I get you some refreshment?"

"I had a glass. I left it on that windowsill. Let me see if it is still there or has been removed by a footman."

They made their way to where she indicated. Mr. Marfleet handed her the half-empty glass.

"Thank you. Do you not wish to drink anything?"

He remained watching her. "I am fine for the moment."

She took a sip.

"How have you been?"

"Very well, thank you, and you?" she replied evenly, annoyed that he must be thinking of her indisposition. At least she was not drinking champagne, so he could not comment on *that*.

"I haven't seen you much lately."

Her gaze wandered over the crowd. "Despite your mother's kind invitation, I am still not invited to all the best parties of the ton. I am sure I must be grateful to her for this one. You must extend her my thanks."

"I'm sure her favor has done little. It's your company that has done the rest."

She eyed him over her glass. "La, Mr. Marfleet, is that a compliment?"

His cheeks flushed. "It is only the truth."

Once again she lifted an edge of her skirt in a mock curtsy. "Thank you, sir. I shall not let it go to my head."

At that moment she sensed someone approaching her. She turned, and her breath caught. Rees stood in front of her, looking so handsome she felt her loss afresh.

"Good evening, Jessamine. You look beautiful." His gray eyes crinkled up at the corners and affection shone from their depths. Before she could regain her composure, he turned to Mr. Marfleet. "I hope I am not interrupting."

"Not at all," she whispered. Clearing her throat, she made the introductions.

Mr. Marfleet's brows drew together. "Phillips? Are you Miss Phillips's brother?"

Rees smiled. "The very one."

"I'm pleased to make your acquaintance, sir. She has spoken highly of you."

"She is the best sister one could hope for."

After a slight pause, Rees said, "If you would permit me, I would like to take Miss Barry away from you for a moment." He looked at her. "Would you honor me with this dance?"

She stared at him, feeling she could drown in his silvery gaze. With a supreme effort of will, she nodded once, feeling as if she were in a dream where her mind's commands would not reach her limbs.

He took her hand and led her onto the dance floor. She didn't even remember to excuse herself from Mr. Marfleet.

The dance was a cotillion. She walked through the steps like an automaton, thankful it was a dance she was familiar with.

"I wanted to compliment you on your season," Rees said when they came together. "You seem to be taking to London as if you'd been born to it," he added with a smile.

She smiled faintly. "I would not go so far."

"Céline says you were riding in the park at the fashionable hour with a very handsome gentleman, looking for all the world like a young lady accustomed to admiration and flattery."

What else had Céline said about her? "Your wife exaggerates."

"I think you are being too modest, since Megan backs her claims."

They moved apart. When the dance brought them back together, he continued. "I wanted to tell you how glad I was. When I said good-bye to you, I never meant to hurt you—yet I knew I was being the worst blackguard—"

It was pity that drove his compliments. She feigned a careless laugh. "Please, Rees, you are the one to exaggerate now. We never had an understanding, and I didn't know my own heart, if truth be known."

His gray eyes scanned hers a moment as if to gauge the sincerity of her words. She didn't let her gaze waver. Finally, he smiled. "I am glad to hear that. You were—and still are—very young. I feared I had tied you down too long for naught. But your success in London reassures me that you will make a good match." He nodded in the direction they had come from. "The young man you were with. He seems a worthy sort."

She glanced toward Mr. Marfleet and found him observing them. "Yes, he is," she said. "He is Sir Geoffrey Marfleet's younger son," she couldn't help adding.

Rees lifted a black eyebrow then chuckled. "Much better than a penniless merchant's son. You relieve me of all guilt I had been carrying around concerning my treatment of you."

So, he merely wanted to alleviate his guilt. She kept her smile in place. He would never know how much he'd hurt—and continued to hurt—her.

When they came together again in the dance, he said softly, "I am glad you were able to meet Céline. I hope you feel kindly enough toward us to visit. I know Megan misses you, and I'm being selfish for wanting her to stay with us." A shadow crossed his features. "I don't want Céline to be alone when I leave, which is why I've asked Megan to remain. I know it is not fair to you since you came together to enjoy the season. Would you not consider staying with them at the town house?"

They drew away, and she had a chance to recover her breath. The hurt she'd experienced at his first remark had transformed into a cold fury, but she vowed not to let it show. She would not be humiliated by him again. All he cared about was Céline. She would be a fool to harbor any notions to the contrary.

When they came together, she managed to look sorrowful. "I'm sorry, Rees, but I cannot leave Lady Bess. She was so kind to invite me to spend the season in London with her. It would be cruel of me to desert her. She was already complaining of how empty the place felt when Megan left."

"I hope she is not offended with Megan."

"Not at all," she hurried to assure him. "She understood perfectly and is happy that you are able to spend a little time with your only sister. But she did grow fond of her while she was there."

"I'm sorry you cannot stay with us, but I fully understand your obligation to your godmother."

When they next came together, she asked him about the situation in Belgium.

His eyes took on a worried cast. "Not good. Wellington doesn't trust Napoleon an inch."

"I can scarcely believe he would have a hunger for fighting after so many years of campaigning."

Rees's mouth tightened. "Once a military commander, always a commander, it seems."

"I—if . . . if it comes to battle, you aren't expected to accompany the duke, are you?"

"No, but I hate to think of the chaos in Brussels if people panic. There are so many British there right now—I'm surprised anyone is left here to enjoy the season. They think it's one grand party."

Her anger forgotten for the moment, she wished she could relieve his worry. Then she remembered herself. He had Céline for that. When the dance was over, he escorted her back to Mr. Marfleet and bowed over her hand. Straightening, he smiled at her. "Thank you for the honor. Now, I will leave you in the very capable hands of this young gentleman and hope you continue dancing. I know you will not lack partners."

A ridiculous urge to cry suddenly beset her. Afraid her lips would tremble if she attempted to speak, she remained silent. But Rees seemed unaware. He turned to Mr. Marfleet and exchanged a few words and then excused himself.

She watched him make his way across the ballroom, straight to Céline.

"How long have you known Miss Phillips's brother?"

She jumped at Mr. Marfleet's quiet question. "What? Oh, for years, ever since he and his family moved to our village."

"You must have been very young."

She nodded. "But five. Megan and I became fast friends."

"You care for them very much."

She wasn't sure it was a statement or a question. "Yes, our two families are very close. They have a cottage next to the parsonage. His mother has been a widow all these years, and naturally my father—as vicar—and my mother look after her when . . . when Rees has been away."

He continued looking at her with a steady regard until she felt uncomfortable. Would he discern her feelings? To her ears, her words sounded natural. But she didn't trust his keen, slate-blue gaze.

To her relief, Mr. St. Leger stepped up to them. "You are finally free. I was hoping I could lead you out in a dance."

Her eyes widened. "I thought you didn't dance."

He smiled lazily. "After seeing you waltz, I have decided an exception to my rule is warranted."

She accepted at once to escape Mr. Marfleet's scrutiny and to show Rees that his wishes were already fulfilled—she did not lack dance partners of the first water.

"You are looking ravishing as usual," Mr. St. Leger said as he led her out.

"Thank you."

"I see my competition grows stiffer with each ball."

She fluttered her eyelashes, basking in the look of admiration in his dark-blue eyes. He was tall and broad-shouldered like Rees, and for a moment she could pretend it was he with whom she was dancing. At the very least, they should be quite visible to Rees and Céline.

When the dance ended, he asked her to accompany him in to supper. She agreed but excused herself for a moment to freshen up. She looked around for Megan but saw her with a young gentleman. Jessamine had noticed during the evening that Rees and Céline had been busy introducing her to their many acquaintances.

Jessamine fixed her hair and inspected her gown before leaving the retiring room. As she crossed the carpeted hall silently in her kid slippers, she passed other rooms left open for the guests' disposal.

Hearing a woman's soft voice through an open doorway, she paused. "What a sweet young thing she is. I think I could be jealous." Jessamine hardly dared breathe, recognizing Céline's voice.

Rees's low tone, laced with amusement, followed. "No need, my dear. There was never any passion in me for her. Unlike you, who drove me insane the first time I saw you."

11

Rees's low chuckle was swallowed up in silence.

Jessamine brought her hands up to her flaming cheeks, too shocked and humiliated to move. *Dear God*, she prayed, *help me to get out of here unseen.*

Her feet wouldn't move. She stared down at them as if she were looking from a great height.

The silence in the next room lengthened, and suddenly she knew. He was kissing her! Her embarrassment grew. What if they should find her here?

She must go! She commanded her feet to move. Finally, as if coming unstuck, she took a step forward. She made it past the doorway, not pausing to look into it, hoping they were not looking her way. Of course they weren't, locked in an embrace!

She flew the remaining length of the corridor and down the stairs, slowing only as she rounded the curve.

She paused there to catch her breath. Willing her pulse to slow, she took hold of the banister and descended the remaining steps at a stately pace.

Mr. St. Leger was waiting for her just inside the ballroom. He raised his quizzing glass. "You look pale, my dear."

"I . . . I need some air . . . that is all." Her hand at her throat, she looked around for somewhere to flee.

"Come, I know just the place." Snagging a glass from a passing waiter, he held out his arm to her.

She let him lead her, not caring where they went as long as she needn't face anyone. He took her down the stairs to the ground floor. They entered a drawing room at the back of the mansion and exited the French doors. Finally, blessed darkness and cool night air met her cheeks. She drew in gulps of it.

Mr. St. Leger guided her across the stone terrace and down some shallow steps. She stumbled once and his hold tightened. "Careful there," he said.

They stopped in an area shadowed by high-clipped yews from the lights of the ballroom and the torches set on the terrace.

He put the glass in her hand, and she took it in both of hers with a murmured thank-you before taking a large swallow. She sputtered, realizing it was champagne.

"Easy does it."

Flushing in consternation, she drank the rest more slowly.

After a moment, he said, "Feeling better?"

"Yes, much, thank you." She lowered the empty glass from her lips, not caring how sick it made her as long as it helped her obliterate the words she'd overheard. He took it from her and set it on the ground. She had a sudden urge to giggle, thinking about the servants having to search high and low tomorrow for all the missing crystal.

"I am relieved you are beginning to find something humorous again."

She glanced up at him through her eyelashes. "You may thank the champagne. It has made me realize I mustn't take things too seriously, least of all myself." Poor, pathetic little creature she must appear to the likes of a former countess. The thought brought another laugh. The champagne made her feel like two people, one acting and one observing. Was this what was meant by light-headed? She laughed again, hard-pressed to stop.

Mr. St. Leger brushed back a wayward curl from her cheek.

Her breath caught at his featherlight touch. His dark head and shoulders, his face in shadow, could have been Rees's. Was this what it would have been like if he'd never met Céline?

"You have skin as soft as a kitten's fur," he purred like the kitten he was describing, the back of his fingertips stroking her skin in a rhythmic motion. She found herself spellbound, unable to move even if she had wished to.

But she didn't wish to. Spurned and forgotten by the man who'd held her heart for so many years, and now worse—mocked by the woman who had stolen his heart—Jessamine was willing for anything to blot out those two people. Here stood a man who found her beautiful and desirable.

Rees's words echoed in her mind. *"There was never any passion in me for her. Unlike you, who drove me insane the first time I saw you."*

Her breast rose and fell in hypnotic cadence with St. Leger's touch.

"Do you like that?"

"Mm," was all she could manage.

His fingers moved downward to her jaw, cupping it and drawing her closer.

She stood transfixed, never having experienced a man's touch like this. Rees had only ever briefly taken her hand. Her body wanted to sway toward St. Leger's warm touch. She didn't know whether it was the effects of the champagne or her own desire to be held.

A distant alarm sounded in the recesses of her mind, but it was too far away to heed.

With an impatient sigh, Lancelot put his spectacles back on, needing to see more clearly since he'd been unable to spot Miss

Barry by the color of her dress alone—a dress cut scandalously low and of a deep amber usually reserved for married ladies.

His concern had deepened ever since Mr. Phillips approached them. Lancelot had observed the conversation between him and Miss Barry. He'd sensed an undercurrent between the two from the moment Miss Barry opened her mouth. The longer he stood there, the greater his conviction grew. When Mr. Phillips asked her to dance, it struck Lancelot then by the look in Miss Barry's eyes. She was in love with him.

He wondered if the feeling was returned but could detect nothing more than brotherly affection in Mr. Phillips's look and tone.

With his spectacles on, Lancelot watched them dance, and his fears were confirmed. Though there was nothing unusual in Mr. Phillips's conduct, Miss Barry stared up at him as if he were the only man in the room. Perhaps Lancelot was imagining it or perhaps he would have noticed nothing if he hadn't been observing her so closely, but now it was as if blinders had been taken from his eyes and he saw the abject longing in her gaze.

It brought a strange sensation to his chest, as of losing something he'd never had. Lancelot frowned, unable to tear his gaze away. Mr. Phillips was quite a bit older than Miss Barry, he judged, over thirty, though a handsome and distinguished-looking gentleman, to her twenty or one-and-twenty. She was young enough to look up to him in admiration, Lancelot thought in growing misery.

As they danced up and down the line of dancers, promenading or holding hands, the constriction in his chest grew.

He snatched off his spectacles, tucking them back into his case, just as the dance drew to a close, even as he chided himself for his vanity.

His questions to her after the dance drew little from her. It was clear she was keeping her feelings hidden, but she hadn't been able to mask her longing as she'd watched Mr. Phillips return to his wife.

Before Lancelot could do anything to console her, Mr. St. Leger had come to snatch her away.

Lancelot left the ballroom, disgusted with himself for wanting something—someone—clearly not meant for him.

But now as the supper hour drew near, he found himself once more searching for Miss Barry.

His concern mounted when he didn't see her anywhere. Nor did he see Mr. St. Leger. Had she been indisposed once more?

He put his spectacles back on, not caring who saw him. Harold had left ages ago, probably to some gaming den, having told Lancelot he was on his own.

"I've taken you about like a child on leading strings. It's past time you stood on your own two feet." He laughed derisively at his pun. "Make love to any one of those frippery young misses who are hanging out for a husband. The second son of a baronet is nothing to sniff at. You'll make Mama and Papa happy." Harold's lips twisted in a smirk. "We are all depending on you to carry on the family line. Perhaps Rosamunde and I can adopt your firstborn if it's a boy."

The thought left Lancelot cold. Although the remark was uttered in jest, now that it had been voiced aloud, he had no doubt between his brother and his wife and his parents, they would not hesitate to set such a plan in motion. It was done all the time—a wealthier relative taking a poorer one's offspring to bring up and educate, especially when the former was childless as Harold and Rosamunde were.

The thought flitted through his mind: what would Miss Barry think if she knew she had to give up her firstborn?

He pushed the nonsensical thought from his mind and continued to look for her.

By the time he had searched every floor, he wondered whether Miss Barry could have gone outside. With Mr. St. Leger? The thought brought him to a stop, worry bringing a constriction to his chest. St. Leger had an unsavory reputation.

Determination edged with desperation filled him as he headed for the ground floor.

The back of the house led to the service stairs. But an opened door revealed a drawing room facing the rear. He was not the only person seeking the outdoors. He followed a couple who headed to the terrace through a pair of French doors.

Once he stood outside, Lancelot paused a moment, adjusting his eyes to the darkness. With the light from the torches as well as that spilling from all the windows above, he made out several people milling about the formal gardens. He walked down the steps, his eyes scanning the area.

He discerned a couple half hidden behind a yew hedge. The gown was the amber shade of Miss Barry's, and the man was certainly tall enough to be St. Leger.

He hurried across the garden, his alarm and anger growing as he saw how closely the man stood by her. By the time Lancelot drew near, the man had bent his head as if he were on the verge of kissing her.

Lancelot took a step forward and cleared his throat. "Miss Barry?"

She jumped away as if he'd shouted at her. St. Leger straightened more slowly and finally turned an eye toward Lancelot. "Marfleet? What the deuce are you doing, startling the lady like this?"

"I should say rather what are you doing bringing the young lady to such a secluded spot?" Lancelot answered shortly.

St. Leger evinced no contrition. "The lady felt the need of some air. I was merely obliging her."

Lancelot ground his teeth at the faint mockery in his tone. He forced his attention to Miss Barry. "Are you all right?"

"Yes, I am fine now."

"May I escort you back inside?"

She looked from one to the other, as if unsure what to say.

Lancelot took another step forward, offering his arm. "May I? Supper is being served."

St. Leger stepped back with a flourish. "By all means, Sir Lancelot, do escort the lady to her supper."

Ignoring the nickname he'd endured since his public school days, when he'd stuck up for the younger and weaker, Lancelot tucked Miss Barry's hand into the crook of his elbow and led her from the secluded spot. St. Leger's low laughter followed them.

He said nothing until they were both in the drawing room. Thankful that no one was in the room, he disengaged himself from her. "It was not prudent to go with Mr. St. Leger outside."

She stepped away from him, her green eyes snapping. "It is not your concern, Mr. Marfleet. Were you following me again?"

"I was worried when I didn't see you or St. Leger anywhere." He cleared his throat, uncomfortable with maligning someone's character. "He has a certain reputation."

"I'll thank you to stay out of my business. Do you think you have an interest in my affairs because you—you rescued my belongings?" She clutched at her necklace. Suddenly she reached behind her and began to unclasp it. "If that is the case, you can have it back until I can redeem it myself!"

"I don't want it back!" Seeing she continued to struggle with the clasp, he was forced to take her forearms and bring them down to her sides.

She glared up at him, her breathing hard, her green eyes shooting sparks at him.

He forgot all those things in the feel of her, her proximity reminding him of their waltz. This was a hundred times worse, his chest almost touching hers, his hands grasping her wrists.

With effort he let her go and stepped away, his own breathing uneven. "Keep your necklace. It has nothing to do with my concern." His glance descended from her face. "If you persist in dressing like a Cyprian and going off with men like St. Leger, you'll need more than me watching over you."

She sucked in her breath. The next second her hand came up,

and he received a resounding slap across the cheek. He stepped back from the shock, his hand going to his stinging cheek.

They stared at one another. She seemed as shocked as he by her action.

"If you will excuse me," she said in shaky tones and turned on her heel, leaving him nursing his cheek.

As frustrated and angry with himself as with her, he wished he could smash something. Before he could do anything, the door from the terrace opened and St. Leger entered.

Seeing Lancelot alone, he lifted a black eyebrow. "The lady didn't appreciate your role of knight errant, I presume?"

"You were taking advantage of a well-brought-up young lady."

St. Leger leaned against the glass panes of the door and examined his fingernails. "The lady is old enough to know what she wants."

"That is unworthy of you."

A slow smile curved his lips. "I realize you are suffering a bout of jealousy and perhaps covetousness, which you must control, *Reverend* Marfleet, but I insist, the lady was in no danger. I could hardly ravish her in so public a place."

"And if the next place is not so public?"

St. Leger shrugged a shoulder. "I cannot answer for hypotheticals." With a small salute, he straightened and walked toward the door opposite. "If you will excuse me, I must go in to supper. I find my appetite is unsatisfied . . ."

Jessamine reentered the ballroom, not knowing what she should do. She felt humiliated twice over. The conversation between Céline and Rees was bad enough but to be found by Mr. Marfleet and then pulled away as if she were a child!

Her face burned, wondering if Mr. St. Leger would have kissed her if they hadn't been interrupted. What would she have done? She didn't know.

Putting her quizzing glass up to her eye, she scanned the ballroom, searching to see if Rees or Céline were anywhere, and felt relieved when she didn't see them. In truth, most people had left the ballroom to go in to supper.

"Are you ready to face the hordes at the supper table?"

She jumped at the sound at her shoulder then turned in relief, recognizing Mr. St. Leger's voice. "Perhaps not, but I wouldn't mind some refreshment."

He eyed her with amusement. "Refreshment it will be."

He led her to the supper room, and she resisted the urge to look back to see if Mr. Marfleet had followed her. She would not let him dictate her behavior. And she would show Rees that she was well over her childhood dreams.

By the time she left the ball that evening, she had agreed to another ride with Mr. St. Leger the following day.

Lancelot spent the morning closeted in his room, staring at his botanical notes. He had a stack of watercolors Delawney had completed, and he needed to compile the descriptions that went with each one.

After last night, he had decided to forget about females for a while, particularly one infuriating, green-eyed vicar's daughter who was determined to harm herself. If she didn't know better at twenty, then he washed his hands of her.

This didn't mean he hadn't prayed for her last night and again this morning. Only God could show her the folly of her ways and set her on the right path before it was too late.

He had seen too many of St. Leger's types through his years at school to have any illusions about his intentions. He didn't know him too well, but he had seen him often enough when he'd sought Harold out at his clubs and gaming dens.

Another wastrel, spending his parents' money, he concluded. What mystified him was the attention he was giving Miss Barry.

Those types usually confined their conquests to actresses and ballet dancers or lowborn shopgirls who had no one to look out for them.

Unless . . . St. Leger thought Miss Barry had no one to defend her, being far from home with only an older, somewhat scatter-brained godmother to protect her.

St. Leger's words came back to him. His blood ran cold at the blatant mockery in them.

But if she repudiated Lancelot's help, there was little he could do. Maybe he could talk to Delawney and ask her help. She'd probably balk and want to know why. He was reluctant to expose his interest in Miss Barry, since he didn't understand his feelings himself.

Praying for guidance, he sat staring out his window, his botanical notes forgotten.

Megan came to visit Jessamine the next morning. Jessamine had slept late, since she hadn't gotten to bed until almost dawn. She was still in her room, just finishing her toilette, when Megan knocked on her door.

"Good morning, I hope I'm not too early," she said, peering around the door.

Jessamine twisted in her seat. "Nonsense. But I'm surprised to see you. I would have imagined you still abed like any good member of the fashionable world."

"I guess my good bourgeois habits have not left me," she answered with a sunny smile, coming to sit on Jessamine's bed.

"Did you have a good evening?" Jessamine asked, continuing to arrange her hair.

"Very nice, thank you. I must admit, having Céline and Rees for sister and brother opens many doors. Rees has many acquaintances at the Foreign Office, and since he is a junior secretary to Wellington, it is like waving a magic wand; everyone comes flocking at the name of the Iron Duke. And Céline—well, you'd never known she'd been gone from London. She is as sought after as ever." Megan's eyes shone. "That is one reason I've come to visit you so early."

Jessamine looked at her friend's reflection in the mirror, her hands suspended on her coiffure. "What has happened?"

"Céline insists on giving me a ball to signal my coming out. She says I need an official event, since I cannot be presented at court." She made a face. "My poor papa being in trade. That means vouchers to Almack's are also beyond my reach. Without those, I may as well be invisible to society."

Before Jessamine could express her sorrow, Megan laughed. "Céline says this silliness doesn't exist in Paris. Anyone with style is admitted to the best hôtels. But that is neither here nor there. Céline has convinced Rees that a ball in my honor is the only remedy."

Megan sat back with satisfaction. "She is sure if Lady Jersey or one of the other patronesses of Almack's has a chance to see me—or *us*, I should say—she will want to issue us vouchers."

Jessamine turned around to face her friend, unsure how she felt about the news. "My goodness, I'm happy for you."

Megan's smile only broadened. "Didn't you hear me? After Céline managed to convince Rees that she was perfectly fit to plan a ball, I ventured to suggest that perhaps the two of us could be presented together."

Jessamine's mouth fell open. "You didn't!" Dismay filled her at the thought of being helped by Rees's wife yet again.

Megan nodded vigorously. "You heard me. How would you like a massive ball in your honor with all the best of society in attendance?"

"Haven't we attended a couple already?" she said, stalling for time.

"Yes, but as nobodies. Here, we shall be the center of attention." She beamed at her.

Jessamine began shaking her head. "I . . . I couldn't possibly." To be beholden to Céline! The humiliation would be too great. "Rees is right; it's too much for his wife to take on two young ladies. Be happy that she is doing this for you. You can invite me, of course," she added with a smile to offset any suspicion that it was because the dance would be hosted by Rees's wife.

"Oh no you don't." Megan came to stand over her. "You are going to appear with me and that is final!" A smile took away the menace from her words.

"I am going to run out of ball gowns to so many exalted events," Jessamine said, turning back to her mirror.

"That's all right. Céline says she has a niece through her late husband, the earl. She was presented two seasons ago and has a heap of ball gowns I am to look through. She has put them at our disposal since she has no need of them now."

"I couldn't possibly. I don't know her, and more importantly, she doesn't know me."

"Of course you may. Céline says we are of similar height and build to Kimberley—Lady Huntingfield now. Céline is visiting her this morning to explain the situation."

Jessamine looked at her in dismay. "That's awful. To have someone lend us her gowns out of pity. What if someone recognizes them on us?"

"We can alter them. Besides, I doubt if anyone would remember them from two seasons ago." When she saw Jessamine's lips firm and her head begin to shake, she took her hands in hers. "Please, say yes. Céline is bringing her best modiste to see the gowns after we've tried them on. She will suggest all kinds of ways to change them. We can do most of the work ourselves. Céline says we are doing her a favor by keeping her mind on this. She's very worried about Rees returning to Brussels. The latest word is Napoleon has left Paris."

Jessamine scanned her friend's face, her objections appearing petty. "Must Rees return?"

Meg nodded sadly. "Yes, he is needed. He leaves tomorrow. I promised him I'd do everything I could to keep Céline occupied—

without tiring her out, of course. And he truly doesn't mind having Céline plan a ball for me. He has left me money for a new ball gown, as a matter of fact. He feels he's neglected me since he left for France. Of course I told him that was absurd, but he truly wished to give me this."

Jessamine squeezed her friend's hands. "Of course he did. Will this dressmaker design it?"

She nodded.

"How exciting. Have you met anyone you fancy at any of the events we've attended thus far?" She'd been too caught up in her own affairs to notice if anyone had begun to pursue her friend.

"Not yet." She laughed. "I may spend my entire season not meeting anyone and go back home and marry one of the gentlemen I've danced with at the local assemblies. Wouldn't that be ironic?" She tilted her head, pursing her lips. "Although Mr. Seymour is very nice and Mr. Crofton has a pleasing manner," she said, mentioning some of her dance partners. She focused back on Jessamine. "What about you? Mr. St. Leger continues attentive?"

Jessamine looked away. "He is . . . charming." And made her feel beautiful and worthy of notice, she added to herself. "He is coming to take me for another ride in his phaeton this afternoon."

"Hmm."

Jessamine was thankful her friend didn't bring up Mr. Marfleet's name again. Perhaps she finally understood that Jessamine was completely indifferent to him.

A few afternoons later she accompanied Megan and Céline—reluctantly—to Lady Huntingfield's house. She was Céline's great-niece from Céline's first marriage to the late Earl of Wexham. The earl's nephew had inherited the title upon his death, and this was his daughter.

Lady Huntingfield's residence was a large town house on Curzon Street. After they were admitted by a dignified butler, they were shown into a small parlor.

The room was richly appointed with plush French carpets, gilded furniture, and sumptuous oil paintings against striped wallpaper. Céline didn't notice her surroundings at all. She and Megan were chatting like old friends—or older and younger sister now.

They had tried to include Jessamine in their lively conversation during the carriage ride, but when Jessamine limited her responses to friendly but brief ones, they had finally left her alone.

In a few moments, a maid appeared and led them up a carpeted staircase to an even more lavish lady's dressing room, where a young blonde woman came to greet them, hugging and kissing Céline. "Hello, Aunt Ceci, how lovely to see you. You look beautiful—glowing, in fact."

The two women laughed and eyed each other with obvious affection. Jessamine then noticed that Lady Huntingfield was also expecting. It gave her a pang to see two mothers-to-be. Lady Huntingfield looked to be Jessamine's age, perhaps even younger, and she'd already been married a year.

Céline explained that she had helped her niece with her coming-out a couple of years ago. She was now happy to see the fruits of her labor in the brilliant match Lady Huntingfield had made.

Two years ago. That would have been when Rees had met Céline in London.

The two ladies discussed briefly their conditions, but even from the little they said, Jessamine could tell that their coming motherhood was foremost in their minds.

That was where she should be, Jessamine thought to herself. Married and awaiting a child, not trying on an array of past season ball gowns and pretending she was a lady of the ton on the market for a titled gentleman.

But she was not allowed to wallow in her morose thoughts. A couple of maids soon brought out the ball gowns. Another maid served tea and cakes, and the other women were so enthusiastic that Jessamine could not demonstrate any ill humor when they were doing her this favor.

So, she dutifully tried on a half dozen or more ball gowns in a variety of soft colors and silks and fine muslins. They all fit very well with little need for alterations. The maids were armed with pins and took in what needed to be taken in.

"They are so beautiful," Megan said with awe, running a hand down an ice-blue half-dress of sheerest taffeta over a cream satin underskirt.

"I'm so glad you are able to use them," Lady Huntingfield said from a velvet settee, where she sat sipping her tea and admiring both Megan and Jessamine as they came out from behind the screen where a maid had helped them into the gowns. "I can't wear any of them anymore, and I don't foresee too many London balls for me in the near future. We are planning to go to our country seat as the time draws near for my confinement, and then we shall stay there for the winter, perhaps longer." She smiled at Céline. "We shall be retiring to the country as if we were already in our middle years."

"Having a child doesn't mean you must retire from society," Céline said, "although I certainly understand your wish to lead a quieter life."

"I have never enjoyed society much, you know that." She addressed Jessamine and Megan. "Thanks to Aunt Ceci, I am able to navigate the waters of society. I was such a shy young thing, and my mother was determined to arrange a marriage for me. It was Aunt Ceci who hosted my coming-out ball and made sure to introduce me to several eligible gentlemen. That's how I met Lord Huntingfield and am happily married today."

Jessamine looked at each of the women. Lady Huntingfield seemed to dote on Céline, the way Megan was coming to. What was it about this Frenchwoman that attracted everyone? Jessamine gritted her teeth, her smile wearing thin, and turned to the mirror to see herself in a pale-yellow silk.

"It's beautiful on you," Megan said at her side.

"Yes, it looks adorable," Céline agreed from her place in a comfortable armchair.

Adorable. Like a puppy.

Jessamine studied her reflection. She looked almost beautiful. She was tempted to pull her spectacles out of her reticule, but she was able to see well enough to appreciate the color and cut of the gown on her.

As the afternoon wore on, it became harder for her to maintain her anger against Céline, who seemed genuinely pleased to help her and Megan enter society. Jessamine could not detect by either look or word any mockery in Rees's wife. The brief interchange she'd overheard between her and Rees still rankled, but she could not say that Céline seemed to look at her any differently than she did Megan. Certainly not with any jealousy. Jessamine was beneath her consideration in that, she realized, remembering Rees's words.

Nor was Céline lording it over Jessamine that she'd won Rees's heart.

They dropped Jessamine home late that afternoon, extracting promises from her that she would accompany them on the morrow to shop for ribbons and other decorations to begin the task of altering and modifying the gowns.

It was hard to hate someone who seemed to harbor no ill feelings toward her and was doing everything to help her.

12

During the fortnight before the grand ball at Céline's house, Jessamine found herself more and more in the Frenchwoman's company. After Rees's return to Brussels, Céline chaperoned Megan at all her social engagements, of which there were many, thanks to Céline's many acquaintances. They insisted on collecting Jessamine in their carriage, which was more convenient than having Lady Bess obliged to hire a carriage. Lady Bess seemed content to leave the social whirl and return to her quiet card parties with her own circle of friends, although she always wanted to hear about Jessamine's evening the following day.

It would have seemed more practical to move to Céline's town house altogether. They invited her, but Jessamine was firm in her refusal, and was brought back to Lady Bess's each evening. Although many times this was in the wee hours of the morning and she knew she was being inconsiderate to Lady Bess's household, she couldn't bring herself to be more beholden to Céline than she already was.

She had not seen Mr. Marfleet at all and wondered at his absence at the assemblies, soirees, and theatrical events she attended. Did he travel in different social circles? Or was he avoiding her as much as she dreaded seeing him again?

Since that night he'd come upon her and Mr. St. Leger, she'd spent hours humiliated and incensed all over again. He deserved to be slapped, she told herself, and then admitted to herself he'd acted out of concern for her safety and reputation.

His words still rankled, though. Behaving like a Cyprian . . . going off with men like St. Leger . . .

She was horrified she'd slapped his face. She'd never behaved so toward Rees, but then, he'd never done anything to make her lose her control.

The next moment, shame filled her again. Neither had she ever done anything to warrant intervention like Mr. Marfleet's. Her thoughts went in circles. She would not return to being a dutiful vicar's daughter but neither did she want to behave unseemly. There seemed to be no middle ground. She wanted to be like Céline and Lady Dawson, women who commanded the attention and admiration of men but who also knew how to keep them in check.

She lacked no dance partners now. When she mentioned Mr. Marfleet to Mr. Allan one evening, he only said, "Oh, Lancelot is busy at work on his book. You know he's an amateur botanist, don't you?"

"Yes, he told me."

"He is quite an academic sort. I was surprised to see him at any of these society events. He usually considers them too frivolous." He grinned. "I had heard rumors that his mother and father are pressuring him to marry. I suppose he was looking over the latest crop of young ladies on the 'marriage mart.'" He colored, as if realizing whom he was addressing. "Oh, I beg your pardon, I didn't mean you, of course."

She forced herself to laugh. "Of course you didn't."

"He must not have seen anyone to catch his interest and has gone back to his musty books and greenhouses."

"I suppose so." She said nothing more but mulled over the information she had received. So, he had been merely looking for a wife. Had she caught his interest? The fact that she hadn't seen him in over a week meant she had been found wanting. She colored, remembering again how he had found her the last time in the garden, on the verge of kissing Mr. St. Leger.

She cringed anew. She didn't know why she had behaved so except that she'd been so upset at overhearing Rees and Céline. She couldn't abide their pity and their amusement at her expense.

As far as Mr. Marfleet, good riddance! She didn't need someone who was going to be her conscience tagging after her. If she chose to misbehave, that was her own affair.

In the meantime, Mr. St. Leger continued to be attentive and had suggested no more promenades in the garden, proving he was a serious suitor. Jessamine looked forward to their rides in the park and his witty sallies at dances.

She must put Mr. Marfleet out of her thoughts and continue cultivating the admiration of Mr. St. Leger and those gentlemen of his circle, without falling in love with any of them.

Lancelot sat up and lifted his spectacles, rubbing the bridge of his nose. His neck hurt from being hunched over his notes for so long.

But he was satisfied that he'd made a measurable amount of progress in the last week. He was ready to show a partial of his manuscript to the publisher Sir Banks had recommended. Delawney had completed dozens of watercolors, and the best ones now sat in a stack on his desk. He would collect everything in a portfolio and go to the Strand tomorrow to the publishing house.

He also needed to finalize his notes for the address he was going to give at the Royal Institute. He would take some of his sister's paintings as well as a few plants.

He stood now and stretched, walking to the window to look at the fading day. He looked over the backyard, which ended in a wall and the mews beyond. The sky faded to a pale gray blue, the sun setting on the other side of the house.

Although he'd tackled his work with a will and single-mindedness he'd only had to exercise on himself a few times in his life, he'd not managed to exorcise Miss Barry from his thoughts.

He'd deliberately avoided any place where he might run into her. To his relief, racing season had started and Harold had left for Newmarket, so he would not be carrying tales if Lancelot absented himself from the season's activities. His mother was visiting friends, so only he and Delawney remained in town with their father.

His father was busy in the House of Commons, what with the alarm over Napoleon's threat, so he didn't have time to interest himself in Lancelot's affairs.

But he knew it was only a matter of time before they would begin to pressure him once more about proposing to a young lady.

Dear Lord, You know I would like to marry as much as they would like me to. But I want it to be the woman You have chosen for me, and thus far, I don't feel You have presented her to me. I thought . . . but no, I realize now, she was not the one. Help me to put her from my thoughts. In Your name, Lord Jesus, I ask this.

His hand went absently to the cheek where Miss Barry had slapped him. He could still feel the impact. He'd never provoked a lady to slap him. It shook him to the core that he could have caused such violence in her.

His thoughts turned to the present uncertainty of his own life. When would he be offered a new living as a vicar?

With an impatient shake of his head, he returned to his desk, determined to work until it was time to change for dinner. Instead his gaze drifted to the invitation that had arrived the day before yesterday. It sat propped against a stack of books on his desk, where he could stare at it every time he sat down.

Céline Phillips requests your company at 9 o'clock on the evening of the 29th of May, 1815, at a ball given in honor of Miss Megan Anne Phillips and Miss Jessamine Elizabeth Barry at 12 Berkeley Square.

With the former Countess of Wexham hosting a ball for her, Miss Barry would no longer need his mother's help in gaining entrée into society. This ball would seal both her and Miss Phillips's coming-out. They needn't have a court presentation. He had no doubt the countess could even drop a hint in one of the patronesses of Almack's ears and have them invited to an assembly.

Lancelot started at the sound of a knock against the doorjamb. He usually left his door ajar, but Delawney would never walk in unannounced.

"Come in," he told his sister, turning in his chair.

She carried a couple of watercolors in her hands. "I brought you these, which I think are satisfactory."

"Let me see," he said eagerly, reaching out for one of the stiff sheets of paper. It was of an orchid specimen he had brought back. "Perfect," he murmured, happy with how well his sister had captured the exotic greenish-yellow flower with black specks and crimson tips. *Paphiopedilum venustum* was written in a tiny gray script at the bottom with the year and her name to one side.

"It really is quite exquisite—the original, I mean," she was quick to amend. "How timely that it blossomed now. The painting doesn't do it justice."

Lancelot glanced up at her with a quick smile. "It's exquisite—the watercolor. It will do very well indeed. I think I shall take this one to the lecture."

"Yes, both orchids will garner attention. They will please all the matrons going there to educate themselves," she added dryly.

"I think it's a nice thing, this current popularity of science with the general public."

She rolled her eyes. "All they want is to be entertained—made to laugh at a whiff of nitrous oxide, watch a balloon ascend, see a man's leg be amputated in Guy's surgical theater." She shook her head in disgust.

"Nevertheless, if it helps educate the public, I am all for their attending the lectures of the Royal Society or the Royal Institute."

She said nothing more, and Lancelot examined the other painting.

"Are you going?"

"Hmm?" His eyes were on a watercolor of a cluster of tiny pink and white flowers resembling lilacs but more pendulous. *Dendrobium aphyllum*, although the name was disputed.

"To the ball."

He looked up, feeling his skin warm. His sister's gaze was not on him but on the invitation displayed so prominently against the books. Why had he left it there?

"I haven't decided."

"It's a golden opportunity."

He grimaced. "For what? To be turned down once more by Miss Barry? She has made it plain on more than one occasion that she does not welcome my company." *Especially when she is in the arms of another man.* He touched his cheek.

Delawney leaned a hip against the edge of his desk and folded her arms. "I think if a man showed a certain amount of persistence in pursuing me, I would take a second look, even if I had at first dismissed him as nothing but a diffident vicar without a pulpit, a bookish second son who blushes too easily, an amateur scientist who can't see more than two feet in front of him without his spectacles—"

"But who nevertheless wears them in public much to the consternation of any young lady forced to be seen in his presence."

She laughed. "But of course you must present yourself as who you are without varnishing the truth. I, for one, would respect such a man."

Lancelot's lips twisted. "The irony is she wears spectacles too."

Delawney's eyes widened and she clapped her hands. "No! In public?"

"Well, no—or only occasionally since coming to London. She has actually taken to wearing a quizzing glass, to great effect, I might add."

Her smile deepened. "I think I should like to get better acquainted with this young lady who has taken your fancy." She reached over for the invitation, and he had to restrain himself from stopping her. Would she decide to attend the ball with him? He didn't know if he welcomed that or dreaded it.

"You may as well go," he said.

He stared at the invitation in her hands, the only sound the edge of the paper rubbing against her fingers.

"Would you like me to accompany you and give you my opinion on"—she read from the invitation—"Miss Jessamine Elizabeth Barry, for I confess I paid scant attention to her at Mother's dinner. She and her young friend seemed as forgettable as any two young ladies descending upon London in the spring to make their come-out."

He attempted a careless laugh. "You, grace a ballroom? I'm afraid you'll intimidate them both—"

"As well as the company at large?" she added with a wicked gleam in her eye.

He lifted a corner of his lips. "Won't you?"

Her expression sobered. "I should do nothing to embarrass you or your young miss, that I can promise."

He touched her hand, again resisting the urge to take back the invitation. "Of course you wouldn't, and I apologize." He sighed. "Very well, if you think you can stand it for an evening, I should appreciate the moral support."

She handed him back the invitation, which he set in its place, resolving to put it away in a drawer as soon as she left the room.

"Speaking of 'moral,' has anything been decided for your future? No living opened up yet?"

His lips flattened at the topic that vied with that of Miss Barry for his attention. "Do you realize that more than half of clergymen never receive a living? Even with Father's influence, the chances are not the best that I shall be offered something soon."

"A pity his own is tied up for the foreseeable future. When you went off to India and he found himself short of funds, he was forced to sell it when it came available."

He gazed back down at the two watercolors laid on his desk. "I had thought of going back to teaching, perhaps as a fellow at Cambridge."

She drew in a breath. "But then you couldn't marry."

"That is so. Mother and Father wouldn't be pleased about that."

"You are seven-and-twenty now. High time you did marry."

He crooked his lip. "I could say the same for you at five-and-twenty."

"Father's inheritance does not depend on my offspring."

He tapped his fingers lightly on the desk. "It makes one consider becoming a dissident preacher. As a Methodist I could open a chapel anywhere."

"Do be serious."

"I am. I met and worked with many fine Baptists, even Catholics, in India."

"Or you could become a full-time botanist."

"That would mean traveling the world over on my small allowance—which I wouldn't mind. But I don't think I could marry with that life."

"That is true." She sighed. "Pity Miss Barry doesn't possess a fortune. Then you could marry her and set up as an amateur botanist right here in England."

"I wouldn't marry someone for my ease and comfort. Besides, as either a vicar or the second son of a baronet, I do not seem to be an attractive candidate to Miss Barry."

"The more fool she then," his sister asserted.

Jessamine stood with Megan and Céline in the receiving line, greeting the guests at their ball. She'd lost count of how many titled ladies and gentlemen she'd curtsied to, even some foreign dignitaries including a prince or two from principalities in the far-off eastern reaches of the continent.

Jessamine could only stare in wonder at how many people greeted Céline as a long-lost sister—and not as someone who had possibly spied for Napoleon only a couple of years ago.

Jessamine and Megan were acquainted with many of the people from the events they had already attended, Megan more so now that she was living with Céline.

At that moment, the butler announced Mr. St. Leger.

The next moment he was bending over her hand. "Good evening, Miss Barry. You look good enough to eat," he added for her ears alone. To her shock, she felt the pressure of his lips against the thin kid of her gloves. She blushed, pleasure stealing through her like warm syrup.

Since the evening in the garden, he had not attempted anything so intimate. Jessamine looked quickly at Céline, who was standing next to her in the receiving line, but she was in animated conversation with an old gentleman in uniform whose chest was covered with medals.

"I . . . I'm happy you were able to attend," she said to Mr. St. Leger.

He cocked a dark eyebrow. "And miss your official launch? Not for the world." Amusement played in his eyes. "I hope I may be privileged to dance a waltz with you this evening."

"I'm not very adept."

"Let me be the judge of that."

"Does that mean you will dance tonight?"

"I think . . . tonight is the night for rules to be broken." He gave her another enigmatic smile before moving away to greet Megan.

He puzzled her. He was attentive, taking her for a drive a few times a week, conversing with her for several minutes every time they met in public, but never paying her the kind of interest that would give rise to gossip.

It made it hard to know if he was courting her. His attempt at a kiss the other night had led to nothing. No declaration nor diminution or increase in his attentions. What did he mean? Did he like her more than any other young lady he conversed with?

"He certainly has turned the charm on you," Céline commented dryly when he had moved off.

Jessamine frowned, not sure if she liked Céline's remark. It made it sound as if Mr. St. Leger's attentions were false. Was it because as a beautiful woman who never lacked admirers, Céline couldn't fathom that such a handsome man could find anything pleasing in Jessamine?

"Ah, well, enjoy it while you may. I suppose there is no harm in being admired for a season."

"Is that all it is, flattery?"

Céline fixed her honey-hued eyes on Jessamine. "I didn't say that. Just have a care. Some men's charm is merely that—surface only."

"How does one tell the difference?"

"Ask the Lord to reveal it to you."

Jessamine stared at her. "You . . . you sound—"

"Like an evangelical?" She laughed her lilting laugh. "If I do, it is thanks to Rees." Her smile died. "He . . . he brought me to understand how very close God is to us if we allow Him in."

Not liking the direction of the conversation, Jessamine turned to greet the next person in the line. She would not be preached to by a . . . a Frenchwoman, possible spy, and traitress.

Her mouth felt stretched thin and her words were now a repetition of the trite phrases she had taken pains to practice the day before.

When the line of guests had dwindled, Céline glanced at her and suddenly winked. "It's almost over and then you may go and dance."

She forced herself to smile, wanting to feel grateful for all Céline had done for her. Of course, she'd done it for Megan. Still, having to sponsor one more young lady couldn't be easy, especially for someone in her condition. "Are you tired? You've been on your feet some hours now."

"Thank you, dear. I am beginning to feel it, but I shall sit down soon. Most of the guests are here. There will always be latecomers, but the butler can attend to them."

Seeing that Megan's attention was occupied with a pair of young gentlemen, Jessamine dared the question she had been dying to ask for so long. "You met Rees when he was the butler here?" She held her breath, wondering how Céline would reply.

A faraway look filled her eyes. She had beautiful eyes, large, fringed by dark lashes, and of a hue not quite brown but something between golden amber and rich, aged cider.

"Yes, he was pretending to be a butler, but I must say I don't think I ever really thought he was a butler."

Jessamine's eyes widened. "You didn't?"

She smiled. "No. I don't think I thought it consciously, until my maid began to arouse my suspicions. But I sensed it on a deeper level. He was too dignified in his manner. Of course a butler is supposed to be dignified. But, with Rees it was different. He would look at me as if he were my equal. It was nothing I could put my finger on but something which I sensed."

Jessamine stared, wanting to know more. What had it been like? When had Rees begun to fall in love with this beautiful woman? At once, she could well imagine. She took a deep breath. "When did you suspect you were in love with Rees?"

Again, Céline looked away from Jessamine, as if she were looking into the past. "It was so gradual I can hardly pinpoint when I admitted it to myself. I think I could no longer deny it to myself when he was shot. I was terrified he would die. Suddenly it didn't matter whose side we were on in that awful war."

Jessamine could hardly breathe. "He was shot?"

Céline's gaze fell on hers. "You didn't know? I'm sorry, I should have realized. We . . . don't speak much of those months . . . before I left France." She looked down at her hands. "Megan and I have talked somewhat at length in the last weeks, since she is Rees's sister and I know he'd want me to trust her. I forget you haven't heard it all. I know you and she are close."

Megan turned her attention to them then but remained silent.

Jessamine expected her to say that Jessamine and Rees had once been close, but Megan didn't intimate it by so much as a look.

"What happened?" Jessamine was on tenterhooks, wanting to hear about Rees.

"He took a bullet when we were on our way back from a visit to my mother. It seemed to be highwaymen at the time." She shook her head as if to clear it of those details and proceeded. "It was a harrowing journey to London. Thankfully we were not far by then. The bullet hit no organ, and the surgeon was able to extract it. I believe it was after that, during his recovery, that we both began to admit we had . . . growing feelings for one another." She moistened her lips, looking down again. "Although I know he had feelings for another, and he was too honorable a man to . . . to pursue one woman while another held his heart."

Jessamine relaxed a fraction. Perhaps Céline had not been told of her friendship with Rees. The next second the meaning of the Frenchwoman's words penetrated. Rees had had "feelings" for Jessamine, only those feelings had not held his heart, she realized sadly. She bit her lip to keep from betraying herself.

Céline drew in a deep breath. "In any case, with the war on, neither of us could act on any feelings we may have had. He was working for the British government, while I—" She gave a small laugh and shrugged her shoulders in a very Gallic way. "I had my own loyalties and was more concerned at that time with what hands France would fall into once Napoleon was defeated."

"Now that he is back, do . . . do you support the emperor?" Jessamine whispered, hardly believing her boldness.

At Megan's sharp intake of breath, Céline only smiled. "Good heavens, no!" She pressed her lips together in an impatient gesture. "France is trying to recover from decades of war. The last thing we need is a general ready to fight for the glory of an empire again."

With a shake of her head, as if to dispel talk of the past, Céline motioned them toward the dance floor. "I believe we can enjoy the ball ourselves now. You mustn't keep the young men waiting to dance."

A gentleman in a naval uniform appeared in the doorway at that moment and spoke to the butler.

The butler announced in resonating tones, "Captain Alexander Forrester."

Céline held her hand out to the latecomer, her face breaking into a smile. "How do you do? You were a friend and shipmate of my husband, Rees Phillips, were you not?"

He returned her smile as if in relief. He'd removed his bicorne, which he carried under his arm, and his dark, honey-blond hair had a slight wave to it. "Yes, though it was many years ago, and I was but a cabin boy when we first met and he already a midshipman."

"You have come along since that time, I see, Captain."

He grinned, making his already handsome face more attractive. "The advantages of war, if one survives."

"Welcome to our home. I am so glad you were able to come to the ball for my sister-in-law, Megan Phillips, Rees's young sister, and her best friend, Miss Jessamine Barry."

He bowed over each hand but lingered a few seconds longer over Megan's as his eyes scanned her face. "You look like your brother." He glanced at Céline. "He is not here, I take it?"

"Alas, you have just missed him. He had to return to Brussels. With things so uncertain . . ." She splayed her hands.

His jaw tightened, the look in his eyes turning grim. "Yes, quite.

I myself have just arrived in London and found your invitation. I wasn't sure if Rees was back in London. We haven't been in the same port in quite some years." He turned to Megan. "But I believe all is not in vain if I am able at last to make the acquaintance of his sister."

A rosy tint filled her cheeks. Jessamine felt a spurt of hope. Perhaps Megan had at last met the person of her dreams.

"We were just about to go into the ball, Captain," Céline said. "Would you accompany us?"

"It would be an honor. And if these two young ladies"—he inclined his head first to Megan then to Jessamine—"would honor me each with a dance, my evening would be complete."

"I think that may easily be arranged," Céline replied with a chuckle.

They proceeded into the ballroom, Megan on Captain Forrester's proffered arm. Céline followed with Jessamine.

Jessamine couldn't help one glance back. Mr. Marfleet had not appeared. She turned quickly away. She didn't care. He had not forgiven her behavior at the last ball. In that case, she should be grateful she would be spared his grave countenance.

Mr. St. Leger was going to waltz with her. It would go much more smoothly than the first time with Mr. Marfleet. She would wager Mr. St. Leger waltzed superbly.

She danced the first set of country dances with Mr. Allan, all the while watching Megan and Captain Forrester. They seemed to be in animated conversation whenever the dance permitted, as if they'd known each other all their lives.

Feeling a pang of envy, Jessamine shook herself and replied to one of Mr. Allan's questions.

When he led her off the dance floor, she halted at the sight of Mr. Marfleet. She was even more surprised to see his sister at his side.

"Hallo there, Marfleet, haven't seen you about lately," Mr. Allan said in a careless tone.

"I've been busy. Good evening," he said with a bow to Jessamine. "You remember my sister, Miss Marfleet?"

She curtsied. "Yes."

Miss Marfleet waved a hand. "Please don't bother. I'm neither royalty nor a dowager yet."

"I should say not," Mr. Allan teased. "You're just Marfleet's annoying younger sister."

She ignored his sally, her eyes fixed on Jessamine.

Jessamine wondered how she appeared to the severely-dressed young woman. Jessamine wore one of the made-over gowns, this one an aqua silk with seed pearls sewn about the neckline and capped sleeves.

Mr. Marfleet wore his spectacles, and she wondered if he no longer cared how he appeared at these social functions.

She fiddled with the ribbon of her quizzing glass, feeling foolish for her vanity. "I—I didn't know you were here."

"We just arrived. I'm sorry we are a little late." He smiled wryly. "My sister doesn't normally attend balls."

"I'm honored you should attend this one," Jessamine told her.

"Anything for a brother," she muttered. "I must say, Lady Wex—that is, Mrs. Phillips, knows how to put on a grand affair." She looked around the room. "I congratulate you and Miss Phillips on an impressive attendance. It should ensure the success of your season."

Unsure if it was a compliment, Jessamine murmured, "Thank you." Did Miss Marfleet see her as a nobody riding on a noblewoman's coattails?

Mr. Allan excused himself. "I must find my next partner." With a bow at them, he left her alone with the Marfleets. Jessamine swallowed, wondering how to proceed with the man she'd slapped in the face the last time she had seen him and his caustic sister.

13

"How are you enjoying your season?" Miss Marfleet asked Jessamine.

"Very well, thank you."

"Have you been to the theater?"

"Twice."

"My brother says your father enjoys botany."

"Yes," she answered cautiously, thrown off by Miss Marfleet's questions, which sounded more like an interrogation than polite conversation.

"Lancelot is giving a lecture on the plants he brought back from Andhra Pradesh, Orissa, and Bengal. Perhaps you'd be interested in attending."

Jessamine glanced to Mr. Marfleet. "You are? When is this lecture to take place?"

"At the Royal Institute on Saturday afternoon."

When Mr. Marfleet said nothing more, she wondered if he wanted her to attend—or was his sister interfering where she wasn't welcome? Jessamine couldn't tell anything from Mr. Marfleet's expression since he kept his eyes fixed on the dancers.

"I—perhaps I can ask my friend Miss Phillips to accompany me."

"It is open to the public, so you may ask anyone you wish," Miss

Marfleet said in clipped tones. "Well, I shall leave the two of you. I see an acquaintance across the room." With a nod, she stepped away from them.

Jessamine wondered if Miss Marfleet had really seen an acquaintance or if she was merely maneuvering to leave them alone. If so, it was awkwardly done.

"You needn't feel obliged to attend the lecture if you'd rather not," Mr. Marfleet said stiffly, bringing his gaze to her at last.

She fiddled with her fan, wishing she could apologize for slapping him, but preferring not to allude to that evening if he didn't. "If I do attend, it will not be because I feel 'obliged to,'" she replied equally stiffly.

"My sister's watercolors are quite accurate if you would care to see them."

"I should like to."

Silence descended once more. Jessamine continued to fret about apologizing, but her mouth remained closed.

"Would you care to dance?"

Relieved that he did not expect an apology, she acquiesced with a tilt of her chin.

As he led her out to the dance that was already in progress, her confusion only increased. That he still wanted to be seen in her company filled her with relief. That he obviously had not forgotten that evening was clear from his disinclination to talk to her.

Would he take this opportunity on the dance floor to bring up her conduct on that awful evening? Her lips firmed in anticipation of his assault.

"Are you enjoying yourself?" Mr. Marfleet asked her as they came together in the dance.

His question caught her by surprise. Her eyelids fluttered upward. "Yes, of course. Why do you ask?"

His lips twitched. "Because you looked so ferocious, I was afraid for a moment my cheek would be the recipient of your palm once again."

At his reference to her slap, she stumbled. He quickly caught hold of her arm.

"Thank you," she managed, heat suffusing her neck. When she found her place once more in time to the music, she said, "I . . . I am sorry for that. I lost my temper. You provoked me and I . . . I . . ." Her voice dribbled away as she stared into his eyes.

He studied her face as they performed an allemande. "I apologize for provoking you. I, too, lost my temper that evening." He cleared his throat and broke his gaze from hers at last.

The tightness that had lodged in her chest since that evening eased as she studied his profile. Even his ears turned red when he blushed.

They spoke no more after that, and she turned her attention to the couple dancing down the line. Cubby came to stand behind her and chatted with her a few minutes as she stood in line. Another gentleman approached Mr. Marfleet and engaged his attention.

When it was their turn to dance down the line, Mr. Marfleet took her hand in his and led her in the chassé and pas jeté assemblé. They both performed their steps with much more ease than they had the waltz, and she could see he was accustomed to dancing the country dances.

"I meant what I said earlier—please don't feel you must attend my lecture."

"Not at all," she answered without thinking. "I am very interested in hearing about the plants you saw in India. I only wish my father could be there."

"Is it too far for him to come?"

"Yes, for he dislikes to travel. Besides, there is no place for him to stay. He has a brother in London, but he is not presently in town."

"That is a pity."

"I shall write him all about it, however. He will enjoy that."

"Do you enjoy gardening yourself?" he asked as they were performing another allemande.

"Yes, very much." She was so relieved that he seemed to have forgotten her conduct the other evening that she answered with enthusiasm. "I love to plant seeds and watch them sprout, then tend the seedlings until they become full-fledged plants and produce flowers or fruit or vegetables or whatever the case may be. My mother and I tend quite a large kitchen garden, and then we have several flowering beds and fruit trees, of course. And then I help my father in his greenhouse with all his experiments." She laughed. "He has had many more failures than successes."

Mr. Marfleet seemed interested in all she was saying. "That is to be expected. What was one of his successes?"

"He has named a peony he produced. It's a beautiful pink shade, a double blossom."

"I should like to see it."

They separated for a few moments.

When the dance ended, she felt so in charity with him that she didn't object when he went to fetch her some refreshment. She didn't know whether to be amused or piqued that he didn't ask her what she wanted and then brought her a glass of lemonade.

She strove to detect some censure in his demeanor but found none. They continued discussing gardens and gardening. He told her of some of the exotic flowers he'd seen in India. "*Jasminum*—or jasmine," he said, startling her with the use of a form of her name, "is a flower much in evidence in India. You catch its scent everywhere on the hot, humid air."

She listened with interest.

His brows drew together. "Unfortunately, in India, so many flowers are used as offerings at temples. White and fragrant flowers like the jasmine are used particularly for worship of deities."

"What was it like to convert these people?"

He smiled ruefully. "That is not a question I can answer in a few minutes on a dance floor."

"Oh." She felt chastened for her naïve inquiry.

"But it is a question I should like to attempt to answer." He cleared his throat. "Perhaps . . . we could make an excursion to Kew Gardens. I mean you and Miss Phillips, of course. There is quite a collection of exotic plants there—if you are interested."

She didn't reply right away, mulling over the idea. She would indeed enjoy visiting another part of London. And if Megan came along, it should be all right. "Thank you," she said at last. "I shall discuss it with Megan and . . . and we can give you our reply at the lecture, unless"—she felt her cheeks burn—"you will be too busy then."

His slate-blue eyes smiled down into hers, and she could almost forget he wore spectacles. "I shall not be too busy. I shall see you there."

Lancelot bowed and forced himself to walk away from Miss Barry although he should have liked to stay and talk more with her. But others had approached her, and he felt it best to withdraw for now. He still felt on fragile ground with her, like a gardener coaxing a seedling in a heavy soil.

His heart was buoyed up, however, after their conversation. It confirmed what he'd always felt about her—that they were kindred spirits, in spite of her quickness to take offense with him.

He relished talking to her about his missionary experience. He sensed she would understand and that with her he could be honest and forthright, sharing his hopes and disappointments, the many failures and few bright spots of success.

His optimism didn't last long. His spirits plunged when he saw St. Leger escorting Miss Barry onto the dance floor for a waltz.

Wanting to walk away yet powerless to do so, Lancelot watched the same movements he had put Miss Barry through so awkwardly. St. Leger was an accomplished waltzer, and Miss Barry's movements were more graceful in response. He held her even more closely than Lancelot had, transforming the dance into a sinuous, seductive courtship.

"They look so well together."

He ignored his sister, who'd appeared at his side.

"Why didn't you ask her for the waltz?"

"I've already waltzed with her."

"And?" she prompted when he was not forthcoming. "What happened?"

"We bumbled our way through it."

"She's improved since then."

"She is with a vastly more competent dance partner."

"Mm." Her single syllable neither denied nor confirmed his statement. After a moment she said, "She's comely enough, though I don't see what has you all tied in knots. But then I scarcely spoke to her."

He glanced at her. "Precisely. You don't know her." The words came out more harshly than he'd intended.

She placed a hand on his arm. "I don't. I am sure there is more to her than first appears." When he said nothing, continuing to watch as his hope diminished with every pirouette and pas de bourrée across the dance floor, his sister asked, "Do you think she'll come to the lecture?"

"She said she would." He added, "She may even come on an excursion to Kew Gardens. She said she'd discuss it with her friend Miss Phillips."

"That would make a fine outing." Delawney's voice quickened with enthusiasm. "It would be a daylong excursion. You could even take a picnic."

"Yes, perhaps." He battled hope and despair as he followed the dancers. Mr. St. Leger's arms lingered around Miss Barry far longer than Lancelot's had in the same movements.

Jessamine felt like a princess or a fine porcelain figurine of a ballerina being led in the precise dance steps, one moment in her partner's arms, the next facing him, each dancer performing his individual steps one after the other in perfect succession.

It made her think of marriage—two people joined as one in God's sight, distinct yet moving in synchronization.

"You look deep in thought," Mr. St. Leger whispered in her ear when he had his arm around her in a close embrace for the pirouette.

"I'm merely concentrating on my steps lest I shame you on the dance floor."

"You could never do that." He smiled down into her eyes as he twirled her around, making her feel as if he saw only her of all the women present in that vast ballroom.

She smiled tremulously in response. "It is only my second attempt waltzing."

He drew an eyebrow upward. "They do not waltz in your village?"

She shook her head. "And if they did, Papa would be scandalized to see his daughter doing so." She giggled. "Remember, he is a vicar."

"Ah. It wouldn't do for a vicar's daughter to be held by a man like this." He took her once more in an embrace, closer this time than the previous one.

"It is unfair you should dance so well when you never practice," Jessamine said with a pout.

"Who says I don't practice?"

When the dance ended, Jessamine was breathless but not from the exertions, which were far less strenuous than those of a country dance.

Mr. St. Leger brought her a glass of champagne and said, "Perhaps you would care to take a turn outside." His dark-blue eyes held hers. "I believe we left unfinished what we began the previous time . . ."

She tried to laugh, but it came out sounding like a nervous choke. "Perhaps some things are better left unfinished." She took a sip of the sparkling liquid to hide her embarrassment.

"Do you think so?" His gaze seemed to measure her. "I would not have taken you for one to retreat from a . . . challenging experience."

Her cheeks flushed. "Perhaps it is because I am only a vicar's daughter."

"I think you are much more than a simple vicar's daughter." His gaze lingered on her lips.

At that moment she was saved from replying by the approach of Megan and Captain Forrester. "How brave you were to dance the waltz. You looked so graceful together," Megan said.

"I didn't dare ask Miss Phillips to dance it myself," Captain Forrester put in with a rueful smile. "She may have had lessons, but I shall have to hire a dance master myself now that I have a reason to dance it."

Mr. St. Leger looked at him in his braided blue uniform. "I take it you have been away from London these past years if you missed the introduction of the waltz. Now that it has received the nod of approbation from Almack's, it is even acceptable to a vicar's daughter." He ended with an amused glance at Jessamine.

Captain Forrester laughed, missing the significance of the reference to vicars, though Megan gave her a curious look. "That is so." He held out his hand to Mr. St. Leger. "Captain Alexander Forrester, lately of the HMS *Pelican*."

"St. Leger. Pleased to make your acquaintance," he replied, clasping Captain Forrester's hand. "You must have seen some action."

"My fair share. In recent years, though, I have been mainly in the West Indies amassing my fortune," he said with a smile, the corners of his eyes crinkling. "Capturing privateers and their prizes." His gaze rested on Megan. "Now I am ready to retire from the navy and settle down."

They discussed a little more the battles he'd seen before he and Megan moved away to dance a Scottish reel, which Captain Forrester declared to be more in line with his abilities.

Before Mr. St. Leger left her, he invited her for another ride in the park, which she accepted with pleasure, relieved he'd forgotten his suggestion to go onto the terrace.

Jessamine spent that night with Megan. It had seemed foolish, even churlish, for her to turn down the invitation when the ball was being held partly in her honor at Céline's house, and they all knew it would go until dawn.

After their maids had left them, she and Megan sat in their night rails on Megan's wide bed.

"Captain Forrester seemed very nice," Jessamine began, curious to hear Megan's impressions of the dashing naval captain.

Megan's face shone. "I feel as if we've known each other forever and are only now meeting." She shook her head in wonder, twirling the end of her braid in one hand. "It is very strange, I admit, to say that. Perhaps it's because he knew Rees and we spoke a lot of him at first." She lifted her shoulders. "And from there, everything else just seemed to follow naturally."

"I'm so glad. I was beginning to fear the season would be over and no gentleman had tugged at your heartstrings."

"What about you? You seem quite fond of Mr. St. Leger."

Jessamine looked down at the bedcover, her finger following a curve of an embroidered pattern, as she struggled to articulate as clearly as Megan had but not feeling nearly as sure. "He makes me feel beautiful and . . . desirable," she said finally.

Instead of looking shocked that a vicar's daughter would use such a word, Megan's tone was gentle and understanding. "I suppose we all want to feel that."

Jessamine smiled sadly. "You know, Rees never made me feel that way." Before Megan could refute her words, she added quickly, "He was everything that was kind and respectful, but there was always such reserve in him. He treated me much more as an older brother would, not as a suitor."

Megan sighed. "I'm sorry. I know he cared very much for you, even though, you are right, he was always very reserved about his feelings. He never confided them to Mother or me."

"I don't think he was ever in love with me." There, she'd said it, and felt no sharp stab of pain.

Megan pursed her lips. "I don't think he knew what it meant to be in love." It was the first time Megan had expressed such a thought. She and Rees's mother had been Jessamine's staunchest allies in wanting a union between the two.

Megan continued soberly, hugging her drawn-up knees, as if only now coming to these conclusions. "He spent so many years just taking care of Mama and me and paying off the debts left by Papa that he learned to put aside his own wishes."

"Until he met Céline."

Megan's gray eyes met hers. She tried to say something, but no words came.

"It's all right." Jessamine touched her hand. "It's funny. It doesn't hurt quite so much anymore to acknowledge it."

Megan smiled. "Because you met Mr. St. Leger."

Jessamine shook her head slowly. "I think more because I met Céline." She smiled sadly. "Could any man help falling in love with her?" There was no bitterness in her tone.

"I suppose not. And don't forget, Rees was living under her roof, seeing her every day, and before long, he suspected she was in trouble. You know how gallant he is. He cannot resist protecting someone."

"Yes." She sighed again, turning away. "If he felt anything for me, it was because of that chivalrous side of him."

"I think he saw you as a shining example of womanhood, the kind of woman he wished for a wife and helpmate—devout, modest, caring, and generous-hearted. He has seen what a fine daughter you are, following your mother's example, helping your father with both his church duties and in his botanical pursuits."

"But that 'ideal' of womanhood is not what men fall in love with. It is not what he saw in Céline."

"Yet she has grown in her devotion to God since meeting Rees.

We have gotten to know each other better now that I live here, and she has told me how her faith has deepened, especially when she and Rees were forced to part and she thought never to see him again."

"I scarcely know her but can find no fault in her," Jessamine was forced to concede.

Megan took her hand in hers. "And you will grow to see that even more and come to care for her as I do. As for that 'type' of woman men don't fall in love with, do not be so sure. Mr. St. Leger certainly seems attracted to you, even if he doesn't see you the way Rees did."

"What do you mean?"

Megan seemed to consider before she replied. "I mean I think Rees saw your worthiness to be a good wife. I-I'm not sure that is what Mr. St. Leger sees."

Jessamine mulled on her words. "If Mr. St. Leger sees me as a beautiful and desirable woman, I prefer that," she said at last.

Megan's gray eyes seemed troubled. "I think Mr. Marfleet does see and appreciate those good qualities in you, but he is not hampered by all the constraints Rees suffered under."

"I think Mr. Marfleet sees nothing but things to reproach in me." Jessamine shook her head. She squared her shoulders. "Besides, if I am ever interested in falling in love again—which I am not—the man must see me with all my faults and sweep me off my feet and lose all his reason because of his overwhelming passion for me."

"He must be an extraordinary man indeed!"

They both fell back on the bed laughing.

As she lay on her back and stared at the ceiling, she thought of the heady way Mr. St. Leger made her feel when he'd held her in the waltz.

"I believe we left unfinished what we began." She shivered. When would he seek to finish that kiss?

14

Jessamine and Megan entered the imposing doors of the Royal Institute a few afternoons later. They followed the crowd that had gathered on the pavement outside.

Jessamine remembered their first sight of the Institute so many weeks ago. She had avoided this street and nearby Grafton Street since that embarrassing day when Mr. Marfleet had caught them lurking outside his residence.

How silly and naïve she had been then. In the ensuing weeks of parties, balls, and theatrical events, she felt she had changed much from that brokenhearted girl who'd run to London to begin a new life.

"Your father would enjoy seeing the inside of this place," Megan whispered at her side.

"Indeed," she whispered back then wondered why she was whispering. There was a growing drone of voices around them as more people filled the vast marble entryway.

They continued following the crowd until they entered a semicircular theater with a lectern down at the center.

"To think we know someone who belongs to this august scientific body," Megan said once they were settled in their seats. They were about halfway up since the best seats had already been taken by those arriving ahead of them.

"Yes . . ." She felt awed by her surroundings and was trying to reconcile her image of the slightly stammering, slightly clumsy man she knew as a missionary and clergyman, with the image of a respected man of science. The comparison shouldn't have been so difficult since her own father had a similar dual role. But her father was a simple country parson with no claim to scientific renown, content to putter in obscurity in his greenhouse and gardens.

A quarter of an hour later, a gray-haired gentleman, his powdered hair in an old-fashioned queue, was pushed to the stage in a wheelchair. He introduced himself as Joseph Banks.

Jessamine turned to Megan. The eminent naturalist Sir Banks was introducing Mr. Marfleet? As she listened to his liberal praise, calling Mr. Marfleet one of his most promising protégés, entrusted by him as one of his emissaries sailing the globe and collecting plant species wherever they went, her amazement grew. He boasted that Mr. Marfleet was one of their youngest members, having been invited to become a fellow at the age of twenty-three for his contributions in Linnaean taxonomy while at Cambridge.

Amidst applause, Mr. Marfleet stepped up to the platform. Even from where she sat, Jessamine could see that his color was high and his gaze lowered as if he were uncomfortable with the praise.

Several plants were arrayed on the stage near him. He began his discourse with a self-deprecating remark in response to all the accolades given him by Sir Banks.

Then his tone grew serious, and he began to talk of his travels in India.

Jessamine became enthralled as he described his introduction to the fauna and flora of the Indian subcontinent from the first stops his ship had made on the western Malabar coast to his longer sojourns in the eastern regions of Madras and Orissa, until his final destination in the province of Bengal.

"From the hot, humid climate of the southern regions to the snow-capped heights of the Himalayas, it is a land of incredible variety in its plant life. I feel I have only glimpsed a mere fraction of this land . . ."

His descriptions conjured up for Jessamine an atlas of exotic and mysterious plants and animals and geographic marvels.

Then he went into more specific detail on the plants he'd seen, from familiar roses and marigolds to wholly unknown specimens. He held up various illustrations of these plants which he explained would be used in a book he was currently working on for publication.

Jessamine had worn her spectacles, yet she strained to make out the detail of the watercolors. How she wished she could see them up close, especially when he had spoken so highly of his sister's talent.

When the lecture was over, there was resounding applause, to which she and Megan joined in wholeheartedly. Jessamine's estimation of Mr. Marfleet had risen. She could almost forgive him his red hair and officiousness. Except for the very beginning when he seemed embarrassed by Sir Banks's praise, he had shown no hesitancy nor diffidence once he'd begun speaking on his subject. He'd appeared knowledgeable and authoritative in a quiet way.

It made Jessamine wonder what he was like delivering a sermon. He seemed to have the same quiet authority her father had in the pulpit. She'd heard more fiery sermons which had moved her, but her father's quieter delivery never failed to convict or encourage her.

But she was not interested in someone who reminded her of her father, she reminded herself. Or of Rees. Mr. Marfleet's reserve reminded her too forcibly of Rees. Like him, Mr. Marfleet was a dutiful son, looking for a wife because it was what he was expected to do at that point in his life. What better helpmate for a vicar than a vicar's daughter?

She got up with a decisive swish of her skirts and followed Megan. When Megan began to turn down toward the platform,

Jessamine tugged on the sleeve of her spencer. "Perhaps we should leave. He looks much too busy to attend to us now."

"But I'd like to see the specimens and watercolors up close."

Jessamine bit her lip, eyeing the crowds ahead of them. "It may be a long wait."

"I don't mind if you don't."

"Very well."

The line of people moved slowly downward since most of the audience seemed inclined to do the same. When they finally reached the bottom, they had to wait still longer before drawing close enough to the watercolors and plants to see them.

Jessamine blinked at the sight of Miss Marfleet in back of the long exhibition table. When she saw them, she smiled. "You came then."

Jessamine smiled and nodded, becoming accustomed to her abrupt manner.

"Yes, and so glad we did," Megan answered at once. "How fascinating it all sounds. It makes me want to join the missionary society and take the next boat to India."

"It does sound like a fabulous adventure until you hear how many of those who have gone out have perished from various illnesses they contract there," Miss Marfleet said. "The natives seem to survive them, but the Europeans rarely do. Perhaps it has something to do with being accustomed since birth to these sicknesses."

They both sobered, remembering that her brother had been quite ill. "Mr. Marfleet contracted one of these, did he not?" Jessamine ventured.

"He nearly died but was too stubborn to return home until forced to by the missionary society. When he first arrived, he looked like a wraith." Miss Marfleet shuddered. "Even if he were inclined to go back on the mission field, it would kill my mother to risk losing him again. For now, Father has forbidden it, though Lancelot hasn't expressed any desire to go against our father's wishes."

Jessamine examined a pretty watercolor of a pink flower labeled as an orchid. "Has he expressed what he wishes to do now that he is back?"

"No, he is quite reticent of his plans," Miss Marfleet said with a short laugh. "He has always been so to us. Perhaps he confides more to those clergy friends of his he went to school with."

He sounded more and more like Rees, Jessamine concluded. She said no more, moving to the next watercolor. "These are very pretty. Did you really paint them all?"

Miss Marfleet only gave a curt nod of her head.

"You are very talented," Megan put in. "Did I hear correctly that they are to be published in a book?"

Miss Marfleet shrugged. "It is what Lancelot hopes. I think he may be successful. He is very close with Dr. Banks and others of the Royal Society. Do you know of him?"

Megan shook her head, but Jessamine nodded. "My father admires him greatly. We have read of his travels with Captain Cook."

"You assist your father in his work?"

Jessamine colored. "A little. Mine is much more an amateur love of flowers."

"That is what botany is in its simplest form—a love for all plants."

They continued looking at the plants and watercolors. Miss Marfleet became busy answering other people's questions.

They had waited perhaps a half hour when at last the crowd thinned and Mr. Marfleet was able to join them. He had been unable to approach them sooner, surrounded as he was by a group of men eager to discuss his talk.

"I do apologize for keeping you waiting so long. I'm glad to see you still here." He smiled at Megan and her, though his gaze lingered on Jessamine. "You exhibit an awful amount of patience."

"Nonsense," Megan said. "We wanted to see all these beautiful watercolors and plants, so the time has gone by quickly."

"We didn't wish to disturb you, however. We could have seen you on another occasion," Jessamine hastened to add.

"No, no, you are not disturbing me at all. I wanted to see you . . . as I said, so that we could discuss our . . . outing to Kew Gardens." His words grew more hesitant as he continued.

Megan clapped her hands. "An outing to Kew. How lovely!"

"Yes, didn't Miss Barry tell you?"

Jessamine flushed. "It slipped my mind." She'd been reluctant to mention it to Megan, not wanting her friend to read more into the outing than it merited.

Miss Marfleet spoke up from her position behind the table. "I suggested you make it a picnic."

"Oh, even better," Megan said, a sparkle in her eyes. "Would you mind very much if I invited someone along?"

Mr. Marfleet shook his head. "Not at all. And Delawney, you are welcome as well."

Miss Marfleet waved away the suggestion. "I am too busy, dear brother. This is your outing. Enjoy it with your friends."

Jessamine turned to Megan. "Did you wish to invite—"

Before she could finish Megan nodded. "Captain Forrester, if no one minds, and if he wishes to come."

"Not at all, although I am not acquainted with him," Mr. Marfleet said at once.

"He is a most charming gentleman. My brother and he knew each other aboard ship several years ago, so it is like finding a long-lost brother."

"Well, not quite a brother," Jessamine said softly.

Megan blushed and smiled. "No, not quite a brother."

Mr. Marfleet rubbed his hands together and smiled, making his lean, bony face almost attractive. "Well, it's settled then. Is the day after tomorrow too soon, if the weather is nice? That gives me time to ask our cook to prepare a picnic for us."

"That would be perfect. I can in the meantime ask Captain Forrester."

Mr. Marfleet's gaze turned to Jessamine as if awaiting her confirmation. "Perfect," she echoed.

They arranged to go in Céline's barouche, which comfortably sat four and was open, allowing them to enjoy the ten-mile drive out toward Richmond. They collected Mr. Marfleet, who brought a large picnic hamper with him, then drove down to Captain Forrester's lodgings near the Admiralty.

Then they left the congested streets of London and traveled the turnpike road west past Hyde Park and Kensington.

Jessamine breathed in deeply of the fresh air of the cultivated fields and walled nursery grounds edging the road. The only disturbances occurred when they were forced to pull to the side to allow the stagecoach or mail coach to pass at their greater speed.

Captain Forrester and Megan kept up a lively conversation during the first part of the journey. She told the captain about the lecture they had both attended.

Captain Forrester grinned ruefully. "I should know more about exotic plants since I have seen so many on my travels and tasted of many wonderful fruits, particularly in the West Indies, but I confess I learned very little about them."

"It's thanks to Sir Banks, the president of the Royal Institute, that our knowledge has increased so much in recent decades," Mr. Marfleet said. "It's he who has commissioned so many of the samples brought back from ocean voyages."

"Indeed?"

"During your time in the West Indies, you doubtless tasted of some of the fruit that originated in the Pacific, which Sir Banks had taken there to cultivate for food—the breadfruit, the mango, and spices such as cloves and nutmeg."

"Yes, though I didn't realize they originated in the Pacific."

Captain Forrester shook his head. "They are quite prolific in Jamaica—at least the breadfruit and mango. I shall endeavor to improve my education at the botanical gardens of Kew." He turned to Megan, who sat beside him, with a smile. "I hope you remember all that our learned friend here had to say to you the other day."

She laughed. "This is not to be a learning excursion today. It is to be a day of walking and breathing the fresh country air."

"Nothing could be better. The air of London makes me miss the bracing air aboard ship."

"You are retiring from the navy?" Mr. Marfleet asked.

Captain Forrester was not in uniform but looked very handsome nonetheless in a dark blue cutaway coat and buckskin breeches with top boots. "Yes. I have collected enough prize money from the privateers we've captured to be able to buy some property and become a gentleman of leisure the rest of my days."

"Perhaps you should learn a bit about botany if you plan to farm your estate," Jessamine said.

Captain Forrester chuckled. "Yes, perhaps you are right, especially considering I have never lived in the country. I must be attentive and follow you about, Mr. Marfleet, like an obedient pupil."

"How is it that you met Miss Phillips's brother?" Mr. Marfleet asked.

The captain settled himself comfortably against the velvet squabs to recount the story. It was a well-sprung coach and the day was very pleasant, so they waited eagerly.

"I ran away to sea when I was twelve. I was an orphan in Portsmouth and escaped one day when I couldn't bear life in an orphanage anymore. It was that or be sent to the workhouse anyway.

"I met Rees Phillips on my first ship, a frigate patrolling the coast of France to enforce the blockade. Rees was an ensign by then and I but a ship's boy. He took me under his wing, you could say, and I quickly took to the life aboard ship." His demeanor sobered slightly. "Our ship was sunk just off the coast of Brittany by a French privateer. I would have drowned if not for Rees. But we both ended up in a French prison."

They listened spellbound as he narrated this adventure. "I wouldn't have survived the French prison if it hadn't been for Rees. He always encouraged me to hope. His faith in God was unshakable. When there was virtually no hope left, his faith sustained him—and me. He taught me to pray not based on my feelings but based on God's Scriptures." Captain Forrester grinned. "Thankfully, he had spent a lot of time reading the Scriptures when the rest of the crew would spend their free hours on board and in port drinking, gaming—and"—he reddened with an apologetic look at the ladies—"seeking other diversions. When we were imprisoned in our cell, with no Bible, much less the diversions we'd sought, he knew so many Scriptures from memory he was able to call them to mind. Every time he prayed, I came away feeling fortified because it was as if I'd heard directly from God."

Jessamine swallowed a lump in her throat. All he said about Rees brought him so forcefully to mind—and the reasons she'd loved him so and had dreamed of a life with him. Would she ever meet such a man again? She shook away the yearning, reminding herself she would not risk her heart again.

Captain Forrester continued. "The strangest thing was that his prayers were answered. I'd grown up in the orphanage and come to hate the hypocrisy of so-called Christians. We were force-fed the gospel and treated so cruelly by those who had oversight over us that I wanted nothing to do with the church when I escaped the orphanage.

"But in Rees Phillips I met a truly godly man. He never preached to me when he knew me aboard ship. But once we were in a tight spot, in the French jail, his faith shone through. It was no more than a year and a half later that we were released and repatriated during the Peace of Amiens in '02.

"Rees left the navy then because his family needed him at home," he said with a glance at Megan, "but I signed on again, having little prospects on land but plenty of opportunities at sea as long as we were once more at war." He heaved a sigh. "The Lord has kept me whole of limb and prospered me during the last decade, though I have seen plenty of action." His brow clouded. "And have watched many perish beside me."

He was silent a moment, then he roused himself. "But I would prefer to hear some tales of your journey to India. Miss Phillips has been telling me you were there as a missionary." He smiled. "I was not even aware our nation sent missionaries to so far and foreign a land. I'm as ignorant as I am on our shipments of exotic fruits and plants."

Even though it was clear Mr. Marfleet didn't want to make himself the center of the conversation, Captain Forrester's questions soon brought out many an interesting adventure he had experienced. The time passed quickly, and before they knew it they had arrived at the bridge at the village of Brentford.

"Look!" Megan pointed. "That must be the new palace the king started to build at Kew."

A white stone castle's crenellated towers and turrets peeked above the trees on the opposite riverbank.

After paying the toll, their coach went over the arched bridge into the village of Kew until it reached the main entrance to the vast parkland.

There they descended from the barouche and Mr. Marfleet gave the coachman some instructions. "I told him to go around to the southern end of the park and wait for us there with the picnic. That will give us time to explore the park."

They walked past the gatehouse and entered the park. Jessamine drew in a breath at the acres of sloping lawns and stands of trees. She could just make out a lake in the distance. Beautiful buildings and classical Greek temples were visible through thick foliage.

"It's beautiful," Megan exclaimed, turning to Mr. Marfleet. "Do you know it well?"

"I have visited several times, before I went out to India, with Dr. Banks. Most of my time has been spent in the botanical gardens and arboretum over there by Kew Palace," he said, pointing off to his right. "If you have comfortable walking shoes, we can walk around the pleasure gardens first. There have been several landscape architects over the years, and I can point out some of the interesting features and trees. Later, if you are up to it, I can give you a tour of the botanical gardens I mentioned. You must be accompanied by a gardener to enter them, but as I am known there, I will be able to act as your guide."

"I am sure you know as much if not more than any of their official gardeners," Megan told him with a smile.

He gave a self-conscious shrug so Jessamine quickly said, "We have worn good walking boots, besides which we are both used to walking in the country, so your plan sounds like a fine one."

"Show us the way, sir," Captain Forrester said, "and we'll follow you without complaint."

"Very well. Shall we?" Mr. Marfleet offered her his arm. She took it, and Captain Forrester did the same for Megan. They made their way toward the lake.

Along the way Mr. Marfleet pointed out many trees of note. Jessamine was impressed that he always knew the Latin name under the Linnaean system.

"This is *Robinia pseudoacacia* or false acacia," he told them, pointing to a tall tree. "It was introduced to Britain over a hundred years ago from the American colonies."

The tree was covered with white hanging clusters of flowers. "It smells like orange blossoms," Captain Forrester commented, "but much larger than the orange trees I've seen in Gibraltar."

"Then it is apt that it should be beside the orangery." Mr. Marfleet indicated the white-framed glass building beside it.

"How are all these plants watered?" the captain asked.

"With an Archimedes screw which is pulled by a horse. It pumps water to the lake and all the ponds as well. It's not far from here and quite a marvel."

"It sounds like an amazing piece of engineering," Captain Forrester murmured.

Farther on, they admired a folly by the edge of the lake built by the former Princess of Wales, Augusta, mother of the present king. "It is a temple to Confucius," Mr. Marfleet explained and pointed to a small Greek temple half hidden by the trees on a mound above the lake. "That's the Temple of Aeolus, also commissioned by Princess Augusta. Sir William Chambers designed it. He was the chief landscaper and architect of the gardens at the time. A good portion of the lake was filled in by our present king for agricultural land. These fields you see are oat and buckwheat."

The remaining lawns had sheep grazing over them. "He introduced the merino sheep from Spain to improve our British strain."

"Farmer George," Captain Forrester quipped.

"Yes, he has earned the reputation with his serious hobby of agriculture. Thanks to his patronage, botany as a field of study has flourished in the latter part of the last century and into this. It is sad that he fell ill. The queen still comes out to the palace, but she is getting older and is not as active as she used to be in oversight of the gardens." Mr. Marfleet sighed. "The regent does not take an interest in plants and farming. If it weren't for Sir Banks and a few other botanists, we would lose the ground we've gained over the last decades."

"I suppose it's hard for people to understand why exotic plants should matter," Jessamine ventured, "unless you are a gardener."

Mr. Marfleet nodded down at her. "Yes. They little appreciate how much the king has done to promote the farming of some of these exotic crops to raise the income of the British. Tea, indigo, coffee all bring in revenue to British coffers and create new millionaires every day."

"On the backs of slaves," she added involuntarily, accustomed to hearing her father's views on this.

"Yes," he agreed sadly. "But that will end someday. It must." There was quiet conviction to his words.

They continued walking along paths that bisected lawns and wound through copses.

"How long is the garden?" Megan asked.

"Almost a mile in length. Of course, we're traveling a longer distance since the paths are meandering. Are you getting tired?" Mr. Marfleet asked in solicitude. "There are many places we can stop and rest awhile."

"Not at all."

"We are almost at the end where there is a Chinese pagoda. It's quite tall, and if you are up to it, we can climb to the top. It affords quite a view, especially with the day being so clear."

"I would love to climb it."

They soon arrived at the tower, which rose up from a stand of evergreen trees. Jessamine craned her neck up the red brick tower, whose octagonal sides seemed to diminish with each story. "How tall is it?"

"Ten stories." Each story was separated by an overhanging slate eave.

As they approached it, she could smell the piney resin of the trees surrounding it. "What kind of trees are these?" she asked.

"Cedars of Lebanon."

She raised an eyebrow. "And their official name?"

"It has not been classified separately from other cedars as yet as far as I know, only of the family *Pinaceae*, genus *Cedrus*."

"I see," she said meekly and followed the others as they entered the tall narrow tower.

They were breathless by the time they reached the top, but the climb was worth their while. They could see for miles around.

"That is London, is it not?" Megan pointed to the hazy distance where a denser cluster of buildings could be made out.

Jessamine leaned against the elaborate red woodwork balcony and looked over undulating green fields and woods, the curving Thames snaking through the landscape.

When they finally returned to the ground, Mr. Marfleet looked for the coachman. He found him with the barouche in a shady spot between some fields just at the edge of the park. He brought back the hamper, and they chose a nice spot on a wide swath of lawn near some thick shrubbery that afforded them privacy. They had seen other small groups of people walking about the grounds, but the park was so vast that they felt isolated from them.

"What about the coachman?" she asked.

"He is going to a local hostelry to have some lunch."

He was mindful of others, Jessamine noted.

"I am famished," Megan announced, peeking into the basket as soon as Mr. Marfleet had opened it.

"That's good. I told our cook to pack a lunch for four, and I know she tends to err on the side of too much food rather than too little."

"May I help you set things out?" she asked.

"Be my guest. I am not an expert on setting out a repast although I ate my share of meals en plein air while I was in India."

Jessamine joined Megan as soon as he'd given her leave, and the two quickly set out all the array of foods. "Goodness, there is enough to feed a small militia here."

Captain Forrester and Mr. Marfleet had already spread out a cloth and now took the dishes and packets of food that she and Megan handed them. "I say keep them coming, I'm as famished as you sound, Miss Phillips," Captain Forrester joked. "I had naught but a cup of coffee before you collected me this morning."

"May I say a blessing?" Mr. Marfleet asked when they had settled down with their portions, ranging from thick sandwiches to cooked eggs, small custards, fruit, and cheeses.

"Of course." The captain immediately sat attentive as Jessamine and Megan bowed their heads.

"Thank You, Lord, for this bounty, not only of the food and refreshment but for allowing us to partake of this beautiful park, to enjoy Your creation. Thank You for the company. Please bless this food to our bodies' use in the name of Your Son, Jesus. Amen."

"Amen," they echoed softly then dug into their food.

They didn't speak much for a while, too hungry to talk. As their hunger was sated, Captain Forrester began to throw crumbs to nearby birds and squirrels.

Mr. Marfleet lay back and closed his eyes. Jessamine toyed with the rest of her food. She was glad she'd come. She sneaked a peek at Mr. Marfleet. He looked so relaxed in his pose. She wondered if he'd fallen asleep. He had worn his spectacles, but with his eyes closed, she noticed the length of his eyelashes. They were pale red, matching his eyebrows.

She started and looked away. It would not do to have him suddenly open his eyes and find her staring at him.

She brushed off the crumbs from her skirt and threw the remains of her bread crusts to the birds, then began to collect the things.

Megan helped her, and soon they had put everything back in the basket. Mr. Marfleet had sat up. "You should have told me. I didn't expect you to clean everything up."

Megan laughed. "We are used to helping out at home. After all, I'm just a cit, don't forget, and Jessamine is but a poor vicar's daughter."

Captain Forrester said immediately, "Well, you both outrank me, who am nothing but an orphan rescued from the streets." He spoke the words simply as if unashamed of his origins. "It's only by God's grace that I have anything to call my own at the ripe old age of seven-and-twenty and can appear as a gentleman."

Jessamine stole a look at Mr. Marfleet. "It seems you are the only one of gentle birth among us."

"And if he's gone off to India as missionary," Megan put in, "he has lived poorer than any of us."

They laughed. "He's the only saint among us then," the captain added.

"Saint Marfleet." Megan bowed her head his way.

Mr. Marfleet looked truly pained at the joke. "Please, I'm no saint."

Jessamine's heart squeezed with compassion. She knew what it was like as a vicar's daughter to be expected to be "good." "Why don't we continue our tour? I don't know about all of you, but I need to walk off some of this food. It seems we've only seen one side of the park." She inquired of Mr. Marfleet, "What about the other side?"

He looked at her with gratitude, and she felt a spurt of pleasure well up in her chest. She turned away, not wanting to feel more than a casual goodwill toward him.

15

Lancelot stared at Miss Barry, sensing her withdrawal. Up to that moment, she'd seemed so amiable. He had not dreamed the outing to Kew would go so well. She was all he could desire in a companion, enjoying the plants and trees as much as he.

As the others teased him about being a saint, she was the one who'd sensed how uncomfortable the undeserved praise made him. But when he'd tried to convey his thanks, she'd turned away from him.

"There is a very nice walk along the river—the remains of Capability Brown's landscaping," he told them, attempting to regain her interest in the tour of the park.

As they displayed their willingness to continue the walk, he picked up the basket and took it back to the barouche. When he returned, they continued on their way. This time the walk led them through a thicker wood. In a clearing the ladies both gasped at the sight of a timbered Elizabethan cottage with a thatched roof.

"This is Queen Charlotte's cottage," he told them. "The king had it built for her in the middle of the last century."

It was fenced off from the public so they enjoyed the field of bluebells growing in a sunny meadow surrounding it. Butterflies fluttered among the flowers, and bees hovered over the blue mass.

Lancelot then led them to a path along the banks of the Thames. "This is called the Hollow Walk. It will take us back to where we began, where we can finish our day with a tour of the botanical gardens."

"What a perfect time of year to visit Kew," Miss Barry said, admiring the profusion of white blossoms covering a thick laurel hedge along the path.

"Yes. I enjoy it any time of year, but for an avid gardener, spring and early summer are best, I must admit."

Miss Phillips and Captain Forrester moved ahead of them on the path, and Lancelot began to relax again, seeing Miss Barry's enjoyment in her surroundings.

After a few moments of companionable silence, he glanced sidelong at her. "You are enjoying yourself?"

"I can't think of a better day I've had since arriving in London."

He was gratified by her words, which seemed heartfelt. Without thinking, he patted her hand in the crook of his arm. "I'm glad. It's worth more than one visit. There is too much to see for one day."

"I can well believe that."

His hopes rose that perhaps she would agree to come with him again, though he remained silent for now.

They arrived at the unfinished castle they had seen from across the river and rejoined Miss Phillips and Captain Forrester, who were standing admiring it. "How sad to see it so empty," Miss Phillips said. "It could be from a gothic novel."

"The Prince Regent has not been interested in completing the palace his father started some years ago," Lancelot explained.

"I'm afraid the government isn't disposed to spend any more money on palaces, not when we were at war so many years," Captain Forrester said. "Carlton House and the Royal Pavilion have strained the national coffers sufficiently."

"I've heard the king already spent a hundred thousand pounds on this one," Lancelot added.

The captain whistled.

"It's a good thing there are sheep around to keep the grass tidy," Miss Phillips said as they turned away from the lonely castle. "Imagine how forlorn it would appear if the yard around it were left to wrack and ruin."

Next they passed a pair of red-coated soldiers standing guard at a small gatehouse in front of Kew Palace, the three-story red brick structure with three Dutch gables across the roof. "There's a pretty formal garden at the rear, but it is for the queen's private enjoyment," Lancelot told them as they paused to admire the palace a moment.

They had made a full tour of the park and now arrived at a brick-walled area.

"The physic garden and arboretum are in there," Lancelot said. "If you are not too tired, I can give you a tour and show you some of the exotic plants. There are over five thousand specimens, many started from the seeds brought back from all over the world."

They marveled at the number.

"Shall we?" he asked.

"As amazing as that sounds," Captain Forrester said with a smile, "I should very much like to see this Archimedes' screw you were telling us about earlier. I feel if I've seen one tree, I've seen them all." His grin broadened. "You may be an amateur botanist, but I fancy myself a frustrated engineer. I find it fascinating that all these gardens are watered by this one pump."

Feeling a sense of relief that he would be able to show the botanical gardens to Miss Barry alone, Lancelot pointed to the east. "It is over that way, not far from the orangery we passed."

Captain Forrester turned to Miss Phillips. "Care to accompany me, or do you prefer the exotic plants in the physic garden?"

"I shall accompany you to this engineering marvel, and perhaps we can still see some of the gardens before we leave?" She lifted an inquiring brow to Lancelot.

He agreed readily. "I shall inform the gardener on duty to allow you entry. I'd be glad to show you the most valuable species before we go."

The afternoon had waned, and Lancelot knew they needed to be getting back in the next hour or so. As soon as Captain Forrester and Miss Phillips had walked off, Lancelot led Miss Barry to the walled garden area.

He spoke to an older man at the gate who greeted him in recognition and waved them through with a curious look at Miss Barry.

She stopped as soon as they'd entered the garden. "It's enormous! I never imagined . . ." Her gaze roamed over neat beds of labeled plants. "I've never seen botanical gardens so immense."

He felt almost a pride of ownership. "The biggest in the world to my knowledge, though the Germans have started a garden to rival it. This one is about nine acres."

"Goodness, we'll scarcely get to see a portion of it."

"We can always come back," he said, warmed with the notion of returning with her.

"Oh yes, I should like that."

Encouraged by her enthusiasm, he began walking toward the beds. "I thought you might like to see how decorative the herbs are."

They walked along the paths between the beds. She stooped down to peer at the various metal plaques stuck in the soil, though the names were all in Latin. She'd worn her spectacles on this outing—a fact he had refrained from commenting on but which had pleased him. It showed him she was interested in seeing everything clearly and that she did not feel embarrassed wearing them in front of him.

She stopped before a bush with spindly yellow flowers. *"Hamamelis virginiana."*

"Witch hazel from the American colonies."

She touched a rough leaf. "Yes, I recognize it."

Many of the herbs were beginning to flower; others had the fresh, bright shoots of new growth. There were a couple of weathered wooden benches beneath some apple and crabapple trees.

But she ignored these and continued examining the different plants. "Seeing so many varieties puts my own herb garden back home to shame. We have but the most ordinary herbs."

"You don't have the advantage of having world travelers bringing back every species they find."

She smiled and conceded his point.

"It's a pity I can't show you the physic garden in Chelsea. It, too, has a fine collection." He wrinkled his brow. "Unfortunately, ladies are not permitted to enter its hallowed acreage."

She made a face. "How archaic. Is it run by monks?"

"No, just men of science," he said with a smile.

"I would think they would be more progressive."

"Perhaps not in everything." When she returned his smile, he said, "Would you like to see some of the things Dr. Banks has brought back?"

"Oh yes."

"We'll go to the arboretum portion of the gardens just beyond the Temple of the Sun over there."

She scarcely spared a glance at the round, colonnaded Grecian temple with a domed roof, her attention on the various trees and shrubs planted beyond it.

"Here is something your father would doubtless recognize." He stopped at a flowering bush. "*Paeonia moutan*, tree peony, a native bush of China first introduced to England from one of the first collectors commissioned by Dr. Banks at the end of the last century."

"It's beautiful." She touched one of its large pink blossoms so like a cabbage rose.

"It has become very popular in Europe since its introduction."

"I can well believe it. My father has planted several bushes."

They examined the varieties around them. "They have followed a very scientific arrangement of plants as you may have noticed, the different species of the same genus and family arranged together," he pointed out to her.

"Yes, I noticed that in the herbarium."

"Here is another ornamental bush. *Hydrangea hortensis.* First named by Swedish botanist Carl Linnaeus and brought over from Japan by another of Banks's collectors, in the late 1780s."

She smiled at the beautiful pink clusters. "I adore hydrangeas. We have one in our garden, though we must protect it from the cold."

"Yes, they cover this one in winter." He motioned her forward. "Come, there are more plants in the glasshouses." They reached the first greenhouse and he held the door open for her.

He showed her the pretty pink flowers of the fuchsia first introduced by Banks, as well as other plants from New Holland and New Zealand from the voyage of Captain Cook.

"This is one of the most exotic looking, *Strelitzia reginae*, or bird of paradise."

"It's beautiful," she said, gingerly touching one of its sharp, pointed leaves. "It truly looks like a waterbird ready to take off in flight."

He enjoyed watching her pleasure at each new exotic plant. It was like seeing them for the first time himself.

Eager to see her reaction to one of Sir Banks's most illustrious acquisitions, he led her to the glasshouse that was full of pools of water.

She looked around in wonder. "Are they water lilies?"

He smiled at what most people surmised when they first saw these waxy, pale, pinkish-white flowers floating on the water among lush green foliage. "I saw many of these in India. They call it the 'sacred bean.'"

She raised her eyebrows in question.

"The lotus flower," he said, watching her.

She drew in her breath, drawing closer to the water. "I have heard of it but have never seen one."

"Banks brought back the first samples in the 1780s after his trip with Captain Cook."

He took her to the final glasshouse, where Miss Barry gasped in awe. It was full of palm trees of every height. The sunlight overhead felt hot through the glass, the air thick and moist around them.

"In winter all these houses are heated from a marvelous system called the Great Stove." He smiled. "Captain Forrester will want to see that, I'm sure."

"Indeed." She touched several of the tree trunks. "They are so different in texture, some smooth, others as rough and shaggy as burlap."

"Yes, there are many varieties."

At last they came to a corner filled with a vine that covered one glass wall. He stood silent, watching to see if she would recognize the small, star-shaped flowers.

She bent down to a small cluster and sniffed. "It's jasmine."

"*Jasminum*," he murmured the Latin name.

She turned around with a smile and nearly bumped into him. "Oh—I'm sorry. I didn't expect you so close."

Lancelot stared down at her, feeling his heart begin to thud. Her lips were half parted, her green eyes staring up at him through her spectacles, wide and filled with the same wonder she had shown for the plants. Was it now for him?

His gaze moved downward to her pert nose and half-parted lips. The warm air around him enveloped them, making breathing difficult. The blood pounded at his temples, and he felt powerless to step back. "I'm sorry, I didn't mean to startle you." His voice came out hoarse and reedy. He cleared his throat.

"You—didn't." She shook her head imperceptibly then moistened her lips, deepening their rosy hue. He felt like a hummingbird drawn by the nectar of a red-shaded flower.

He inclined his head closer to her, feeling as if the two of them were wrapped in a warm cocoon of steam. Nothing else existed outside of it. Before he could decide whether to remove his spectacles, he closed the gap between them, and his lips touched hers. To his surprise, there was no clashing of spectacles. She closed her eyes and seemed to sway toward him.

Her lips were soft and pliant. He deepened the pressure against them, marveling at how perfectly they molded to each other.

He held her by her arms, her body touching his. The scent of jasmine filled his lungs, intoxicating him, making him want more.

After a moment, her hands pushed against his chest. He loosened his hold, searching her face. But her eyes were closed, her dark lashes curved against her delicate skin.

Her cheeks were flushed, her lips still moist and parted as if she were hardly aware of where she was or what had happened.

He brought a finger to her face and traced her downy cheek. "Do you know what I discovered?"

Slowly she opened her eyes and shook her head slowly.

"That two people wearing spectacles can kiss without knocking against each other." The moment he uttered the words, he knew he'd made a mistake.

Consciousness seemed to fill her eyes. A second later she shifted away from his embrace.

Feeling a yawning hole grow in him as her distance grew, he could do nothing but loosen his hold and watch as the wonder on her face disappeared and her expression transformed to horror.

Was she mad? Allowing Mr. Marfleet to kiss her! And leaning into him like that! As the realization of her position dawned on her, she pushed against him and would have landed in the jasmine bush had he not steadied her with the grip on her arms.

What had begun as a sudden, unexpected moment, when she'd felt suspended in time like a lotus flower on the water, had ended with Mr. Marfleet pressing his lips to hers in a shocking, intimate way.

She hardly heard what he said now as her thoughts tossed about in a confused jumble of sensation and consternation.

A sinister thought occurred to her, even as her senses continued to be roused. Did he think he could kiss her because he thought she was free with her favors? Did he think because he had found her alone with Mr. St. Leger that she would allow any gentleman to kiss her? What had he called her—a Cyprian?

The thought so stunned her, she staggered. "I—I need some air—I c-can't breathe—" She pushed away from him, wanting only to find a way out of the hothouse, whose cloying air now choked her.

"Here, let me." He grabbed her by the arm and pulled her after him, through the sharp palm fronds which a moment before had appeared exotic and now appeared lethal, like knife blades keeping her imprisoned in the airless enclosure.

They reached the door, and he thrust it open.

She held the doorjamb and gulped in the blessedly dry air of the June day.

"Come, there is a bench over there."

Her breathing steadier, she allowed him to lead her. She sat down ready to move away from him if he sat down, but he remained standing, looking down at her with concern.

"Are you all right?"

She nodded, too ashamed to look at him. How could she have allowed him to kiss her? There was no excuse of too much champagne or the magic of a dark terrace.

She put her hands up to her cheeks as she continued to look away from him.

After a few moments of silence, he coughed. "I—I beg your pardon for—for my behavior in there."

His voice sounded stilted and formal, with only a slight stammer. She let her hand fall to her lap and dared to peek up at him from under the brim of her bonnet. But as soon as her gaze met his, her cheeks flamed again as she remembered her conduct.

Try as she might, she could no longer deny that she had not fought him off. She was not yet ready to admit she had kissed him back. No! He had taken advantage of her passivity.

"Please say something."

He seemed truly repentant. But was it only because she'd appeared to be ready to suffocate? She breathed in deeply, her hands clutched together on her lap. "You shouldn't have." She couldn't say the word *kissed*. It would bring up the feel and taste of him too vividly, and she wanted to erase it from her memory. What kind of wanton woman was she that she was accepting a kiss from a man whom she had no regard for?

"I know," he said softly, looking down at his feet.

She almost sobbed with relief at the sight of Megan and Captain Forrester entering the physic garden. She stood to wave and almost lost her balance. Mr. Marfleet was quick to steady her, but she jerked out of his light grasp. "They're here."

He turned, then seeing them, said, "Let me go to them. Why don't you sit here and collect yourself?"

She wanted to protest but then had the horrible thought that Megan might discern something in her countenance. She plopped back down on the bench and tried to steady her breathing, praying her friend would notice nothing out of place in her appearance.

Mr. Marfleet walked across the garden beds, his long stride taking him rapidly to the entrance. They all smiled and greeted each other as if nothing untoward had happened.

Her world had tilted, but everyone else was in perfect equilibrium. Even Mr. Marfleet had quickly regained his composure.

She hugged herself, mortified afresh. How could he think he could take such liberties when he knew she was interested in Mr. St. Leger? Mr. St. Leger! What would he think if he knew of her behavior?

When the threesome walked toward her, she attempted to smile. Megan hurried on ahead. "Are you all right, Jessamine? Mr. Marfleet has told us you were feeling a bit faint."

Jessamine's gaze flew to Mr. Marfleet. "I'm fine. The air inside the hothouses was rather close."

"It has been rather a long, warm day," Captain Forrester said, gazing down at her in sympathy.

"I'm perfectly fine. The air was just too thick." She stumbled with an explanation, her mind going back to Mr. Marfleet leaning toward her, his lips touching hers. No—she must purge that image from her mind, from her senses!

"I'm much better now," she said in a determinedly cheerful voice. "Why don't you show them around, Mr. Marfleet"—it cost her some effort to say his name without a tremor—"while I sit here in the shade?"

"We don't have to see anything more. We can leave," Megan said, but Jessamine shook her head.

"Don't be silly. I feel perfectly fine now, but I have seen the glass-houses already and there are really some spectacular things you should see. It won't take you more than a quarter of an hour or half an hour at most and that will give me plenty of time to rest."

"If you are sure," Megan began, her gaze studying her friend closely. Megan knew she was never faint or ill from walking too much or being inside a greenhouse. Jessamine lifted her chin and kept her smile in place.

Mr. Marfleet didn't say anything, his slate-blue eyes focused on her.

Finally, they moved off, promising to be no longer than a half hour.

By the time they returned, Jessamine managed to appear her normal self. They left the park soon afterward and found the barouche waiting for them at the main entrance.

Once they were on their way home, Jessamine lapsed into silence, watching the scenery go by. Thankfully, Megan and Captain Forrester kept up a lighthearted conversation to which Mr. Marfleet contributed occasionally.

She stole an occasional look at him, but he seemed his normal, quiet self. The kiss had clearly not overset his nerves.

She was the first one they brought home, since everyone assumed she was done in. She was not done in in the least but made no demure, relieved to be away from Mr. Marfleet.

Nodding at Megan's admonitions to lie down, she bid farewell to her and the captain, and gritted her teeth as Mr. Marfleet took her hand to help her down.

He insisted on walking her to the door even though she said it was unnecessary.

He looked at her in concern, but the maid had already opened the front door. "I will call on you tomorrow to see how you fare, if you do not object."

She bit her lip, refusing to meet his eyes directly. "It is not necessary."

Before he could reply, she turned to go in.

Once in the house, she was relieved to hear that Lady Bess was out. She made her way to her room, although she knew lying down would not be in the least helpful. Her thoughts refused to be still. If she were at home, she would go and work in the garden. Garden—that would only remind her of that disgraceful kiss.

That kiss. It had become an entity, an obstacle, in her mind, and it was all she could think about no matter how much she tried to push it from her thoughts and pretend nothing had happened.

She headed to her washbasin and dashed cool water against her cheeks and lips, wishing she could scrub the memory away as easily as she could scrub her mouth.

16

Lancelot was afraid Miss Barry wouldn't receive him when he knocked on the door to her house early the next afternoon. The young maid looked him up and down then closed the door to see if "Miss Barry was in."

He stood awhile on the front stoop before the door reopened. "You may come in," she said with a motion of her chin. She took his hat and gloves and bid him follow her up the stairs.

He was shown into the drawing room, where to his surprise he found Miss Barry alone. He'd expected to have to make inconsequential conversation with Lady Beasinger.

"Good afternoon," he said with a hesitant smile, entering farther into the room. She nodded from her place in an armchair.

"Good afternoon, Mr. Marfleet."

All he could think about and all he had thought about since yesterday was the kiss they'd shared. He peered at her now, hoping she had come to a more favorable view of it herself. But her face gave little away as she sat with her hands primly folded on her lap.

He'd asked himself over and over again why he had kissed her. Because she looked so delectable there in the glasshouse. He hadn't meant to scare her away just when she was beginning to warm to him.

He hadn't thought but acted, he who prided himself on self-control and circumspection. Had he ruined all chances with her? If she hadn't turned away from him yesterday, he would have proposed. He came prepared to do so this afternoon, wanting her to know he did not kiss a woman he was not prepared to marry.

She looked as delectable as she had yesterday. Today she wore a pretty pink frock with a white chemisette with a high, frilly neckline.

When she said nothing, he looked around the room. "Lady Beasinger is indisposed?"

Miss Barry cleared her throat, her gaze focused on her hands. "My godmother is not at home. I would not have received you . . . but I needed to speak with you."

His heart leaped. Perhaps she was waiting for his proposal.

He took another step forward. "I appreciate your receiving me. I shan't stay long, but I, too, wanted—needed—to see you."

She looked up in alarm at his last words. Before he could reassure her, she stood and faced him squarely, her chin tilted up. "You shouldn't have taken liberties with me yesterday."

He flushed. "I know I shouldn't have. I just lost my head. I am sorry."

Too spots of color rose in her cheeks. "Did you think because you saw me that evening with Mr. St. Leger that I would welcome any man's advances?"

He staggered at her words. "Did I think . . . ?" Jabbing a hand through his hair, he gave a harsh laugh. "Mr. St. Leger was the last person on my mind."

She looked away from him, her hands twisting together. "I—I wouldn't want you to think I allow such liberties."

His eyes narrowed at her, his thoughts going back to that night he had found her alone with St. Leger. "Why *did* you allow him such liberties?"

"How dare you, sir!"

"How dare I question a young lady who seems to allow an awful lot of liberties with the gentleman she is with?" Although his voice came out calmly, inside he was seething. He remembered her response to his kiss—for she *had* responded initially—and could not believe she was comparing him to St. Leger.

"You are impertinent, sir—with your disapproving airs, pretending to be so holy and then taking advantage of me—"

"Taking advantage of you!" He gave a bark of laughter. "Excuse me if my recollection differs. You were hardly fighting me off." His words amazed even him, but he seemed unable to get his tongue under control. This was not the way this interview was supposed to go. About now he should be down on his knee proposing. Instead he felt like shaking her.

She gasped and knotted her hands into fists.

He lifted his chin, not having meant to insult her. "My intentions were fully honorable—unlike that blackguard's."

They stared at each other. Did she understand what he meant?

Instead of realizing the honor he was bestowing on her, she stepped back and said with a sniff, "As were Mr. St. Leger's."

He hesitated, his heart thumping painfully in his chest. "Were they? Has he proposed to you?"

She flushed. "That, sir, is not your affair."

He lifted his chin. "It is if I am intending to propose."

"I would never consider marrying a vicar."

She said the word *vicar* as if it were *leper*. If her previous words had hurt him, nothing came close to these.

He bowed stiffly from the waist. "I see. Then it is fortunate I have not proposed. Do not bother to ring the bell, I shall see myself out. Excuse me for having troubled you."

As the door clicked softly behind him, Jessamine's shoulders sagged. She had not meant to belittle his calling. She brought a hand to her mouth, ashamed of the disdain in her words. It was too late to do anything about it now. She should be thankful she had prevented an unwanted proposal.

She sank down on the edge of her armchair, her fingers going to her lips, which despite all her attempts to forget still felt the pressure of his mouth.

What would she have done if she had not said such spiteful things to him and he had proposed?

Even though Megan had teased her about Mr. Marfleet's attentions, and even after the shock of his kiss yesterday, Jessamine had never seriously considered that he cared for her to that degree.

A thought occurred to her. Perhaps he only meant to propose to her because of his kiss. There had been no hint of any deeper feeling in him but a sense of honor and obligation. He was a vicar. He would feel he'd dishonored her if he didn't offer for her. He must have realized that as they were driving home yesterday. That was why he'd sounded so resolute on the front stoop when he'd told her he would call on her today. And why he'd looked so ill at ease when he'd first walked through the door.

Even yesterday after their kiss, he'd spoken no avowals of love, only made a silly remark about their spectacles. She cringed, remembering his tone of detachment. She could never marry a man so cold and scientific. She must be grateful he had never actually proposed.

And she wouldn't marry an older man. She, who had always looked up to Rees, as someone so much older and wiser—she would not repeat that mistake! Mr. Marfleet must be almost thirty, too old for her almost one-and-twenty.

In short, she would not marry a man like Mr. Marfleet—a cross between her father and Rees. She shuddered at her near escape.

No, best not to think those things. She got up from her chair and paced the room. What was done was done. It didn't matter what she'd experienced during his kiss. It was no different than Mr. St. Leger's—or would be if he ever did kiss her. Mr. Marfleet had interrupted them before anything had happened.

How dare he think she went around kissing any gentleman who approached her! She would not be tied to a man who preached holiness and purity—and then little practiced them!

That evening she dressed for another ball. She no longer bothered to keep track of the names of the great lords and ladies. It seemed ever since Céline had taken Megan under her wing, life had become a round of parties and balls. The one thing Céline would probably not be able to secure for them were vouchers to Almack's, the most prestigious assembly room, but Jessamine didn't really care anymore.

Who would have thought these entertainments would pall so quickly? The only thing to look forward to was seeing Mr. St. Leger. Her conscience pricked her ever since Mr. Marfleet had challenged her about receiving a marriage proposal from him.

In truth, she still had no idea if Mr. St. Leger was pursuing her. He seemed so aloof at times. She reminded herself she didn't care, for she did not intend to fall in love herself.

But she couldn't help feeling a frisson of excitement every time Mr. St. Leger focused his dark blue, mocking eyes on her. He made her feel like a beautiful, desirable woman.

When Céline's coach arrived to collect her, Megan greeted her with a squeeze of her hand. "How are you? I meant to call on you today, but I decided to stay at home with Céline. She received a letter from Rees."

Jessamine's glance went to Céline, who sat in the shadows across from them. "Is everything all right?"

"Yes, all is well, thank God, but there is so much uncertainty. He can't tell me much since he himself doesn't know, but it seems to be a daily waiting game."

"Does no one know what Napoleon intends?"

"He has issued a new constitution which France must vote on, and because Louis ran to Belgium, it is clear that Napoleon intends to stay as leader of France." Céline sighed. "Whether the allies allow that is dubious to say the least."

"Does that mean war?"

Céline spread her hands. "I cannot see how they can avert it. I think they are only waiting for Wellington and the other allied commanders to decide *when* not *if* to invade France once again."

Jessamine forgot her own personal affairs in the light of this sobering reality across the narrow English Channel. She prayed for Rees's safety as the coach continued on its way.

When they arrived at the large, brightly-lit building on Cavendish Square, they followed the guests streaming into the imposing mansion which occupied all one side of the square.

By now she and Megan felt at ease entering into these grand ballrooms. They both had become acquainted with enough ladies and gentlemen of their own age that they no longer feared standing ignored.

She had only a moment's trepidation wondering if she would see Mr. Marfleet, but she shook aside the worry. With so many people milling about, it would be easy to ignore each other if he were present.

As if reading her mind, Megan leaned toward her. "Have you seen Mr. Marfleet since our outing to Kew?"

"He stopped by briefly yesterday afternoon to . . . see if I had recovered from the excursion."

"How nice of him. Have you recovered?"

"Of course. It was nothing, just a touch of heat."

"I had such fun on that outing. It was so nice of him to arrange it for us. And such a delicious picnic luncheon!"

"Have you seen Captain Forrester?" Jessamine decided to turn the conversation to a topic Megan surely wouldn't wish to avoid the way she did that of Mr. Marfleet.

Her friend blushed. "He did call on us yesterday."

They smiled at each other. "The captain seems very nice," Jessamine said.

"Mmmhmm." Megan's gaze was roving the ballroom, whether to avoid Jessamine's gaze or to look for the gentleman in question.

"If he is wearing his uniform, he should not be too difficult to spot," Jessamine murmured.

"What's that?" As her meaning penetrated, Megan tapped Jessamine with her fan. "You mustn't plague me about him. We have hardly known each other a week."

"Perhaps sometimes it takes no longer." Jessamine sounded wistful. "Love at first sight."

"I always thought that was only in novels, but now I'm not so sure . . ." Megan's voice trailed off as she continued to search the room. "Ah, there he is."

Realizing her friend's attention was captured now, Jessamine followed along as she made her way toward the captain.

After greeting them, Captain Forrester said to Jessamine with a smile, "I saw Mr. Marfleet earlier."

She kept her smile in place. "Indeed." Did he think Mr. Marfleet was her suitor?

"I told him how much I enjoyed our outing to Kew. He mentioned a couple of other noteworthy gardens in the area. Spring Grove is one. It belongs to Sir Joseph Banks."

"How interesting."

She was saved from saying anything more by the arrival of Mr. St. Leger. She turned to him in relief.

He bowed over her hand. "I was hoping you would be here."

She smiled shyly. He was so handsome he took her breath away. "It is nice to see you again."

He turned to greet Megan and Captain Forrester. After exchanging a few pleasantries, St. Leger turned to her. "I hope you have saved the first dance for me."

She blushed. "If you care to dance, I am free."

He held out his arm. "Come then."

She danced the first set with him. As she walked off the dance floor, she saw Mr. Marfleet.

He nodded but made no move toward her. She acknowledged him but kept moving, her heart pounding as she waited to see if he would follow her. But when she finally stood facing the dance floor again, she no longer saw him.

Her heartbeat eased, but she didn't know if she was relieved or sorry.

Why did he have to ruin the lovely time they had had at the gardens? She had felt in such sympathy with him and could believe that a friendship was forming before he went and kissed her!

She had only allowed it and kissed him back because she was feeling so in charity with him, she told herself for the hundredth time. He had misinterpreted what had only been feelings of friendship.

Mr. Allan stepped up to her with a smile. "I hope you are not too tired to dance this next one with me."

"Of course not," she answered immediately, though she was feeling a bit tired after the two long dances. But she'd rather be on the floor than standing where Mr. Marfleet could approach her.

By the time the next sets ended with Mr. Allan, Mr. St. Leger was awaiting her with a glass of champagne. "It is almost time for supper."

"I could use a few moments to sit down." She took the glass although she wished he had brought her a glass of lemonade. But she didn't wish to disappoint him, so with a grateful smile she took a sip, fanning herself at the same time.

The champagne was not as refreshing as she liked, and she wished once more she had a glass of lemonade.

"Is something the matter with it?" he asked at her elbow.

She realized she'd been staring down at the rising bubbles. "Not at all." She took another sip then smacked her lips a few times. "It seems just a little bitter, that is all."

"Not all champagnes are the same. You probably had a sweeter one before. This one is 'brut,' a dry one. I thought it time to educate your palate," he added with a lazy smile.

She returned his smile, not wishing to appear unsophisticated. "I see." She took another sip. "That must be the reason."

When she had finished the glass, he said, "Shall we go into the supper room?"

She looked around for Megan or Céline but didn't see them immediately. As if guessing her thoughts, he said, "I saw your companions enter the supper room already."

"Oh." How strange they hadn't waited for her, but perhaps Céline had needed to sit down and they hadn't cared to wait for the set to end. "Very well, let us go. Perhaps there will be room to sit with them."

"I wouldn't be too optimistic. There is quite a crowd by the looks of it. But Cubby promised to save us some seats."

She merely nodded. When she took a step, a wave of dizziness passed over her. She brought a hand to her forehead.

St. Leger's hand was immediately at her elbow, his other taking the empty glass from her. "Steady there."

"I . . . felt a trifle light-headed."

"A bit of food and some more champagne should take care of that."

She laughed. "Perhaps no more champagne. I must remember not to drink it as if it's lemonade."

He chuckled and led her to the supper room. When they entered it and stood a moment surveying the crowded tables, she felt relief at stopping. The room had begun to move in waves around her as they walked.

She leaned against her companion's arm, feeling as if she were on a ship.

St. Leger touched her hand, which rested in the crook of his arm. "Is everything all right, my dear?"

She shook her head to clear it. "Yes, I think so." She attempted to stand straighter but only felt the floor moving beneath her. "Goodness." She giggled, finding it funny that she should be on a ship and no one else aware of it. She didn't think she'd ever been on a ship before. Once on a small boat when her family had made a trip to the seaside.

This feeling reminded her of its pitching up and down as each wave hit the prow.

"Here, you'd best sit down." St. Leger helped her into a seat at the table filled with his friends. A young lady sat across from her with Reggie Layton. Jessamine smiled at them.

St. Leger bent close to her. "I shall bring you back some refreshment and victuals."

"Some lemonade," she said.

"If you say so, my dear."

Cubby, who sat beside her, smiled. "Can't drag you from the dance floor, can we?"

"I do like to dance." She opened her fan. "But it does get a little warm in there."

"That's why I believe in sitting back and partaking of the food and drink."

The young lady said, "Of which you have partaken more than your fair share." He laughed uproariously and turned back to his plate. Jessamine continued to fan herself, not feeling at all well. The room was taking on a strange aura as if the people looked wavy. She blinked to hold them in place.

St. Leger returned and set a plate and glass before her. "Eat something so you may get a second wind for dancing and I shall return in a thrice with my own."

"Thank you." She took the glass, thinking for a moment it would give way in her hand. What a funny thought. She took a sip, glad to find it was lemonade. Since she'd drunk that champagne, she was not feeling at all herself. Perhaps if she had this, it would counter the effects of the spirits.

"You must have been dashed thirsty," Mr. Layton said across from her.

She looked at her glass and realized she'd downed half of it. "Yes, it was all the dancing."

She took up her napkin and unfolded it and focused on her plate. It was filled with miniature tarts and custards, a few slices of ham, a roll, some pats of butter and dollops of mustard to the side. She squinted because everything seemed to be moving.

She reached out and tried to spear some of the ham, but she missed. The tines of the fork clacked against the china.

She smothered a laugh and quickly looked around to make sure no one had noticed. The lady was looking at her strangely, and she smiled before quickly looking down at her plate again.

This time she tried for a tartlet. Slowly, she reached out and aimed for it. She breathed a sigh of satisfaction when her fingers touched the fluted pastry.

She brought it to her mouth, afraid she would miss her mouth. A second later the tart hit her lips and she smothered another laugh, realizing she had miscalculated the distance between her hand and her mouth.

She nibbled on the crab-filled tart, savoring the flaky pastry and flavorful insides, hoping the food in her stomach would make everything right.

St. Leger returned and took the seat beside her. "How is everything?" He looked at her intently until she blushed, hoping she didn't have crabmeat around her mouth. Where had she put the napkin?

"Delicious." She looked around for her napkin. It was on her lap but appeared to be floating, a big white blob. Where was her quizzing glass? She couldn't remember.

She managed to bring the napkin to her mouth.

St. Leger turned away from her, setting to his own food.

She reached for another tart, and with a bit of fumbling she grasped it.

She continued eating with difficulty, allowing the lively conversation to go on around her without trying to join in. Her vision seemed more fuzzy than usual. Generally she could see fine near at hand, but now even the things on her plate appeared blurry.

The meal seemed interminable, but finally it was over, and the others began to stand. She was gearing herself to stand, hoping her legs wouldn't wobble beneath her, when St. Leger placed a hand under her elbow.

"Thank you," she said breathlessly, holding onto the edge of the table and heaving herself up.

"Are you quite sure you are well?" he said in a low voice at her ear.

"I'm not sure," she whispered. "I am feeling a . . . a bit strange," she admitted with an embarrassed smile.

He tucked her hand into the crook of his arm, and she felt tethered. But as soon as she took her first step, a wave of dizziness washed over her so strongly she stopped and gripped his arm. "I don't know what is wrong. I've never felt this way before." Even her words sounded as if they were coming from far away. The floor looked far down below her feet.

"Perhaps you are overheated. It is infernally warm in here."

She shook her head and then regretted it, since it made her feel as if she were underwater. "I never feel this way after dancing, and I'm accustomed to dancing several sets without pause."

He chuckled. "Perhaps out in the country but not in London. The air is stuffier and dirtier, if you haven't noticed. Come, my dear, I shall take you out to enjoy some of that 'fresh' city air."

"I don't know . . ." She tried to look around him for Megan or Céline but couldn't manage it around his broad chest.

He began leading her toward the door. "I think some fresh air first, and then if you aren't feeling better, I'll send a footman to look for Mrs. Phillips and let them know you are indisposed."

"I'm so sorry. I feel such a nuisance. Perhaps something I ate . . . although I began to feel . . . funny before . . ." Her words sounded slurred, and it was taking too much effort to form them, so she allowed herself to be led out of the supper room. In truth, she didn't care where he took her as long as it was away from everyone, somewhere she could sit and the world could stop spinning.

She was hardly aware of where she was going until the cooler night air hit her face. She took in great gulps of it, smelling its whiff of coal smoke, refuse, and greenery. She had no idea where she was since the night was so dark. The torchlight flickered and wavered in the distance. Maybe she was in outermost space among the stars, though she couldn't see any stars in the murky sky.

Instead of leading her to a bench, St. Leger kept walking, his arm now around her shoulders to steady her.

"May . . . may I . . . sit . . ." Those simple words had caused too much effort to form in her brain, she was hardly aware if she'd uttered them except that he murmured close to her ear, "In a moment, my dear."

Then she heard something like a latch of a door or gate, and then his voice, more commanding but still low.

She was being led up a step. The sway of something—was it a coach?—and finally, blessedly, she was able to sink down on a seat.

Her body immediately slumped to the side. The smell of leather reached her nostrils. The next moment she heard the sharp voice of St. Leger then a more forceful swaying of the seat she lay across. Then he was beside her again, propping her against him, his arm once more around her.

"There, you will feel better in a moment."

Besides the dizziness within herself, there was more movement. Was she in a carriage? Was that the clop-clop of horse hooves? How had she gotten here? She brought a hand to her head and felt a thick strand of hair tumbling across her neck and shoulder. She must appear a fright.

She giggled at the thought. What mattered was not how she looked but that she wouldn't be sick in front of this elegant gentleman. What he said about champagne—there was sweet and . . . dry . . .

"W-where are we . . . going?" she mumbled. As if in a dream, she felt her words were not coming out so as to be understood.

"Someplace where you will feel better," he murmured against her temple, smoothing her skin with his fingertips. The rhythmic movement eased her for a while. Her eyelids felt heavy. Her head felt heavy. With a slight pressure of his hand, her head easily dropped against his chest.

17

Lancelot craned his neck to look into every nook and cranny of the ballroom, which was beginning to fill up again as couples returned from the supper room.

Every time he had seen Miss Barry this evening, she seemed to be with St. Leger. The man had taken her in to supper, and he had departed the supper room with Miss Barry leaning on his arm.

Lancelot's disquiet grew as he continued scanning the ballroom and saw no sign of Miss Barry. Where had St. Leger taken her? He pictured her once again in St. Leger's arms in a secluded garden.

His conscience smote him as he remembered his own conduct. But he knew his kiss had not been premeditated. It had been broad daylight where anyone could have seen them. But more importantly, Lancelot had made clear the next day that his intentions were honorable. That Miss Barry had spurned him in no uncertain terms was beyond his control.

"I would never consider marrying a vicar."

Her words still hurt as much as when she'd uttered them. They'd shocked him too. With them she'd repudiated her own father and all Lancelot valued most.

She'd intimated that St. Leger had also proposed.

The thought didn't sit well with Lancelot. Yet that would be preferable to Lancelot's suspicions about St. Leger. His instincts continued to tell him a man with the proper intentions wouldn't take a young lady out to a dark terrace and embrace her.

Lancelot circled the ballroom as these thoughts dashed about his brain like a fly looking for an outlet. He reentered the supper room, his glance never still. But few people lingered. Waiters moved about, clearing away the remains of food and setting chairs right.

He returned to the ballroom. With a sigh of relief he spied Miss Phillips standing with Captain Forrester.

The captain smiled broadly. "I haven't seen you dance all evening. We must find you a partner."

He tried to smile but couldn't manage it. "You haven't by chance seen Miss Barry?"

Miss Phillips looked sympathetic. "Not since supper. By the time we came in, she was sitting with Mr. St. Leger and his party. When we had finished, she had already left. Céline and I did find it strange she had not sought us out to go into supper, but since she sat with a group, we thought she would be all right."

"Yes, I saw her then too," he said distractedly. "But I have been looking for her since they left the supper room and have not seen either of them."

Miss Phillips bit her lip. "Perhaps she is in the retiring room. I could look for her if you think it's necessary."

Captain Forrester gave him a keen look from under his dark blond brows. "Is this St. Leger a decent sort of chap?"

Lancelot hesitated to say anything in front of Miss Phillips. Better he allow them to believe he was only a jealous suitor. But he needn't have said anything. The captain seemed to understand and turned to Miss Phillips. "Why don't you search the rooms set apart for the ladies? Marfleet and I can find Mrs. Phillips and inquire of her. If she hasn't seen Miss Barry, we'll scout outside a bit. Maybe she needed some air. We can meet in a few moments at the entrance of the ballroom."

Miss Phillips nodded, a frown furrowing her brow.

"Thank you," Lancelot said to the captain when they parted from Miss Phillips.

"No need. So, this fellow's a bit disreputable?"

Lancelot nodded grimly. "Let us just say he is not the marrying sort, to my knowledge. But he usually does not interest himself in respectable young ladies."

They searched for Mrs. Phillips as they spoke in undertones.

"Why Miss Barry, do you think? Her dowry?"

"No—none to speak of. All I can think is that she has little protection here in London, only Lady Beasinger, an impoverished widow."

Captain Forrester nodded.

They approached Mrs. Phillips, who sat with some matrons in a quiet parlor. When she saw their serious faces, she excused herself.

"Is something the matter?"

They told her and she began to move toward the ballroom. "Let me help you search for her."

"Miss Phillips will rejoin us at the entrance there. We're going to search outside."

A quarter of an hour later they met again. Lancelot's gut tightened in worry when he saw Miss Phillips and her sister-in-law standing alone.

"No sign of her?" he asked.

Mrs. Phillips shook her head, glancing at each of them in turn. "You didn't find her either?"

"No," Captain Forrester answered tersely. "We've looked both in the front and back of the house. We even asked your coachman if he'd seen her. Nothing."

Lancelot didn't want to speak but felt he must say what he found most significant. "We've seen no sign of St. Leger either." He squared his shoulders. "I'm going to inquire of the footmen if they saw any couple matching their description leaving."

Up to now they had been discreet in their search.

Mrs. Phillips drew in a sharp breath. "You don't think—"

She left the thought unspoken, but Captain Forrester said, "It's too soon to know what to think, but we must locate Miss Barry without delay."

Lancelot addressed Mrs. Phillips. "Perhaps if you pleaded fatigue, you can make your excuses and depart. If the captain will make inquiries of some of her dance partners with the excuse that you are leaving, I can ask some of the servants for any information."

When they agreed to this plan, Lancelot went in search of the footmen. He questioned the porter, all the footmen, and even the butler to no avail. He began to question the coachmen and grooms loitering outside with their owners' carriages, but no one had noticed a lady and gentleman leaving. It would be too common a sight to cause undue notice.

His alarm growing with each passing minute, he finally descended the service stairs to the kitchen area, where he was able to get information from a kitchen maid.

"I saw a gent escorting a young lady out the back way," she told him.

After giving her some coins for her trouble, he raced outside to the mews. When he flashed some coins to a stable hand, the man grunted. "Seen a lady and gent leave from here." He jutted his grizzled chin down the alleyway leading out to the main street.

"Did you glimpse their faces at all? I mean, did they appear to you as a young couple or an older couple?"

"Oh, young for certain, sir. The lady appeared a bit unsteady on her feet as if she'd imbibed a bit too freely o' the punch." He chuckled with a shake of his head. "The gent had 'is arm around her, steadying her like."

Lancelot's stomach lurched. "How long ago?"

The man removed his cap and scratched his head. "A half-hour ago, mayhap less, mayhap more."

Lancelot gave the man the half crown and turned away, his insides feeling scraped raw. Could it have been St. Leger and Miss Barry?

He remembered the man's description. The lady appeared unsteady. Had she drunk champagne again, enough to make her foolish enough to leave alone with St. Leger? What could she have been thinking?

Fear clawed at his throat even as anger threatened to obliterate his reason. If St. Leger dared lay a hand on her—

He found the others standing together at the entrance to the ballroom. "Have you found out anything?" Mrs. Phillips asked.

He stepped closer with a glance around to assure he was not being overheard. "A young couple left in a carriage parked in the mews perhaps a half hour ago."

Miss Phillips stifled a gasp, but Mrs. Phillips maintained her steady gaze. "Just about when supper was over. Do you think it could have been St. Leger?"

He chose his words carefully. "I must assume it was since we haven't found them anywhere."

"Then we shall have to track them down."

He had already thought what best to do. "Madam, I think you should go home with Miss Phillips. Everyone will assume Miss Barry has left with you. You mustn't overtire yourself," he added without embarrassment. As a vicar and missionary, he was accustomed to addressing topics others would find unmentionable in polite society.

Before she could protest, Captain Forrester said, "Marfleet is right. I will go with him to search for Miss Barry. Perhaps you will find her home when you arrive."

Mrs. Phillips shook her head. "She wouldn't have left without informing me."

Miss Phillips spoke up. "Do you think she could have gone to Lady Bess's instead?"

"She had plans to spend the night with us. She would not have changed anything without informing us."

Lancelot hadn't wanted to mention the other thing, but now found himself forced to. "A groom told me the lady appeared . . . unsteady on her feet."

Both females turned wide eyes on him. "She appeared unwell?" Mrs. Phillips asked.

He hesitated before nodding. "Perhaps she was too unwell to make her way to you."

"Then St. Leger would have informed me—if he was any kind of gentleman," Mrs. Phillips said between her teeth. She looked at him directly as if coming to a decision. "Very well, I shall call for my carriage. If you could send word as soon as you know anything. We shall be up. If you find her, you must bring her to my home straightaway . . . before any harm is done."

"Don't worry, either of you. We shall find them. Come, I've already called for your carriage."

After they had seen the ladies off, Lancelot said to the captain, "I'm going to talk with some of St. Leger's set and see if I can find out where his lodgings are."

"I already inquired of them. None had seen her since they sat together at supper." He frowned. "I couldn't help noticing a bit of reticence on the part of a couple of them. That fellow—Cubby, I think they call him—and another one, Layton. Do you wish me to accompany you?"

"Better not. We need to be as discreet as possible. I fear already we've probably raised people's curiosity."

"I shall call a hackney if you wish."

"I shall be with you directly."

Lancelot made his way through the ballroom. He spotted Cubby standing with Layton.

They nodded to him. Both men seemed to observe him with

amusement. Lancelot gritted his teeth, praying for a civil tone of voice. "A word, if you please," he managed in a low tone.

They moved apart with him.

He didn't bother with a preamble. "I need to know where St. Leger takes his lightskirts."

Displaying no surprise at his question, Reggie Layton flipped open his snuffbox and took a minuscule sniff before looking at Lancelot again. "You will pardon me if that is not a question I choose to answer lightly. Point of honor, you understand."

Lancelot gave him a level look. "When it involves a young lady, it no longer becomes a point of honor to hide his haunts from someone concerned with her welfare."

"Perhaps you should ask his man."

"A valet will hardly divulge his master's whereabouts to an outsider."

The man turned away from him with a sigh. "I'm afraid I cannot satisfy your—er—curiosity, no matter who is involved. Point of honor," he repeated, his voice fading away in the din.

Lancelot ground his teeth. Cubby was watching him with uncertain eyes.

Knowing he wouldn't speak to him in front of the other man, Lancelot made a slight indication with his head and then made his way out of the ballroom.

With effort he kept from pacing the floor. Instead, he prayed. *Dear God, have mercy on Miss Barry, wherever she is, whoever she is with. If it's with St. Leger, help me find her. Let me find her in time.*

He stood by the doorway, ignoring the people who walked in and out, the laughter and conversation floating by him.

Too engrossed in praying—and imagining what was happening to Miss Barry—he didn't notice Cubby approach him until he cleared his throat beside him.

Relief poured through him like a sluice of water. He straightened from the wall and motioned to an anteroom. "There's a small parlor here."

As soon as he'd closed the door behind him, Lancelot faced Cubby. "Can you give me any information about St. Leger's whereabouts?"

Cubby looked pained and didn't quite meet his eyes. "All I know is Miss Barry didn't seem to be feeling well and he told me he was taking her home."

"Not feeling well—not inebriated?" He forced out the last word through stiff lips.

Cubby puffed out his cheeks, a shadow marring his guileless blue eyes. "Hard to say. She did seem a bit giggly, but so do most of the young ladies present here." He shook his head, pondering. "Didn't seem quite herself though. Strange-like, even at supper."

Lancelot narrowed his eyes, trying to fathom his meaning. "'Strange-like'—how?"

Cubby tipped his head up and scratched his chin under the high cravat. "Can't remember precisely, apart from the giggling." He snapped his fingers. "I know! She went to take something off her plate and didn't connect with it."

Lancelot frowned. "What do you mean?"

"You know." He made a motion to illustrate. "Say I'm going to spear a piece of meat and my fork clean misses it."

Lancelot's frown deepened. "That sounds like intoxication."

Cubby lifted one shoulder. "Perhaps . . . still, it didn't seem that way. But could be. You give a young lady one glass of champagne and it goes to her head."

"Was she drinking champagne?"

Cubby blinked. "Yes. I remember seeing it because it was the pink variety. Oh, not at the table. St. Leger brought her lemonade there, but before we went into the supper room, I remember seeing her with a glass of the bubbly." He nodded, growing more sure. "But she wasn't garrulous or overly loud the way one would expect with someone . . . you know . . . who's—" He made a motion of bringing an imaginary glass to his lips.

"Thank you." Lancelot's worry grew as Cubby confirmed his fears. He hesitated, deciding how to return to his first question but mindful that time was passing. "Do you know if there is anywhere St. Leger would take a woman . . ." He left the question dangling.

Cubby's plump cheeks turned pink, and he looked to the side. "Well, ahem, you know . . . uh . . ." Finally, he sucked in a breath and said in a low voice, "There is an inn, the Apple and Thistle on the Knightsbridge Road. He's been known to go there."

"Thank you."

As he moved past him, Cubby held him back with a touch on the elbow. "I hope you find her." The words were halting, but there was a look of genuine sympathy in his eyes.

"So do I."

He needed no further confirmation of his own suspicions, but the fact that St. Leger's own friend believed the worst only deepened Lancelot's sense of urgency.

Let me be in time. Dear God, let me be in time. Jesus, protect her . . .

Jessamine woke to flickering shadows on a low plastered ceiling, its dark, thick beams giving the room a medieval cast.

She shifted her gaze, sensing someone beside her.

Mr. St. Leger gazed down at her, his head propped on his hand.

She backed away from his proximity. "Mr. St. Leger—w-what are you doing here? Where are we?" She brought a hand to her head, but the movement took effort. Her limbs felt heavy. Why was she lying down? She attempted to sit but couldn't muster the strength to lift herself from the soft bedding.

Why was she on a bed, a straw-filled mattress by the rustle and deepness of it? And why was Mr. St. Leger lying beside her, his body touching hers?

Panic welled up in her. She sought Mr. St. Leger's eyes once more.

He smiled, the soft candlelight reflecting off his eyes, their pupils wide. "Shh," he whispered, trailing a finger along her cheek and playing with a tendril of her hair.

"W-what are you doing? Where am I?"

"At an inn. Waiting for you to wake up, my dear."

His answers confused her. "An inn?" she echoed.

He nodded slowly, his eyes half-lidded.

Her heart thudded, drowning out the last word. Had he said an *inn*? "Why?"

His fingertip continued its trip along her earlobe and down to her jaw. Blood coursed through her eardrums. "Please," she whispered, but her lips had trouble forming words. She still felt woozy, as if she'd been drugged.

Drugged. The idea took hold in her confused thoughts as fear sent pinpricks tingling over her skin. She remembered feeling dizzy. Where had that been? Hadn't she been at a ball?

His lips curled upward, deepening their sinister cast. Why hadn't she noticed it before? "Please what? Stop? Or . . ." He paused, drawing his head closer until his lips almost touched hers.

The breath from his nostrils fanned her face. A scent of a masculine cologne like sandalwood tickled her nose.

Then he closed the gap between their mouths.

She brought her two hands up but could do little against his weight atop her. Her movements were weak and sluggish. She remembered feeling as if she were on a boat.

That dizziness seemed to have passed, but her limbs now felt like sodden blankets, too heavy to lift.

How long had she been sleeping? Had Mr. St. Leger done something to her while she slept?

A scream filled her throat, but it had no outlet. She was suffocating, but he didn't draw his lips away. Instead they ground against hers, his chin abrading hers.

She began to writhe, but her movements brought his hands up to encircle her wrists. He pinned them down above her head.

She began to buck him, her panic overwhelming her, blotting out all ability to think but giving her strength.

Save me, Lord, she cried silently, tears trickling down her temples. *Jesus, help me!*

Her efforts seemed to have no effect on her captor. "You won't get away from me, my sweet, so stop fighting me," he murmured along the side of her mouth, his lips moist.

She moved her face away. "Please, let me go," she whimpered when she could find breath.

He was everywhere she turned.

Her brief burst of energy left her, and her body seemed incapable of obeying her commands. "Please, Mr. . . . St. Leger . . . please," she begged whenever she could get a word out. "Please . . ."

He made no reply but continued to kiss her, his lips traveling down her neck. One hand loosened around her wrist, but her relief was short-lived as it began to move over her body.

Even as he began to grope her gown, she realized with a gasp of relief that she was fully dressed.

St. Leger began pushing down her low neckline.

The worst nightmare that could befall a young lady was happening to her, and she could do nothing about it. All those silly gothic novels she'd read flashed through her mind. What had seemed heart-stopping but fascinating reading while sitting on a window seat or reclining in her bed, knowing there would be a rescue for the heroine, now appeared horrific in reality.

She was ruined. No hero would come charging in the door for her. St. Leger had her pinned down so effectively she could scarcely breathe, let alone move. The heaviness of her limbs was more effective than ropes would have been.

Tears soaked the pillow cover beneath her as she continued to beg God for help.

"Don't cry, my sweet. You will see how pleasurable it all is, I promise you," St. Leger murmured, kissing away her tears.

Muffled voices sounded through the door. Jessamine's breath hitched as she tried to gain enough air in her lungs to call out.

Before she could utter a sound, loud pounding shook the panels. St. Leger lifted his head, looking toward the door. "Go away—this room is occupied," he bellowed.

The next second it burst open, splintering the wood around the simple lock.

Jessamine gasped at the sight of two men striding into the room. She squinted, wishing she could see more clearly.

"You swine!"

It was Mr. Marfleet's voice in a roar she'd never heard. The next instant he hauled St. Leger off her and threw him to the floor.

The other man—Captain Forrester—bent over her. She cringed with shame, drawing her body up close.

"Easy there," the captain crooned, bending over her.

Her hands clutched at her gown, pulling it up.

"Did he hurt you?"

She shook her head, her breath coming in gasps. He helped her sit up. She strained to look around him, hearing a loud thud from the floor.

The two men were rolling on the plank floor, grunts and angry exclamations issuing from them.

"Pardon me—if you are sure you are all right." Captain Forrester rose.

She nodded. "Please, help Mr. Marfleet."

He bent over the men and tried to separate them. "She is unharmed. We must go."

Jessamine groped at her waist and found her quizzing glass still tied to its ribbon. She brought it up to her eye and saw Mr. Marfleet straddle Mr. St. Leger, his arm lifted. Captain Forrester caught his fist and held it back.

Marfleet and St. Leger eyed each other, panting heavily. Mr. Marfleet was rumpled, his spectacles askew, his hair wild, but otherwise he appeared unhurt. A trickle of blood slid down the side of St. Leger's mouth, a mouth that had so recently mauled hers. Jessamine scrubbed at her lips.

"We must get her away from here," the captain said, his words finally penetrating Mr. Marfleet's understanding.

Slowly, he lowered his arm and rose, keeping his gaze fixed on St. Leger. Captain Forrester helped Mr. St. Leger to stand.

"Before he challenges you to meet him on Hounslow Heath, I urge you to leave here and keep silent of what has transpired tonight. Not a word will leave your lips—or those of your friends," Captain Forrester told St. Leger, his voice quiet but deadly serious.

When St. Leger said nothing, the captain glanced toward her. "It appears we arrived in time to prevent any lasting harm. If we hadn't, be assured we would haul you up before the magistrates and force you to honor Miss Barry. As it is, I am sure she will be satisfied never seeing your dishonorable face again."

St. Leger wiped his mouth, shifting his gaze to Mr. Marfleet before coming to rest on her. She cowered, crossing her arms in front of her. "Miss Barry is here willingly."

Mr. Marfleet growled, his fists coming up. Captain Forrester held him back. "Give us your word that no breath of scandal will touch Miss Barry's name."

Mr. St. Leger straightened his waistcoat, then reached for his jacket on a chair. As if he were going out for a stroll, he donned the jacket then took up his greatcoat, hat, and gloves.

"If I hear so much as a whisper of anything touching Miss Barry's name, be sure I shall hunt you down," Mr. Marfleet said in a voice of steel to Mr. St. Leger as he stood near the door, one hand upon the handle.

Placing his hat upon his head, Mr. St. Leger looked in her direction. "Good evening, Miss Barry. I will not say it has been a pleasure." Before the other men could move, he addressed them. "You have my word."

The next second he was gone, the thud of his boots fading down the corridor.

Jessamine huddled on the edge of the bed, wishing she could hide.

18

Lancelot wished he didn't have to face Miss Barry. He hadn't thought of much beyond rescuing her when he and Captain Forrester had rushed here from London.

As the blinding rage faded, all he felt was cold disdain and the most profound disappointment in the woman he'd given his heart to. He didn't think he could ever erase the image of her pinned under St. Leger.

He wiped a hand over his eyes to dispel it.

"Miss Barry, come, we'll take you home." Captain Forrester's soothing tone shook Lancelot from the stupor he seemed to be in.

He lifted his gaze until it met hers. She looked disheveled but still clothed. Captain Forrester was right. They had come just in time. Overwhelming relief filled him. If that swine had ruined her, Lancelot would have killed him. He still felt the anger hovering dangerously close to the surface of his reason.

He could only watch as Captain Forrester put a hand under her elbow to help her stand. "Good, you still have your shoes on. Now to find your cloak."

She put a hand to her head. "How long have I been here?"

"You don't know?" Captain Forrester's gaze met his across Miss Barry's head. "Do you mean you were unconscious?"

"I . . . think . . . so. I remember so little."

"You can tell us in the coach. We need to get you back home before anyone suspects you were not at the ball."

At the last word, she put a trembling hand to her lips, and tears started to trickle down her cheeks. Lancelot felt more pain than any blows St. Leger had given him. He clenched his fists in an effort not to be softened by her tears.

"I can't go home—I can't go—"

"Shh," Captain Forrester whispered. "We're taking you to Mrs. Phillips. She's waiting for you. No one knows anything and no one need know anything. It's thanks to Mr. Marfleet here that we found you in the nick of time. The ball is still going on, no one need be the wiser that anything happened to you."

Slowly she raised her head and met Lancelot's gaze. There was a stunned, lost look in her eyes. Her mouth quivered, and she covered it quickly with her hand.

He felt frozen, unable to go to her and comfort her. Why had she gone with St. Leger? How could she?

Captain Forrester looked about him for her cloak, and seeing it at the end of the bed, he wrapped it around her. Then he led her to the door, his arm around her since she appeared unsteady on her feet.

At that hour, the inn was quiet and Captain Forrester was able to escort her out without anyone seeing her but the innkeeper, who eyed her as she passed him.

Lancelot walked behind them with a sharp nod to the man. The man quickly looked away and turned his attention back to wiping down the bar. They'd had to bribe him and threaten him before he'd divulged St. Leger's presence.

Once in the carriage, Lancelot sat facing Miss Barry. The coach swayed along the bumpy road. Everything was dark save the small light cast by the outside lanterns.

"Can you tell us what happened?" Captain Forrester asked once they had gotten underway and he'd tucked a travel rug about her.

"I can . . . can hardly think . . . straight." Her words were slow, as if she had a hard time forming them. Once again she brought a hand to her head. "I scarcely remember. My . . . my head feels . . . like lead."

"Perhaps something was given you?"

She raised her head, frowning.

Captain Forrester enunciated each word, as if speaking to a child. "Someone may have put something in a drink, something to cause you to lose consciousness."

She brought a hand to her mouth. "How . . . ?"

"Did you have anything to drink?"

She hunched over, her hands to her temples as if it hurt to think. Lancelot kneaded his knuckles, wishing he'd caused St. Leger more harm. If that man had drugged an innocent young lady . . . A wave of revulsion swept through him.

He'd seen much vile conduct among young gentlemen, both at college and among officers in India, but he'd never known a gentleman to take advantage of a young lady of gentle birth. Among women they considered beneath them socially, they exercised no scruples.

"I . . . seem . . . to recall . . . something—champagne." She looked up as if having solved a puzzle. "He . . ." At the mention of St. Leger, she averted her gaze. "He brought me some," she finished in a low tone, forcing Lancelot to lean forward to hear.

"I saw him," Lancelot found himself saying.

They both looked at him. "I was looking for you," he said with difficulty, "to—to ask you in to supper. I saw him bring you a glass of champagne." The words sounded accusatory even to his ears.

Her gaze fell and she nodded. "I . . . I remember drinking it." She gasped.

"What is it?" Captain Forrester asked, bending near her. Lancelot wished he were the one sitting beside her to put his arm around her. She looked so forlorn, so lost.

"I remember saying it . . . tasted differently."

Captain Forrester met Lancelot's gaze across the shadowy interior. "Was it bitter?"

"I don't remember . . . only that it was not sweet." Her words continued slowly, as if she were still having trouble remembering or stringing the words together. "But he said it was a . . . different kind of . . . champagne."

"He must have put something in it to make you more . . . compliant," Captain Forrester said in a grim voice.

"Do you remember anything more?" Lancelot asked, striving to make his tone more gentle.

She swallowed, looking toward the window. "I . . . remember walking into . . . supper. I think I began to feel—yes, yes, I began to feel dizzy." She clutched a hand to her breast. "I thought the room was swaying. But he took me by the arm. I remember sitting down, and the food seemed to be moving on the plate. But I tried to eat—he said I may have danced too much, become overheated."

She turned to Captain Forrester, her look imploring. "But I've danced as much before—I think I told him that—and never felt so. I remember very little more—I think he took me outside. I remember the night air, but I just wanted to sit down . . . and then I was in a coach . . . and then . . ." She fell silent, swallowed, and turned anguished eyes toward Lancelot.

He wanted to erase that haunted look. "It's all right," he managed softly even as his heart felt wrenched in pain. "We arrived in time."

"Thanks to you," Captain Forrester said. He smiled at Miss Barry. "Mr. Marfleet here was the one who noted you missing. He was quite concerned about you. I don't think much time had elapsed since dinner when he asked Miss Phillips and me if we had seen you. He had seen you last with St. Leger and didn't trust him."

Miss Barry stared at Lancelot from the moment the captain mentioned his worry.

"None of us had seen you since supper," the captain continued when Lancelot said nothing. "We immediately began to look for you. As soon as we realized you weren't anywhere in the house, Marfleet here didn't rest. He bribed or browbeat the servants until he found a groom who had seen a carriage leave from the mews."

She shook her head as if to clear it. "From the mews? That's why . . . I seemed to be in a garden and it was dark."

"You must have lost consciousness soon after. I don't think you were at the inn too long. We wasted no time in coming after you once Marfleet found out from one of St. Leger's cronies where he—er—takes . . . ahem . . ."

Her round eyes looked up at him. "Young ladies?"

Even Captain Forrester's cheeks looked ruddy in the semidarkness.

"I'm sure he usually limits his pursuits to lowborn women who can't defend themselves—servant girls, shopgirls, young chorus girls," Lancelot finished for Captain Forrester, capturing Miss Barry's shocked attention once more. He coughed. "That's why it seems so incomprehensible that he should pursue his wicked intentions so far with a young lady."

She brought her hands to her cheeks. "How horrible." She shuddered. After a moment she lifted her gaze to him once more. "But why me?"

"Perhaps he just saw you as a defenseless young woman—your father is not here. You have only Lady Beasinger—a careless chaperon at best, with no real weight in society. I hate to disillusion you about the wiles of men, but he was probably bored and saw you as an easy mark." Lancelot had kept his tone dispassionate, even hard, but he couldn't help himself. He wanted her to realize how close she'd been to utter ruin.

Captain Forrester flicked a look at him. "What he didn't count on is that you had a defender in Mr. Marfleet." The captain pressed her hand. "He may not flaunt his credentials, but never fear, my dear Miss Barry, the Marfleet name is one to be reckoned with in society. St. Leger, whose fortune is indifferent, will keep his word, I am certain."

As the words sank in, she dropped her head in her hands. "I am ruined! How shall I face Papa and Mama?" As if remembering their presence, she shook herself and sat up, looking away from them. "Forgive me—it's not your concern. You have already done more for me than I merit. I deserve whatever comes to me. How could I have been so foolish?" she murmured as if to herself.

Captain Forrester patted her hand that rested in her lap.

Once again Lancelot longed to reach for her and offer her comfort, but something held him back. He could not forget her disdain of him and how she had encouraged St. Leger's advances.

"We are confident there will be no scandal. Unfortunately, it means that we will not be able to do anything to St. Leger directly. If St. Leger has the audacity to show his face in a drawing room or ball, we can only use underhanded means to keep him out. We shall certainly inquire at the clubs and see if he owes money anywhere. If he does, we can use that as leverage to insure his silence."

His words roused her. She clutched his arm. "Please don't do anything, don't say anything! I can never hold my head up again in public."

"There, there, don't fret. Mrs. Phillips and Miss Phillips will be able to comfort you more than we, but be assured, they will be of an opinion with us. We were very discreet this evening, and not too much time elapsed since St. Leger spirited you away. I am sure the ball is only now breaking up." He took his watch out of his waistcoat pocket. "It is going on three. They may not even have played Sir Roger de Coverley yet. Mrs. Phillips pled fatigue and made it clear she was leaving the ball early with both of you. Even if they didn't see you, the guests will assume you all left together. When you appear in public again, no one will be the wiser."

Miss Barry's brief outburst seemed to have cost her all her energy. She lapsed into silence, her gaze fixed on the window for the rest of the ride.

Lancelot spent the time praying to overcome the anger and bitterness lodged in his chest. *Show me what to do, Lord. You see the extent of the vileness, the villainy of that scoundrel. He mustn't be permitted to escape scot-free—to do the same thing to countless other defenseless women.*

By the time they arrived, Miss Barry's head was slumped forward, either from exhaustion or the lingering effects of whatever drug St. Leger had laced her drink with.

Lancelot rose as soon as the coach came to a stop and opened the door and let down the step. There was no footman at the door, for which he was grateful. Surely, Mrs. Phillips had shown wisdom in not alerting the staff. The lamps were still burning. Captain Forrester roused Miss Barry and helped her down. As Lancelot approached the front door, it opened.

Miss Phillips peered round the edge, and when she saw them, she opened it wide. She was dressed in her nightgown and dressing gown, her dark hair braided down her back under a nightcap.

She drew Miss Barry in, hugging her. "Thank God you are all right." She looked at the two of them with a question in her eyes.

Captain Forrester nodded in reassurance. "Apart from the aftereffects of whatever drug she was given, she is unharmed. The best thing is to get her to bed."

Miss Phillips gasped at the word *drug*.

Before she could say anything, Lancelot said, "We will not keep you."

She gave them both a heartfelt thank-you.

Captain Forrester said, "Get some rest, both of you. How is Mrs. Phillips?"

"She is fine. I insisted she go to bed, that I would watch for your return."

"That was wise," the captain said, reopening the door. "We shall be around tomorrow to see how everything is."

He shut the door behind them, and they returned to the carriage.

When they were on their way, Lancelot having given instructions to the driver to drop Captain Forrester at his lodgings, Captain Forrester spoke in the dark interior. "What do you think—will any hint of scandal arise from this night?"

Lancelot drew in a breath, pondering. "It all depends upon how good St. Leger's word is." He motioned toward the front. "I shall pay the jarvey a generous sum, although I don't think he saw Miss Barry, bundled up as she was. She doesn't reside with Mrs. Phillips, so cannot be linked to this address."

"I don't think St. Leger's friends will talk," the captain said. "Why should they wish Miss Barry ill?" He shifted in his seat as if debating. "It's hard to say if speaking to them will have a beneficial or adverse effect."

"Yes." Lancelot rubbed his jaw, feeling the fatigue. "That's what's so frustrating. We don't want to make enemies of them. Yet, I find it hard to countenance allowing St. Leger to walk blameless. But anything we do will only bring attention back to Miss Barry, no matter how innocent she was in the matter."

"You do realize that, don't you?"

Lancelot stared at him in the predawn light. "Why do you say that?"

Captain Forrester shrugged. "At the inn you looked like someone had clobbered you—and that was before your tussle with St. Leger. I would hate to think you have put any of the blame upon Miss Barry for finding herself in this situation."

Lancelot blew out a long breath, wishing the captain had not been so discerning.

"Men like St. Leger use any means, flattery, charm, sympathy, to win a woman's trust," he added. "Incapacitating her with a drug is beyond the pale."

The captain said nothing more, allowing Lancelot to mull on his words. After a moment or two, Lancelot said, "What you say is true. My anger doesn't originate with tonight, however. It has been growing since the evening I saw Miss Barry alone in St. Leger's company—after drinking champagne. I warned her then about him."

"She's very young and innocent about men."

"Yes." The single word expressed his frustration at her dilemma. "But she has been courting disaster for some time now. She should have known better than to go outside alone with a gentleman."

Captain Forrester took his time to respond. "I don't know Miss Barry so I cannot judge her conduct. She and Miss Phillips both seem modest, chaste young ladies."

"Miss Barry's father is a vicar. She has been brought up in a small village vicarage her whole life." Lancelot's voice rose. "Since she arrived in London, she has behaved as if she had conveniently forgotten all she was taught."

"Perhaps all the more reason she was fooled by someone like St. Leger."

Lancelot made an impatient gesture. "Then why hasn't Miss Phillips behaved in the same manner?" Without giving the captain a chance to respond, he shook his head in disgust. "Listen to me! I should be the one who speaks in a careful, reasoned way, not with anger and resentment. After all, I am the clergyman."

Captain Forrester issued a low chuckle. "But my emotions are not involved. If it had been Miss Phillips . . ." He let the words hang in the air a second. "You would not have been able to pry my hands away from St. Leger's neck before snuffing out his last breath."

Megan hugged Jessamine tightly as soon as the door was shut behind them. Jessamine buried her head in Megan's shoulder, the tears finally letting loose. She had had time to piece everything back together during the coach ride, and the horror of it all only grew.

She'd had to rein in her misery and desolation, too embarrassed and humiliated before Captain Forrester—a virtual stranger—and Mr. Marfleet, a man who had admired her to the point of being willing to offer for her. She shuddered, her sobs increasing at the thought of this godly man, whose honor and integrity reminded her of her father's, having witnessed her degradation.

"There now," Megan said in a soothing voice, her hand patting her back. "There now, you're safe," she continued murmuring as she nudged Jessamine away from the door.

Jessamine's legs still felt rubbery, and without Megan's help she didn't think she would have made it up the stairs. Megan led her to her own room and shut the door.

"Come, let's get you undressed and into bed. I brought up some milk which I've kept warm on the hob. It will help calm you."

"D-does everyone know?" Her lips trembled so she could hardly speak.

"Only Céline. She went to bed because we didn't . . ." Megan's voice faltered. "We didn't know when they would find you. Thank God they found you as quickly as they did. I have never been so thankful for anyone as I was for Mr. Marfleet this evening. If it hadn't been for his concern . . ." She shuddered.

Jessamine sat on the edge of Megan's bed, too lethargic to do anything, her heart sinking further at the words.

"I insisted Céline go to bed," Megan continued, "because I knew Rees wouldn't want her up so late, in her condition. But she wanted me to wake her the moment we heard anything."

Jessamine shook her head. "Please don't—"

Megan patted her hands, which lay limply on her lap. "No, I shan't. Here, let's get you out of your gown. Captain Forrester proved himself just as trustworthy and dependable, too, tonight, a true friend."

As she spoke, she helped Jessamine off with her cloak. "Oh, good, you have everything . . . your shawl, your reticule. Let's get your slippers off. Oh, you're cold." She rubbed her hands. "Come, stand by the fire. Your night rail is laid out on the chair here, nice and warm."

Jessamine did as she was told like a child. A naughty one who knew how badly she'd behaved and now wished only for the earth to swallow her up so she'd never have to face anyone again. Why was Megan being so nice to her?

Finally, she was in bed, her face washed, her teeth cleaned. Megan climbed in on the other side and turned to her. "Do you want to tell me about it?"

At Megan's sympathetic look and gentle tone, tears welled up in Jessamine's eyes again. She bit her lip, looking away. She didn't deserve such consideration.

"I'm sorry. You don't have to say anything if you'd rather not."

Jessamine shook her head. "It's so awful." Her voice came out a rough whisper.

Megan laid a hand on her shoulder. "I'm so sorry. We should have been more attentive, more watchful. We saw you having a good time, dancing. We never imagined anyone could behave so vilely—not a gentleman of the ton." She shuddered. "Céline blames herself," Megan added after a moment. "She said she should have been more vigilant of you, knowing St. Leger has a bit of a rakish reputation."

Jessamine's eyes widened in shock. "Why didn't she say anything?"

"It was only a little gossip and no worse than what is said of most of the young blades about town. She never dreamed he'd behave that way with a young lady. She said those gentlemen mostly confine their . . . their philandering to women . . . you know . . . of a certain class." Megan's cheeks reddened and she looked down, plucking at a corner of her pillow. "That is why they are able to behave with decorum with the young ladies they are considering for marriage."

"Mr. Marfleet said he was not trustworthy." If she had only heeded him before it was too late.

Megan's sad gaze met hers. "Yes. Céline doesn't approve of such behavior among the gentlemen of the ton, but said that is the way it is for the most part in London society—and Parisian, as she was quick to add. That's why she was happy—and I was too—when Mr. Marfleet seemed to like you. He is not like that. His older brother is considered a bit fast, but there is no hint of gossip about Mr. Marfleet. If anything, he is teased about being a proper parson."

Jessamine reddened, remembering the way Mr. St. Leger's friends mocked Mr. Marfleet. "That's what makes it worse," she whispered. "Why did it have to be he to see me in such a shameful way?"

Megan put an arm around her. "Shh, you mustn't fret. Thank God it was Mr. Marfleet, that he was so concerned about you. It might have been awhile longer before we noticed that you weren't on the dance floor. I was too taken up with Captain Forrester . . ." Her voice slowed. "I'm so sorry."

"Don't be, please. It's no one's fault but my own. If I hadn't been so flattered by Mr. St. Leger's attention—if I had drunk lemonade instead of champagne, I would have tasted that something was wrong with my drink."

Megan drew away and scanned her face. "How could someone do something so horrible?"

Jessamine shook her head. "As soon as I drank the champagne, I began to feel strange."

She continued speaking, knowing she owed Megan an explanation, however little she wanted to recount the events. How she wished she could blot everything out. She still wasn't feeling wholly normal.

Megan seemed to sense this because she didn't ask any questions, and as soon as she told her how Mr. Marfleet had burst into the room, she patted her hand. "Thank God they came in time. Captain Forrester told me you appeared unharmed . . . and that nothing worse than . . . than inflicting his kisses . . ." She appeared too embarrassed to continue.

Jessamine nodded quickly and looked away. "Yes, that's what they told me. I . . . I had only just come to." She put a hand to her head. "Everything still seems strange. My head feels like a ball of wool."

Megan moved away. "And here I am keeping you up. It's best you sleep and don't fret about anything tonight. Tomorrow we'll sort things out with Céline. She'll know what to do."

"I wish she hadn't been dragged into this," Jessamine said with a moan.

"Don't worry. Céline has been through so much herself, she will not judge you harshly." She turned down the lamp, though dawn was already lightening the room.

Grogginess swallowed Jessamine up in sleep almost immediately, but sleep lasted only a few hours.

She awoke dreaming of dark, malignant creatures. St. Leger's smiling face loomed over hers once again, and she clawed at the air, fending him off.

She opened her eyes with a start and stared at the light seeping in from the heavy curtains.

Megan's even breathing beside her checked her movements, and she fell back on her pillows, relieved that it had only been a dream. But the next moment everything came back to her, and despair and shame overwhelmed her.

Dear God, what have I done? How could I? Why? Dear Lord, why?

Tears filled her eyes, and she stifled the sobs that threatened to erupt. Megan deserved to sleep. She'd been up most of the night because of Jessamine's folly.

Turning carefully in the bed to face away from Megan, Jessamine burrowed under her covers and continued praying. She asked the Lord's forgiveness but felt no solace. She'd courted disaster and now she had to live with the consequences. Her father was a kind, gentle man, but he had brought her up to understand that fact. A person reaped what she sowed.

She had wanted to prove that she was attractive to men as handsome and charming as Mr. St. Leger—and all she'd proved was how vain and shallow a creature she was, her head turned by a handsome face and a few crumbs of attention.

Mr. St. Leger had never had any honorable intentions. She buried her head in her pillow, overcome with humiliation. She couldn't imagine marrying such a despicable, debauched man as that. A man who hid his true character behind a lazy smile and witticisms. She shuddered at how easily she had been duped.

How different from a man of honor and character . . . like Mr. Marfleet, a man she'd disdained from the moment she'd met him but who had been nothing but attentive and gentlemanly. She thought of his anger the night before, how he'd fought Mr. St. Leger.

But then she remembered the look of pain and reproach when he'd met her eyes. She didn't think she could ever face him again.

He had warned her about Mr. St. Leger, and she had willfully scorned him. Well, he'd been vindicated last night. Her face heated. Nothing could punish her more than the fact that he'd witnessed her degradation.

But she would have to face him, no matter how little either of them wished it. For of course, he would never want to be in her company again. He must be thanking the Lord that she had repudiated his near proposal. She stifled a sob in her pillow. She who'd scorned to marry a vicar was now not even worthy of receiving a proposal from a deacon!

Captain Forrester had said something to Megan about coming around today to see how she fared.

Would Mr. Marfleet accompany him? Would his sense of duty, his good manners, compel him? She couldn't face him.

She couldn't bring further shame to Céline and her household, nor taint Megan's season with any association with her. No matter what they said to convince her that scandal could be averted, Jessamine knew it was a false hope. St. Leger might not talk, but his friends all knew.

She remembered their laughing and joking over supper and on other occasions. What had seemed like high spirits and innocent fun now took on lewd and sinister implications. What a fool she'd been—a green girl from the country.

She must leave. Today.

19

She must go home. Jessamine crept out of bed, the resolve forming and hardening in her mind. Though it was early, surely she could find a maid or footman to order a hackney for her.

She began to gather her few things and then changed into the simple morning gown she'd brought when she'd planned to stay the night with Megan.

When she closed the door softly behind her, her valise in her hand, she turned and halted at the sight of Céline outside her own door down the hall.

"You startled me," she said, her hand at her chest.

Céline smiled and approached her. "I'm sorry. I didn't mean to." A frown formed between her brows as she looked at the valise in her hands. "But what is this? I expected you to sleep till noon at least. You don't mean to leave this minute, do you?"

Jessamine's throat closed, and she could hardly get the words out. "I—I must."

The next second Céline put an arm around her and led her away from Megan's room. "Come to my sitting room. I shall ring for some tea or hot chocolate and you will tell me why you must leave. I'm sorry I was not up when you came, but I thank God, from all appearances, they brought you back safe and sound."

The reminder of Mr. Marfleet and Captain Forrester brought the tears to her eyes again.

Céline drew apart from her and looked at her. "He didn't harm you, did he?"

She shook her head. She knew she looked a fright, but it no longer mattered. "No, but . . . but I am ruined, all the same."

Céline tightened her hold around her shoulders. "Nonsense. There is no ill that doesn't appear a bit smaller and manageable after a cup of chocolate and a warm croissant. Thank goodness I woke when I did, since it looks like you were going to abscond without telling a soul, when this is the time when you most need your friends rallying around you."

She brought Jessamine to her private sitting room, a cozy, feminine space, and led her to a comfortable armchair by the fire. "Now, you sit here, put that valise down. I shall ring for a maid to stir up the fire and bring us some breakfast."

"You are too kind," Jessamine said with a sniff. "I don't deserve such consideration."

"Of course you do." Céline tugged on the bellpull. When she returned to her side, she squatted down, taking both of Jessamine's hands in hers and chafing them. "Your hands feel like icicles. I know you feel terrible about yourself right now, but soon you will put things in a better perspective."

Her golden-hued eyes stared up into Jessamine's with a wealth of understanding. "Believe me, my dear, I know what it is to make mistakes and be filled with regrets and heartbreak and to think the world has come to an end as far as one's part in it is concerned. But one thing I will insist you listen to me about."

Jessamine's heartbeat quickened, wondering what this older woman who was so beautiful would say to her. What did she know about heartbreak?

Céline drew in a breath, squeezing her hands, and looked at her steadily. "You are not to blame for St. Leger's abominable and ungentlemanly conduct."

As Jessamine began to shake her head, Céline held her hands

tighter. "Do not reproach yourself. What he did was unpardonable. He deserves a thrashing for absconding with you. I still do not know what happened so you must tell me, although I know you probably wish to forget it all."

"Please, ma'am, sit down. You shouldn't be kneeling there."

Céline smiled and rose from her position. At that moment, there was a soft knock and the maid popped her head in.

After the fire was burning brightly and Céline had given the order for hot refreshment, she sat back in the other armchair. "Now, tell me what happened last night."

Jessamine drew in a breath and braced herself to once more recount the awful course of events as she remembered them. She kept her eyes on the burning sticks of wood in the grate, watching as the hunks of coal ignited.

When she had finished her short recital, Céline nodded. "It could have been much worse. Thank heaven Captain Forrester and Mr. Marfleet were able to locate you so quickly." She tapped her forefinger to her lips, her gaze going to the flames. "I think you can plead indisposition for a few days and then reappear in society. I don't think anyone will be the wiser. St. Leger and his few cronies won't speak. They have a strange code of honor. It may be all right in their book to deflower a defenseless young woman, but they won't brag to polite society about it. They know they would be ostracized."

What about anyone else who might know? When Céline paused, Jessamine said, her voice low but resolute, "I thank you for your understanding—and for trying to help me make the best of things now—but I wish to return home."

At that moment the maid returned and set the breakfast tray on a low table before Céline. After they'd been served and were alone again, Céline said, "Lady Beasinger will still be abed. Trust me, she won't realize a thing has happened—"

"No, I mean I wish to return to Alston Green. Today, if at all possible."

Céline's fine eyebrows rose. She studied Jessamine several seconds. "Do you think that's wise? A precipitous departure might raise gossip more than remaining out of society for a few days."

Jessamine looked back at the fire. "Whether it is wise or not, I feel I must return home. Whatever my responsibility in this—" Her voice choked, and she had to pause a few seconds. "I cannot return to society. I cannot bear to see . . . see speculative glances. Someone will drop a careless word. Or perhaps someone noticed my leaving the ball with him." She drew in a breath as another thought occurred to her. "Surely a servant saw us leave by the back . . ."

She shook her head, her resolution growing. "I must return." She met Céline's gaze once more, her own entreating. "If I could beg you for one more indulgence, I would ask your help in returning to Lady Beasinger now before . . . before anyone else is up. Captain Forrester said something to Megan last night when he brought me home . . . that he—they—would call today." She brought a hand to her mouth. "I really can't bear to see them."

She could speak no further. Tears coursed down her cheeks.

"Oh, dear, don't distress yourself." Céline was at her side, caressing her bowed head. "Of course I shall help you if that is truly what you wish. I know the two gentlemen do not judge you. They are the ones who did their utmost to find you. Why, Mr. Marfleet wouldn't rest until—"

Jessamine sniffed, wiping her nose with her handkerchief. "He looked at me with such shock—and hurt. I cannot subject him to any more." She bowed her head into her hands, bursting into sobs again.

"There, there," Céline soothed, drawing Jessamine to herself. "If he was shocked, it's because he cares so much for you. I could see it in his eyes, in his manner last night when he grew so worried about you. Believe me, upon reflection, he will lay all the blame at Mr. St. Leger's door, not yours, my dear."

Jessamine quieted at last, knowing tears would do no good.

She blew her nose and wiped her eyes. "I must go. I've collected my things. If I've overlooked anything, Megan can bring it to me when next she comes to Alston Green." As she spoke she drew away from Céline and rose from the chair.

"At least finish your croissant."

Jessamine touched her stomach. "I really couldn't eat anything."

With one last searching look, Céline gave a brief nod. "Very well. Let me instruct the footman to call for the coach."

"I can take a hackney."

"Nonsense. It will only take a few more minutes. Sit there." She went to the bellpull once again. Jessamine sat staring into the fire, whose flames had died down to blue flickers and red, glowing coals. She felt too spent to do anything but stare.

When Céline had spoken softly to the maid, she closed the door once more and approached Jessamine.

"If you don't mind, my dear girl, I should like to pray for you before you leave."

Jessamine looked up, startled. "I'm too ashamed to pray."

"That's all right. I shall pray for you. Believe me, when I found myself at the lowest point in my life, I turned to the Lord and He delivered me out of all my distresses." She quoted the psalm with a tender smile.

Jessamine stared at her. How could this beautiful, self-possessed lady have any distresses comparable to her foolishness?

As if guessing her thoughts, Céline's smile deepened. "I thought I had lost everything—and all through my own reckless and carelessly made decisions. I, too, fled London . . . for France." Her features sobered, and she seemed to be looking into the past. "At a time of war when the city was being cut off from the rest of the world. I didn't know what I would find, where I would go . . . and most of all, I was filled with the hopelessness of having lost the only man whom I could truly trust and honor. My heart had been deadened to love for so long. I had no right to this man . . . he belonged to another, and our two countries—our loyalties—kept us apart."

Jessamine knew from the moment Céline began speaking that she would hear of Rees. Her breath caught and she listened spellbound, hearing how it had been from this woman's perspective—Jessamine's rival, the one who had succeeded in stealing the man she'd loved and waited for for so long.

"But this man had given me an invaluable gift." Céline's smile returned as her gaze met Jessamine's once more. "He gave me the gift of his faith. I know you have that same faith, which is one of the reasons Rees had pledged himself to you. You were the only young woman he found honorable and pure and worthy of his love. He would never dishonor you or break his pledge to you, and that was one of the reasons I loved him."

Jessamine caught her breath. Céline had known it was she.

The next moment Jessamine shook her head. "He had never pledged himself to me. There was no betrothal, no understanding."

"Perhaps not spoken, but he honored his commitment just the same."

Jessamine hesitated, but Céline's confession spurred her own. "I wanted to hate you."

Céline pushed a lock of hair away from Jessamine's forehead with a fingertip. "I'm sorry for any hurt I caused you."

"I didn't want your pity. You treated me—and continue to treat me—so nicely. More than I deserve."

Céline smiled. "If I do, it's because I can understand how you feel. Did I not want to hate you, too, at one time?"

They stared at one another a few seconds longer as Jessamine felt the icy shards imbedded in her heart begin to melt. But with the thaw came deeper pain.

"Now, with your permission I will say a prayer for you. The Lord brought me out of my grief, he turned my mourning into dancing, put off my sackcloth and girded me with gladness." Again she quoted a psalm, astonishing Jessamine, who as a girl brought up in a vicarage prided herself on her knowledge of Scripture. She would have thought Céline as a worldly Frenchwoman knew little of the Scriptures.

Céline bowed her head, and Jessamine followed suit.

"Dear heavenly Father, I come before You by the precious blood of Your dear Son, Jesus. He is our justification, our righteousness, and the only plea we have before You. I thank You for protecting my dear sister from evil. Thank You for sending Mr. Marfleet and Captain Forrester to her rescue. Thank You for leading them to where she was and saving her in time. Thank You for Your angels who guarded her during her ordeal.

"Now I ask You, dear Father, that You would continue to guide her. Lift the sadness from her. Fill her with Your joy—the joy of her salvation. Bring peace to her heart. Help her to understand how much You love her, how much You understand her distress.

"Go before her now as she returns to her family. Make the way straight for her and prepare them for her homecoming. Guide her heart so that she may understand the path You have for her. You know the desires of her heart. I pray that You make those desires conform to Your desires for her.

"Now may You bless Jessamine, and keep her, protect her on the road. Silence the voices of gossip and scandal. Give her the right words to explain her homecoming to her mother and father. In the name of Your Son, Jesus, we pray. Amen."

Stillness reverberated in the room. Jessamine slowly opened her eyes and looked up at the other woman. "Thank you. I . . . I feel better." It was the truth, she realized as she uttered the words.

While she was still feeling the warm effects of the heartfelt prayer, she smiled tentatively. "I'm glad Rees found you." Perhaps she wouldn't feel the same tomorrow, but for now, her heart was filled with the love she felt Céline's prayer had imparted to her.

Céline returned her smile. "Thank you. I thank the good Lord every day for him." Her smile disappeared. "I pray for him more than ever now and try to keep my faith. I received a message that Napoleon is heading to the Belgian front."

Jessamine drew in her breath.

"There is bound to be a battle. No one knows how or when, but it will be any day . . . if it has not already occurred. Pray for him."

Jessamine nodded her head. "Of course." Her own situation paled.

"Come, the carriage should be ready."

As Jessamine stood and bent to pick up her valise, Céline spoke again. "I will pray that the Lord send you the right young man, one who is worthy of your love."

Jessamine straightened, her lips twisting. "I am afraid I have dishonored myself beyond repair and am no longer worthy of any honorable man's love."

"Then I shall pray that you feel the Lord's forgiveness and cleansing love. And that you will recognize that young man's love when he appears before you."

Disbelieving her words, Jessamine said nothing but followed her out the door.

Lancelot woke with a start, his hands clutching his covers. He'd been throttling a man's neck. St. Leger, his eyes bulging, pleaded with them for his life.

Reality returned like a wave of bracing seawater, making the sweat on his brow feel clammy. He lay back against the pillow, remembering all that had transpired the evening before: his growing worry and desperation when he realized Miss Barry had left with St. Leger, and then the reality that had hit his eyes when Captain Forrester had opened the door of the room at the inn.

Even now his gut heaved with revulsion at the sight of St. Leger's body covering hers, Miss Barry struggling futilely. If they hadn't arrived then—

He put a hand up to his face, covering his eyes, wishing he could wipe the image away.

He remembered what the new day would bring. He would see her. Captain Forrester said he'd stop by in the early afternoon so they could go together to Mrs. Phillips's town house.

He dreaded seeing Miss Barry in the sobering light of day. Of course he wanted to assure himself that she was all right. She'd been drugged last night. He wanted to ascertain that St. Leger had indeed not harmed her more than what they'd witnessed. Would she remember any more? He'd heard of some drugs—belladonna, for one—which caused memory loss.

Dear God, he prayed, *let there not have been more harm than what we saw. If St. Leger stole her virtue, make him pay, Lord.*

Lancelot ground his teeth, burying his face in his hands, pleading with God.

He remembered the verse: *"Dearly beloved, avenge not yourselves, but rather give place unto wrath: for it is written, Vengeance is mine; I will repay, saith the Lord."*

His own wrath last night and this morning in his dream came back to him like a flood.

Forgive me, Lord, for my wrath. I give it over to You and trust You to right the wrongs that have been done to Miss Barry. I don't want to let go of my anger. I want satisfaction—as any honorable man would in these circumstances, even though I have no right to demand satisfaction. I am nothing to Miss Barry. She will probably despise me even more now since I have witnessed her degradation.

His prayer turned to her, and he asked for God's healing and mercy for her.

Then he sat up and picked up his Bible and spectacles and began to read his daily portion of Scripture.

By the time he rose to dress, he felt stronger in his spirit. The anger was not completely gone, but he felt master of it by God's grace.

When Captain Forrester called for him, Lancelot was impatiently pacing the front hallway. The house was silent; both his parents had returned to their country estate. He hadn't heard a word from Harold in weeks and assumed he must be doing well at the races.

He said a quick prayer for his brother before his thoughts returned to Miss Barry. He'd have gone around to Mrs. Phillips earlier to inquire after her, but Captain Forrester had reminded him last evening that the two young ladies, as well as Mrs. Phillips, would doubtless be exhausted today.

So, it was nearing three o'clock when their carriage finally pulled into the square.

They were obliged to stop behind a couple of other curricles and phaetons which were already stationed directly in front of the large house.

His lips turned down at the thought of having to jostle his way between all the other gentlemen callers who were paying their respects the day after a ball.

The ball seemed an age ago. What was Mrs. Phillips's butler telling these callers? Surely Miss Barry would not be up to receiving anyone?

They made their way to the door just as it opened and a young gentleman emerged, placing his high-crowned hat on his head, his walking stick and gloves still in the other hand. "Good day," he said with a smile as they stood aside to let him come down the steps.

He and Captain Forrester presented their cards to the starchy butler. "Are the ladies receiving today?" the captain asked.

"One moment, sirs, and I will ascertain."

He left them in a small side parlor.

Captain Forrester raised his eyebrows to Lancelot, and Lancelot shrugged. "We shall soon see," he murmured.

The butler returned shortly and indicated they might ascend to the drawing room.

They heard voices through the half-opened doors. When they entered, Lancelot's gaze quickly scanned the room, looking for Miss Barry.

Only Mrs. Phillips graced a settee. The rest of the company were a few gentlemen. She was smiling and responding to what one had said. She appeared as if she had not a care in the world.

She greeted them across the room as soon as they entered. "Good afternoon, gentlemen. I am sure you are both here to call upon my sister, Miss Phillips, and her dear friend Miss Barry." Her smile disappeared, replaced immediately by a sad look. "Alas, the two young damsels are indisposed this morning, both too fatigued to leave their rooms this day."

She turned to the other gentlemen. "I fear Miss Barry has contracted an influenza, so I have told her in no certain terms to stay abed. We've had maids running up and downstairs with hot toddies and broth." She smiled at Lancelot and Captain Forrester again. "It's a wonder any young lady survives the season without falling ill. Going out till the wee hours then shopping, teas, and rides in the park the next day." She clucked her tongue. "I must avow I am glad that I am long past that."

Lancelot was torn between worry for Miss Barry and the suspicion that Mrs. Phillips was fabricating her illness. But how to find out what was the true situation?

There was nothing for it but to wait. Thankfully, Captain Forrester was more adept than he at making idle conversation. Lancelot found it difficult just to sit and pretend interest in all the latest society on-dits.

After some minutes, the other gentlemen rose. Mrs. Phillips rang for the butler. As the men bid their farewells to the captain and him, she signaled the butler and whispered a few words to him.

When the door had closed behind the men, she turned her attention to them with a smile. "I told him not to admit anyone else." She clasped her hands on her knees and leaned forward, her manner all businesslike. "Now, I know you are anxious to hear how Miss Barry fares. She is fine—physically."

Her amber-hued eyes focused on Lancelot. "She is understandably quite broken up emotionally—and spiritually. She has given me only a cursory summary of how much she remembers, which is precious little, thank goodness."

She held up her hand, stalling any questions. "But before I go any further, I must tell you that she is gone."

Lancelot's jaw dropped open.

"What?" Captain Forrester demanded.

Mrs. Phillips nodded. "She was up at dawn. As was I, thank goodness, or she should have sneaked out before any of us was aware." She smoothed down the silk of her gown. "She felt so badly that she wanted nothing more than to return to her home." Again, her gaze went to Lancelot before including the captain. "Her home in Alston Green."

Lancelot swallowed, hardly believing what he was hearing. "You can't mean you allowed her to make the trip today alone?"

She nodded sadly. "Believe me, I tried to persuade her otherwise, but she was adamant. I insisted she take my coach first to Lady Beasinger and tell her she was feeling overtired and homesick. I shall pay her a visit later and explain things more fully . . . though we both agreed that the less Lady Beasinger knows, the better."

They nodded.

"I lent her my traveling chaise although, again, she insisted she could take the stage. But never fear," she reassured them with a smile, "I prevailed. She promised to write to me as soon as she arrived."

The door startled them both, and they turned to see Miss Phillips entering. She smiled at them, though her smile lingered at Captain Forrester, and Lancelot felt a pang that the two of them seemed to have formed an immediate attachment. Why was it so difficult for him to have found the same?

He'd thought . . . but now . . . He brushed aside these futile longings in order to hear what Miss Phillips said.

"Thank you for alerting me that they were here," she said to her sister-in-law, then she turned to them with an irrepressible smile. "I've had to cool my heels up in my room, pretending indisposition." Her mouth turned downward. "But Céline and I decided it best to pretend both Jessamine and I are too fatigued after the rigors of the ball."

Her sobered look fixed on Lancelot. "Céline has told you that Jessamine left?"

He nodded, unsmiling, still finding it difficult to absorb. "I wish you had notified me—us." He felt himself color to the roots of his hair. "I mean, perhaps one of us could have persuaded her to remain. I fear this will be worse if we hope to stem the gossip."

"That is what I told her," Mrs. Phillips said. "I would have sent word to you immediately, of course, but it was so early—barely after dawn—and believe me, she would have been gone before you had time to arrive. She was resolute. She'd already packed her things and would have a hailed a hack."

"What shall we put out in society, ma'am?" Captain Forrester asked, bringing their attention to the most pressing problem.

"I think since I have been telling all her callers today that she caught the grippe, that we must maintain the fiction that she is with me. After a fortnight, I can inform visitors that she has been transported back to her home to recuperate. If word is out that someone in this household has the grippe, believe me, I shall have few visitors."

"What about the servants?"

Her lips firmed into a serious line. "I shall ask for their secrecy. I trust most of them, though some are new." She sighed. "It is almost impossible to assure oneself of total confidentiality from the servants." She looked down at her hands. "The truth is, Miss Barry told me she doesn't care what conclusions society draws about her." Her gaze rose once more. "She realizes that if not St. Leger, then one of his companions may let something slip—when they're in their cups or over the gaming tables.

"She says she is through with London and will retire to her village." She spread her hands. "She was determined, and I could see that nothing would convince her at this point. Perhaps it is best for her to be at home with her parents for a time. By next year, there will have been plenty of larger scandals, and she can come back if she wishes for another season."

Lancelot curled his fingers into fists, angry at the unfairness of it. Miss Barry had had a lapse in judgment in allowing her head to be turned by St. Leger, but she had certainly committed no crime. She had behaved as many innocent, naïve young ladies did their first time in London. She should not have been prevented from enjoying what any young lady dreamed of enjoying.

"What a pity," Captain Forrester murmured. Miss Phillips had taken a seat next to him, and she addressed something to him. Mrs. Phillips turned to Lancelot as if to give the couple time to visit with each other.

"Please tell me what transpired last night. I didn't want to press Miss Barry too much, and she remembers little at any rate."

Lancelot nodded, though he didn't want to relive the episode either. But he quickly and as dispassionately as he could related all that had happened after they had left the ball.

"So you are sure St. Leger did nothing worse than kiss her?"

He nodded. "Yes. She was fully clothed though disheveled." He drew in a breath. "If we'd been a few minutes later . . . I shudder to think." His hands clenched and unclenched as he recalled his dream. "Believe me, ma'am, if I thought he had done anything else, he would not be alive this morning."

She searched his eyes and finally nodded. "I see. You relieve me." She moistened her lips, her look earnest. "You must pray for her. She will need it."

A shaft of guilt pierced his heart. He had prayed for her but with anger and bitterness in his heart, blaming her for her predicament. "I shall."

"I prayed for her before she left. She is very hurt and confused right now. Only the Lord can heal her heart so that she may enjoy the love of a worthy man, the way any woman aspires to."

Their gazes locked a second longer before he gave a curt nod.

He wished he could excuse himself then. What he wished most of all was to get on a horse and ride all the way to Miss Barry's village and see for himself that she was well. But he pretended patience, allowing Captain Forrester an adequate visit with Miss Phillips. After another quarter of an hour, the captain finally stood, bending over Miss Phillips's hand. Her face fairly glowed at his attentiveness, and once again Lancelot felt a stab of jealousy and longing.

When they left the Phillips's residence, Lancelot excused himself from Captain Forrester and walked home. The captain seemed to understand his desire to be alone. His only words at parting were, "She'll be all right, you'll see."

Lancelot swallowed and gave a curt nod.

He ignored the sights and sounds around him until he finally turned down his street. He climbed the steps wearily, feeling the fatigue of the night before. He too had risen early and slept poorly.

The footman opened the door for him. He nodded in thanks and removed his hat.

"Mr. Marfleet, sir, you've received this message. It was delivered not a half hour ago."

He turned in the act of removing his gloves and took the note.

"It's from Kendicott Park."

Wondering what his parents wished to communicate to him, he stepped into the nearest room and broke open the crested seal. The letter was in his father's handwriting.

Dear Son,

Come home at once. Your brother is gravely ill. Notify your sister and bring her. Do not delay. Pray.

The last word was underlined, which struck a note of fear into Lancelot's chest. His father was not given to hyperbole or to invoking divine intervention.

Lancelot began to pray immediately. What could have befallen Harold? When had he gone home?

He left the small room and made his way up the stairs, calling down to a footman as he went, "Prepare the traveling chaise for me. I must go to Kendicott Park. Send Alfred to me," he said, naming the footman who acted as valet for him when he was home. "Where is Miss Delawney?"

The young man jumped to attention. "Yes, sir. Immediately, sir. Miss Delawney is in her room, I believe."

He took the rest of the stairs two at a time and headed there, his mind in a whirl.

All thoughts of Miss Barry's dilemma fled for the moment as his thoughts and prayers focused on his older brother.

What catastrophe had at last befallen Harold? For so long he'd prayed for him, counseled him, cajoled him, reproved him. Lancelot quailed with dread. The last thing he wished was for God's judgment to befall his errant brother.

20

Jessamine had been home a fortnight, and the despondency that had descended on her the morning after her debacle with Mr. St. Leger refused to lift.

She had arrived home after a whirl of packing and explaining to poor, confused Lady Bess her sudden departure for home. But Jessamine felt as if hounds were on her heels. She refused to admit it, but deep down she was fleeing from seeing Mr. Marfleet again. He would feel duty bound to inquire after her, but she couldn't bear to have his censorious, pitying gaze on her once again.

He would make a good vicar, the way he beheld a sinner with that sad gaze—just like her father. A good swat of a switch would be preferable to that quiet, compassionate look, she'd often thought as a child.

She'd finally managed to convince Lady Bess that she was not out of her mind. "I must return home. I feel so terribly homesick," she said, ending on a half-smothered sob. The sob had been real enough, but not for the reason she claimed—though a part of her longed for her parents' embrace and the quietness of the parsonage.

But it had convinced Lady Bess. The older lady had patted her hands. "There, there, dearie, I understand. But must you leave today?"

"Yes—yes—I must. Mrs. Phillips has lent me her traveling coach, and I do not want to impose on her kindness."

"Very well. Let me help you pack."

"Betsy will help me, ma'am. You mustn't trouble yourself."

"Well, I shall order a nice luncheon basket packed for you then."

The last thing Jessamine wanted was food, but she realized in that second how empty her stomach felt. It would be better to nibble something in the privacy of her coach than stop at a coaching inn. "You are too kind, Lady Bess."

"Nonsense. I've enjoyed having you, my dear." The lady's eyes filled with tears. "I shall miss you."

The two hugged, and Jessamine felt remorse for leaving her so suddenly. First Megan and now her. "I shall miss you awfully, as well." She couldn't promise to visit her soon, because she never wanted to return to London. She would write to Megan and ask if she would visit Lady Bess occasionally.

"There, there," the old lady said, withdrawing gently. "You mustn't cry. It's been my pleasure to have you."

In less than an hour, Jessamine had packed and was ready to leave London. She leaned out the coach window to wave to Lady Bess and Betsy, who stood at the door, and gave a last look at the neighborhood she and Megan had come to know so well.

Hours later, when the coach finally pulled up at the door of the parsonage in the dark, the sight of her childhood home brought tears to her eyes.

Her parents had no idea she was coming home. The last letter she'd written was a cheerful account of her town activities—just as every letter had been. She had not expressed any of her disillusions about society, since they had sacrificed so much to give her a season in London.

The footman opened the coach door and let down the step. Taking his hand, she stepped down, her legs feeling stiff from sitting so many hours.

"Will you have me knock on the door?" the man asked her in the dark.

She glanced toward the lantern at the door and the evidence of light between the curtains. Her father always left the entrance lit to welcome callers at any time of the day or night. She felt a burst of gratitude for this now, when in the past it had inconvenienced the family many times when someone in trouble had come knocking at the door well into the night.

She straightened her shoulders. "No, thank you."

With a nod, he turned away and went about getting her trunk. She opened the low wooden gate, leaving it wide for the footman, and proceeded up the flagstones.

What would her parents say? What would she tell them? She'd thought much of this during the tedious journey, and she still was not sure. Megan would not betray her. Lady Bess—she would only express her regret at Jessamine's sudden departure.

Jessamine pushed open the door. She heard a voice coming from the parlor. Her father reading to her mother. Hopefully any visitors they'd had had already departed for the night.

She left the door open and walked slowly down the carpeted wooden planked floor. There was a louder bustle behind her as the footman jostled the trunk through the doorway, loud enough to alert her parents.

She hastened her steps and entered the parlor.

They were already standing. Her mother gasped, bringing her hands to her breast, and could move no farther.

"My dear, what has happened?" Her father reacted more quickly, increasing his pace until his concerned face looked into hers, his hands grasping her arms.

Her lower lip trembled as she opened her mouth to speak. Then he took her in his arms, hugging her close, not demanding any words. Her mother joined him, putting an arm around Jessamine's back and patting it.

"There, there, dear, you are home."

She regained her wits enough to motion behind her. "The coachman—my trunk—"

Her father pushed himself away from her gently, giving her to her mother's arms. "I'll see to him."

"Come, dear, what is this?" Her mother steered her toward an armchair by the fire. "Why didn't you write us to let us know you were coming home?"

She lifted a tear-streaked face to her mother. "I didn't know until yesterday—last night." She fumbled for a handkerchief in the pocket of her pelisse.

Her father came back into the parlor, closing the door softly behind him. "There, the coach is off to the public house, and you are safely home." He rubbed his hands, approaching them. "Well, I see you are in one piece, the Lord be praised, so physical harm has not precipitated your return. I don't think Lady Beasinger would have turned you out of her house." His gray eyes twinkled down at her. "So, I surmise it is a matter of the heart that has brought you home."

She clutched the handkerchief to her lips. "I—it is worse . . ."

He lifted a dark brown eyebrow. Her father was still a handsome man at fifty, though his lean cheeks were craggy and there were laugh lines between his nose and mouth and at the corners of his eyes. "Worse? Mary, I think this calls for strong tea."

Her mother rose from where she had been bending over Jessamine. "Of course. The water is simmering nicely here on the hob," she said with a smile to Jessamine. "I shall just prepare a fresh pot."

"It's not necessary." Her parents only employed a couple of servants, villagers who went home in the evenings, so they were used to fending for themselves a good part of the time.

"Nonsense," her father said. "We can all use some refreshment while you compose yourself to tell us what calamity has befallen you. My throat is parched from an hour's reading." He picked up the book from the small table by his chair. "Frances Burney's last novel, *The Wanderer*. I was going to mail it to you once we finished. I think as a woman you will find it of particular interest."

As if realizing he was forgetting the matter at hand, he cleared his throat. "Yes, well, let us have our tea and find out what brings you to our doorstep at this hour of the night."

Her father's commonplaces had given her time to dry her eyes. She recognized how he put so many parishioners at ease with his chatty, absentminded manner. But she knew he was neither. All the while he would be observing the person who'd come to him in trouble while seeming to be distracted by trivial things.

She blew her nose a final time and straightened in her chair, receiving the cup of hot tea from her mother. "Thank you. I am thirsty," she admitted.

She set it down on the lace doily on the table at her side to let it cool a bit. When her parents were settled in their chairs, drawn up close to her, she folded her hands on her lap and looked at each in turn, knowing she had to be fully candid with them. She felt their love encompassing her and knew even if what she had to say was tenfold worse than it was, they would still regard her with the warm, sympathetic, concerned look in their eyes.

"I have been very foolish," she began in a low tone. Her throat tightened.

"We have all been so at one time or another in our lives," her father said quietly as her mother murmured agreement.

Jessamine moistened her lips. "I allowed myself to be flattered by a . . . young gentleman—someone who appeared to be a gentleman." At the intake of breath on her mother's part, she knew she must get through this quickly before they conjectured the worst.

She kneaded her hands as she began to tell them about meeting Mr. St. Leger. She didn't pause except to draw long breaths, until she came to leaving the ball. She looked at each parent in anguish.

Her mother clutched her hands to the shawl around her shoulders, her father looked serene, but his eyes watched her keenly.

Unlike Mr. Marfleet, who dressed in regular clothes, her father wore a narrow white clerical collar. She quickly averted her thoughts from Mr. Marfleet, the way she had all day each time he intruded into them.

Her narrative ended, and by this time her handkerchief was damp. "I don't remember anything else . . . except when I awoke and found myself in a strange place . . . weighed down by someone atop me."

At another gasp from her mother, she hurried on. "I was fully clothed, but he was trying to kiss me—" She gulped in some air. "I came to my senses enough to try to push him away, but he only laughed and continued teasing me as if . . . as if what he was doing was a normal . . . thing."

"What happened, dear?" her father asked.

Her eyes met his. He no longer looked serene. His eyebrows had drawn together, forming a line between them, his gaze razor sharp.

"There was a pounding on the door, and the next thing I knew, Mr. Marfleet and Captain Forrester burst into the room. Mr. Marfleet began to fight Mr. St. Leger. Then Captain Forrester came to me and helped me up and asked me if I was hurt."

Her mother sat back, visibly calmer. Before she could speak, her father said, "Thank the good Lord for these gentlemen. Who, pray, are they?"

Relieved now that the worst was over, she took a sip of tea, debating how to describe the two gentlemen. She would have no trouble telling them about the captain, but she feared what they might think when she described her acquaintance with Mr. Marfleet.

She was finished with love. First had been her unrequited love for Rees Phillips, and then she'd been flattered by the attentions of a handsome but unscrupulous rake. The last thing she wanted was for her parents to get false ideas in their heads about Mr. Marfleet.

"They must be more than a pair of gentlemen you've danced a few dances with if they rode out to this inn to rescue you," her father said.

She swallowed, glancing briefly at her father before looking as quickly away. "They are very worthy gentlemen. Megan made Captain Forrester's acquaintance only a week or so ago through her new sister-in-law, Céline Phillips, Rees's wife."

She paused, then resumed before her parents would think it was painful for her to mention Rees's name or that of his bride. "Captain Forrester is an old acquaintance of Rees's from his days in the navy. I don't recall him—I was too young, but perhaps you might have met him."

Her gaze went from her mother to her father, and she was thankful that her tone sounded normal, as if she were only inquiring something about an old neighbor of theirs.

Her mother narrowed her eyes behind her spectacles then shook her head. Her father looked thoughtful, rubbing a forefinger over his chin. "As I recall, Rees brought home some sailor friends on occasion for brief visits, but I don't remember any individuals. It was quite some time ago."

"Yes. Well, Captain Forrester has come home for good. He is retiring from the navy now that the war is over. He seems a most worthy gentleman." She hesitated, unsure whether to add the rest, then decided to go ahead. "He seems quite taken with Megan—and she with him."

"How lovely," her mother said, bringing her hands together.

Glad to lighten part of her mother's load from all she'd told her this evening, Jessamine plowed on. "Yes, I am happy for her."

"And Mr. Marfleet? Does he have an eye on Megan too?" her father asked in that tone of dry wit she recognized so well.

She rubbed the palms of her hands over her skirt. "He is a . . . a vicar," she answered carefully, "recently returned from a couple of years as a missionary in India."

"Indeed?"

She risked a look at her father, and to her dismay but not surprise, he looked more interested than he had when she had mentioned Megan and Captain Forrester. "Yes. He . . . he would likely still be there but for the fact that he contracted a fever and almost died. I don't believe he will return. His family needs him home." She briefly described his family.

When she finished telling them about Mr. Marfleet, her mother's eyes were wide. "Son of a baronet? That is an exalted knight to your rescue."

"I am more thankful for the perseverance he showed in seeking you. I should like to thank him personally," her father said.

Jessamine's heart sank. If her father were to write Mr. Marfleet, he might construe it as an attempt on her part to rekindle their friendship.

"I should say so!" her mother exclaimed. "We must express our gratitude."

"I'm sure he does not expect any communication from us," Jessamine began, rubbing her arms in growing agitation.

"If he is the kind of man he appears from your narrative, then I don't imagine he does expect any thanks. But that is no reason not to convey it."

"I have no address for him," she told her father in a low voice.

"Did you have an opportunity to see him before you left London—to thank him?" her mother asked.

She flushed and looked at her handkerchief. "No. He and Captain Forrester were to call today . . . to see how I fared. It was very late when they brought me home—that is, to Mrs. Phillips's."

Now came the most difficult part of all.

"When I finally woke up, it was just before dawn. My mind finally felt clear and when . . . when I remembered everything I had done, I couldn't face anyone, much less these two gentlemen." She brought the handkerchief up to her mouth. "I was so ashamed."

"Oh, dear, I'm so sorry," her mother said. "You did right to come home. You'll be safe here. I worried so having you in London. Such a wicked city."

Jessamine looked at her father again, awaiting his verdict.

"Much as I am glad you have come back, I cannot help but think you did so precipitously. It was more as if you were running away than that you were returning home to your family."

The mantel clock ticked as Jessamine found herself unable to look away from her father's knowing eyes. "Yes, sir," she whispered before dropping her gaze. "I just couldn't bear to see the disappointment in their eyes. They were both such upstanding gentlemen. I had done wrong to . . . to flirt with Mr. St. Leger."

"You are not a young lady to flirt. Did London society go so quickly to your head, my dear?" her father asked gently.

She shook her head, still looking down.

"Carl . . ." her mother began in a remonstrative tone.

"No, it's all right, Mama. Papa has a right to ask me, as do you." She spoke slowly, her gaze meeting theirs. "I flirted with Mr. St. Leger because . . ." Her voice threatened to break once more. "I wanted to know that I was attractive to a gentleman. I was so hurt . . . and angry at Rees."

Amidst her mother's protest, she bowed her head once more into her damp handkerchief. "I wanted to prove I could be like Céline—Rees's wife—the kind of woman that men give up everything for."

"And what did you discover?" her father asked gently.

She studied the pattern on her gown, unable to meet her father's gaze. Her thoughts went to Mr. Marfleet, a worthy man whose regard she had spurned in an effort to prove something so foolish. "That I have no wish to be the kind of woman I thought Céline was. She has had her own burdens to bear." Jessamine inhaled deeply. "I have no wish to be anyone but who the Lord fashioned me to be."

"Then I would say your time in London has been of value," her father said.

She stared into the fire, glad for the peace and quiet that reigned in their sitting room. The old Jessamine would never have wished to be anyone but herself. Or, was the person she'd become in London the real Jessamine? Selfish, vindictive, caring only about her hurt and pride?

Silent tears rolled down her cheeks.

Her parents allowed her to cry silently, her mother approaching and hugging her, as she murmured endearments.

When she felt spent, her father said, "Let us pray for you, Jessamine, and then perhaps you should go up to your room and get some sleep. Things always appear better in the morning."

He approached her chair and laid a hand on her shoulder. He gave her a soft smile, but there was a trace of sadness in his eyes. She knew he had forgiven her, and her load felt lightened. But her own sadness and disappointment in herself was not alleviated.

He took a hand in his and her mother took her other one. They bowed their heads and closed their eyes. Her father's prayer was one of comfort. It was as if he knew exactly what she needed and was confident the Lord would provide it for her.

He asked the Lord to heal her wound and wash away her shame and guilt and show her that her sins and disgrace were taken away by the shame Jesus bore on the cross.

Then his prayer turned to Mr. Marfleet and Captain Forrester. Her father asked for a blessing upon them for all they'd done for her. He ended with, "Whatever sentiments compelled Mr. Marfleet not to rest until he had found my daughter, I pray, Lord, that You will restore them to him if they have been shaken by my daughter's disgrace. Prove him and what is in his heart so that he may be able to forgive Jessamine's conduct, her errors—as well as the perfidy of the man who took advantage of her naiveté and innocence."

With a final squeeze of her hand, her father ended his prayer and then opened his eyes and smiled down at her. "Don't forget, God's grace is sufficient for you."

"Yes, Papa."

"Now, off to bed with you."

She obeyed him, hugging and kissing her parents good night. She felt much lighter in her spirit as she walked up the stairs to her old room, but the sadness remained.

Her disappointment in herself was a burden she would have to carry. Time would ease it, but in the meantime, she must live with the person she had proved herself to be.

Lancelot and his sister arrived at Kendicott Park several hours after departing London. They had hardly spoken on the journey, each one preoccupied by their own thoughts.

The sky had already deepened to an inky hue although the western horizon still showed a band of lighter blue where the sun had recently set.

Tired and dusty, Lancelot turned to help Delawney descend the carriage. Together, they hurried up the wide, shallow steps of their ancestral home.

The door was opened immediately by a footman, who greeted them, then held the door open wide for them.

"How is Harold?"

A shadow crossed the young footman's face. "I do not know, sir. He is in his room. I believe his wife and your mother are at his side. Your father wanted to know as soon as you arrived. He is in his study at the moment."

"Thank you." Lancelot divested himself of his hat and greatcoat then hurried up the wide, curving staircase, Delawney at his heels. After a knock on the study door, he entered at his father's bidding.

"Lancelot, Delawney, thank God!"

"Hello, Father. How is he?" Lancelot asked at once.

Their father briefly kissed Delawney on the cheek before gripping Lancelot's arm and replying, "Not good."

"What is it?" Delawney spoke up. She had not even bothered

to remove her hat and pelisse. "Your note told us nothing. How did he fall ill?"

"He was visiting the Langdons at Rossmore—in Kent, you know—and contracted what he thought was a catarrh. He came home to recuperate. In a matter of days it had turned into the whooping cough. We've called in the best physicians, but he has only gotten worse. That's when I wrote you." His father shook his head. "It looks grave . . . grave indeed."

"May we see him?" Lancelot asked.

"Yes, pray don't delay. Your mother is with him now."

Lancelot hesitated. "How are she and Rosamunde holding up?"

"Rosamunde only arrived the day before yesterday. She is shocked at his appearance. Your mother has hardly left your brother's side."

Without another word, he and Delawney left the library and made their way down one wing of the house to his brother's room. With a soft knock, he opened the door and held it open for Delawney to precede him.

The curtains were drawn, and the room had the stuffy, medicinal smell of a sickroom. His mother looked up from where she sat near the bed. A lamp was turned down, giving her enough light to sew by but keeping the bed in shadow.

A maid carrying a basket of dirty linen looked at them in surprise, dipped her head in acknowledgment, and hurried past them.

"Hello, Mother," he said softly, bending down and kissing her on the cheek.

She rose and grasped their arms. "Thank God you've come."

Delawney gathered her in an embrace as Lancelot glanced over at his brother's sleeping form. His face looked pale, his eyes sunken, his golden hair lank, though combed neatly away from his forehead. *Dear Lord, touch his body and bring Your healing*, Lancelot prayed, shocked at his brother's appearance.

"He's resting quietly now, but he is exhausted from the coughing." She shook her head, her eyes watering. "It comes on him and won't stop. I don't know how his body can support it much longer though he is so big and strong." She brought her handkerchief up to her nose and sniffed. "But they rack his body so it seems his ribs will crack and . . . and that he'll . . . suffocate."

Lancelot put an arm around her shoulders and squeezed. "He's strong as you say. I'm sure he'll get better." He refused to acknowledge the possibility of anything else.

"You should have summoned us sooner," Delawney whispered at her mother's other side.

"We didn't know it would come to this. It happened so quickly from one day to the next." She shook her head, bringing the handkerchief to the corner of her eye. "How can a man, so healthy and hale one day, be brought so low?" She started to cry quietly.

"There, Mother, you are tired," Lancelot murmured against her hair. "You probably haven't slept. Why don't you go and lie down a little and we shall sit with him awhile?"

Urging her little by little, he led her to the door. "Father said Rosamunde had arrived. How is she?"

Her mother made a moue of distaste. "She has been to see Harold but is lying down now." She looked away from Lancelot. "They have been . . . estranged for the past few years, as you probably know."

He nodded sadly. Having been away, he knew little of Harold's private life, but the fact that they seemed to live primarily apart had not demonstrated a close-knit bond between the two.

Theirs was not the kind of marriage he envisioned for himself. He remembered when his brother had married. Both their parents had been the ones primarily involved in arranging the union of the two illustrious families.

When Lancelot had questioned his brother about his feelings for his bride-to-be, Harold had shrugged and laughed. "Love is not for those in our realm—at least not for the firstborn," he added with a knowing look. "It's not to say I cannot enjoy my life after

I'm married. All I need concern myself with my future wife is begetting an heir, and then we may go our merry ways. I've nothing against Rosamunde. She's comely enough. That should guarantee fair progeny. Who knows, perhaps we'll end up falling in love after we're wed."

Lancelot gazed at his brother's still figure now. Had they ever fallen in love?

"Come, Mother," he urged, focusing on his mother once more, "why don't you rest for a bit? I'll sit with Harold."

He and Delawney finally persuaded her to leave. He closed the door and faced his sister. Did he look as sober as she?

"Let's pray for him," she said.

He nodded and drew closer to the bed. His tall, hearty brother looked dwarfed in it. Lancelot had a sudden, gut-wrenching premonition that his brother would not survive. As soon as the thought came to him, he squelched it with the thoroughness he would an impure or faithless thought.

He bowed his head and began, "Heavenly Father, we beseech You for my brother, Harold. Please heal his body, his spirit, his mind." Lancelot never forgot his brother's waywardness and knew his spiritual well-being was as critical as his physical. He continued to pray for a few moments, then lifted his head with a final "amen," which was echoed by his sister.

He reached out and touched her arm. "Why don't you settle in and let me sit with him a while? When you have rested, you can relieve me."

She debated a moment, her gaze going to Harold, but finally nodded. "Very well, but call me if . . . if . . ."

He nodded so she didn't have to finish the thought.

When she had left the room, he sat down in the armchair his mother had vacated. He felt tired but not sleepy. Glad to see a Bible on the table beside him, he took it up and opened to the satin bookmark between its pages.

It was placed in the book of Psalms. His gaze skimmed the thirty-fourth psalm, the psalm of promises. Had his mother been reading it? Neither of his parents were pious, only attending church when they were in residence here as an example to the villagers.

> I will bless the LORD at all times: his praise shall continually be in my mouth. . . .
> I sought the LORD, and he heard me, and delivered me from all my fears . . .
> This poor man cried, and the LORD heard him, and saved him out of all his troubles . . .

His brother stirred. "Who's there?" he asked in a raspy whisper.

"'Tis I, Lancelot," he replied in a soft tone.

A ghost of a smile graced Harold's bloodless lips. "'Bout time."

"Don't try to speak. Just know I'm here, old man, and I shall be praying for your speedy recovery," Lancelot said in a light tone. Internally, he was shocked at his brother's ashen complexion and weakened state. He was a shadow of the way he'd seen Harold last—hearty, confident, full of vibrant life.

"Do that." His brother's hoarse words made him start.

He leaned forward and squeezed his hand. "I will." He bowed his head. "Dear God, I pray for Your mercy and grace for my brother. Bring healing to his body." He continued praying, hardly aware of the words, interweaving Scriptures with his petitions. "Amen," he ended softly.

His brother silently echoed his word. "What . . . d'you think?"

Lancelot covered one of his brother's hands, which lay atop the coverlet. "I think you need to rest. Don't exert yourself. Just know I'm here."

His brother lapsed into sleep for a time. But not an hour had passed when he began to cough. He hunched over, his hand covering his mouth.

Lancelot grasped him and helped him sit up against the pillows.

His body shook with each cough. Putrid matter spewed out. Lancelot grabbed a handkerchief from a pile at his bedside.

He prayed silently as his brother's body was battered by the coughing fit.

A serious-faced woman came into the room, whom Lancelot took to be a nurse.

"What can I do?" he asked.

"Nothing, sir." She nudged him aside and held a glass of water to Harold's lips when there was a moment of respite.

He had only taken a swallow when another fit began.

She set the glass down and held his shoulders. "Hand me another handkerchief, if you please."

Lancelot obeyed her immediately.

"There is little you can do right now," she told him over her shoulder. "Your mother tells me you are just returned from London. If you care to freshen up after your journey, I shall be here. You may return when he is quieter."

"Yes." He moved away from the bed reluctantly. But he wanted to settle in and change out of his traveling clothes. "I shall return in a little while."

"Very good, sir."

Lancelot stood a moment longer, staring at his brother. Sadness engulfed him.

21

Jessamine slipped back into her previous life with hardly a glimmer of disturbance. The weeks slipped by, summer days warm and sunny with an occasional shower to freshen the gardens.

To her parents she strove to appear her old, cheery, obedient self until she felt sure she had convinced them that she was fine again.

Her mother fussed and cosseted her the first few days until Jessamine wanted to shout that she didn't deserve such consideration. Instead she clenched her teeth and smiled, knowing it was the least she could do as part of her penance.

Even though her father had taught her about grace since she'd sat on his knee as a child—that God's forgiveness was given her for free because of the cost already born by her Savior on the cross, she could not free herself now of the desire to pay for her sins and shortcomings.

She'd never had a serious reason to doubt the grace of God until now, for she'd never really done anything to be ashamed of. All it took were the gentle admonishments of her mother to learn to share her dolls with other little girls who visited her, or that sad look in her father's eyes to make her repent of any desire to disobey.

But since the day she'd found out Rees had married another woman after telling Jessamine there was no hope for the two of them, her world had turned upside down, and she'd wished to hurt someone as she'd been hurt. And that someone, she was coming to understand now, was God Himself.

These troubling thoughts loomed foremost in her mind in the stillness of the night when she lay in her old bed, gazing up at the plaster ceiling, sleep nowhere to be had.

They came to her on long walks between the hedgerows that cut through meadows dotted by sheep, as she meandered through orchards filled with short stunted trees and ripening fruit, and breathed in the scent of tilled fields, wooded copses, and deserted heaths.

She walked until she was too exhausted to dwell on vain thoughts of "what if."

What if she'd sought God's Word for her pain? What if she'd resolved to forgive Rees for hurting her and trusted God to work that forgiveness out in her heart, so that she would have arrived in London with an attitude of humility and trust in God to lead her to the right person?

Had the right person been Lancelot Marfleet? Had she been too obstinate to see that? She had scorned him because he was a vicar—yet what man had she ever admired more than her father in his calling? Never more so than now.

Her father never brought up her conduct in London. He treated her with compassion and understanding, as if he knew all too well the frailties of the human heart.

Her mother had been sensitive as well. Only once or twice did she bring up Mr. Marfleet's name, wanting to know more, but desisted when Jessamine answered in monosyllables.

When by herself, however, she couldn't help wondering where Mr. Marfleet was and whether he ever thought of her. Megan wrote to her but said only that she hadn't seen him lately. She reassured her that she had heard no gossip surrounding Jessamine, but she had not attended many balls, so she was not caught up in society's on-dits.

Her letters were full of references to the captain. He came to dine several times in the week. He accompanied her and Céline to the theater, museums, and on outdoor excursions.

But her most recent letter was filled only of news of the large battle that had been fought on the field of Waterloo just south of Brussels.

Rees sent word as soon as he could to Céline to tell her that he is fine. He was in Brussels, never in any danger, but the city became chaotic as soon as news was received that the French had crossed the border. Napoleon took them all by surprise, even our great commander Wellington. He was at a ball, Lady Richmond's, on the eve of battle, can you imagine? Rees attended the ball and wrote how composed Wellington remained even as he continued receiving dispatches from the field and ordered the officers to rejoin their regiments and be prepared to march by three (in the morning!).

The battle occurred the next day. It was closely fought and the entire campaign lasted three days, but in the end on the field of Waterloo, our English and the Prussian armies routed the French.

It's finally over, according to Rees, but the carnage was horrific. He must stay on awhile longer but hopes to return to England as soon as things are more settled in Brussels.

Céline, as you can imagine, is overjoyed that he is safe. She has put on a brave front the past few weeks for my sake, but her thoughts have been across the channel.

We hope to see him soon.

I miss you awfully and hope you are well and keeping busy.

Jessamine's breath caught at the sight of Mr. Marfleet's name in the next sentence.

I have seen neither hide nor hair of Mr. Marfleet since you left. I don't know what could have happened to him. I certainly am out and about, but he seems to have disappeared off the face of the earth. I have not seen his sister so I can only deduce that they must have left town. Many families have already left with June more than half over. The season will soon be at an end.

My biggest news is that amidst all his concerns, Rees has invited Captain Forrester to visit us in Alston Green when we leave London and Rees is back among us.

So, I am looking forward to that day of having all my favorite people in the world united at Alston Green.

Jessamine's gaze skimmed Megan's closing and then rose, taking in the gently rolling hills of the meadow, where she'd come to read her letter in solitude.

Had Mr. Marfleet left London?

After several minutes of pondering his whereabouts and what he was doing and thinking, Jessamine realized she had been more concerned about his fate than Rees's.

Her heart began to thud in her ears at the significance of this. Of course she was concerned about Rees and his well-being. She thanked God he was safe and would soon be reunited with his wife.

But it was not the concern of a woman in love.

"Dear Lord," she whispered through the chirping of birds flitting among the trees and hedgerows behind her, "have You healed my heart?"

It had happened so gradually she had not been aware of it.

Had her love for Rees been so quickly replaced by concern for another individual?

She turned away from the pleasant scenery, her heart heavy.

If so, she had no claim on that individual's affection. He had clearly put her behind him.

When she returned home, the woman who came to clean and help with the housework every day looked up from dusting a table in the entry hall. "There's a letter for you there just came by the afternoon post."

Jessamine halted in front of the basket where the post was placed. "Thank you, Mrs. Miller."

She picked up the letter, curious to see who had written her. She didn't expect any correspondence from Megan since she had just received her letter that morning. Perhaps Lady Bess, though Jessamine owed her a letter.

She saw at once that the letter had been originally sent to Lady Bess's address in London. That address had been crossed out by Lady Bess and the Alston Green one written below it.

She did not recognize the original handwriting or the crest imprinted in the sealing wax when she turned it over. Her curiosity growing, she broke open the seal with her fingernail and unfolded the single sheet.

Dear Miss Barry,

Forgive me for writing to you in this way. We only met a few times, but I feel I should let you know that my brother Lancelot and I have been called away from London to be at our elder brother Harold's side. He is gravely ill with whooping cough, contracted during a visit to a house party in Hampshire.

We are very concerned for him and have not left his side. Lancelot prays for him continuously and would covet your prayers, I have no doubt.

Since I am uncertain whether my brother had time to inform you of our leaving town so suddenly, I did not want you to take it amiss if you had not seen him again.

He has scarcely had time for anything since he spends his time at our brother's bedside.

Please keep us in your prayers.

Jessamine closed her letter with her scrawled signature, Delawney Marfleet.

"Not bad news, I hope."

Jessamine jumped at Mrs. Miller's voice at her side. "Yes—no—I don't know. I mean, someone—a relative of an acquaintance is ill."

"That's too bad." The older lady shook her head and moved on down the hall with her dust rag.

Jessamine refolded the letter and went up the stairs toward her room, determined to get down on her knees at once to pray. Poor Mr. Marfleet, how worried he must be for his brother.

The whooping cough killed many infants and was not so usual with adults, but she had known of some who had contracted it—and some who had not survived it.

Why had Miss Marfleet seen fit to write her? Did she suspect something between her brother and Jessamine? If she believed her brother had not been in contact with her, did it mean Miss Marfleet had an inkling of the scandalous incident in Jessamine's life?

Had she written her because Mr. Marfleet still had feelings for her? Or only because the situation with Sir Harold was so dire they desired her prayers?

With more questions in her head than answers and little confidence in the power of her prayers, Jessamine entered her room and knelt by her bed, determined to do all in her power to respond to Miss Marfleet's plea.

Lancelot looked up at the slight movement from his brother. The days had blurred one into another so that he'd lost count of how many had passed since he and Delawney had arrived from London.

All he knew was that his brother had not recovered, despite Lancelot's prayers and the efforts of the best physicians from London.

He stared at Harold's still face. His valet kept his cheeks

smoothly shaved. The lack of beard only accentuated their pallor and gauntness.

Harold's lips began to move.

Lancelot leaned forward, touching his brother's hand to let him know he was there. "What is it?" he asked softly.

"I must . . . give up . . . the reins, old man," he managed with effort, the words barely distinguishable.

"Nonsense," Lancelot said with more assurance than he felt. "You'll rally yet."

A breath issued from his brother's chapped lips, a ghost of a laugh. "You'll have to . . . step into . . . my shoes. I'm sorry . . . know you don't want to . . ."

Lancelot's throat constricted. He squeezed his brother's hand. "I could never step into your shoes! You're Father's heir."

"Beg pardon . . . no longer . . ." After a moment, he continued. "You'll make a fine . . . baronet. Marry that dark-haired chit . . . carry on the family name."

Lancelot pictured Miss Barry—Jessamine, as she was to him. His heart constricted with a longing to be with her right then, her sympathetic eyes on him, her hand clasping his.

He drew in a shuddering breath. She didn't want him. If he'd ever had a chance with her, he'd destroyed it that night of her rescue with his arrogant, judgmental attitude. He'd condemned her as surely as the Jews the woman caught in adultery. Why had he turned away from her when she'd most needed a friend?

He pulled his attention back to his brother, who appeared to have fallen asleep again.

But a moment later, his lips moved once more. "Funny . . . I'll be . . . seeing your Lord before you . . ."

The words stopped all thoughts about Jessamine. If he was talking eternity, Harold must be serious indeed.

Before Lancelot could think how to reply, his brother said, "Pray for me . . . that it be so . . ."

Lancelot swallowed. “I will . . . I do. I shall pray for you now.” Keeping his eyes on his brother’s face, he began, “Dear Lord, be with my brother, Harold. Let him feel Your presence. Grant him Your grace. Fill him with Your Spirit.”

Feeling compelled by something deep within him, Lancelot leaned closer. “Harold, if you can, pray after me, ‘Lord Jesus.’”

“Lord . . . Jesus.” The words were hardly audible.

“Forgive my sins.”

Lancelot waited, his breath held until his brother said, “Forgive . . . my sins.”

“Wash me with Your precious blood.”

“Wash me . . .” was all Harold managed, but Lancelot squeezed his hand.

“Our Lord can hear you even if you can’t speak the words aloud.” He continued. “I receive You as my Lord and Savior.”

“I receive . . . You . . .”

“I believe You died for me.”

“I believe . . .”

“And rose again.”

“And rose . . .”

“So I may have eternal life.”

“So I may have . . . life.” The last word was said on an expulsion of breath. He lay still after that, and Lancelot did not press him to say more but continued praying softly.

He sensed peace in Harold and thanked God for imparting His Spirit to him.

Tears filled Lancelot’s eyes and spilled quietly down his cheeks as he sat there, his hand covering Harold’s, his lips murmuring snatches of Scripture.

When he could tell by his brother’s breathing that he had fallen asleep again, Lancelot slipped from the chair onto his knees and bowed his head upon his arms on the bed and let the tears come more fully.

I don't know why he must die. He had so much life to live. He could have lived it a changed man. Why, dear Lord, must You require his life? Perhaps he is wrong and so am I. Will You raise him up? Will You please heal his body? Please, dear Lord . . .

All he heard were the lines of Scripture when Martha answered Jesus about her brother Lazarus. *"I know that he shall rise again in the resurrection."*

Lancelot tried to gain hope from the story of Lazarus's resurrection from the dead, but instead all he could hear was Martha's reply.

He continued praying until his mother came in to relieve him. Two nurses were ever present, hovering in the shadows of the room.

The house was quiet, the servants seeming to walk more silently than usual.

That evening, Harold breathed his last. His parents, his wife, Lancelot, Delawney, and his faithful valet surrounded his bedside. One moment they heard his labored breathing, the next there was stillness.

Lancelot spent the following days walking the vast parkland, remembering childhood moments with Harold. Sometimes Delawney accompanied him, but they spoke little, their thoughts never far from their brother.

Neither wanted to speak of the future. Neither dared contemplate it.

"Do you ever think of Miss Barry?" she asked him one afternoon as they stood leaning against a wooden stile, contemplating the sheep grazing on the deep green field of grass beyond it.

After a quick glance at his sister, he fixed his gaze on the sheep and let out a breath. "I try not to."

"I presume that means you are unsuccessful."

He didn't bother to reply, his mind conjuring up Miss Barry. She was always there, hovering at the edge of his thoughts, no matter how much he tried to fill his mind with edifying Scriptures, devotional works, prayers for his brother and now his bereaving parents.

"Have you written her at all since leaving London?"

His sister's question was so blunt, he let out a laugh.

She continued her steady regard of him, no trace of humor in her eyes. "Well, have you?"

He shook his head. "I have no permission to write to her, and even if I did, what would be the point?"

"The point, brother dear, would be to see if there is any foundation to the attraction you clearly felt for her. Now that some time has passed since you left London, the least you can do is to see how she goes on."

Lancelot had told no one about that night in London.

"She is no longer in London."

"I know."

"You know?" Delawney narrowed her eyes. "Since when have you known?"

"Since I left." He turned away from her. "It's a long story—one I am not free to divulge. Suffice it to say, she returned home to her family right before I came here."

"I wrote to her awhile back," she said. At his look of surprise, she continued in a calm tone. "I wanted to inform her that you—and I—were called from London suddenly on account of Harold. I addressed my letter to Lady Beasinger's residence, supposing that she was still to be found there. I merely wanted to let Miss Barry know why she had not seen you anymore in town—if in fact she had noticed your absence."

"You had no right to do this without my knowledge," he said, his thudding heartbeat belying his stiff tone.

"I am sorry if you are offended, but I thought you would want to know that she replied to me, apologizing that it would have been sooner, but that my letter had had to be forwarded on to her father's parish before she received it."

He swallowed, in fear and anticipation. "What else did she say?"

"Merely that she was sorry to hear about Harold's illness and promised to pray for his recovery—as I had asked her to. She thanked me for news of you but confessed that she had not missed seeing you in London for the simple fact that she had left London about the same time."

His gaze drifted back to the bucolic meadow scene, his thoughts nowhere near as peaceful. How was she? He had received a short note from her father shortly after arriving at Kendicott Park, thanking him for his assistance to his daughter, so Lancelot knew Miss Barry had confessed all to her parents. But how had they greeted the shocking news?

Overlapping all his questions about Miss Barry's welfare was a longing to see her, a longing that superseded all his days of blotting her from his thoughts.

"She said little about her present life, only that she was well and her parents were well, that is all. She did ask me to give you her best wishes and to let you know she would not forget to pray for your brother. Her exact words, as I recall, were, 'Tell him I shall be constant in prayer.'"

His shoulders slumped, relieved that she was well. But his thoughts continued dissecting the scant information. Miss Barry had sent him greetings and said she was well. That was something. But was it? Wouldn't any polite person do the same? It told him little of her real state.

He had to know. Had she gotten over St. Leger and that horrific ordeal?

He jabbed a hand through his hair, letting out a frustrated sigh. He could not go to visit her.

"Why don't you write to her?"

His sister's words startled him. He hardly remembered she still stood there. "I—no." A note would not suffice. He needed to see her in person—and see if there was any hope for them.

He had discovered in the days since leaving London that his feelings had not changed.

The anger and disgust he had felt on the night he'd rescued her had faded, leaving only a still unfulfilled longing for her presence.

He remembered the times she'd seemed to return his feelings—at least feelings of regard. The afternoon at Kew, the time they had waltzed together, and a few others like that.

Would a handful of occasions when he'd felt her warmth suffice to build something more lasting?

22

Jessamine's face felt warm by the time she returned home from a walk to a heath where she had spotted clumps of harebell in bloom on her last walk.

She carried a bouquet of the lavender-colored flowers in one hand when she turned onto the narrow lane lined with elms that led to the vicarage. A carriage stood before the front door.

She quickened her step, wondering who had come to visit. There were always visitors stopping by in the afternoon, but she didn't recognize this fine-looking coach.

As she drew closer, she noticed a liveried servant by the horses' heads. Except for the local squire, there were no great families in the vicinity. This was a traveling coach, its sides dusty from the roads.

Her heart began to thump as she realized the footman's livery resembled that of the Marfleets' footmen. But it couldn't be the same.

Her fingers trembled as she struggled to untie the ribbons of her bonnet. She would need to go up to her room and change her old muslin gown before entering the parlor.

She stopped in front of the hallway mirror to remove her bonnet and arrange the curls framing her face.

"Jessamine, is that you?" her father asked through the parlor doorway, which stood open, voices audible through it.

Her heart sank. She wouldn't have time to go to her room and freshen up. "Yes, I've just come in." She smoothed down the last wayward wisps of hair, patted her shiny cheeks and forehead with her handkerchief, and straightened her ruffled collar. Squaring her shoulders, she headed to the parlor, then paused at the entrance to see who the visitors were.

Mr. Marfleet rose from his chair as soon as she appeared.

Her hand at her throat, her heart tripping, she could only stare at him.

Her father's face was wreathed in smiles. "Look who's come to visit you. Come in and have a seat. We've done our best to entertain your friend while you were out."

Gathering her wits about her, she took a few steps into the room and tried to smile.

Mr. Marfleet came to meet her, his hand held out. "Hello, Miss Barry. I hope I am not intruding on you."

She shook her head, allowing her hand to be engulfed in his, all the while feeling as if she were in a dream. "Not at all." Reason began to return. "Your brother, how is he?"

She bit her lip at the shadow that crossed his features. "He is no longer with us."

She drew in another breath. "I am so sorry," she said, pressing his hand.

"Thank you. We—none of us—have accustomed ourselves to his absence."

He relinquished her hand, and she clutched it with her other, embarrassed that she had held his so long.

"Please, be seated." She moved forward, her gaze darting from her mother to her father, wondering how long they had been alone with him.

Her mother smiled in reassurance. "You must be parched after your long walk. Come, let me pour you some tea. Mr. Marfleet has been with us nearly an hour and no sign of you." She chuckled, lifting the cozy off the teapot and touching its sides to see if it was still warm.

"You've been here an hour?" she asked Mr. Marfleet after taking the cup her mother served her.

"Yes, an hour that has passed all too quickly with my tales of life in a country parsonage and Mr. Marfleet's missionary journeys in India," her father replied for him. "I can assure you we have only scratched the surface of the latter topic, of which I hope to hear much more."

Mr. Marfleet smiled. "Nothing would give me greater pleasure, unless it be to hear more of your life as a village pastor."

She sat down, flustered to think her father might have brought up her disgrace in his wish to thank Mr. Marfleet. What was he thinking of her? "How is your sister?" she asked.

"She is well, considering our loss. She told me only recently that she had written to you."

Jessamine looked down at her cup. "Yes. I—I hadn't realized till then that you had left London."

"Yes. I received a summons from my father that my brother was gravely ill."

"I see," she said quietly. "I . . . hope he didn't suffer."

"He suffered some, but he was at peace at the end."

She studied him as he spoke, wishing to know more.

Her father, as if sensing Mr. Marfleet's reluctance to repeat what he'd already told them, spoke for him. "The Lord gave Mr. Marfleet the ineffable privilege of ministering to his brother in his final days, and of being assured of his eternal salvation."

Jessamine stared at Mr. Marfleet as her father spoke. He had told her father all these things at their first meeting?

As if reading her thoughts, he said, "Your father is a very easy man to unburden oneself to. You were right when you said he is a true shepherd to his flock and would thus not want to leave his post here for a larger parish."

Her gaze went from one man to the other, her amazement growing. "I see," was all she could think to say.

"Perhaps when you finish your tea, you would like to show Mr. Marfleet the garden," her mother put in, a hopeful look on her face.

"I promised him a tour of our modest greenhouse," her father added, "but perhaps that can wait another day."

As she was nodding to her mother's suggestion, and draining her cup, her father's words penetrated. Another day? How long would Mr. Marfleet be staying? What had brought him? She peeked at him over the rim of her cup, all her questions hinging upon this last one.

Despite finishing her cup, her throat felt parched.

Realizing her parents were waiting for her to initiate the walk in the garden, she set her cup down and addressed him. "Would you like to . . . to take a turn about the garden?" Feeling acutely embarrassed at the ploy so many hopeful parents used to allow a suitor to be alone with their daughter, she cringed at how her question must sound. Her cheeks flushed as she thought of the last time she had taken a turn about the garden with a gentleman. The day Rees had come to tell her not to pin her hopes on him.

She pushed aside the memory. As Mr. Marfleet met her gaze, she wished she could tell him she didn't mean it like *that*. She was only inviting him because he came from so far away, and he was her acquaintance.

He stood at once and nodded. "I should like that very much."

If she didn't know better, she would say he exhibited relief and eagerness. Perhaps he was only bored with her parents' company and had been waiting for this moment to see her, dispatch whatever message he had come to give her, and be gone.

She rose and smoothed down her gown, wishing once again that she had had a moment to wash her face and brush her hair before having to face him. "Very well. Won't you come with me then?"

Mr. Marfleet followed her down the corridor and into the breakfast room at the back of the house, which had a door leading into the garden. He held the door open for her, and she murmured her thanks, conscious of his arm so close to hers as she passed through.

Glad that the garden showed to such advantage in late June, she proceeded to lead him down a graveled path, not bothering to identify anything since she knew he could easily name all the flowers, which were common ones to be found in any English garden: foxglove, Canterbury bells, pinks, peonies, larkspur, iris, forget-me-nots, and roses, roses everywhere. Lattices with climbing ones, small bushes with miniature ones, bushes with large, cabbage-like heads too heavy to support on their stems, their fragrance filling the walled space like vapor in an enclosed room.

"It's beautiful. Do you have a gardener or is it just you and your father?"

"Just my father and I. He does employ a couple of men to cultivate the glebe, but he reserves our own private gardens within these brick walls for ourselves. Gardening and his botanical experimenting are his passions—aside from ministry, of course."

"He is a very wise man in ministerial matters, thus I'm sure he is also in botanical things."

She looked sidelong at him, but his gaze was fixed on a bed of lavender that was beginning to blossom. "I'm glad that he was able to offer you some comfort in your recent loss."

He swallowed.

She longed to reach out and touch him, but she curled her fingers into her palms. "I'm so sorry. I only met your brother but a few times, but I can scarcely believe he is gone."

He turned to her then, his slate-blue eyes looking intently into hers. "Yes, I am having the same difficulty no matter how much I believe that someday we shall be together again in eternity. But by rights it should have been I to depart prematurely. I was the one who hurried off to India and was struck down with more than one kind of pestilence." His tone turned bitter as he looked away again. "I should have died, not he."

She couldn't help reaching out then and touching his forearm. "Don't say that! Neither of you should have been struck down. We don't know why the Lord takes some before their time. We can only trust in His infinite wisdom, and in eternity."

His throat worked as if finding it hard to speak. She tightened her hold on him, wishing she could say or do more.

His gaze fixed on her hand, and she realized what she was doing. Quickly she let go of his arm.

His gaze lifted to hers, and for a moment they only gazed at each other. Her heartbeat threatened to drown out the sounds of buzzing bees around the lavender.

"Do you believe that?"

She swallowed, sensing he was asking her, not because of any lack of belief on his part, but to ascertain hers. "Yes, I do."

He seemed to relax and resumed walking. "My brother had not been living an exemplary life for many years, ever since he came of age. He was a typical young man of the ton, living for his own pleasure."

She didn't know what to say. The little she'd observed of Sir Harold showed her a carefree gentleman of society.

Mr. Marfleet shook his head. "But he was no longer a young blade. He was a married man of one-and-thirty, whom my father was grooming to take over the reins of his estates. I had spoken to Harold on more than one occasion about his gambling, drinking, and generally dissipated life. Excuse me for mentioning these things, especially to a young lady. I do not wish to speak ill of the dead—"

"Of course you don't. Please tell me. I shan't repeat any of what you are telling me." She bowed her head. "Believe me, I have nothing to reproach anyone for. I know too well the consequences of sin."

To her surprise he touched her chin with his forefinger and nudged it upward. Too stunned to speak, she could only stare at him. "Whatever you did was done out of innocence. My brother had long lived the life of a reprobate, unmindful of my parents, of his wife, or of his good name."

He let her chin go, and she felt bereft. "I only mention these things to explain God's grace to him in the end. He—Harold, that is—truly repented and received Jesus as his Lord and Savior right before the end. He departed in peace. I didn't want to . . . to . . ." Mr. Marfleet had difficulty continuing for a few minutes and turned away from her.

She remained still, giving him time to compose himself.

He drew a breath. "At first, I didn't want to accept his end, when it became clear Harold was not getting better. I railed at God, pleaded with Him, spent hours on my knees at Harold's bedside."

He bowed his head. "Then it occurred to me—or perhaps the Lord revealed it to me—that I was praying more for my own sake than Harold's."

She drew in a breath. "What do you mean?"

His blue eyes met hers again. "Isn't it clear? I didn't wish to step into Harold's shoes. I never have. It is the last thing I wished, to be heir to Kendicott Park."

Her hand came to her mouth to stifle a gasp. Of course—someday he would be the baronet and inherit the family seat.

His lips twisted up. "Didn't you realize?"

She shook her head. "No—it was stupid of me. I was just so shocked over your brother's death—and how you must feel . . . I hadn't thought about that." Her gaze rose to his once more. "Oh, I'm so sorry—you have only ever wanted to be a minister of the gospel. How awful for you!"

He looked at her as if he had never seen her before. A second later he shook his head as if waking up. "You know, you are the first to express such a sentiment."

"I didn't mean—" She stopped, confused, not sure what she wanted to say.

"No one has said anything directly. My family is still too full of grief. And no one expected Harold not to continue the line. He has always been so healthy, escaping most childhood diseases that afflicted me. Still less has anyone expected me to fill Harold's shoes. I have never had the distinction of knowing how to carry on in society."

He smiled without mirth. "But the unthinkable has happened. Harold is gone without leaving an heir, and underlying everyone's grief is the sense of relief that my father has another son to inherit. It never occurs to anyone that I never wished—nor wish it now—this title and all it implies for my life."

He let out a breath. "That sounds very selfish of me, I know. I shouldn't be thinking such things, not now. My father is hale and hearty and will live many decades still, I expect."

Jessamine chose her words carefully, groping for something that would comfort him. "Yet you will never be a simple vicar again. Even if you are able to continue as a clergyman, it will surely be in some exalted position befitting a baronet's son." She swallowed on the last words, still unable to conceive of such titles for Mr. Marfleet. "And not as my father, a simple country vicar."

He nodded slowly at each word, his gaze not wavering from hers.

As if by mutual accord, they continued walking. At the end of the brick path, she motioned to a wooden bench under the beech tree, and they sat down.

"How is your sister taking your brother's departure?"

"As I am. Shocked, gradually reconciling herself to his absence. She didn't see too much of him—like me—in recent years, since the two of us had little in common with Harold and his way of life. Yet, he always loomed in our lives. He was the next head of the family."

"I'm glad she found time to write me . . . to tell me of your brother's illness. I did pray for him."

He rubbed his chin, looking away. "I'm sorry I didn't write you myself—"

"Oh no, that's not what I meant. I didn't expect you to write me." She stopped, embarrassed by the memory of their last meeting.

His gaze rose to meet hers. "I should have. I received a note of thanks from your father shortly after I left London." Before she could decipher his reception of her father's letter, he continued. "I could use the excuse that I was too preoccupied by my brother's condition, but it wouldn't be the truth." He watched her steadily as he spoke, his voice soft.

She maintained his steady gaze with effort. "I had no reason to expect to hear from you ever again—" Her voice caught on a sob at the last word, and she clamped down her jaw to control her emotions.

He covered her clasped hands with his hand, dwarfing hers. His hand felt warm, causing a yearning to feel it upon her cheek. She remembered his lips touching hers that afternoon in Kew.

"You had every reason to hear from me. I was very concerned for you after that . . . that evening. Well, I shan't refer to it except to say that Captain Forrester and I called upon you the next afternoon only to hear from Mrs. Phillips that you had decided to return here. You can imagine our shock. I had no idea your state of mind the next day. Then as soon as I returned home, I received a summons from my own father to come to Kendicott Park without delay."

He took a deep breath. "Yet, I continued to wonder why you had left London in such haste. I know you perhaps didn't wish to see"—he cleared his throat, his cheeks reddening, then rushed the next words—"Mr. St. Leger again, but you had no reason to fear scandal. No one but Captain Forrester and I knew anything, and you can be sure we would never breathe a word."

As he spoke, Jessamine's eyes filled with tears, and she didn't dare move her hands to swipe at them. Try as she would to stem them, as Mr. Marfleet continued in his gentle tone, the tears welled up, until they spilled from her eyes onto his hand.

Before she could move to seek a handkerchief, his eyes met hers with concern. "I didn't mean to distress you. Forgive me." He pulled his own handkerchief out of his waistcoat pocket and patted her cheeks, first one, then the other as if she had been a child.

She sniffed and tried to sit back. "I'm sorry, I shouldn't be crying. I—I've put that . . . evening behind me."

"It's because I'm being very clumsy at explaining why I didn't write you." He smiled crookedly. "I wished to, and yet didn't dare."

Her eyes widened. "Didn't dare?"

"I wasn't sure what to say. I didn't know your state of mind, and . . ." He shrugged as if not finding the right words. "I was angry and . . . and disappointed in you at first, but that's long since past. You are not to reproach yourself for anything. That blackguard took advantage of you."

She wiped her nose with her own handkerchief and looked away from him. "You had—have every right to reproach me. I was foolish and naïve—and willful—and deserved what happened to me, and can only thank God that He sent you and Captain Forrester to rescue me that night so that I suffered nothing more than a headache."

"Shush. Do not reproach yourself, Miss Barry. You behaved no differently than any young lady of the ton. He is the blackguard. But I don't wish to speak of him. He has left London, and you have no need to worry about him ever again. I only beg your pardon for not corresponding with you sooner to see how you fared."

With a sigh he drew back from her. "And then so much time had passed—and so much has happened, that I decided the only thing for it was to see you in person."

She shook her head, still amazed that he had made this trip just to visit her. "You had no need to make such a journey."

He raised a light red eyebrow. She had once thought that shade so unattractive and now found herself admiring it. His skin was pale. Her gaze lowered. His lips were well shaped, not too narrow, neither too fleshy. His chin had a faint cleft.

"I had every need." His lips tilted slightly on one side. "I wanted to meet your father, for one thing."

She was able to return his smile. "He seems to like you."

His smile broadened. "I am relieved to hear you say so."

"My father likes everyone—but he would be particularly interested in someone who shares his love of botany."

"He promised to show me his collections tomorrow, including his *Gelsemium sempervirens*."

Her eyes flew to his. "Yellow jasmine?"

"The very one." Amusement crinkled the corners of his eyes. "I asked particularly about it."

"It is just an ordinary vine. It is probably not even in bloom."

"That's all right. I have enough bloom before me."

As if conscious suddenly of having said something flirtatious, his face filled with color and he looked away, clearing his throat.

She would have pitied him if she wasn't so relieved that he didn't witness her own flushed cheeks.

"Shall we return to the house?" she asked.

"If you wish." His tone returned to the polite, sober one he'd used in the parlor. He stood and held his arm out to her.

She complied, trying to hide her disappointment that their walk was at an end.

When they arrived at the house, he paused before the door. When he didn't open it right away, she looked up to find him regarding her. "Is something the matter?" she asked.

"I hope there is not. I merely wished to ask you if I might call upon you?"

"Call upon me?" she echoed faintly. "But . . ." She placed a hand to her throat, feeling her quickening pulse. "I—you live away."

"I was thinking of staying in the neighborhood a while."

"Oh."

"Unless it would be distasteful to you. I don't wish to remind you . . . of things you'd rather forget."

She shook her head. "No, of course not."

"Then perhaps tomorrow. Your father promised to show me his greenhouse."

"Oh, yes, of course." That must be his reason, his desire to see her father's collection. She hoped he wouldn't be disappointed. "It is nothing like Kew."

"That's all right. I look forward to seeing it."

Without another word, he opened the door and held it for her.

They found her parents still in the parlor.

Her father rose and rubbed his hands together. "They aren't much, but I hope you derived some pleasure from the gardens."

"They were most enjoyable," Mr. Marfleet said at once. "Very nicely laid out and full of variety. Thank you for the opportunity to see them, in such agreeable company."

Her father bowed his head, his twinkling eyes meeting Jessamine's.

"Well, I shall make my way to the village now. I believe I saw an inn there as we drove through."

"Yes, there is a nice inn there, but please, I hope you will stay with us while you are in Alston Green."

Jessamine's gaze flew to her father. He was inviting Mr. Marfleet to stay in their humble parsonage? She turned to see how Mr. Marfleet would react.

"I wouldn't wish to put you and your wife to any trouble. There is my coachman and a groom, though they, of course, can stay at the inn."

"Capital," her father said, rubbing his hands again. "We haven't a lot of room for a retinue of servants, but we would certainly wish to have you stay with us during your visit. And of course to sup tonight."

Mr. Marfleet looked to Jessamine as if asking her permission, and she could only offer a small smile, too confused by the rapid turn of events to do more.

It seemed to be enough because he turned to her parents and thanked them again for their hospitality. Her mother then took charge, going with him when he left, to give his servants directions to the inn.

"Well, my dear."

"Well, what?" she asked carefully, afraid of what her father would say.

He took her by the elbow to lead her toward the window, where they watched the footman unload Mr. Marfleet's baggage. "I do believe you have a serious suitor."

"I think he is only here to see your plant collection. I . . . I told him much of it when I knew him in London."

Her father chuckled. "I shall be pleased to show it to him if that is the reason he claims."

"I don't know if that is what he *claims*." She didn't want to make Mr. Marfleet out to be a deceitful person. "I was only deducing that from his words."

He patted her hands, which she realized she had begun to wring. "Never mind what you think he means by his visit. I am just happy that he seems a fine young gentleman. A man both your mother and I could be well pleased with *if* our only child has caught his favor."

She looked into her father's loving gaze, unable to find any words to refute him.

23

The days went by quickly—too quickly for Lancelot. He'd been at the parsonage five days already, days spent in the bosom of a family such as he'd never known, a family filled with love and warmth for each other and for anyone under their roof. They had received him as one of themselves.

All except Miss Barry.

He still didn't know her true feelings. He glanced sidelong at her now as they trudged along one of the turf paths in the countryside. She took him on one of her long walks each day, except the one day when it had rained, which they had spent in the greenhouse helping Mr. Barry transplant some seedlings of a species he was propagating.

Miss Barry was unfailingly friendly and sympathetic, showing interest in whatever topic he spoke of. She was everything a good friend could be, but was there hope for more?

Anytime he broached anything approaching his own feelings, she changed the subject in such a polite, gentle way that he could not take offense, yet still he felt rebuffed.

He had not pressed the point because he, too, wanted to make sure of his heart. Taking his sister's advice, he used the days to ascertain whether what had drawn him to Miss Barry in the first place had in any way diminished.

It had not. Each day brought new delight in her company and a greater certainty that this was the woman God had for him.

But he could not deny the reluctance in her.

Was he yet so distasteful to her? Was her resolve never to be a vicar's wife unchanged? But he would not always be a vicar, she must realize that now.

He drew out a breath, knowing whatever her sentiments, he could wait no longer to express his own. His parents needed him home. And he needed to make a decision on his own immediate future.

He felt the letter that lay folded in his pocket, the one he'd received that morning.

The bishop needed an answer.

"May we sit awhile?" He pointed to a grassy area under a large oak tree in the nearby meadow.

"Yes, that would be nice."

Once they were settled under its shade, he knew of no way but to go directly to the point. "Do you know why I came to visit you, Miss Barry?"

She looked away from him and made a vague motion with her hand. "I supposed you wished to see my father's collection."

"Your father's . . . ?" He let out an abrupt laugh, which he cut short as soon as he saw her look of alarm. "No, that was *not* the reason—though I have enjoyed discussing botany with him and seeing his achievements."

He drew in another breath, hoping his next words wouldn't repel her. "I wished to see if you . . . you returned my feelings."

This time she didn't look away but repeated faintly, "Your feelings?"

He nodded. He edged closer to her and took one of her hands in his. He loved the feel of her smaller hands the few times he'd been able to hold one of them. They were so soft . . . and felt so right in his. "I wished to ask you to be my wife."

Her lips parted, and her green eyes scanned his. "I didn't think you'd—" She shook her head and pulled her hand away, leaving him with a sense of dread. She half turned from him, giving him her back. "You can't want me for a wife, not after how I behaved with Mr. St. Leger. You will be Sir Marfleet some day. Your parents would never accept me." She waved back toward the way they'd come. "You see how humbly my parents live."

He reclaimed her hand and held it firmly. "But what do *you* wish, Miss Barry?"

She shook her head. "It's too late for what I wish," she said in a choked voice.

His heart sank. Did she still have feelings for Mr. St. Leger? "What is it?"

She bowed her head. "It's too late for me to wish for things."

"Because of what happened that night?"

She nodded, not looking up.

"I've told you—*you* did nothing wrong. And if you showed poor judgment in encouraging Mr. St. Leger in any way . . ." He struggled for a way to express what he wanted to say. "It is perfectly understandable. You were a young lady enjoying her first season. Perhaps you flirted a bit with St. Leger. It's not wrong to be flattered by a young man's attention." It was coming out sounding all wrong.

But as he spoke, she slowly turned to face him again, and he tightened his hold on her hand, feeling encouraged. His heart hitched at the sheen of tears he detected in her eyes.

"My father wouldn't have condoned flirting with Mr. St. Leger." She sniffed. "I allowed my vanity to believe he found me attractive—pretty enough to compete with the other young ladies of the ton." She brought a fist up to her mouth. "I was so hurt by . . . by . . ." She struggled once more and he waited, his breath held.

Drawing in a shuddering breath, she continued. "When Rees—Mr. Phillips—fell in love with Céline and left me for her."

For a moment, he felt confusion. Then he remembered meeting Mr. Rees Phillips. The revelation was like a clanging bell in his chest. So, he had been right—she did love Mr. Phillips!

The next second, his hopes plummeted. If he could scarce compete against a rogue like St. Leger, how could he ever think to banish a ghost like Rees Phillips from her heart?

"Do you still love him?" he asked with great difficulty, every fiber in him tensed in preparation for her answer.

The tears overflowed her eyelids, and she gave an angry shake of her head. "No—no! But I felt unloved and unlovable for so long. When Mr. St. Leger began paying me special attention, it helped me forget how . . . how Rees had spurned me."

She began to cry quietly, biting her lower lip to restrain herself but unable to stop the flow of tears.

Thinking only to comfort her, he brought his hand up to her face and brushed away the tears with his thumb. Her skin felt as soft as he'd imagined.

"I—I'm sorry—"

"Shh," he murmured, continuing to stroke her cheek.

She didn't pull away from his touch. Emboldened, he wrapped his arm about her shoulders, drawing her toward him.

She continued to cry and he sat quietly, stroking her back until the shudders ceased.

He prayed quietly for her peace and comfort, setting aside his own feelings. When she sat still within the circle of his arms, he was reluctant to move. He shifted only enough to extract his handkerchief and bring it up to her face. She took it from him and wiped her cheeks. But she didn't move away from him, and he took heart from that.

Unless she viewed him only as a brotherly shoulder to cry on. The thought disheartened him, but still he didn't move.

Should he or shouldn't he carry on with what he came for? He prayed for courage.

"I'm sorry for being such a watering pot around you. I usually am not so," she said in a more matter-of-fact tone, drawing away from him enough to meet his gaze. He loosened his own hold but kept his arm around her.

She was so close he could detect the soft rise and fall of her chest. Her eyes and nose were red, her cheeks flushed, but she looked so beautiful it took all his control not to close the gap between them. But he wouldn't scare her the way he had that day at Kew.

Dear Lord, help me!

But then it seemed it was she who tilted her face upward. Scarcely daring to trust what he saw, he inched downward. The next instant, whether it was he or she or both of them who moved, his lips touched hers and he heard her small sigh.

Encouraged, he deepened the kiss, all rational thought fleeing in the sheer sensation of touching and tasting her once again.

When she didn't push away, he ventured to put his other arm around her and draw her closer once again. His eyes were closed, so he didn't see when her arms came up. With a start, which quickly transformed to pleasure, he felt her fingers entwining in his hair.

"Jessamine," he breathed against her lips before pressing them once again.

His passion intensified as it found an outlet at last. He'd dreamed of this moment with her for so long. Realizing she was doing nothing to halt him, he at last broke apart, panting.

His eyes scanned hers, his arms still around her, seeking any fear or disgust in her green eyes. But he saw only wonder and acceptance.

"Will you do me the honor of becoming my wife," he said in an unsteady voice.

The wonder gradually died as the meaning of his words penetrated. Her arms came down and she drew away from him.

A sharp stab of disappointment pierced him, and he kept his thoughts in check, refusing to believe she would deny her feelings for him.

"I don't know what to say . . ." she said, bringing her fingers to her lips as if still trying to understand what he had done.

He quirked his lips upward. "Say yes."

Her gaze flew to his. "You can't want to marry me."

"I've wanted to marry you for quite some time."

"But that was before."

"Before what?" He tried to keep his tone light but was having a hard time keeping his hope alive.

"Before my . . . shameful behavior."

He caught her hand in his. "I thought we'd already discussed that and put it aside."

She continued as if he hadn't spoken. "And before your brother's passing." Her eyes gazed earnestly into his. "You were only a simple vicar, not a future baronet."

"I am still only a simple vicar." He patted the letter in his pocket. "In fact, I have been offered a living in Reading, and I must inform the bishop forthwith of my reply."

Her eyes widened, and for a moment they glowed. He was heartened that she seemed pleased by his appointment. Her words confirmed this. "That's wonderful. Will you be able to accept—I mean, with your new situation in life?"

"I think so. My father is healthy. I don't expect him to expire anytime soon," he quipped, though his tone immediately sobered. "It's true I didn't expect Harold to succumb so quickly, but he had lived a rather dissipated life for quite some time, so despite his looks, I think his body was weakened."

"I'm sorry."

He took in a breath. "But as for my father, I have no reason to suppose he shall not be lord of his manor for many years. I do not believe he will object to my accepting this living in the meantime.

It's a large church—that can only help train me to manage a large property someday."

"You don't feel reluctant to be a landlord one day?" she asked slowly.

"It is not what I would have wished." He clasped his hands loosely between his knees, trying to formulate an honest reply. "I have spent many hours in prayer and in the Scriptures since my brother's death—to try and understand why this change in my family's circumstances. I felt called into ministry and now it is as if that has been pulled out from under me.

"I find it hard to accept that the Lord would take me from that, first by ending my career in India, and now by making it clear that my ministry here in England will not be a permanent call. But, I have come to an acceptance of whatever the Lord has for me to do. I can be a minister of the gospel in whatever role—be it vicar, landowner, member of the House of Commons, as long as I am true to my convictions."

When he risked looking at her, she nodded slowly as if processing what he was saying.

To his surprise, she reached out a hand and covered his clasped ones. He sat still, afraid to frighten her away.

She took a deep breath. "I am honored by your proposal."

He held his breath, anticipating a refusal.

"I should be happy to accept—"

His heart soared until he heard her next words.

"But for two things."

"Which are?" He felt he was waiting on the edge of a cliff ready for someone to push him off into the abyss.

She moistened her lips, and he remembered the taste of them. "First—and most importantly—I wish you were not to be your father's heir. I hate the thought that you might think I am disposed to marry you now because of what you may inherit and not because of who you are."

Her words brought a burst of feeling in his chest. "I wish there was something I could do to reassure you, but I cannot change my circumstances."

"I know," she whispered with a sad smile.

"If it makes you feel any better, I don't believe you are marrying me for my future position."

"Thank you. But what makes you so sure?"

He faltered, finding it hard to put into words. It would sound presumptuous of him to claim he knew what was in her heart. "The person I have gotten to know in London is not a person who would marry because of a man's position in society. You are the product of the two fine people who have raised you. You are a sweet, dear woman with strong principles of right and wrong."

Her sad smile returned. "Are you sure you are describing me? It would seem my actions were not those of someone with strong principles."

"We all fall at times. I have not been free of all sin since surrendering my life to my Lord."

She seemed content with his words.

"And your second reason?"

She took a deep breath and looked away from him. "I fear to cause a breach between you and your parents. I cannot believe they will accept me as your choice for bride. You can have anyone you wish."

"And I wish you." He took her hand in his. "They will be so happy that I am finally marrying that they will be very pleased to accept my choice. They have already met you and approved of you."

She didn't return his smile. "What if they don't like me upon further acquaintance? I doubt they will think me good enough for their only son."

A wave of sadness at the description of "only son" passed over him. "They used to be very high in the instep." He smiled ruefully. "When Harold entered society, they examined the pedigree and portion of every young lady on the marriage mart that season. Only a handful of young ladies qualified."

"You prove my point."

"I said *used to*." His smile deepened, his thumb tracing a pattern against the back of her hand. "Since Harold married Rosamunde, a young lady of impeccable pedigree and sizable portion, and who proved barren after a decade of marriage, they have altered their views."

He glanced at her figure. "Forgive my indelicacy, but now they will only be concerned about your capabilities for breeding."

"Oh!" Color flooded her cheeks. "I see. But . . . how can they tell?"

He pursed his lips, continuing to eye her. "I haven't a clue."

She shifted away from him as if trying to hide from his scrutiny.

"I beg your pardon," he hastened, realizing how indelicate he was being and averting his gaze. "I didn't mean to stare."

"What if I don't . . . measure up . . . in their estimation?"

He shrugged, offering a reassuring smile. "It doesn't matter. Any future heirs are completely in God's hands. What matters is my love for you." He paused, his heart in his throat, gauging her reaction to his declaration. "And yours for me."

Instead of giving him the words he longed to hear, she returned to the issue of children. "But what if we . . . were to—ahem—marry and . . . a few years later, I were to prove like your sister-in-law?"

"I shouldn't worry too much. The Bible says that children are a blessing of God, and I trust His goodness and grace toward us in that area. But children or not, it won't change my love for you."

Her eyelashes swept down over her eyes. A few seconds later, she looked straight ahead of her, off into the meadow, and said quietly, "Thank you. It does reassure me."

Any disappointment he felt that she didn't acknowledge or return his declaration of love, he didn't let show. Instead, he rose and held out his hand to her. "I'm glad. Come, I should get you back."

As he tucked her hand into the crook of his arm and walked back along the path homeward, he said, "I hope you will think about my proposal and be able to give me a reply before I leave."

She glanced at him. "You are leaving?"

He nodded. "I must. My father and mother need me there for the time being. I must give the bishop a reply and make arrangements to take up my post in Reading."

She turned and focused on the path before them. "Would you mind very much if I waited until you have gotten your parents' permission to marry me?" She turned to him, as if a new thought were occurring to her. "Have you spoken to my father?"

He nodded. "Yes, I spoke to him the day I arrived."

Her eyes widened. "He hasn't said a word to me!"

"He didn't seem at all surprised by my request. I wish you were as accepting as he and your mother."

She smiled. "Perhaps I am trying to save you from yourself."

"I can assure you, my dear, that I know my own heart and mind and think you would make me an excellent wife."

Her lips turned downward. "I wish I had all your confidence."

He sobered. "Ask the Lord to show you."

"I will," she whispered.

Jessamine was torn. Not because she didn't wish to marry Lancelot—it still sent a shiver to say his name to herself—but because she felt unworthy of him. Despite his reassurances to the contrary, she doubted his parents would approve of her, and she didn't wish to cause a rift between him and his parents, not now when they had lost their oldest son.

Mr. Marfleet announced at dinner that he was leaving in three days' time.

Two days later, to her surprise and joy, Megan appeared at the vicarage.

"Megan!" Jessamine ran to her friend, her arms outstretched, when she saw her walking up the path to the front door.

The two girls hugged tightly.

"When did you arrive?"

"Late yesterday," Megan said with a wide smile. "Rees returned from Brussels. We were so overjoyed, we decided to come home immediately so that Mother could see him as well and be assured that he came to no harm."

At the mention of Rees, Jessamine's heart gave a small lurch. "Thank God he is safe."

"Yes, we praise and thank the good Lord. He said he was never in any danger—except perhaps to be run over by the carts and coaches filled with panicked British leaving the city the night before battle." She sobered. "But he said the battle was ghastly from all he has seen and heard in the aftermath. So many soldiers were slain and left on the battlefield, their things looted."

Jessamine clutched her hands together. "Dear me," she murmured. "Is it truly over now?"

"Yes, he believes so. The French army was in disarray once the Prussian army and our own army under Wellington, as well as the Dutch under the Prince of Orange, managed to divide the French."

"Thank God for that at least." Jessamine drew in a breath. "So, Rees and Céline are at your house now?"

"Yes, I expect they will be over soon to say hello." Megan's cheek dimpled. "I heard from Mama that you have a young gentleman visiting you at the parsonage."

Jessamine's own cheeks warmed. "Yes. Mr. Marfleet stopped by unexpectedly a few days ago."

Megan's smile deepened. "My, my, what a surprise." She didn't sound surprised at all.

"I was quite surprised, you can well believe."

"Were you indeed?" She lifted a brow.

"Indeed I was," she maintained, her face growing warmer.

"I must say hello to him. Is he still here?"

"Yes, though he is leaving tomorrow."

"What a pity." Megan tilted her head, observing her. "You sound sad."

Jessamine attempted to smile. "I suppose I am. I . . . I've grown used to his company."

Megan reached out a hand to her. "He must be quite fond of you to come all the way here to visit you."

Jessamine wanted to tell her about Lancelot's proposal, but something held her back. Until she gave him her answer, she felt protective of him and didn't wish anyone speculating or commenting on his proposal. Instead, she said, "He lost his brother—you remember Sir Harold?"

Megan looked down. "We read the notice in the paper. I'm so sorry."

Jessamine briefly filled in the details of his sudden illness. "But come inside, I've left you standing out here in the garden all this time. You may greet Mr. Marfleet yourself and give him your condolences."

It was later that afternoon that Rees and Céline stopped in. They were all in the parlor—Jessamine's mother and father, Lancelot, and Jessamine—when they called.

After the enthusiastic handshakes, hugs, and greetings, they all sat over tea to hear about Rees's time in Belgium and the somber reports he brought back from the Duke of Wellington and other returning soldiers and aides-de-camp who had survived Waterloo.

Jessamine listened, her gaze going from Rees to Céline. Céline's waistline had increased so it was very evident now she would soon bear his child.

The knowledge did nothing to upset Jessamine, as it had a few months—even weeks—ago. All she felt was joy over Rees's safe return and their anticipation of the impending event.

Her glance strayed more than once to Lancelot, and she colored each time she found his eyes on her. Was her complacence over Rees and Céline's obvious happiness due to her newly discovered feelings for Lancelot?

Jessamine traced the rim of her teacup with her forefinger, continuing to analyze her feelings as the talk went on around her. She felt a burden lifting from her shoulders. She had not dared confess to Lancelot her budding love for him as long as she was weighed down from the twin burdens of guilt—her past behavior and her fear that her girlhood infatuation for Rees had left her unable to give her heart fully to another.

She still feared his parents' reaction to a betrothal, but she grew impatient now, as the afternoon waned, for an opportunity to speak alone with Lancelot before he left. She wanted to give him the words she knew he longed to hear.

Her heart constricted with the fear that despite his declarations of love and his proposal to her, once he returned home and spoke to his parents, she would never see or hear from him again. The realities of his new responsibilities as heir would extinguish his feelings for her.

Instead of a moment with Lancelot later that afternoon, she found a moment alone with Rees.

When he and Céline stood to leave, she walked out with them, intending to accompany Megan to the gate.

But when they reached it, Rees held back, allowing Megan and Céline to precede him and continue to their house next door. With a smile, he turned to Jessamine.

"I wanted to tell you how much Mr. Marfleet impressed me," he said when they stood alone. His gray eyes smiled warmly into hers.

Jessamine swallowed. "He is a very worthy gentleman," she said through dry lips.

"It is apparent he adores you. He can hardly take his eyes off you." Rees lifted a dark brow. "May I ask if you return his feelings?"

She found herself nodding her head. "I hardly feel worthy of his love. My own feelings have grown so gradually, I was hardly aware of them until he arrived here." She looked down. "He has asked me to marry him."

"Have you accepted him?"

She shook her head. "Not yet."

"Only you know your own feelings. Let me just tell you it would give me great joy to know that you have found the kind of love I have found with Céline."

Slowly she lifted her head and nodded. "Thank you. That means a great deal to me."

He smiled, and she was able to return the smile. "I hope we will be invited to your wedding."

"You may be sure of it." Her smile disappeared. "That is—if his parents approve of me."

"I have no doubt they will."

"You don't know who they are. They are very proud."

"If this is the man the Lord has for you, He will give you favor with them." With those words, he winked and left her with a wave.

She continued watching his departing figure a moment longer before returning slowly to the house.

Lancelot looked up at her when she returned to the parlor, but she only smiled and took a seat next to him on the settee.

"Is everything all right?" he murmured when her mother turned to say something to her father.

She smiled. "Yes, very much so."

He questioned her with a lift of his brows and finally returned her smile when her own didn't waver.

After supper, in the warm summer evening, she invited him for a walk through the garden.

When they reached the end, they sat on the bench the way they had at the beginning of his visit.

With a boldness she had not displayed to him up to now, she

took one of his hands in both of hers. If he was surprised, he said nothing.

"I will miss you," she said softly.

He covered her hand with his free one. "As I will you—but it won't be for long." He cleared his throat before continuing. "That is, if you decide to accept my proposal. Then I shall be back here as soon as possible and fetch you and your parents to visit me and meet my parents at Kendicott Park."

Her gaze rose to his and she read the fear and uncertainty in his. She moistened her lips. "I do."

He continued regarding her a few seconds as if uncertain what she meant. Slowly, understanding filled his blue eyes. They widened before uncertainty filled them once again. "Do you mean that you agree to be my wife?"

She nodded slowly, her gaze never wavering from his. "If you still want me . . . after you've spoken to your parents."

For answer, he wrapped his arms around her tightly and laughed. "Have no fear of that changing."

She hugged him back, burying her head against his chest, feeling shy all of a sudden with this man who would share her future.

"Are you sure?" He tilted her head up with his fingers, his gaze scanning hers.

She nodded. Drawing in a breath, she braced to tell him all that was in her heart. "I realized this afternoon when I . . . I saw Rees again that my heart was truly free . . . to love you," she ended in a whisper.

Before he could speak, she continued. "I think I had been afraid of trusting my feelings for you until I was certain I no longer felt anything—not in that way—for Rees." Her eyelids fluttered downward. "I had been infatuated with him for so long that I no longer trusted my feelings. You have every right to think me a most fickle creature, first pining after Rees and then allowing Mr. St. Leger to cause me to forget my better judgment."

He drew her up to face him once more. "Your feelings for Mr. Phillips only do you credit, proving your faithfulness. We shall speak no more of St. Leger, since you acted out of your hurt—and he took advantage of that."

Her heart felt it would burst with emotion at the tenderness and understanding reflected in both his words and gaze. "I love you, Lancelot Marfleet, and hope I can someday be worthy of your love."

For reply, he bent his head closer, closing his eyes. She drew in a breath of happiness as his lips touched hers. "Your sentiments echo my own for you," he murmured, drawing apart a hairsbreadth from her before kissing her once more.

Epilogue

AUGUST 1815

Yesterday had been her wedding day. Jessamine looked over the lawns of Kendicott Park in the misty dawn, still awed by their beauty.

She had awakened early and stared some moments at her beloved's sleeping face.

Not wishing to waken him and too restless to fall back to sleep herself, she had crept out of bed and quickly dressed, wanting to go outside and spend some time alone with the Lord before the start of the day.

Her heart was full to overflowing, and only by lifting her head heavenward and singing her silent praises to Him could she hope to fathom something of what she was experiencing.

The summer had passed quickly, with letters back and forth between the parsonage and Kendicott Park almost daily. Then she and her parents had traveled there and spent a few weeks with Lancelot and his family.

That first visit had not proved nearly as daunting as Jessamine had feared. Her father had been able to console Sir Geoffrey in his grief over his firstborn son. Her mother's peaceful presence seemed to be a balm to his wife.

Lancelot's sister, Delawney, enjoyed showing her father the botanical gardens and her watercolors. That interest created a bond between her and Jessamine too.

Instead of being intimidated by Delawney, Jessamine felt a tug of compassion. She sensed behind her gruff exterior a shy woman who longed for the kind of love she witnessed between Lancelot and Jessamine.

After much discussion and prayer, Lancelot and Jessamine had decided they would not postpone their wedding until his family was out of mourning for Harold but would marry by the end of the summer. Lancelot felt his brother would have wanted it so.

As the day drew closer, so did Jessamine's impatience. Her love and admiration for her future husband had only deepened with each passing day. She watched his conduct with his parents and sister, with the vast army of servants at Kendicott Park, and with the tenants he'd taken her to visit, and grew more and more proud of this shy, self-effacing man and knew he would be about the Lord's business wherever they lived and in whatever station he was placed.

His parents had welcomed Jessamine with no hint of disappointment and strove to make her feel welcome. She hoped, prayed, and trusted in God to be able to bring them the joy of grandchildren one day soon.

Lancelot and Jessamine's wedding had been a small affair with only the closest family and friends.

Rees and Céline had been blessed with a daughter a few weeks ago, so Céline had not been able to attend the wedding. But they hoped to all be together in a few months' time in Alston Green when her father joined Megan and Captain Forrester in matrimony.

Jessamine smiled now as she saw her new husband approach across the dewy swath of green lawn.

"Good morning, dear wife," Lancelot said with a smile, his head still sleep-tousled, before leaning down to kiss her.

She wrapped her arms around him, feeling only a trace of shyness. "Good morning, dearest husband of mine. Are you feeling rested for today's journey?" They were traveling to Scotland later in the morning to spend a month at a hunting lodge in the Highlands.

He gazed at her through half-parted lids. "Well, as to that, I am not so sure. But I will likely nap in the coach."

She blushed under his gaze. "I am sorry to have disturbed your sleep," she murmured, looking at his chest.

"I am not," he replied, nuzzling the side of her neck. She leaned back to allow him more access.

"If you are so hungry, we had best be going to the breakfast room," she said then giggled as his bristly cheek tickled her skin.

"I am famished and hope you are too." Again, there was a teasing look in his eye.

She paid him no heed but took his hand in hers and turned toward the house. "We should be on the road soon, since we have a long journey ahead of us."

He merely nodded, squeezing her hand.

As they reached the door, he held it open for her, staying her a moment with his hand. "Are you happy, my dearest love?"

She gazed into his eyes and smiled. "Most happy and blessed, indeed."

Ruth Axtell has loved the regency period of England ever since discovering Jane Austen and Georgette Heyer in high school. She knew she wanted to be a writer even earlier. The two loves were joined with the publication of her first book, *Winter Is Past*, a Regency, in 2003.

Since then she has published several Regencies, as well as Victorian England and late nineteenth-century coastal Maine settings.

Besides writing, Ruth always yearned to live in other countries. From three childhood summers spent in Venezuela, a junior year in Paris, a stint in the Canary Islands as an au pair, and a few years in the Netherlands, Ruth has now happily settled on the down east coast of Maine with her college-age children and two cats.

LEARN MORE ABOUT
Ruth Axtell
RuthAxtell.com
RuthAxtell.com/Blog